THE NINTH GRAVE

STEFAN AHNHEM grew up in Helsingborg, Sweden, and now lives in Stockholm. He is an established screenwriter, whose credits include adapting Henning Mankell's *Wallander* series for TV. He also serves on the board of the Swedish Writers Guild. His first novel, *Victim Without a Face*, won Crimetime's Novel of the Year in Sweden in 2014, and became a top-ten bestseller in Germany, Sweden and Ireland. Stefan Ahnhem has been published in thirteen countries to date.

Follow him on Twitter @StefanAhnhem

PAUL NORLEN is an experienced translator of Swedish fiction. He was awarded the American-Scandinavian Foundation Translation Prize in 2004. He lives in Seattle.

Also by Stefan Ahnhem

Victim Without a Face

STEFAN AHNHEM

THE NINTH GRAVE

Translated from the Swedish by Paul Norlen

BAINTE DEN STOC
WITHDRAWN FROM DLR LIBRARIES STOCK

Leabharlanna Dhún Laoghaire - Ráth An Dúin

First published in Sweden as *Den Nionde Graven* in 2015 by Forum

This translation first published in Canada in 2016 by
House of Anansi Press Inc

First published in the UK in 2017 by Head of Zeus Ltd

Copyright © Stefan Ahnhem, 2015
Translation copyright © Paul Norlen, 2016

The moral right of Stefan Ahnhem to be identified as the author of this work has been asserted in accordance with the Copyright, Designs and Patents Act of 1988.

All rights reserved. No part of this publication may be reproduced, stored in a retrieval system, or transmitted, in any form or by any means, electronic, mechanical, photocopying, recording, or otherwise, without the prior permission of both the copyright owner and the above publisher of this book.

This is a work of fiction. All characters, organizations, and events portrayed in this novel are either products of the author's imagination or are used fictitiously.

9 7 5 3 2 4 6 8

A catalogue record for this book is available from the British Library.

ISBN (HB) 9781784975524
ISBN (XTPB) 9781784975531
ISBN (eBook) 9781784975517

Typeset by e-type, Aintree, Liverpool

Printed and bound by CPI Group (UK) Ltd., Croydon, CR0 4YY

Head of Zeus Ltd
Clerkenwell House
45–47 Clerkenwell Green
London EC1R 0HT

WWW.HEADOFZEUS.COM

THE NINTH GRAVE

TEN YEARS AGO

IT WAS SO DARK he could barely see what was right in front of him. The prisoner transport vehicle lurched forward so vigorously on its way through the difficult terrain that the letters he was trying to write were almost illegible. But that couldn't be helped. It was his last chance to record his story of the love affair that made him leave everything behind before the pool of blood under him got too big. He would describe how he was shot down and captured by his own people and how he was now on his way to almost certain death.

He had found the pen in the Israeli military camp at the Huwwara Checkpoint that was in the uncontrolled part of the West Bank. The paper came from some empty diary pages he had found in Tamir's backpack, along with the used envelope he could turn inside out.

Once he was finished writing, he folded up the pages of the letter with his bloody hands, slipped them into the envelope, and sealed it as best he could. He had no stamp – or even an address. All he had was a name. But he didn't hesitate to push the letter out through the thin crack in the truck and let it go. *If it was God's will, the letter would get there*, he thought, giving in to fatigue.

The envelope didn't even have a chance to hit the ground before it was sucked up by the strong winds and pushed higher and higher up into the black, starless sky that was starting to resemble a storm above the Nablus mountains. The time between dull rumbles and flashes of lightning diminished and a feeling of rain was hanging in the air. In only a matter of seconds, the imminent rain would hammer the envelope down to the ground and transform the dry earth to wet clay. But no rain ever came, and the bloodstained envelope continued its journey over the mountains and across the border towards Jordan.

SALADIN HAZAYMEH WAS LYING on his sleeping pad looking up towards the sky, where the light of dawn was making its first hesitant attempts to peak out. The strong winds from the night's storm had finally calmed down and it looked like it might be a beautiful day.

It felt as if the sun had decided to clean up the sky for his seventieth birthday. And though his birthday was the reason for this ten-day-long hike, Saladin Hazaymeh was preoccupied by something else.

When he first noticed it up in the sky, he thought it was an airplane several thousand metres above him, but then he decided it must be a bird with an injured wing. Now he had no idea what was floating down to the ground some fifty metres ahead of him, glistening in the light from the sun.

Saladin Hazaymeh got up and noticed his usual morning back pain was gone. He hurried to roll up his sleeping pad and put it in his backpack. Something was about to happen – something of great significance – and he felt full of energy.

It could only be a sign from the God he had believed in for as long as he could remember, telling him that he was on the right path. For this birthday, he'd retraced the steps of Jesus all the way from Jerusalem to the Sea of Galilee.

Yesterday he had visited the holy grotto in Anjara and had hoped to spend the night there, just as Jesus had done with his disciples and the Virgin Mary. But the guards had discovered him and he had been forced to sleep under the open sky. *But there was a meaning to everything*, thought Saladin, hurrying off with a light step across the uneven land towards the olive tree, where the sign from God was caught among the branches.

When he got there he saw that it was an envelope. *An envelope?*

As much as he tried he could not come up with a logical reason to explain its origins. He finally decided that *Heaven* would have to do. And perhaps that wasn't completely wrong. His inner voice kept repeating how important it was that he took care of it, like a mantra. It was how things were intended. That – and nothing else – was the real point of all his wandering.

After a number of attempts, he managed to hit the envelope with a stone and catch it before it hit the ground. It was dirty and full of small tears and looked as if it had survived the end of the world against all odds. It was also heavier than he'd expected.

All doubt had now blown away. God had chosen him. This was not just any old envelope.

He inspected both sides for clues, but found nothing other than a name written in small, sprawling letters: *Aisha Shahin*.

Saladin Hazaymeh sat down on a stone and laboriously sounded out the name, but it meant nothing to him. After some hesitation he took out his knife and carefully slit open the envelope. Unaware that he was holding his breath he pulled out and opened the letter, examining the long rows of handwriting.

It was Hebrew, that much he could tell. But he could barely read Arabic, so how would he able to understand this?

What was God trying to say? Was he punishing him because he never learned to read? Or was the letter not intended for him at all? Was he only an insignificant middleman whose sole purpose was to pass it along? He tried without success to dismiss the disappointment, while he folded the letter and put it back in its envelope. He continued his wandering northward toward Ajloun, where he reluctantly put the letter in a mailbox.

MANY WOULD SURELY THINK that Khaled Shawabkeh had behaved shamefully and was deeply immoral. He, on the other hand, did not feel guilty at all when he picked up the envelope without a stamp, sender or complete address. Letters where the sender had failed to do their part became his property. It was a practice he had applied without exception during the forty-three years he had worked sorting mail.

At home he had many boxes filled with stray letters, one for each year. He liked nothing more than fishing one out at random and studying the contents that were meant for someone else. This particular envelope was something out of the ordinary.

The oxidation confirmed that the journey itself must have been an adventure. Moreover, someone had already slit the envelope open, but left all the contents inside – for him and no one else.

Exactly ninety-eight minutes earlier than usual, Khaled Shawabkeh arrived home and locked the door. He had skipped afternoon tea, even though he'd brought harissa cakes, and jogged the whole way home from the bus. Now he was out of breath and could feel the sweat trying to penetrate his tight polyester shirt. Dinner could wait. Instead, he poured a glass of wine from the bottle hidden behind the books on the bookshelf, sat down in the armchair, took out the envelope and solemnly coaxed out the letter.

'Finally,' he said to himself, reaching for the wine, blissfully ignorant of how the blood clot, which had been building up in his left leg for several years, loosened and followed the blood flow all the way up to his lungs.

EVEN THOUGH IT HAD been more than a year since Maria's uncle died from a lung embolism, she still had not set foot in his house. Her two brothers had challenged the will and done everything they could to pressure her to refuse the inheritance. Even her own father had tried to convince her, arguing that Khaled Shawabkeh had gradually lost his mind over the years and had left his house in disarray. He also didn't think women would ever be able to manage property.

But Maria held her own and now, finally, she could put the key in the lock and go inside. In the negotiations she'd become estranged from her brothers and parents. The house would be cleared out and sold, and with the money she could afford to quit her job at the tailoring shop, move to Amman and start working her dream job at the Jordanian National Commission for Women.

IT SHOULDN'T HAVE BEEN possible. There was really nothing to suggest that the letter would ever reach its recipient. With all the obstacles, the probability was so slight it was impossible to calculate.

Yet that was exactly what happened.

One year, four months and sixteen days after the letter had been pushed through a crack in the prisoner transport vehicle and taken hold of by the winds in the black nights it ended up in Maria Shawabkeh's hands. A few hours later, she had succeeded in piecing together most of the missing information.

Three sleepless nights after reading the horrific story from the letter, she made a few Internet searches, put a stamp on the envelope, wrote down the complete address and left it at the nearest post office – without any idea of the consequences.

Aisha Shahin
Selmedalsvägen 40, 7th Floor
129 37 Hägersten

Sweden

PART I

16–19 December 2009

Many people will be horrified by the things I've done. Some will see them as revenge for all the injustices that have been committed; others as an unlikely game to trick the system and show how far one person can go. But the vast majority will believe that these are the actions of an extremely sick person.

All of them will be wrong.

TWO DAYS AGO

SOFIE LEANDER WAS SITTING in the waiting room at Stockholm South General Hospital waiting for an ultrasound. She was browsing through a well-thumbed copy of *We Parents* filled with page after page of beautiful, happy mums and dads and she wanted nothing more than to be one of them. But after so many fruitless rounds of IVF, she'd started to doubt that her egg production would ever get started.

This was her absolute last chance. If the procedure didn't work this time, she would have no choice other than to give up – something her husband already seemed to have done.

He had promised to be by her side when she needed him, but he'd missed today's appointment. She turned on her cell phone and read his message again: *Have a conflict and unfortunately won't make it.* He treated the whole experience like it was shopping for milk on the way home from work. He hadn't even said 'good luck'.

She had hoped that the move to Sweden three years ago would revive their relationship, especially since he had chosen to take her surname. She'd seen it as a declaration of love; proof the two of them were united, no matter what happened. Now, she was no longer so sure and she couldn't escape the feeling that they were slipping further and further away from each other. She had tried to bring it up, but he persistently avowed his love for her. She could see it in his eyes though; or, more correctly, in the way he avoided her eyes.

Now, the man who had once saved her life suddenly had *conflicts* and hardly looked in her direction. She wanted to call and confront him, to ask if he'd stopped loving her or if he'd met someone else. But she didn't dare. Besides, she was sure he wouldn't answer. He almost never did when he was working, and especially not now when he was in the middle of a new project – something so secret that he couldn't even tell her what it was. Her only chance was a positive report from the doctor. If she could just get that everything would surely be fine again. Then she would finally be able to give him the child they always wanted and he would realize how much he really loved her.

'Sofie Leander,' she heard her name being called. She followed the midwife through the corridor and was shown into a small examination room with closed blinds, a large computer-like apparatus and a hospital bed.

'You can hang up your coat on the hook and then lie down on the bed. The doctor will be here at any moment.'

Sofie nodded and took off her coat and boots as the midwife left the room. Once on the bed, she pulled up her blouse and unbuttoned her trousers. She decided to try her husband anyway and ask what was so important that he couldn't join her. As she was reaching for her handbag the door opened and the doctor came in.

'Are you Sofie Leander?'

Sofie nodded.

'Good. I'll have you start by lying down on your side with your back to me.'

Sofie did as she was told and could hear the doctor opening some plastic packaging behind her. She couldn't put her finger on it, but there was something about the whole situation that didn't feel right.

'Excuse me, I'm here to have my ovaries examined.'

'Absolutely. We just have to take care of this first,' the doctor said, pressing on her vertebrae.

Suddenly she felt a prick in the middle of her back.

'What are you doing? Did you just stick me with a syringe?' Sofie turned around and saw something slip into the doctor's trouser pocket. 'Now I demand to know what—'

'You don't need to worry. This is purely routine. Are those your things?' the doctor said, pointing to her coat and boots, but didn't wait for an answer and set them by her feet. 'We don't want to forget anything, do we?'

This wasn't the first time Sofie had been in for an ultrasound of her ovaries, so she knew that this definitely was not routine. She had no idea what this was. All she was sure of was that she no longer wanted to be part of it and wanted to get away from the doctor, the examination room and the entire hospital.

'I think I have to go now,' she said, trying to get up. 'I want to leave. Do you hear me!?' But her body refused to obey. 'What's happening? What have you done?'

The doctor leaned towards her, smiling and stroking her cheek, before stretching a respiratory mask across Sofie's face. 'You'll understand soon.'

Sofie tried to protest and scream as loud as she could, but the mask suffocated all sound. Before she knew it, the brakes of the bed had been released and she was being pushed out of the examination room and into the corridor.

If only she could grab something, anything at all, and pull herself out of the bed to make everyone realize what was happening. But she couldn't. All she could do was lie there, stare up at the ceiling and watch as the fluorescent lights passed by and doors opened in front of them.

She saw so many faces: pregnant mothers and soon-to-be fathers, midwives and doctors. They were all so close, but still so far away. She heard voices and the sound of elevator doors opening and then closing behind her. Or were they opening? She was disoriented.

Then she was alone with the doctor again, who was whistling a tune that echoed between the hard walls. It was the only sound she could hear other than her own breath, which was starting to remind her of the asthma she had had as a child. Then, she had felt completely helpless when she had to stop playing to gasp for air. Now, she felt both helpless and small, and all she wanted to do was collapse and cry. But she couldn't even do that.

The fluorescent lights on the dark concrete ceiling ended and she saw first her legs and then her upper body being lifted on to a stretcher. *You'll soon understand*, the doctor had said. How could she understand? All she could think about was the story she'd read recently about a plastic surgeon in Malmö who had injected something into his patients so they couldn't resist when he raped them. But why would anyone want to rape her?

She was pushed backwards into an ambulance and tried to focus on the sounds. She heard the driver's side door close and the engine start. They started moving and turned west on Ringvägen and then continued along Hornsgatan towards Hornstull, where she got confused when they went through a roundabout. After that, she lost all sense of direction.

About twenty minutes later, they finally stopped. She had no idea where they were, but she heard a garage door open. The ambulance went in about thirty metres before the engine was turned off.

The ambulance doors opened, and she was pulled out and pushed away on the stretcher. New fluorescent lights chased each other in the ceiling. The pace quickened, and the doctor's steps echoed against the hard floor until they abruptly stopped. She heard keys and a beeping sound, and then an electric motor starting.

She was rolled into a dark room and it sounded as if something was closing behind her. A strong lamp in the ceiling was turned on and was shining right down on to a rectangular table. She couldn't see any windows or figure out the size of the room.

She could only make out the lamp and the table with a number of devices around it. She was pushed forward and could now see that the table was covered with plastic and had a number of straps and an inch-wide hole right below the midpoint. There was another, smaller, metal table alongside the rectangular one that had various surgical instruments lined up on a white towel.

Once she saw the scissors, tongs and scalpels, she understood exactly why she'd been taken away – and what was coming.

1

FABIAN RISK READ THE message over again before he looked up from his cell phone and met the teacher's puzzled gaze. 'I'm sorry, but unfortunately it looks like we'll have to start without her.'

'Really? I suppose if we have to,' said the teacher, very clearly demonstrating her displeasure.

'What do you mean, Mum's not coming?' Matilda looked as if she would rather jump off the West Bridge than undergo a parent–teacher conversation without Sonja. And Fabian could understand the feeling, given that he had missed the last few meetings for various reasons. Although Matilda was now in third grade, he couldn't even remember her teacher's name.

'Matilda, unfortunately Mum has to work. You know how busy she gets when an exhibition is coming up.'

'She said she would be here.'

'I know, and I can promise that she's just as disappointed as you, but I'm sure this will go just fine anyway.' He patted her on the head, and sought support from the teacher, who responded with a neutral smile.

'Stop it.' Matilda pushed away his hand, adjusting the pink hair clips that held her dark, shoulder-length hair in place.

'As far as Matilda's motivation for learning and ability to follow the lessons are concerned, the entire teaching staff only have positive feedback.' The teacher flipped through her papers. 'In both Swedish and maths she's one of the best in—' She fell silent and looked at Fabian's cell phone, which had started to vibrate on the table.

'Sorry.' Fabian turned over the phone and saw, much to his surprise, that it was Herman Edelman. He had been Fabian's boss since he'd started at the National Bureau of Criminal Investigation in Stockholm. Even at age sixty, Edelman was a force to be reckoned with and as hungry for the truth as he'd ever been. Fabian could honestly say that he wouldn't have amounted to much of an investigator without Edelman.

But Edelman hadn't been seen at the department since lunch. By afternoon coffee neither Fabian nor any of the others on the team had heard from him and they'd started to wonder if something had happened.

But now he was calling. And after office hours no less, which could only mean one thing: something had definitely happened. Something that couldn't wait.

Fabian was about to answer, when the teacher cleared her throat. 'We don't have all evening. You're not the only parents I have to see.'

'Sorry, where were we?' Fabian declined the call and set the phone aside.

'Matilda. Your daughter.' The teacher forced a smile. 'As I was saying, the whole teaching staff only have positive things to say about Matilda. But,' she looked Fabian in the eye, 'if it's all right, I would really like to talk with you privately.'

'Yes? Okay. I'm sure that's fine. Isn't it, Matilda?'

'What are you going to talk about?'

'I'm sure it's just some grown-up things.' Fabian turned to the teacher, who nodded with a smile. 'Matilda, can you wait out in the hall? We'll be coming soon.'

Matilda sighed and dragged her feet sulkily on her way out of the classroom. Fabian watched her, but couldn't stop wondering what Edelman wanted from him.

'So, it's like this.' The teacher placed her folded hands on the table. 'I've heard from various people that there are serious signs that Matilda—' Once again she was interrupted by Fabian's vibrating cell phone. Her irritation was impossible to overlook.

'You have to excuse me, but I don't know what's going on.' He picked up the phone and turned it over. This time it was his colleague Malin Rehnberg, who was in Copenhagen at a seminar. Edelman must have called her after him. 'Sorry, but I have no choice but to—'

'Then I think we'll stop here,' the teacher said, starting to gather up her papers.

'But wait. Can't we just—'

'At this school we have a zero tolerance policy for cell phones during class. I see no reason to make exceptions for grown-ups.' She continued to gather up her papers and put them in her briefcase. 'Take your important call. That way I can see parents who are actually interested in their children. Have a nice rest of your evening.' She stood up.

'Wait, this turned out completely wrong,' said Fabian, just as the cell phone pinged a voicemail notification. *Please tell me you left a message explaining what happened*, Fabian thought. 'Sorry. Of course I'm here for Matilda and nothing else.'

The teacher gave him a contemptuous look. 'Fine. We'll give this one last try.' She opened the briefcase again and took out Matilda's folder. 'This is not something we normally get involved in, but we feel it's really important in your daughter's case. We're concerned that if you don't take action, there might be a risk to her studies.'

'Sorry, but I don't think I understand. Do what?'

The teacher set a drawing out on the table. 'Here is one of her latest works. And, well, see for yourself.'

Fabian recognized himself in the picture. He still had the goatee he'd shaved off a few weeks ago. Sonja stood right across from him with a kitchen knife in her hand. Their faces were bright red and they were screaming with their mouths open. He remembered how he'd questioned whether it really was necessary that she worked so much in the evenings. Sonja had flared up and countered with all his late work nights over the past few years and blamed him for only looking after his own needs.

They had agreed to never, ever fight in front of the children. But in the heat of the moment he had even threatened divorce.

'I don't know what to say. This, this is—'

'And here's another,' the teacher interrupted.

This time the image depicted Matilda's bedroom. He recognized the wallpaper by her bed and the stuffed animals lined up in rows across the pillows at the lower edge of the picture, just as they were in reality. A small part of Fabian could not help being impressed by how skilful she was at drawing, while the rest of him struggled to take in what was written in the text bubbles that illustrated the fight on the other side of the wall. This time it concerned sex, and from what he could see, some of the lines were painfully close to the truth.

He wanted to sink down through the chair and get out of there.

'Of course, I understand that there are quite a few fantasies and exaggerations, but this theme recurs in everything Matilda is doing right now, and I thought it might be good for you to know about it. As a parent, I would want to know.'

'Of course,' said Fabian, trying to conceal the cell phone that was once again vibrating in his hand.

ON HIS WAY OUT of the Björngård School, Fabian called Edelman, but got a busy signal. 'Look, Matilda, now there's even more snow.' He gazed out over the schoolyard, which was covered by a thick layer of fresh snow. 'You can all make snowmen tomorrow.'

'By then it will probably only be slush,' Matilda said, starting to go down the steps.

'Matilda, wait.' Fabian hurried to catch up. 'You're not worried that your mum and I are going to separate, are you?'

'So that's what you were talking about.'

'Well? Are you?'

Without answering Matilda ran towards the car, which was parked on the other side of the street.

Fabian held up the car key to unlock it so that she could jump in and sit down. He really wanted to hurry over and keep her company, but he wasn't sure what he should say. She was right, after all. If they continued like this, it was only a matter of time before their marriage would be over. He, who had not only promised Sonja, but most of all himself, never ever to follow in his parents' footsteps – no matter what. However tough it might be for them, he had thought nothing would ever make them give up on their marriage.

Now he wasn't so sure. Even though the air had gone out of the tyres, so to speak, he'd continued to drive around on the rims for so long now it was doubtful they could be repaired. He sighed and stopped in the middle of the schoolyard to call Malin Rehnberg.

'Fabian, where have you been? The only thing that will save you now is the fact that I'm over six hundred kilometres away. Do you realize that Herman has been on me like a flipping leech simply because you can't be bothered to pick up the phone? He's treating me like I'm his secretary or something. Yes, I know that no one cares, but I happen to be in Copenhagen at a seminar that is actually rather interesting.'

'Okay, but do you know what—'

'But the beds here are shit, and besides I feel like a swelled-up sweaty pig.'

'I understand, but—'

'And I don't care that I have two months left – I'm on the verge of doing something illegal if these kids don't pop out soon! Hello? Fabian? Are you still there?'

'Did he say anything about what this is about?'

'He didn't tell me. Evidently it was extremely important, but I think I have an idea.'

'Okay.'

'Try answering next time he calls.'

He heard a click, and Fabian was left nodding in agreement. He also hoped that her pregnancy would soon be over. Fifteen seconds later Malin sent a text apologizing for her harsh tone and promised that she would be her usual self again as soon as the 'pregnancy from hell' was over.

Fabian got in behind the steering wheel and looked at Matilda in the back seat. 'What do you say about stopping by Ciao Ciao and getting pizza?'

Matilda shrugged, but he could see how she lit up a bit, even if she was doing everything to hide it. He started the car and turned on to Maria Prästgårdsgatan, while he made another attempt to get hold of Edelman.

'Hi, Herman, I see that you called.'

'I assume I should be thanking Malin.'

'I was in the middle of a parent–teacher meeting, and I've only now—'

'Yes, yes, that's fine. The reason I'm calling is that I've been summoned to SePo for eight o'clock this evening, and I want you to come with me.'

'This evening? Sorry, but I'm alone with the kids. Why is it so important that I—'

'Who's in charge here? You or me?'

'That's not what I—'

'Listen up: Persson and Päivinen have just found a new lead in the Adam Fischer case and Höglund and Carlén have their hands full with the Diego Arcas mapping. The only people who don't have anything on their desks right now are you and Rehnberg. And as far as I can tell she's in Copenhagen.'

'Okay, but can you tell me what's happened?'

'I assume that's what we're going to be informed about. See you outside SePo at five to. Bye now.'

Fabian took the headset out of his ears and turned on to Nytorgsgatan. He didn't know much about the Adam Fischer case beyond that he was a famous playboy who had recently gone missing. His two colleagues were treating it as kidnap but in Risk's view he could have simply gone on an eight-day bender and not yet come home. Diego Arcas was a name he was more familiar with – a ruthless pimp who ran several brothels in Stockholm. They had been trying to arrest him for years for trafficking or drug-dealing, but he was always too slippery. Risk hoped that Höglund and Carlén would get the evidence they so desperately needed – though privately he doubted it. Arcas was too smart to get caught. He pulled his thoughts back to the road, and the meeting ahead of him. It was far from the first time his paths had crossed with the Swedish secret service, but he had never been invited to a meeting after office hours, which was probably because he was too far down the food chain. Herman Edelman, on the other hand, was there all the time, and wasted no opportunity to underscore how crucial it was to always sit with your back against the wall if you wanted to survive a meeting with them.

And now he wanted Fabian to come along.

'NO, IT'S NOT POSSIBLE, Fabian. I'm sorry. You'll have to work it out some other way.'

'What do you mean "work it out some other way"?' Fabian said, looking out over the snow-covered roof ridges. He could hear Sonja taking yet another cancer-inducing puff and then a sigh of smoke. It was a sign that she was in a really bad mood.

'I don't know. You'll have to improvise. I don't have time to talk more now.'

'But, wait a minute...' Fabian could see Matilda's reflection in the window, listening to them. He took the remote control, turned on the TV and raised the volume.

Eight days after playboy Adam Fischer disappeared without a trace, police have announced that they are treating the case as a kidnapping.

'Sonja, this isn't my decision. It's not like I have a choice.'

'And you think that I do?'

We have criminology professor Gerhard Ringe with us in the studio...

'Should I just drop my brushes and tell Ewa that there won't be an exhibition?'

'No. But—'

'Okay, then.'

'Please, calm down now.'

What caused police to release this information? And why haven't we heard about a ransom?

'I am calm,' said Sonja, doing nothing to conceal the fact that she was taking another puff. 'I just don't understand why it should be such a problem that for once, I'm the one who has to work.'

'Okay, I'll try to arrange something. Do you have any idea when you'll be home?'

'Yes. When I'm done. And please, don't ask me what time, because I have no idea. All I know is that I hate these paintings more and more with every second that passes,' she said with a new puff and a new sigh. 'Sorry. I'm just so sick and tired of these and want nothing more than to puke on all of them.'

'Darling, it will work out. You feel like this before each exhibition, then suddenly you have an epiphany and everything comes together.'

'We'll see about that.'

'I'll figure it out, so don't worry about it.'

'Okay.'

'Love you.'

'Talk to you later.'

Fabian sat down with Matilda in the kitchen and took out his pizza. 'How was the banana pizza?'

'Okay. But I want to ask you something.'

'Yes?'

'Did Mom say that she loves you too?'

Fabian met her gaze and wondered how he should answer. 'No, actually, she didn't.'

'Maybe it's just because she's so stressed.'

Fabian nodded and took a big bite of pizza, which had long since gone cold.

2

THIS WASN'T THE FIRST time Fabian had been to SePo, but he'd never gone through so many security checks and been so far into the building. He had lost his sense of direction completely. Only after numerous elevators and windowless corridors were he and Herman Edelman shown into a large room with faint illumination. As far as Fabian could remember, this was the first time Edelman had had nothing to say.

Just before he had to leave, Theodor had come home from floorball and agreed to take care of Matilda after a quick negotiation. Even though it was an ordinary Wednesday evening, Fabian agreed they could have crisps and soda and watch videos in their bedrooms. His only counter-demand was that they didn't tell Sonja, and that Matilda didn't make a drawing of it in school.

'You must be Herman Edelman and Fabian Risk.' A woman emerged from the darkness and shook hands with them. 'Welcome. Anders Furhage and the others are already waiting.'

The woman led them further down the hall. Once Fabian's eyes got used to the dimness he noticed a number of dark cubes that appeared to be freely floating a metre or so above the ground. He had heard about the eavesdropping-proof rooms, which, according to rumour, had broken SePo's budget by tens of millions, but this was the first time he'd actually seen them. Edelman, though, didn't bat an eye. Instead, he wiped off his small round glasses with a handkerchief and kept going. Fabian hadn't seen him so serious and grim since his wife died of cancer almost ten years before.

'May I please have your cell phones,' the woman said, stopping by a staircase that led up to one of the hut-like cubes. A thick door stood open at the top of the stairs, and, once closed, the cube would be hermetically sealed.

They handed them over and went up the steps and into the cube, which was painted brown and had dark red wall-to-wall carpeting. Three men in suits, each wearing a different-coloured tie, were sitting around an oval walnut table that had some glasses and bottles of mineral water on top of it. Fabian immediately recognized the general director, Anders Furhage, who stood up and greeted them as the door closed behind them.

'Thank you for coming on such short notice. As I'm sure you've understood, everything said during this meeting is completely confidential.'

Fabian and Edelman nodded and sat down.

'Let's get right down to business,' said Furhage, looking them both in the eyes. 'Something, let's call it a situation, has come up which may actually turn out to be a non-situation – an insignificant little trifle.'

Fabian glanced at Edelman, who looked as perplexed as he felt.

'Melvin Stenberg here is responsible for personal security and can tell us more,' Furhage continued, before nodding towards the man with a blue tie.

'At 3:24 p.m. today, about an hour after question time in parliament concluded, Carl-Eric Grimås walked out the west door of the parliament building, where a car was waiting for him. According to our driver, Grimås never showed up and hasn't been seen since.'

'Wait a minute, do you mean that the Minister for Justice is missing?' said Edelman.

Stenberg adjusted his tie and nodded curtly.

'We've searched through the areas around the government buildings and Rosenbad, and have been in contact with both his family and the chief of staff at the Ministry of Justice,' said the man with the green tie. 'But right now everyone is just as confused.'

Silence descended on the room while everyone took in the fact that one of the country's highest-ranking ministers, who was also ultimately responsible for their operation, had vanished without a trace.

'And you're calling this a *trifle*?' Edelman shook his head.

'Herman, that's not what I said at all.' Furhage smiled at Edelman. 'Let's not nitpick here. As you're fully aware, at the present time we don't know whether—'

'He's missing, dammit! How many politicians have to sacrifice their lives in this country before we wake up? I mean, doesn't Grimås have personal protection twenty-four hours a day?'

Furhage turned towards the man with the blue tie, who cleared his throat. 'Well, everything is a matter of resources and priorities. We did a risk assessment that concluded there was no impending threat pattern as long as he was inside one of the parliament buildings.'

Oh well, at least we have an eavesdropping-proof cube to sit and talk in, thought Fabian, as Furhage gave the green tie the go-ahead to press the button on the table's built-in control panel.

A screen lowered along one wall. 'This sequence is taken from the surveillance cameras at the door in question,' he said, starting the projector.

The video, which was not much more than a minute long, showed Carl-Eric Grimås walking towards the double glass security doors with a briefcase in his left hand. Once he got there, he ran his pass card through the reader, opened one door, then the other, before disappearing out into the snowstorm.

Fabian recognized his clothing from pictures in the newspaper: the winter coat with the big black fur collar and an unmistakable hat had become the minister's trademark. The timestamp in the top left corner of the video showed 3:24 p.m.

The projector turned off and the screen soundlessly crept back up into the ceiling.

'And one of your cars was waiting outside to pick him up?' Fabian said. It sounded incomprehensible to him.

The green tie nodded. 'I will add that it was snowing heavily and that the driver did not have a clear view of the whole door.'

'When did he arrive?'

'If you're referring to Grimås, then 11:43 a.m. through the main door of the west parliament building,' the green tie said, looking satisfied with being able to provide a quick, precise answer.

'At 11:38 a.m. he left Rosenbad and walked at a brisk pace along Strömgatan, but instead of taking Riksbron he took a detour over Vasabron to Kanslikajen – with personal protection,' the blue tie said.

'And when did question time start? At twelve?'

'No, not until twelve thirty, but Grimås is never late.'

'And the car that was waiting. What time was it supposed to be there?'

'Three o'clock,' the blue tie said, taking a sip of water.

'So even though he's known for always being on time, he doesn't leave the parliament building until 3:24.'

The men in ties exchanged glances, whereupon Furhage cleared his throat.

'Let me clarify one thing. You're not here to take over the investigation. On the contrary, you are only here to be informed. As long as we are unsure if any crime has been committed, we're the ones who will control the investigation.'

'And what could have happened, if not a crime?' said Edelman, pulling on his beard.

'The fact is, so far there's actually nothing that points to foul play, and just as... excuse me, what was your name again?' Furhage turned to Fabian.

'Fabian Risk.'

'Just as Risk suggests, there are a number of unanswered questions here; questions that we are working hard to get answers to right now. Jumping to a lot of conclusions is pointless in my opinion. Of course, we'll give you real-time updates.'

'I see. You've known about this since three thirty today and you're only informing us now. Is that what you call "real-time updates"?'

'Let me put it to you this way: at the present time we have neither a body nor an explicit threat. There is nothing that suggests this might be a terrorist act, or something along those lines. On the other hand, there are quite a few people who report that he has appeared both stressed and unfocused recently, which suggests that he has disappeared of his own free will and simply wants to be left alone.'

Edelman snorted. 'Have you thought about whether your so-called "threat analysis" is worthless? Maybe all you're trying to do now is buy time for your team to sweep away all the traces of your failure?'

'Herman, might I suggest that we keep this on a seemly level,' Furhage said, clearly unperturbed by Edelman's attack. 'No one here is trying to sweep away anything. We wouldn't be sitting here if that was the case. We're after exactly the same thing as you – to find out what happened. And, sure, it's very possible that we've made a wrong assessment in our threat analysis. But that doesn't change the fact that the investigation stays with us until we can confirm a crime really has been committed.

'I want to underscore that this is not about keeping you on the outside, but only about the benefit of being able to work quietly. Both you and I know the advantages of that, Herman. The moment you start up your machinery this will be out on the front page of every tabloid, and all we'll be able to do is hold press conferences for days on end.'

'And if I don't go along with it?'

'You will. And to save you unnecessary headaches, I've already cleared it with Crimson.'

Fabian observed Edelman, who sat quietly without moving a muscle. The rug had just been pulled out from under him and he knew it. Without his knowledge Furhage had already contacted the police commissioner and got the green light to keep the National Bureau away from the investigation. In all probability, it was on Crimson's orders that they were now here being informed. They'd been outmanoeuvred.

His boss let the seconds tick by without revealing what he was thinking. He calmly took out his cigarillo case with one hand, while he fished out his old Ronson lighter with the other. Before anyone could say a word, the cigarillo was glowing an angry red. Neither Furhage nor any of the ties said anything. Only after two long puffs did Edelman put it out in one of the glasses.

'All right, but we're done here. I look forward to getting ongoing information about how everything develops.'

'Of course.' Furhage extended his hand. 'You're at the top of my list. You know that.'

Edelman ignored the outstretched hand and turned his gaze towards Fabian, who got up and left the cube, reminding himself to never, ever say yes to a management position.

EDELMAN WAS JUST AS taciturn on the way out through the labyrinth of corridors as he'd been when they'd arrived. It was impossible to know if that was because he was worried about being overheard or simply too angry to talk. Fabian kept quiet too, even though he was full of questions.

It wasn't until they were out in the snowstorm on Polhemsgatan that Edelman suggested they get into Fabian's car, although a taxi was already waiting for Edelman. They crossed the street and Fabian unlocked the car, got in and started the engine to get the heat going. Edelman sat in the passenger seat with his eyes aimed straight ahead at the snow-covered windshield.

'I don't know if you're aware of this, but Grimås is—' Edelman took a deep breath. 'An old friend that I still care about.'

Fabian nodded. Long before his time at the National Bureau of Criminal Investigation, Grimås had been Edelman's boss, before he left the police department to devote himself to politics. Everybody at the department had observed the fruitful collaboration between the two and Edelman never missed an opportunity to talk about what he and Grimås had done in their day. But that they still had contact came as a surprise to Fabian.

'Do you have any idea what might have happened?' asked Fabian.

Edelman shook his head. 'But I suspect the worst. So it's of the utmost importance that we find out as much as possible before SePo's cleaning patrols have gone too far.'

'You believe that's what they—'

'I don't believe anything. But the last person I trust is Furhage.'

'So we should start an investigation, even though Bertil Crimson—'

'Not we. You,' Edelman interrupted, turning to Fabian. 'Let me be completely clear: there's no one else at the department who is even close to having what it takes. And both you and I know that.'

'But how could I start a separate investigation when Bertil Crimson has explicitly—'

'Let's not call it an investigation. What I mean is that... if we don't get to the truth, who will? SePo?'

Fabian nodded. Edelman definitely had a point.

'Make sure to keep yourself far enough below the radar. Until we know more, you won't report to anyone other than directly to me.' Edelman got out of the car and slammed the door so hard that most of the snow came loose from the windows. Fabian put on the windshield wipers, which removed the last of it, and turned out on to the street.

He tried to concentrate on the traffic, but his thoughts took on a life of their own. He was so preoccupied with trying to understand what had really happened that he finally had to pull over in a parking lot on Norr Mälarstrand, lower the side window, and take a deep breath of cold night air.

Not only had the Minister for Justice disappeared under mysterious circumstances, Edelman had also chosen him to lead a secret investigation. And he knew just where to start and who to contact.

3

MALIN REHNBERG WANTED NOTHING more than to have a full-bodied glass of red Zinfandel, which felt like the obvious pairing to the steak on her plate. At home in Stockholm she'd had no problem skipping alcohol the moment she got pregnant. The craving had disappeared all on its own. It was a different story here in the Danish capital where it had returned full force. Or maybe it was it because Dunja Hougaard – her new contact at the homicide unit in Copenhagen – didn't seem to have any problem drinking a whole bottle alone.

They had found each other after only a few hours at the conference, where homicide investigators from all over Europe had gathered for two intense days to network across borders. Right then and there they had decided to be each other's respective contacts. It had been so pleasant that Malin suggested they go out to eat together.

Now they were at the Barock restaurant in Nyhavn, and Malin was starting to appreciate why Danish children were the last in the world to learn to speak. After only one glass of wine Dunja Hougaard had left the safe harbour of English and switched to Danish, which got harder and harder to understand as her wine consumption increased. Malin had initially interrupted her and asked her to explain when there was something she didn't understand, but she soon reverted to nodding and smiling, mostly trying to understand context.

She couldn't even manage that at this point. It was as if Dunja's words were squeezed together into one long incomprehensible sludge, and more than once she caught herself thinking about something else entirely – including how envious she was of the Dane who wasn't pregnant and could drink as much wine as she wanted. Or how jealous she was of her bright red jeans and her body, where everything still sat exactly where it should.

Malin hated looking at herself. She had to wear ugly maternity clothes and would exchange her body for just about anyone else's in the blink of an eye. She'd gained fifty-five pounds, and there was still over two months left – two months of hell.

Even if she really tried she couldn't think of a single place on her body that wasn't swollen, aching or generally florid and sweaty. She felt like one big sticky minefield of cramps and complaints that risked blossoming out into something really painful at any moment. Take her belly, for instance. She rubbed it every morning and evening with a cream so expensive that she had lied to Anders about the price. But whenever she lowered her eyes, her stomach was so full of stretch marks that she looked like she'd been run over.

'Are you sure you won't have a little wine?'

Malin jolted back into the conversation. 'Excuse me?'

'Lit-tel wine,' Dunja Hougaard said, attempting to speak Swedish as she held up the bottle.

'Thanks, it's okay. I promised myself not to drink a drop of alcohol as long as I'm pregnant.'

'Why?' Dunja looked sincerely confused, which made Malin wonder whether she was visiting another planet and not just a neighbouring country.

'It's just not good for the foetus. Alcohol enters the placenta and—'

'That's so typically Swedish.'

'What?'

'You have so many rules and prohibitions – you're so scared, to be quite honest. How much damage can a simple little glass of wine do?'

Malin took a deep breath to keep her irritation in check. 'Maybe it hasn't reached Denmark yet, but there is actually quite a bit of research that shows that when the mother drinks alcohol the foetus develops more poorly and the risk of ADHD increases. Besides—'

'No, that's just not true.' Dunja took a gulp of wine and met Malin's gaze. 'Here in Denmark we've just completed a study with several thousand five-year-olds, and doctors could document no difference whatsoever in the children where the mother had two drinks a day while pregnant and the ones where the mother had completely abstained from drinking alcohol.'

'I see, that sounds strange though. On the other hand, they can prove just about anything with those studies. The point is—'

'Do you know what I think?' Dunja held up an index finger. 'I think the only risk of you having a little glass of wine tonight is that your children will have a happy mother.'

'What do you mean "happy"? I'm happy, aren't I?' Malin could feel her irritation winning the battle and was now storming in.

'Okay, Malin. You'll have to excuse me, because I'm a bit drunk, but I just have to say it.'

'I'm listening,' said Malin, realizing that she suddenly understood every word.

Dunja looked Malin in the eyes. 'Unfortunately you don't seem that happy.'

Malin didn't know what to say or how to react. She ought to get angry and leave, tell her newfound Danish friend that she could go to hell with her alcohol-glorifying bullshit, and find another contact in Stockholm. If Anders had so much as breathed anything that might resemble criticism she would have taken the pruning shears and clipped off his nose without batting an eye.

But for some unfathomable reason she did not get the least bit angry. On the contrary.

'Okay…' She emptied the glass of mineral water. 'Give me a little wine then, dammit.' She held out the empty glass and Dunja filled it, laughing, as she signalled to the waiter that they wanted another bottle.

They raised their glasses and toasted. Malin savoured the taste of the wine, and felt a wave of pleasure spread in her body.

'Oh, God, that's good.' She had a little more. 'But you do have one thing completely backwards here – not just you but all Danes. Sweden doesn't have more prohibitions than Denmark. It's the exact opposite.' She took yet another sip. 'Here, for example, you can't live in your summer house as much as you want. Kan jang, an ordinary dietary supplement, is banned, and businesses can't even be open on Sundays. Talk about a nanny state!'

'Okay, okay. I see your point. But—'

'And best of all, did you know that by law Danish contractors are forced to wear lip balm with sunscreen whenever they work outdoors?'

'That's a joke.'

'No! It's the truth!'

They burst into laughter and Malin once again raised her glass. 'Cheers!'

'You know what? I'm very *misundelig* of your pregnancy.'

'*Misundelig?* If that means "envious", then I'm more than happy to switch places.'

'Why? Isn't it completely amazing?'

'What's so amazing about going around like a fat duck and hurting everywhere? I have nothing against having children, truly not. And I see twins as mostly being a big bonus. It's better to reduce the years with small children as much as possible. But pregnancy… if I'm going to be completely honest, I hate it more and more every day.'

'You don't really mean that, do you?'

'You said it yourself. I don't look particularly happy, and what do you think is the cause of that, if not this?' Malin pointed to her belly with one hand and took the wine glass with the other. 'The first few weeks I joked with my husband, Anders, that he got to choose either pregnancy, delivery or nursing. That's not a joke any more. If he doesn't take over soon there won't be any children to raise! So take my advice and never subject your – if I may say so – amazing body to pregnancy.'

'It's probably not going to happen any time soon.'

'What do you mean? Are you single?'

'No, but my boyfriend and I *knalder* way too little.'

'*Knalder?*' Malin illustrated by moving a finger into the space between her thumb and index finger.

Dunja nodded. 'We've tried talking about it and even made a schedule for it at least once a week, but it didn't help a bit.'

'Do you love him?'

'Carsten? Of course I do. We're getting married this summer. The plan is to move to Silkeborg in the autumn.'

'Silkeborg? Isn't that on Jutland? Excuse me, but what the hell are you going to do there?'

'Carsten's going to take over his father's accounting firm.'

'But what about you? You have a career here, right?'

'Yes, but... I don't want to work full-time with small children anyway.'

'Dunja, now you listen to me.' Malin filled both their glasses.

'Maybe you should be careful that the wine doesn't get out of hand.'

'Now I'm the one who's talking,' said Malin. 'And listen to me very closely. I've never said this to anyone and presumably I'm never going to say it again. But... you shouldn't have kids. In any event, not with this Carsten, or whatever his name is.'

'How can you say that?' Dunja set aside the glass.

'If you've got a body like yours beside you in bed, you have to be very peculiar for there to be too little "*knalderi*", if I'm going to be frank.'

'Frank?'

'Either Carsten is homosexual, or he doesn't love you. And the question is whether you love him.'

'Of course, we love each other. What the hell gives you the right to come here and—'

'I'm just telling you what I see.'

'And what's that?'

'I see a woman who... who... okay, I think it speaks for itself. The whole arrangement with this Carsten seems completely...' Malin fell silent and suddenly realized how thin the ice was beneath her. She set aside the glass and covered her mouth. 'Oh, my God, excuse me.' This was certainly not the first time she had just blathered on and said exactly what she thought, but this was the first time she did it to someone she barely knew. 'Forgive me. I'm sorry. I take back everything. It wasn't my intention at all to barge in and... Oh, God, how stupid. I don't know what's got into me.'

'Maybe just a little too much of a good thing?'

'Probably. Besides, my hormones are not to be toyed with at the moment. The best you can do is to keep your distance, which I wish I could do myself.'

Dunja burst into laughter and raised her glass.

4

FABIAN LOOKED OUT OVER Riddarfjärden to the melody of Arcade Fire's 'Black Mirror'. The light from the thousands of illuminated windows from the heights of Södermalm reflected in the water and he was struck by how beautiful it was. The surface steamed, at once enticing and treacherous, almost as if it was warm, when in reality it was only hours from freezing to ice.

The song reached a crescendo.

He lowered the volume and searched for her number on his phone, and pressed dial. It didn't take more than two rings.

'Hey there, it's been a while.'

'Yeah, I guess it's almost two years since you quit. Sorry if I'm calling a little late,' he said, even though he thought she sounded anything but tired.

'No problem. The night is young, and you know me.'

'Maybe you've settled down, started a family and get up early.'

He could hear her laughing on the other end. For Niva Ekenhielm the nuclear family was about as improbable as life on the moon. They had been colleagues at the National Bureau of Criminal Investigation for six years where she worked as an IT investigator, or sci-fi cop, as they'd called it. It had been more of the rule than the exception that Niva was still at work when everyone else had left, slogging far into the night and not going home until the next morning, when people started coming in again.

Fabian had kept her company and spent the night at the department on a number of occasions. Usually it was because he found himself in the middle of an investigation that gave him insomnia, but sometimes it had just been a chance to clear his desk.

On each occasion, Sonja had reacted with a jealousy so strong that it risked corroding their whole relationship. And in a way he could understand it. Niva had both charisma and was incredibly good-looking. Besides, there was something about her attitude. In the beginning he'd assumed she acted that way to all men, but soon he understood that she'd been flirting with him. Even though he'd let it be known that he wasn't interested, she'd kept up her insinuations and done less and less to hide what she was really after.

But this time he was the one who was after something.

'Fabian, what can I do for you? You haven't got divorced, have you?'

'No, we won't have that much fun.' Fabian regretted it immediately, and tried to rescue it with a laugh. 'Joking aside, I need your help with a case that has to be kept outside the building.'

'Can it wait till tomorrow?'

'Preferably not.'

He fixed his gaze on the Münchenbryggeriet Conference Centre on the opposite side of Riddarfjärden and started counting how many windows were illuminated. He could hear Niva walking back and forth in high heels on a creaking parquet floor.

'Okay, tell me.'

5

KAREN NEUMAN HAD BEEN afraid of the dark for as long as she could remember. When she was little, living in a small town outside Copenhagen, she'd believed in monsters that hid under the bed or behind the curtain, so she always kept a light on when she was sleeping. Her parents thought it was normal at that age and were convinced that she would grow out of it. Instead the problem got worse, and when Karen entered her teens she suffered from such severe insomnia that she had to take sleeping pills.

Now she no longer believed in monsters under the bed, but her fear of the dark still held its grip on her and she would never manage without the pills, something that didn't improve now that winter was only just beginning and it was getting darker and darker with every passing day.

They lived in an old half-timbered house, which was no great help either. It was very lovely, situated on the Danish coast with an outstanding view of Öresund, but Karen had never really been able to enjoy it, because however you twisted it, the sea wasn't their nearest neighbour – it was darkness.

The pressure in her chest had alleviated a bit over time because of the many hours she had spent in therapy, not to mention the small fortune Aksel had paid for the outdoor lights. But the feeling was far from gone, even if she could now manage to stay home alone when he was working on his evening TV 2 show three nights a week. On those nights she insisted on keeping every light in the house on, despite Aksel's protests about the high electricity bills.

But tonight the pressure in her chest was more tangible. As soon as she came home from yoga shortly after nine, she'd sensed that something was in the air. She had first noticed the sports car parked a little out of the way down Gammel Strandvej. A parked car was nothing unusual; on the contrary, it was relatively common that people would leave their cars to walk along the shore, but not during the winter months. It was definitely not normal that a car with Swedish licence plates found its way down to Tibberup, even if it was only a kilometre or so north of the Louisiana Art Museum.

She tried to resist the temptation to give in to the fear, just as she'd agreed to with the therapist, and continued to calmly walk through the garden towards the house. But when the garden lighting didn't turn on, even though she jumped and waved her arms in front of the motion detector, she'd felt helplessly lost and her heart rate doubled. She ran as fast as she could up to the door, unlocked it and turned off the alarm with trembling fingers.

Fortunately, the indoor lights were working, and she illuminated the whole house with the remote control. She went into the kitchen and boiled a big cup of water and added some squeezed lemon, a pinch of Himalaya salt and honey to restore her substance balance after the Bikram session. Assuming a fuse had blown, she felt a sense of calm returning.

'I'm sure it was nothing,' she repeated out loud to herself on her way to the living room. She grabbed her tablet that was sitting on the coffee table, and scrolled to Lisa Nilsson, whose voice always calmed her. She pressed play and music started streaming out of the concealed speakers in the ceiling. Aksel had initially struggled to get her to understand the advantage of streaming music instead of putting on a CD. Now she couldn't imagine not having the freedom to take music to any room in the house with a single click.

She walked to the bathroom, where she ran a hot bath, took off her yoga clothes, put up her hair and sank down into the Jacuzzi, letting the massage jets work on her body. She relaxed and closed her eyes. 'I'm sure it was nothing,' she repeated to herself, and sang along with 'Heaven Round the Corner' in the best Swedish accent she could.

Aksel had warned her that he would probably be spending the night in the apartment on Vesterbro and not be home until breakfast tomorrow. There were guests on the programme, who would almost certainly want to have a few drinks after the broadcast. But she would have no problem passing the time at home. After the bath she would add yesterday's chicken salad to some quinoa, settle down in front of the TV and binge watch as many episodes of *Mad Men* as she could, even though Aksel expected her to watch his show.

But as Lisa Nilsson faded out, the uncertainty came creeping back. Had she heard a door closing out in the hall? It couldn't be Aksel, could it? The show hadn't even started yet. Karen pressed on the Jacuzzi's panel so that the massage jets fell silent and reached over the edge to pause the music on the tablet before the next song started. Her hand was too wet and soon Lisa was going on again with 'Never, Never, Never'.

Thoughts whirled through Karen's head. Should she lock herself in the bathroom or venture out into the house and see if there really was someone there? She got out of the tub and dried her hands so that she could turn off the music. The silence fell over the room so abruptly that it gave her a start. Her entire body was now tense as a spring and she felt like a five-year-old again – a five-year-old with a monster under the bed.

She slipped over to the bathroom door and put her ear against it. All she could hear was her own breath. It took all her courage to push down the handle and open the door slightly. It creaked so loudly that the sound cut into her belly. She'd been after Aksel so many times about that door that it had become a standing joke.

Maybe it was just Aksel. After all, the show might have been cancelled for some reason. She stuck her head out and called to him, but there was no answer. And why should there be? She was the only one home – or was she?

She yelled again, this time really loud, but was met by the same suffocating silence. The sound of the door had probably just been in her head. Her father always said she had a lively imagination.

She shook her head and decided to get back into the bath and try to relax, but she changed her mind almost immediately, stood up again and dried off. She carefully rubbed her body butter on herself, especially the area around the scar. She always felt a sting of immorality whenever she stood naked in front of the mirror, even though over ten years had passed. Besides, it didn't seem as if the sensory nerves ever intended to repair themselves. The area was numb, and if she drew her fingers on one place she felt it somewhere else entirely. But she didn't complain – everything had a price.

She put on her silk kimono and left the bathroom, whistling 'Heaven Round the Corner', and continued towards the kitchen. As usual, it was freezing cold in the hall, and she reminded herself to nag Aksel until he agreed to extend the under-floor heating there, too. But this time it was colder than normal. She stopped mid-step and turned towards the front door, which was ajar. Hadn't she closed it properly? She always locked it behind her, even in the middle of the day.

She had been jittery since she came home. First the parked car and then the garden lights that didn't work. *I've just been careless*, she thought, closing the door. To be on the safe side she checked that it was really locked, before continuing towards the kitchen where she arranged a chicken salad plate and put out a carbonated bottle of water. She set everything on a tray and walked to the living room. Then the phone started ringing.

She set the tray aside and went over to grab the phone. Instead of answering, she stared at it as if, by pure mental force, she could get it to stop ringing, but it refused to obey.

Finally, she gathered her courage and picked up the receiver. 'Yes, hello?'

'Why didn't you answer?'

'Aksel? Is it you?'

'Yes, who did you think it would be? I've called your cell so many times. But—'

'My cell?' Only now did she realize that she had no idea where she'd put it.

'I just wanted to check in and make sure that you're okay with me sleeping in town.'

'Do you have to?'

'But, sweetheart, you know how it is. Some guests more or less demand that we go out after the show and Casper is one of them.'

She thought she heard a noise from the hall, but this time it wasn't the door shutting. It sounded like something quite different, almost like something rolling. Or was it just the wind howling outside?

'Sorry, I missed that. What did you say?'

'It's nothing important. Just go to bed. I'll come home with fresh bread tomorrow.'

'No, I really want you here tonight. Please, can you come home right now?'

'Now? How would that work? The broadcast starts in eight minutes.'

'I know, but I feel like there's something or someone… I'm not really sure. Can you just come home? Please, I'm begging you.'

'Sweetheart, I don't know how many times we've been through this: the dark can be tough. We all feel the same way, but there are no monsters under the bed, I promise. There never have been and there never will be either. Okay? If you put on the TV, it will almost be like I'm at home.'

'Okay.'

'I have to go. I love you and I'll see you tomorrow.'

Aksel hung up and Karen set down the phone with a sigh. She went out into the hall and looked around, but saw nothing different – until she lowered her eyes to the floor. The transparent plastic surface protector had been rolled out from the front door all the way through the hall and further around the corner into the corridor.

'Hello?' she yelled, following the plastic around the corner and down the hallway. 'Excuse me? Hello!'

The house was completely silent, except for the plastic film that rustled under her feet. She was surprised at herself for not running in the opposite direction. It felt as if something inside her was tired of being afraid. She was more angry than afraid. Whatever kind of monster this was, she intended to look it right in the eyes – at least that's what her therapist always told her to do.

She followed the protector into their bedroom and looked around. The plastic she was standing on continued across the wall-to-wall carpeting and up on to the double bed.

'Hello, is anyone there? Because if there is come out! Come out, if you dare! Come here and look me in the eyes!' She waited and could feel her legs shaking under her. 'I thought so! When it comes down to it you wouldn't dare!'

She waited but couldn't see anything except the plastic on the bed and under her feet. Then she heard a noise, a hissing sound right behind her. When she turned around and tried to determine its origin she saw white smoke seeping out between the slats in the wardrobe door. She didn't even consider fleeing. Instead she walked up to it, as if she had no other choice than to find out what was inside.

Just as she opened the door, she realized that she'd been right all along.

Someone dressed in heavy dark clothing and boots with their face hidden behind a gas mask came out of the wardrobe.

'Who are you and what are you doing here?' Karen burst into tears and felt her legs buckling under her. 'Answer me. Please! What do you want? Why are you here!?'

But Karen got no answer. All she could hear was the hissing from the gas mask. And never again would Karen need to be afraid.

6

FABIAN RISK HAD BOTH hands on the wheel as he drove out of the city through the burgeoning snowstorm. He was trying to dismiss the uncomfortable feeling that he had absolutely no grasp of his new assignment's potential magnitude. He really ought to decline Edelman's instructions and head home to his kids, but he couldn't turn his back on it.

Edelman had specifically given the task to him, and he knew himself well enough to know that he would pursue it regardless of how many warning lights were blinking. The Minister for Justice had been missing since this afternoon and, like Edelman, he didn't believe for a moment that the minister had chosen to disappear of his own accord and would soon show up again.

Something had definitely happened.

He called home but only got the family voicemail. He left a message for Matilda and Theodor saying that he would be a little later than he'd thought, and that they should just go to bed, which he assumed they must have already done. *It was after eleven thirty*, he thought, putting Harold Budd and Brian Eno's *The Pearl* into the CD player. It was far from his favourite album, but it was one of the first CDs he'd ever bought, and so it always had a place in his collection – like most projects Eno was involved in. It suited his mood perfectly today.

Solemn piano tones filled the car as he drove across the Drottningholm Bridge and made the snowflakes outside feel like a pleasant stage in a private theatre rather than the storm it was in reality. If this storm didn't calm down soon he might never get home at all.

He continued along Ekerövägen to Rörbyvägen, where he turned left and stopped some fifty metres later at a manor-like building with a number of parked cars outside. One of the cars, a red Mazda RX-8, blinked its lights. He parked and hurried through the whirling snow towards the car. He barely had a chance to get into the passenger seat before Niva put it in gear and skidded out on the road.

'Fucking shitty weather,' she said, accelerating as if there was no tomorrow. 'Hi, by the way.'

'Hi, there. Nice car.'

'In this weather it feels more like Bambi on ice than a car. Yours would have been better, but I didn't want to draw a lot of unnecessary attention to us.'

'Are you sure you're okay with all of this?'

'Uh... If I wasn't, why would I be here instead of inside Spy Bar where it's warm?'

'To see me, of course,' said Fabian with a smile.

Niva burst out laughing, turned right, and stopped at a closed gate with a large sign: *National Defence Radio Institute*.

'You're funny,' she said, pressing on a small remote control that opened the gate. 'But I happen to already have a date this evening, so this can't take all night.' She had already parked and left the car before Fabian had time to respond.

They hurried through the snow towards the door of one of the nondescript buildings. Only now did Fabian notice her styled hair, little fur jacket, high heels and glittering gold short skirt. Niva really did intend to go out when they were finished. He couldn't remember the last time he'd gone out himself, especially not on a weeknight.

Niva pulled her pass card through the reader, entered a long code and opened the door. Fabian looked quizzically at the sign on the door in front of them: *Department for Operational Support*.

'Aren't you in the technology development department?'

'Yes,' said Niva, hurrying down a stairway. 'But right now I prefer this route.'

Fabian had a hard time keeping up with her, despite her high heels, and he was struck by how much bigger the building was underneath the ground than above. A few floors down, Niva once again pulled out her pass card, opened a thick iron door and disappeared into the dark. Fabian had no choice but to follow the sound of heels against the concrete floor. Niva flicked on a row of fluorescent lights, revealing that they were in a culvert that was well over a hundred metres long. One more heavy iron door and elevator later they were finally at the Department for Technology Development.

It was NDRI's most respected department, but the general public knew almost nothing about it. The Department for Technology Development did not face the same legal restrictions as all other departments at NDRI and could basically indulge in any kind of eavesdropping, as long as it fell under the designation of 'technology development'.

'Okay. The minister for justice, you said.' Niva had already sat down at one of the desks in the windowless room and was starting up one of the big computers that covered most of their field of vision. 'Do you have his cell phone number?'

'Isn't that why we're here?' said Fabian, pulling up a chair beside her.

She shrugged. 'You're the one who called me.' She entered a number of commands and clicked further into various servers, when her cell phone lit up. 'Hi... Sorry, but I have to help an old friend with something, so I'm going to be a little late... Absolutely... Yes, I promise... Okay ... Bye.' She set down the phone and entered *Carl-Eric Grimås* in the blinking search field.

'Was that your date?'

'Mmm.'

'Was he upset?'

'Who said it's a he?'

'Oh, sorry. I—'

Niva gave Fabian a smile that could just as well mean she was pulling his leg, *which would be like her*, he thought. He looked at the screen that was now filled with rows of names. 'Where are you?'

'In SePo and their department for personal protection,' said Niva, pulling the minister's secure cell phone number to a search field on an adjacent computer screen. Then she pressed *search positioning*. On yet another screen a map of Stockholm started zooming in. A few minutes later, a blinking dot appeared in the water outside the Kanslikajen.

'Is that the last location of the cell phone?'

Niva nodded. 'At 3:26 p.m. earlier today.'

It was two minutes after he'd disappeared through the door of the parliament building, which would mean he must have gone straight there and thrown in his phone, or else jumped in himself. Why would he do that? There were much easier ways to kill yourself than jumping into ice-cold water in the middle of the afternoon. Or did he run into someone on the way?

'Is it possible to see whether he had any calls around that time?'

Niva nodded and brought up a graph on one of the computer screens that showed the activity on the minister's phone number up until 3:26. 'Here are some calls from this morning, when he was still at Rosenbad.'

'Can you see who they were with?'

'Yes, but from what I can tell, there's nothing that stands out. Actually – he had a brief call with Herman Edelman right before nine.'

'Edelman?' Fabian repeated. He couldn't understand why his boss hadn't said anything about it. 'Anyone else?'

'Yes, thirteen minutes later he called the Israeli Embassy, but hung up before they had time to answer. At nine thirty he spoke with a Melvin Stenberg at SePo's personal protection.'

'I'm sure it was about his decision to walk to the parliament building.'

'There are also some calls with the other ministers and one with the chief of staff at the ministry, but nothing all that exciting.'

'Are those calls recorded anywhere?'

Niva laughed. 'You've read too much Orwell.'

'Maybe, but we're talking about the minister for justice. I imagine his phone would be particularly interesting to you here.'

'Absolutely. But even we have our limits. But I can print out a list of all the minister's calls, their times and who they were with. So maybe we're done for tonight?'

'Done?' said Fabian, while he studied the graph of the minister's calls on the screen.

'Yes. What would Sonja say if we got snowed in here?' Niva stood up and went over to a printer, which hummed as it started up. 'Isn't that your wife's name?'

'Yes. But—' Fabian stopped himself, realizing that he was about to walk right into a trap. Even though she had a date waiting she was definitely toying with him. It felt like she had picked up the scent of marital crisis and would sink her claws into him at any moment.

'But what?' She came towards him with a smile.

'Wait a second. What's that?' Fabian turned towards one of the screens and pointed at two markings on the graph. 'Both those calls are right after 3:26.'

'Yes, but they're unanswered.'

'So someone tried to call him after the phone ended up in the water. Is it possible to see who?'

Niva sighed and looked at the clock, her smile gone.

'For my sake.'

'It's going to cost you. Just so you know.' She gave him a look, sat down in the chair, and returned to the keyboard. 'Unfortunately, the caller at 3:28 has a blocked number.'

'So that's not something you can produce?'

'I could, but not now. It takes a bit more.'

'Okay. And the other at 3:35?'

'That number belongs to a... Sten Gustavsson, and he...' Niva's fingers danced over the keyboard as if they never did anything else. Fabian realized how impressed he still was with people who could type without taking their eyes off the screen. 'Works as a chauffeur at Rosenbad.'

'He was probably waiting and wondering where Grimås was,' said Fabian. 'And by the way, what does that mean?' He pointed at a numbered marking on the graph by the call.

'It's a time indication of how long the line was connected. Sten Gustavsson apparently hung up as soon as the voicemail started.'

'But the anonymous caller didn't,' said Fabian, looking more closely at the graph. 'The call was connected for twenty-four seconds, which is more than enough time to leave a message, wouldn't you say?' He turned to Niva, who shrugged without answering. But Fabian did not give in, holding her gaze until the silence became much too insistent.

'Okay,' said Niva, shaking her head. 'But then the fun is over.'

'Sure thing,' said Fabian, taking the printed list of calls while Niva continued working. A few minutes later she'd pulled up the message.

'Carl-Eric Grimås is unable to take your call right now. Please leave a message, or even better, send an email.'

'Hi, it's me,' a female voice said. 'And yes, I know I really shouldn't call this number. I've tried the other one several times, but you don't answer. You may not believe it but I actually have a life too. You're not the only one. So annoying.' There was a click and the call was over.

Niva turned towards Fabian. 'Did you hear the same thing I did?'

Fabian nodded.

Grimås had another phone.

7

DUNJA HOUGAARD DEFIED THE snow and pedalled along Gothersgade. But then she remembered what happened when Carsten had biked home three years before after a night of drinking on Vesterbro, and decided to get off and walk the bike instead.

A wrong assessment of the distance to the edge of the sidewalk, and a fraction of a second later his face was in the asphalt. But instead of waiting for help he'd got up and kept biking as if nothing had happened. Not until the next morning did he discover that several of his teeth were bashed in and parts of his face looked as if they had been run through a meat grinder. Since then, he hadn't touched alcohol – which you couldn't accuse her of. Nor her new contact person Malin Rehnberg either, for that matter. The evening had far exceeded expectations, and it had been a long time since she'd laughed so much.

The Swedish police officer had initially been just as proper and boring as most other Swedes she'd encountered. But after a little wine, her stiffness transformed into a hilarious and to-the-point attitude. Dunja had no problem picturing them in regular contact and perhaps even becoming really good friends in a few years.

Yet something was bugging her that refused to leave her in peace. Malin had charged in like a bulldozer, maintaining that Carsten didn't love her. Although she blamed it on the fact that it was the first time in six months she'd allowed herself a little wine, it still didn't make it easier to take.

The problem was that she couldn't stop thinking about it, even though she was quite sure that she and Carsten were made for each other. Sure, they had their problems, but who didn't? And how often did people really have sex? She'd never doubted that she and Carsten would be together for ever – not until this evening.

Now she no longer knew what to believe. Even just the slightest chance that Malin was right was hard to handle. Maybe she was blowing it out of proportion because she was still drunk, so she tried to get it out of her mind and continued walking over Nørreport where the gathering snowstorm bombarded her with its wet snowflakes.

Once she stepped into the apartment at Blågårdsgade 4 she looked like the snow monster from *Tintin in Tibet*. True to her habit, her clothes were far too thin, and she could feel a urinary tract infection waiting just around the corner.

The lights were on in the living room and she could hear one of Carsten's favourite pieces from the stereo. It was something classical that she'd heard at least a thousand times, but could never remember the name of. So Carsten was still up, working.

Normally she would go in and say hello, and then ask whether there was tea left or if he wanted her to put the kettle on. But not tonight. No, tonight would be something completely different. She would show that pregnant Swede how in love she and Carsten really were.

She slipped as quietly as she could into the bathroom and closed the door without locking it so that the sound from the creaking old lock knob wouldn't give her away. She got into the shower and turned on the water. After lathering up and washing herself, she took out the shaving cream and razor and started to shave her bikini line.

She'd thought about it many times, and read that most men preferred it, but she'd never dared to go the whole way; tonight she decided it was now or never. Once she was fully shaved and had dried herself, she stood in front of the mirror and oiled her body with the olive-scented cream Carsten had given her after his latest trip to Stockholm.

She couldn't tell if it was the heat from the bath, her wandering thoughts, or her soft hands over her body, but she was filled with desire. She put on her kimono and went out into the living room, where Carsten was sitting at the desk with his eyes nailed to the computer screen.

He still hadn't noticed she was there, so she took the opportunity to study him. He looked good – he always did. He looked like he exercised even though he never set foot in a gym. The only thing she didn't like was the moustache that he'd had for the past month. It didn't suit him, and she was sure that he agreed with her, and kept it just to tease her.

'Hi, honey,' she said, walking up to him.

'You're home already?' Carsten said without taking his eyes off the stock exchange listings.

'Hmm... Do you know what I just did?'

'Yes, weren't you going out for dinner with that Swedish policewoman? Where did you go?'

'Not that. I mean now, after I came home.' She waited for a reaction, but Carsten was consumed by the endless number tables. 'I took a shower and I'm all warm and clean.' She started massaging his shoulders. 'So, I was thinking we could... You know, before we get too tired.'

'There's tea, if you want some.' Carsten nodded towards the kitchen.

'No, I'm fine,' she said, wondering how she should continue. She couldn't just stand there massaging for all eternity. 'Do you have much left?'

'Tokyo opens soon and I'm still not done with the figures from Fed.'

Dunja's desire had pretty much disappeared and she wanted nothing more than to creep under the blanket with a cup of steaming hot tea and keep reading Jussi Adler Olsen's *A Conspiracy of*

Faith. But she'd promised herself to do everything she could and so decided to cast herself headlong down the precipice and hope that Carsten was there to catch her.

'Then we'll have a quick second to be together now?' She unbuttoned his top shirt buttons, stuck her hands in and started massaging his chest.

Carsten twirled around on the chair. 'What are you up to?'

'What does it look like?' She continued down with her hands and started loosening his belt.

'Please, not now.' He pushed away her hands. 'I've got a lot to do and besides I haven't showered lately.'

'Forget about that.' *Now I'm jumping*, she thought, and let the kimono fall to the floor.

Carsten looked at her. Or rather stared. She felt like a model in a Helmut Newton photo, but wasn't sure whether that was good or bad. Carsten didn't seem to know what to say, but at last looked up and met her eyes.

'You know perfectly well *that* considerably increases the risk of urinary tract infection.'

Dunja wanted to get away from there as quickly as possible and erase the whole experience, but her legs refused to obey, so she just stood there, feeling more naked than ever, looking like someone who was trying to get her virginity back. Then she picked up the kimono and hurried away.

'Honey, forgive me. I didn't mean to…' Carsten followed her into the hall and tried to open the bathroom door, which she had just managed to lock. 'Listen, I just said that out of pure consideration for you. I think you're really beautiful. But—'

'Carsten, it's okay,' Dunja said, wiping her eyes. 'I'm very tired anyway.' She pulled on a pair of striped men's pyjamas and sat down on the toilet seat.

'Love you, just so you know.'

'Love you, too,' she said, but couldn't stop thinking about how right her the pregnant Swede had been.

8

HAD HE SEEN RIGHT or did it only look like one?

Aksel Neuman was holding on to the steering wheel as hard as he could and cast yet another glance in the rear-view mirror. Dammit – he'd seen right. The police officer was only a few cars behind him. After he'd consumed three beers and one-and-a-half gin and tonics, he suddenly decided not to spend the night in town but to take the car home to Tibberup and surprise Karen. At the time, it had seemed like a good idea: she'd been beside herself with worry and he didn't have the heart to leave her alone for the whole night. And in his recently purchased BMW X3 with its intelligent four-wheel drive, the trip wouldn't take more than half an hour.

It didn't seem like a good idea any more. Why hadn't he chosen to sleep in the apartment on Vesterbro in Copenhagen? Karen's anxiety attacks about the dark were starting to become more the rule rather than the exception. If it continued like this, he would be forced to stop his evening show.

He looked in the rear-view mirror again and noted that the police car was still keeping the same distance. If they stopped him now, he wouldn't stand a chance and there would surely be a scandal. He could already see the headlines: *Famous TV Host Drove Drunk – Spends the Night in Jail*. The media would wait before giving out his name and spread various rumours about who it might be to try to get people interested. Not until a few days later would they release the bomb along with a lot of spicy details about how he'd peed his pants and needed help out of the car.

How in the hell could he be so fucking stupid? He'd promised himself that the last time was it. Maybe he deserved to go to jail and have his driving licence taken away. It could be exactly what he needed – just not right now.

It was crucial not to drive too slowly, which was always the biggest mistake people made when they were driving under the influence. To over-compensate and stay far below the speed limit to avoid an accident was the surest way to attract police attention. Instead it was critical to stay as close to the speed limit as possible, or even better just over it. The hard thing was staying in your lane at the same time. Dammit, he was still drunk, almost more drunk now than when he got into the car. He lowered the side window, took in the freezing air and tried to focus on the markings on the road.

Nice and easy now. There wasn't far to go. In a kilometre he would be at the Louisiana Museum. After that it was just a matter of turning down towards the water after the church. A hundred metres or so later he was more or less home.

Just like in a bad movie, the blue lights came on and penetrated right into the car. Dammit. He would stumble at the finish line. He tried to see how close the police car was in the rear-view mirror, but was blinded by the strong light. He had no choice but to stop and try to talk his way out of the situation, something he was admittedly good at. But the police car rushed past him and disappeared into the darkness.

'Yes!' Aksel drummed his fingers on the steering wheel and burst out in a howl of joy. He had escaped by the skin of his teeth and he promised himself that this was absolutely the last time.

He passed Humlebæk Church, slowed down and turned right on to Gammel Strandvej. He would soon be able to see the house, and his heart rate finally started to reflect the fact that the danger was over. He drove past a silver-coloured Porsche that was parked along the road. Fifty metres later he turned on to the driveway and parked alongside Karen's car.

For some reason, the floodlights didn't come on. When he got out of the car he realized that all the garden lighting was turned off, but Karen always kept the lights on when she was home alone.

He continued along the cobblestone walk through the snow towards the house. He had to support himself against the wall so that he didn't lose his balance when he put the key in the lock. But he couldn't turn it – the door was already unlocked. This was not at all like Karen. First the garden lighting and now the door.

She had undeniably sounded more worried than normal, and went so far as to try to get him to cancel the show. But it hadn't really registered at the time. He could never grasp anything in the minutes before the red light came on. At that moment his entire focus was on the impending broadcast.

He stepped into the hall and wondered how many times he'd tried to explain his process

to Karen, emphasizing that it didn't have anything to do with his love for her. It happened completely in his subconscious. The world could come to an end outside the studio and he wouldn't even realize it until after the show.

But she never believed him and always insisted that his routine was proof of his narcissism and that, when it came right down to it, there was no place for her in his life. He had tried to convince her otherwise again and again, such as when he'd supported her when she was sick, not least financially. If that wasn't proof enough, what was? He pulled off his shoes and almost lost his balance.

The question was whether he would ever sober up again. Right now it felt as if his blood alcohol level was still rising. He looked into the living room and determined that Karen was not still up, which meant that she'd managed to calm down and finally go to bed. But then he heard the bedroom door in the hall open and close and figured that Karen was *about* to go to bed. At least she knew he was home now.

He whistled all the way to the bathroom. Once he got there, he undressed, leaving his clothes in a pile on the floor, and then stepped into the shower and let the hot water stream over him. He set the control to the quiet summer rain setting and reminded himself how much he loved the new shower, which could re-create everything from monsoon rain to dense fog.

When he'd finished rinsing the soap from his body, he dried himself off, pulled in his stomach and studied his body in the mirror both from the front and the side. He was in good shape and had no problem getting down on the floor and firing off thirty-odd push-ups at a rapid pace. He left the bathroom and walked to the bedroom, where he stuck his head into the darkness.

'Hello? May I come in?' He awaited a response, but none came.

So that was the game they would play tonight, he speculated and continued into the room, the wordless game, where body language and physical desire were the only vocabulary. She usually had a lamp on until he came in and lay down beside her, but now it was so dark that he had to feel with his hands along the edge of the bed to find his way. He crept down under the covers on his side and lay on his back. He was still intoxicated and could only hope that she wouldn't notice. In any event, it was her turn to take the initiative, he thought, and tried to sound as if he was about to fall asleep.

Besides the faint murmur of the ventilation system he could hear nothing but his own breathing. Karen was almost completely silent. He had a tendency to snore through the night, and Karen had regularly threatened to have separate bedrooms if he didn't start using his anti-snoring mouthpiece. He had broken this promise more or less every night, he admitted to himself, automatically pulling back the covers. His pounding erection was now completely exposed and pointed right toward his navel.

But he got no reaction from Karen. She couldn't be that upset because he hadn't cancelled the show, jumped into the car and driven home just because she was a little afraid of the dark, could she? No, he was probably the one who was impatient and over-eager. He cupped his hands in front of his mouth and exhaled, but couldn't tell whether he reeked of alcohol.

After yet another endlessly long minute he turned towards her and let one hand find its way under the blanket. Karen was lying on her back. He continued up with his hand and grazed her nipple, something that always turned her on. But this time there was no reaction at all, not even after he started using his tongue.

He pulled back the covers, leaned down over her and drew the tip of his tongue in careful light circles around and on top of her nipple. He still got no response, and he wondered what he was doing wrong. He always initiated foreplay this way. He decided to focus on the lower regions, even if he knew that Karen could get turned off immediately if he was too forward. But what choice did he have? She was forcing him, more or less.

He brought his hand down from her breast and along her ribs and belly, where he felt something sticky that made him instinctively pull back and sit straight up. *What the hell was that*, he asked himself, and turned on the bedside lamp.

His first thought was that he had actually already fallen asleep and this was nothing but a malicious dream to reinforce his guilty conscience about having left her alone. But then the shock hit him with such force that he had a hard time breathing and had to leave the room to get air.

9

FABIAN RISK TURNED ON to Bergsgatan. The morning news hadn't mentioned a word about the disappearance of the Minister for Justice, but instead devoted most of the broadcast to the kidnapping of the playboy Adam Fischer. Apparently no ransom had yet been demanded – puzzling since his father, a diplomat, left a small fortune to the family when he passed away. When the news moved on to a rancorous debate on whether children and pregnant women should be vaccinated for swine flu, Risk turned off the radio.

Hopefully Niva would soon be in touch. On the way home from NDRI she had promised to identify the minister's secret cell phone number and tried to convince him to grab a drink because her date had finally cancelled. *That's the least you can do, isn't it*, she insisted.

But fear of what he hoped the drink would lead to made him decline the invitation and put the blame on his kids who were home alone. *Then we'll do it next time*, she whispered in his ear, and he heard himself promise to treat.

Fabian lowered the side window, pressed the little plastic key against the reader, and drove down into the police station garage. He had hoped to get there first and have time to investigate any of the existing leads before Malin and the others showed up, but his morning had become a textbook example of how not to start the day.

Sonja had spent the night in the studio. Matilda and Theodor didn't seem to have slept at all and it was almost impossible to get them out of bed – or his bed, to be precise. When he had finally come home at twelve thirty, they were both lying tightly curled up under the covers.

At first Fabian couldn't believe his eyes. Matilda and Theodor never played together; the age difference was too great and their only common interest was getting on each other's nerves. Sonja thought they would get more enjoyment from their sibling relationship when they were older, but Fabian wasn't so sure. On the contrary, he thought most signs pointed to them having the same kind of non-existent relationship that he and his older brother had.

Everything suddenly made sense once he saw the cover to the classic *Nightmare on Elm Street* lying on top of the DVD player. When they woke, they were back in their old roles and quarrelled about everything from who had the right to the last package of O'boy chocolate powder to how long it was okay to stay barricaded in the bathroom.

Now it was eight thirty and he could see Malin Rehnberg's car was already in its spot, even though she'd flown in from Copenhagen that morning.

'ANDERS… BUT, ANDERS, PLEASE listen to me now,' Malin said into the phone as she rolled her eyes toward Fabian, who was hanging up his coat. 'If we're going to have the slightest chance to be finished this century we're going to have to bring in real contractors. If you haven't noticed, I'm actually very pregnant… No, now I'm the one talking.' She stopped talking and chugged back her glass of Coke. 'You think I have the energy to spend the whole weekend on all fours tiling the bathroom? What? No, I'm not upset. I'm pregnant!'

Malin slammed the receiver down so hard on the cradle that Fabian was impressed that it held at all. 'Sometimes, but only sometimes, you men have your brain connected, like every other leap year or so.' She shook her head, filled the glass with more Coke and emptied it in one gulp. A few seconds later she picked up the receiver again and dialled. 'Hi, it's me again. Listen, sorry… I didn't mean to… I just don't have the energy to renovate any more now. Love you too. Kiss.' She hung up and turned to face Fabian. 'I was about to call you to hear about the meeting at SePo yesterday.'

'Is everything all right?' said Fabian, sitting down at the desk opposite her.

Malin looked as if she didn't know where to start. 'Whatever you and Sonja do, promise me never to buy a house that needs renovating. And I mean never as in never, ever have the thought. Never look at listings. Never set your foot in a neighbourhood of single-family houses, even if your best friends just moved there, okay? Stay in the city. For God's sake, stay inside the city limits, if you want to survive.'

'Okay. I promise,' said Fabian, starting up his computer.

'On top of that, I have my first hangover since these two came on the scene.' Malin pointed at her belly and refilled her glass. 'But forget about that now and tell me about the meeting.'

'Hangover?' said Fabian, wondering how he could neatly guide the conversation away from the meeting. 'Hangover as in I-consumed-alcohol-even-though-I'm-in-late-pregnancy-with-twins hangover?'

Malin met Fabian's gaze with a tired look. 'You know how the Danes are.'

'I don't think I do. Why don't you tell me? And did you find a contact person?'

'Yes, and she was extremely pleasant. I want to underscore that I didn't have more than one-and-a-half, max two, glasses of wine.'

'And how big was a glass?'

'Can we please drop it and talk about your meeting instead? I want to know everything.'

'Good morning. Did everything go well in Copenhagen?'

They turned towards Herman Edelman, who was in the doorway with a steaming cup of coffee in his hand and the morning newspapers under his arm.

'Yes, it was actually really interesting,' said Malin. 'I intend to tell all about it at the nine o'clock meeting. And speaking of meetings, I'd like to know what—'

'Exactly,' said Edelman, turning toward Fabian. 'Do you have a few minutes?'

'Absolutely.' Fabian got up.

'We'll do it in my office.'

'Is there time to get a cup of tea?' said Malin, also getting up.

'I'm sure. The meeting isn't for twenty minutes,' said Edelman. 'And then we all look forward to hearing more about wonderful Copenhagen.'

Fabian could feel Malin's gaze burning on his neck the whole way down the corridor.

FABIAN ALWAYS FELT LIKE he was going back thirty years in time as soon as he took a step across the threshold into Edelman's cluttered office. Throughout all his years as the boss, Edelman had persistently declined every offer of renovation, to the point that they had now talked about the importance of preserving the office in its original condition for future generations.

Fabian suspected that Edelman only really wanted to retain his rumbling refrigerator that was always stocked with Kalle's caviar, red onions and cold beer. The old TV with the VHS player was perhaps not used as often, but as long as he still had a collection of classic films on the shelf, he evidently didn't intend to get rid of that either.

He'd even opposed having the nicotine-yellow walls repainted because he was worried that they would discover that he defied the smoking ban.

'Please sit down.' Edelman sat in the reading chair by the window and started filling a pipe.

Fabian moved a pillow and a few binders off the worn leather couch and sat down.

'We only have a few minutes. The last I heard is that SePo has now found the cell phone,' said Edelman, getting the flame from the lighter to turn down and lick the pipe.

'In Riddarfjärden outside the Kanslikajen?' said Fabian.

'Yes. How did you know that?'

'We did a positioning last night and it was identified as the phone's last known location. We also discovered that he has another cell phone, but with a secret number. If everything goes according to plan, we'll have a position on it today.'

Edelman thought and sipped his coffee. 'You say "*we*"? I assume that the other person isn't me.'

'It's a former colleague who no longer has any connections here. I thought it was better than bringing in Novak.'

'Former colleague.' Edelman puffed the pipe smoke out in small clouds. 'You mean Niva. And here I thought I was completely crystal clear that no others should be involved.'

'She's not someone you need to worry about. She understands exactly why—'

'Let me decide what I should be worried about.'

Fabian was about to nod, but stopped himself. If he accepted the reprimand now, he risked losing all his freedom in this investigation. Normally he could essentially guide his investigations however he wanted, but this was anything but a normal case, and Edelman evidently thought he could control him like a puppet.

'You had a call with Grimås a few hours before he disappeared,' he said. 'What did you talk about?'

It was clear that Edelman was not prepared for the question, but he recovered quickly and took another puff. 'Nothing important. If it had been, I would have mentioned it yesterday of course.'

'But now I'm the one who's leading the investigation, so let me decide what's important.'

Edelman broke into a smile and laughed. 'That's rich, Fabian. We talked about the question time he was on his way to. And, if I remember correctly, it was about some legislative amendment proposal.'

'Did you pick up on anything that may have to do with his disappearance?'

Edelman shook his head and laughed again. 'No, but I promise to let you know if I think of something. And speaking of phone calls.' Edelman stood up, went over to the desk and came back with an old Nokia 63109 and a charger. 'As of now I want you to use this when you call me. You'll find the number under the Jewish Theatre.'

Fabian looked at the ancient-looking phone, even though it hadn't been much more than a year since he'd had one like it.

'I guess we're done for now, assuming you don't want to continue the questioning, that is?'

'Just one thing. To avoid any misunderstandings,' said Fabian, ignoring the irony.

'Yes?'

'You've put me on an assignment that directly contradicts the explicit instructions of the police commissioner.'

'True. But you know just as well as I do that—'

'Herman, you don't need to go on the defensive. I don't think it's wrong – on the contrary, I consider it our duty to find out what's happened. But if I'm going to step on a wasps' nest, I'm the one they'll sting, not you.'

'That's true. So the best thing you can do is to not make any missteps.'

'Which is exactly what I'm doing. And I intend to follow up with some of my leads. I just want you to be aware of the situation.' Fabian was determined not to let go of Edelman's gaze until he got what he was after.

They sat for a few moments while the silence became more and more insistent. But at last, it came, in the form of a barely perceptible nod.

'It's already two minutes past,' said Edelman, standing up and moving towards the door. 'No reason to keep the others waiting.'

Fabian nodded, stood, and heaved an inward sigh of relief. He'd won, and now he could keep working with a free rein.

10

SOFIE LEANDER OPENED HER eyes and had to squint to avoid the lamp that was shining right down on her. She couldn't do much more than open and close her eyes anyway. Straps were tightened so hard around her from her feet all the way to her hips, lower arms and torso that she'd lost feeling in a number of places. The strap across her neck was not pulled as tight, but prevented her from raising her head more than a millimetre or so.

In a way, she felt like she deserved it. Her attempts to alter reality were a sin so grave that punishment was unavoidable. What did she imagine would happen? That there was a statute of limitations on what she did because so many years had passed without repercussion?

True, she'd harboured a nagging worry that the truth would eventually catch up with her, but she hadn't expected this. Not even her worst nightmares had come anywhere close to where she now found herself: lying strapped to a plastic-covered table with a hole for defecation, a lamp blinding her with its glow. The little stainless steel table beside her was still polished and covered with tools. The apparatus was still turned off, but it only needed a quick flip of the switch to do its job. A drip and feeding tube were fastened in her mouth. Everything suggested that it wasn't a question of *if* but *when* it would happen.

She tried to count the days, but the strong, continuous light along with her irregular sleep pattern made it virtually impossible. If she was to guess, she'd been lying here between three and four days, which should mean the police weren't far off. Her husband, surely, would have contacted them the evening she disappeared and given them all the information they needed to pick up a trail as soon as possible.

The question was whether they would get here in time.

She could hear the humming of the tube feeder starting up under the table and soon her mouth would be filled with that viscous batter that tasted of chemical strawberry. The mere smell of it gave her nausea. On one occasion she'd decided to see what would happen if she tried to spit it out, but the tape around her mouth was too tight and the effort almost choked her. Since then she forced the viscous fluid down in small, quick clumps and tried to think about something else so that she didn't vomit.

This time the process was harder than usual, and she found herself counting the clumps. There were usually between thirty and forty of them. But now she was at twenty-two and couldn't imagine getting one clump over forty.

Twenty-five, twenty-six, twenty— What was that? She lost track and listened. Had there been footsteps, or was it just her imagination? The batter filled her mouth, and she got rid of it all in one big vomit-inducing swallow. If her mind wasn't playing tricks on her, it was the first time she'd heard anyone other than herself since she'd been here.

Once the tube feeder finally stopped and the artificial batter began swelling in her stomach, she determined that someone was definitely walking on the other side of the sheet-metal wall. The steps sounded distant, but they were getting closer.

What if help was on the way? But it was too quiet to be a big team of police. It sounded like a single person on their way right towards her. Was it time now? Maybe this was the end she'd done everything to suppress in her mind, but had actually been anticipating for several days. She heard the steps getting louder and realized now that, contrary to what she believed earlier, she wasn't ready at all. Panic spread like a forest fire through her body. She would have screamed at the top of her lungs if she could.

This wasn't how she intended to react. She broke down in silent tears and visualized the scalpel penetrating her skin. Soon the electric motor that raised the slatted louvre gate that led into her room would start and the truth she'd swept under the carpet for so long would laugh right in her face.

But the electric motor didn't start, and instead of stopping the steps kept going. It was someone else. She tried to whistle and make a sound, any sound at all, but it was impossible and all she could do was lie there and listen as the steps grew fainter.

Apparently it wasn't her time yet.

11

CONSIDERING WHAT HAD HAPPENED, and above all to *whom* it had happened, Dunja Hougaard shouldn't have been the least bit surprised at the media circus that had taken over the area. All the major Danish newspapers were there – *Berlingske*, *Politiken* and *Ekstra Bladet* – and both DR and TV 2 were reporting live. Truth be told, she hadn't expected anything at all – she'd had her hands full just getting through the morning.

She got out of her car an hour later than Jan Hesk and the rest of the team. She suppressed a sour belch and, as she forced her way through the horde of journalists, she promised herself she wouldn't let this happen again. There was nothing worse than a hangover – or meltdown, which might be a more apt description of her current state

She actually had no problem with the headaches, which a few pills could always alleviate. It was the nausea that made her lose her lust for life. Her stomach was turning inside out and refused to keep anything down, terrorizing the rest of her body. She'd had to stop by the side of the road twice, and lost most of the breakfast she'd forced down in front of Carsten, so that he didn't know how bad she was really feeling.

'There you are. Where have you been hiding?' asked Jan Hesk as soon as she stepped into the building.

'There were a few complications on the way over,' she said, noticing that Hesk, who'd always been slender, had now acquired a little belly under his shirt.

'I see. What kind of—'

'I promise. You don't want to know. I'd be more interested in hearing about what you've been doing,' she said, pulling on a pair of shoe protectors.

'Well, I guess it's pretty standard. We have a number of question marks, but none that we won't figure out eventually – assuming we could just work in peace.' Hesk showed her through the house. 'The biggest problem right now is keeping the media at bay. I'll be damned if they're not worse than the mosquitoes at my country house in Sweden.'

Dunja looked around on the way in and realized immediately that her salary would never be enough to afford anything even close to this house, even if she became head of the whole homicide squad.

'The guy was on *Let's Dance*... what was it? Three or four years ago? And he couldn't even dance.'

'But have you found anything?'

'It's better if you see it with your own eyes.' Hesk stopped outside the bedroom door and let Dunja go in first.

She came to an abrupt standstill after the first step and stared at the double bed in the middle of the room. The last time she'd seen Karen Neuman was in a gossip magazine at her dentist. There'd been pictures of her and Aksel from some film premiere, and she'd been struck by how in love they appeared to be, even though they'd been married for over twenty years.

Now she was lying alone in her bed, naked and drenched in her own blood, which had run out from her vagina and the wounds around her torso. When she moved closer she saw that the stabs were so deep that they must have come from something other than an ordinary knife, something bigger and heavier that could penetrate through all the layers of skin, and through the cartilage and bone in some places.

'No, don't turn away. Keep looking.' Predictably, it was Oscar Pedersen from forensic medicine, who came out from the adjacent bathroom in a white coat. 'Humans are creatures of habit. We often don't even notice what's bothering us. The same thing happens with battered human bodies, I promise you. I agree that it looks exciting.'

Pedersen was as exhilarated as a kid at Legoland, except there was a naked, mutilated woman in front of him.

'Have you been able to identify the murder weapon?' asked Dunja.

'It's definitely not a knife.' Pedersen walked up to her. 'If I were to bet my salary, I would say an axe. And I don't mean the toy version.' He measured with his hands. 'We're talking real power that can cut wood in a single stroke. See for yourself how parts of the ribcage are completely shattered, not to mention the inner organs.' He opened up one of the wounds in the abdomen to get a better look inside.

'I think I've seen enough,' she said, feeling the rest of her breakfast on its way up.

'No, come on and look inside.'

Hesk wouldn't rescue her – he had his back turned over by the closet. And under no circumstances did she want to treat the medical examiner to a scene, so she leaned forward and looked down into the mutilated bowels. A sweet, heavy odour hit her and forced her to hold her breath.

'You see? She's completely mutilated, as if someone ran her through a threshing machine.'

Dunja nodded and looked a little longer, before she straightened up and met his gaze. 'And the blood from the abdomen?'

'I haven't got that far yet, but if I were to make a guess he probably had a little fun with her before he went bananas.'

'And by *he*, who are you referring to?'

Pedersen looked at Hesk, who had now joined them.

'Most of the evidence suggests that it's Aksel Neuman,' said Hesk.

'Aksel? Her husband?' asked Dunja. Hesk nodded. 'Are you sure? I can't imagine he would ever subject his wife to something like this.' She nodded toward the bloodbath in the bed and felt like she was starting to regain her energy.

'And what do you base that on? The gossip in *See & Hear*? You've been here for, what, a whole minute?'

Dunja was about to say something, but stopped herself. This was Hesk's investigation, not hers. Officially they had the same job title, but he had more years under his belt, which meant that such a high-profile and complex investigation automatically ended up on his desk. Her task was to assist and offer her thoughts and ideas – not take over. Besides, he'd hit the nail on the head as far as the tabloids were concerned.

'Okay, this is how the scenario looks right now.' Hesk placed himself in the middle of the room. 'Neuman was reportedly seen at the Karriere Bar here in Copenhagen with Casper Christensen, one of the guests on his talk show last night. According to his associates at TV 2, he was supposed to spend the night in his apartment on Vesterbro, but decided to drive home instead. Richter has secured clear traces of his BMW X3.'

'Are you talking about me?' probed crime scene investigator Kjeld Richter on his way into the room.

'I'm just explaining how the leads indicate that Aksel Neuman was here and then left in his car.'

Richter nodded as he scratched his stubble thoughtfully, which, along with his sideburns and eyebrows, was in major need of a trim. 'But it so happens that we've found traces of a third car.'

'What do you mean, a third car?'

'There was another car besides Aksel's and Karen's that was here sometime after midnight.'

'And how do we know it was after midnight?' asked Hesk.

'There was no new snow in the tracks and according to weather reports it stopped snowing around midnight.'

'So there was a third person involved?' said Dunja, and Richter nodded.

'That strengthens my theory,' said Hesk. 'The woman brings someone home believing her husband is going to spend the night in the city, but the old man comes home and catches them in flagrante. Shit hits the fan and he runs out to get an axe, while Don Juan uses the opportunity to flee. We'll have a witness as soon as we find him.'

Dunja shrugged.

'You still don't think it's him?' Hesk now sounded really irritated.

Dunja didn't know what to say. Gossip or not, she was convinced Aksel Neuman wasn't the killer.

'Can you give me a single reason why it isn't—'

'Sorry, my cell phone is ringing,' Dunja interrupted, looking down at the screen. 'Uh-oh, it's Sleizner. It's probably best that I take it. Yes, hello, this is Dunja Hougaard.'

'Now I'm actually a little hurt. Do you really not have my number programmed into your phone?' asked Sleizner in a feigned pitiful voice.

'Of course I saw that it was you,' said Dunja, while she racked her brain to understand why he was calling her and not Hesk. 'But I always answer that way during work hours.'

'I see. Then I guess I'll have to make sure to call a little more often after work hours. Tee hee.'

Dunja responded to Hesk's perplexed look by throwing out one hand.

'But that's not what this is about. The press are all over me like leeches.'

'It's the same here. If your question concerns the investigation, I think it's better that you speak with Jan.'

'If I wanted to talk to Jan, I would've called him. Here's how it is: I've called a press conference in an hour and I'll need something to offer.'

'But—'

'Anything at all. Just so they calm down for a bit.'

'It's too soon. We don't have a clear scenario yet, and Richter needs more—'

'Dunja, it feels as if we're getting off course here. You must have something? What have you been doing for all these hours?'

'There are some indications that a third person may have been involved somehow, but we don't know in what capacity or the role they may have played.'

'So it could be a lover or the perpetrator?'

'Or both,' said Dunja, feeling that she was on such thin ice that it would be a minor miracle if she didn't break through. 'But so far these are only loose theories. If I were in your shoes I would be extremely careful about what I—'

'But, as luck would have it, you're not in my shoes. Tell the others that we'll have a meeting as soon as you're all back. See you.' Then he hung up.

'Excuse me, but what the hell was that?' said Hesk. 'Why does he call you when I'm the one leading the investigation?'

'That's exactly what I'm wondering myself. I have no idea.'

'And you're quite sure of that?'

'What are you trying to insinuate? That I had a secret meeting with Sleizner to take over the investigation?'

Hesk threw out his hands. 'I'm not the one who got here a full hour after everyone else.'

Dunja felt like she needed to sit down. The nausea was back.

12

FABIAN RISK HAD A long list of things he wanted to investigate. He wanted to get in touch with whoever was responsible for security in the parliament building and request a copy of the surveillance video he'd seen at SePo. He wanted to study in detail Carl-Eric Grimås' call traffic from the last hours before he disappeared, and he wanted to meet the chauffeur who'd been waiting in the car. But he couldn't do anything other than pretend he had all the time in the world and sit down with the others around the table in the windowless meeting room.

With their coffee cups in hand everyone pulled out a chair, which after years of wear had become 'theirs', and sat down. Once, a few years ago, Fabian had decided to sit on one of his colleagues' chairs, just to see his reaction, but he'd quickly rejected the idea as much too risky and moved before it was too late.

The thermos went around with coffee that had been sitting on the burner so long that it tasted more like tannic acid than coffee. As always, the tin of Danish cookies stopped with Markus Höglund, who insisted on picking out his favourites, which, Fabian noted, were becoming more numerous. He couldn't understand where it all went. It certainly didn't go to his waistline. Markus wasn't even thirty-five yet, but that couldn't be the only explanation. In Fabian's case the shift in metabolism happened at twenty-five, and every extra calorie had stayed with him ever since.

Carl-Eric Grimås had introduced the cookie tin during his time at the Bureau, and the tradition had survived, like a stubborn cockroach that refused to die. Edelman never had any of the cookies and made a brave effort to end the tradition a number of years ago, but was met with such firm resistance that he reintroduced it immediately. Fabian had been unsympathetic to the protests and was sure that no one really liked the buttery cookies with powdered sugar – no one but Höglund anyway.

'We have quite a bit ahead of us so we might as well get started,' said Edelman, turning toward Malin Rehnberg. 'Malin, you've been in Copenhagen and from what I've understood, it was a huge success.'

Malin nodded as she emptied her glass of Coke. 'Absolutely. I would recommend that everyone take the opportunity to go next time. I think they were talking about Berlin in the spring.'

'Berlin sounds super,' said Tomas Persson, running his hand over his military haircut. 'What do you say, Jarmo?'

'You know how I feel about travelling,' Jarmo Päivinen muttered in his unmistakable Finnish-Swedish accent.

'In any event, I now have a good contact in Copenhagen. She's sitting in the exact same position as—'

'Malin, I'm sure you have a number of interesting experiences to share. But I thought that could be the last item of the meeting, time permitting,' Edelman interrupted, sending her a smile.

'Sure.' She took a cookie and tried to make eye contact with Fabian, who was busy pretending that his cell phone hadn't just started vibrating in his pocket. He had to wait until the meeting had started before he could take it out under the table and look at the text message: *Call as soon as you have a chance. Niva*

There was no way he could leave immediately because everyone, not just Malin, would wonder what was going on. But waiting until the meeting was over was out of the question.

'And we still have no news about Diego Arcas?' Edelman asked.

'No, unfortunately that scumbag is still destroying one girl after the other and laughing all the way to the bank. But what can I do? As long as Inger is on leave, I'm alone,' said Markus Höglund, rinsing down a cookie with a gulp of coffee.

'What should you do? Sorry, but I can't just sit here and keep my mouth shut,' said Tomas Persson, pushing a pinch of loose *snus* inside his upper lip. 'Markus, can you explain to me why you can't seem to do anything other than sit here and consume sugar? There must be any number of things you can take care of on your own.'

Höglund rolled his eyes, looking in vain for support from the others. 'You can think whatever you want, but just because Inger's been home taking care of her kids more than she's here doesn't mean I've been doing nothing. Besides the Black Cat on Hantverkargatan, where he showcases most of his girls, I've managed, with Inger's help, to locate seven different apartments around the city where parties are going on more or less night and day. And, yes, we could go apartment by apartment, but it would be better to carry out a synched operation, and that's not something I intend to do without Inger.'

'All right. Whatever,' said Tomas Persson, shrugging. 'I just think that—'

'I think we'll stop there,' Edelman interrupted. 'If she isn't back on Monday we'll have to try to resolve this some other way.'

Höglund nodded and tucked away yet another cookie while he glowered at Tomas.

'Otherwise, Fabian and I can help out,' said Malin, turning towards Fabian. 'Can't we? Right now we don't have anything on our desk.'

'Why not?' said Fabian, even though he could see in her eyes that she was just teasing.

'As I said, we'll wait until after the weekend,' said Edelman, turning to Jarmo Päivinen and Tomas Persson. 'From what I've heard you have some news concerning Adam Fischer's car. Let's hear about it.'

Jarmo nodded, brought his reading glasses down on his nose, and searched in his documents.

'Do you want to tell them or should I?' asked Tomas, drumming his fingers on the table.

'Take it easy.' Jarmo kept searching, and Fabian was struck by how old he looked, even though he was only five or six years older than him, which placed him in his late forties. His wife had left him four years ago and taken the children with her and it looked like the loneliness was eating away at him. 'As I'm sure you've all heard on the news,' Jarmo continued, 'we've been able to establish that this is a kidnapping.'

'Which is what we suspected all along,' said Tomas.

'This is the last we've seen of Fischer.' Jarmo passed out some pictures of Adam Fischer in his SUV from a surveillance camera.

'Until yesterday,' said Tomas, looking overly satisfied as he flexed his tattooed biceps. 'Because then we got a damned good bite.'

'Maybe you should talk instead.' Jarmo turned to his much younger colleague.

'No, no, it's cool. You go.'

'Sure?'

'Yes, just keep talking,' said Tomas, staring down at the table.

'We should have thought of it sooner, but he lives in a huge bachelor pad up on Mosebacke – it must have cost him pretty much all his inheritance – and we contacted the car parks in the neighbourhood. Finally, we got a bite at the Slussen car park.'

'Was his car there?' said Malin.

'No, but we did get this surveillance video.' Tomas held a DVD in the air and stood up. 'Are you prepared?' He went over to the old TV, put the DVD in the player, and tried to get it started with the remote control.

'The remote doesn't work,' said Höglund. 'You've got to use

the buttons on the TV. Wait, I'll show you.' He stood up and went over to Tomas.

'No, it's okay. I'll take care of it,' said Tomas, searching with his fingers for the right button.

While they were waiting, Fabian's phone vibrated again in his hand: *Going into a meeting soon, and then the curtain goes down for the rest of the day. N*

Fabian could wait no longer and made to leave. 'I'm sorry, but unfortunately I have to go.'

'Okay. No problem,' said Edelman.

'What do you mean, "no problem"?' said Malin. 'What is so important that you have to leave in the middle of a meeting when you don't even have an ongoing investigation?'

'It's from Matilda's school. They want me to call as soon as possible.'

'It's fine. I just hope it's nothing serious.'

'Yes, we truly have to hope so,' said Malin, shaking her head at Fabian as he backed out of the room.

'Okay, you do it then!' said Tomas, stepping aside so that Höglund could press one of the buttons a few times, whereupon the TV came to life.

13

FOR ALMOST A YEAR and a half she'd cleaned regularly at the Black Cat – the notorious strip club on Kungsholmen that, strangely enough, wasn't much more than two stones' throws from the Stockholm police building. Three times a week she'd been let in at the side entrance from Polhemsgatan and made her rounds with the cleaning cart in the murky basement premises, so extensive and labyrinthine that it took her months to get her bearings.

And every time she'd vacuumed and swabbed the floors just as precisely. Fluffed and placed the pillows properly on the couches, and laundered and ironed the pillowcases as needed. She'd picked up condoms, collected lost wedding rings and rubbed away dried semen stains. And sometimes even blood.

Despite explicit orders from Diego Arcas's right-hand man – the burly guy with rings in his ears and eyes in the back of his head – that they should be on the pill or use an IUD, there were always a few girls who refused, hoping to get pregnant. To start with she hadn't understood why anyone would subject themselves to getting pregnant by one of the filthy swine who probably had a wife and kids in the suburbs. But soon she realized that there was no quicker way out of there than a growing belly.

But the blood didn't come only from menstruation. True, violence against the girls was forbidden, but if it was free rein you were after there was a price tag for that too. The fact was that it was all only about how many extra zeroes on the bill you could afford. According to rumour, if you could pony up 300,000 you could rape someone to death. But then you had to take one of the older ones who were on their last legs anyway.

Twice she'd had to disinfect the room afterwards. The first time was after a session in one of the private rooms that got out of hand. It took her hours to get it clean, and the burly guy had given her a tongue-lashing and withheld her pay because she was unable to finish before the club opened. She hadn't protested, just nodded and reminded herself that money was not the only reason she was there.

The second time it was Diego Arcas himself who was responsible for the assault, when it came to his knowledge that one of his chattels had gone and got pregnant. The point was obviously to frighten the others, and frightened was just what they were when they heard about the bloody loose nails and torn-off clumps of hair she found in the room afterwards. About all the bodily fluids and excrement she scrubbed with cleanser so strong that it required both a face mask and protective gloves. The mattress alone had been so soaked with blood that she was forced to discard it. She could have seen to it right then that the club would be closed by offering her testimony to the police, whom she already knew were actively monitoring it. But she hadn't made so much as a comment, simply left the room cleaner than ever and continued her rounds as if nothing had happened.

Only then had they started to trust her. The burly man stopped frisking her and let her go unwatched on her rounds. And it didn't take her long to exploit this newly won freedom. Step one had been to draw out her shift a little longer every day so that she was still there when the doors opened and the customers streamed in. Step two was to make herself invisible in the darkness and go around making a note of everything she saw.

And she saw plenty.

14

FABIAN RISK LOOKED AT himself in the mirror above the sink as his phone started ringing again. So far the circles under his eyes hadn't come back, but it was only a matter of days before the pressure of this new investigation would bring them back and make him look at least ten years older. He yanked out a few nose hairs and realized that his left sideburn was longer than the right one, then he took out the Nokia Edelman had given him and punched in a number.

'Niva speaking.'

'We suspect that SePo is listening, so use this number going forward,' said Fabian. 'Have you found anything?'

'Just wham-bam-thank-you-ma'am, no foreplay here.'

'Sorry, but I think we'll do that another time. Right now—'

'Just say when and where. And in case you've forgotten, you owe me a drink.'

'No, no, of course I haven't. Who do you think I am?'

'I would say that after this, we've probably upped it to at least dinner.'

'Maybe so. But I don't know what you have yet.'

'You'll just have to take it sight unseen and hope for the best.'

'In other words I have no choice?'

'Fabian, you always have a choice.'

She was toying with him, and he should have realized that they would take this route. 'Silence implies consent. So what do you choose?'

'Door number one.'

'Good. That wasn't so hard, was it? And I'm convinced that you're going to be satisfied. The woman who left the message on Grimås' voicemail is named Sylvia Bredenhielm, and only a minute or so later she called the prepaid card number 073 785 66 29.'

'And that's Grimås' secret cell phone?'

'You guessed right.'

'Do you have a call list for that number, too?'

'Yes, but it's just the two of them calling each other, so unless you're thinking about a career with the tabloids, I wouldn't waste your time on it. Now here's your payoff. Are you prepared to take notes?'

Fabian took out a pen and pulled up his jacket sleeve. 'Okay.'

'59.311129, 18.078073.'

Fabian wrote the number combinations on the inside of his arm. 'What is that?'

'The cell phone's most recent position, plus or minus ten or fifteen metres.'

'Is it still on?'

'No, it disappeared at 4:04 p.m. yesterday, which is almost forty minutes after the first one.'

'Amazing, Niva. You have truly been a great help. I'll be in touch.'

'I know.'

Fabian ended the call and left the washroom. Finally, he had something concrete to go on. Without sitting down at his desk, he started up the computer and clicked to Google Maps, where he entered the co-ordinates from his arm. A map of Stockholm came up with a red balloon marker pointing at somewhere over Södermalm. He zoomed down to street level and determined that it was aiming at Östgötagatan 46.

He hadn't initially understood the point of street view on Google Maps. It must have taken an incredible amount of work to photograph every street corner in Stockholm, which was the first city in Sweden to get the service. But when he finally mastered the commands, and aimed the view at the building at the corner of Östgötagatan and Blekingegatan, he sent them his heartfelt gratitude. The building was covered with scaffolding and looked completely uninhabited.

The image was probably taken some time during the autumn, and there was no guarantee the building was still being renovated. If it was, though, or even better, if the renovation had stopped while they were waiting for the financial crisis to ease up, it would be the perfect place to keep a victim hidden.

He cleared his search history, shut down the computer, and walked right into Malin Rehnberg.

'My, what a hurry you're in. And you don't even have anything on your desk – nothing I know about at least.'

'Malin, I'm sorry, but I don't have time for this.' He tried to go around her, but she refused to let him pass.

'That's tough luck because I don't intend to give up until you've told me what the hell is going on.'

Various scenarios fluttered around in Fabian's mind, until he realized that he wouldn't be able to get much further by lying.

'Come with me.'

15

THIS MORNING, JUST LIKE every other morning, Ossian Kremph had been sitting by the corner window having his late-morning coffee and solving a Sudoku to Radio Stockholm's traffic reports. He didn't know why, but for as long as he could remember he'd loved listening to both the traffic and weather updates, especially the long sea reports which described in detail the direction and force of the wind in every corner along the Swedish coastal strip.

But this particular morning was different. Even though he'd listened to the entire sea report he felt far from calm. Worry had slipped in without him noticing and was suddenly very apparent. He'd tried to ignore it and kept persevering with the Japanese number puzzle, but he couldn't write down a single digit. His mind was racing and he couldn't switch off his thoughts.

He'd worked so hard for so many years to get control over his thoughts. Now they were getting stirred up, concentrating on a lot of forbidden things. He turned up the volume on the radio and switched to an easier Sudoku, but that didn't help, and he was finally forced to switch off the radio and set aside his pen.

It occurred to him that this change had started a few weeks earlier, maybe even before that. The more he thought about it, the more he realized that nothing had been the same recently. He'd been in an unusually bad mood, but that wasn't the only thing that was off. For instance, he was wearing a blue shirt, even though it was Thursday and he always wore green. And what had happened on that walk around Årstaviken last Sunday? Did he really take it? He couldn't remember.

That wasn't the only thing he couldn't recall. All of last week was basically one big black hole apart from a few loose fragments. And yesterday morning, he'd stayed in bed too long and hadn't been able to stop thinking about everything he'd promised himself never to dwell on again.

He had no memory of the rest of the day whatsoever.

He'd taken all his medication, he was sure of that. Every day: morning, afternoon and evening he rinsed down the pills with a glass of lukewarm water and felt them make their way down his throat. So that definitely wasn't the issue – or could it be? What if he thought he had taken the pills but hadn't really? Or if the dose was much too low? What was it the doctor said? Should they raise it or lower it? And what was that smell? He hadn't forgotten to take out the garbage on Tuesday, had he?

Ossian Kremph was almost dizzy from all the questions and felt like he needed to lie down and rest. But that didn't help either, especially not with that man and woman walking back and forth on the street. *No one did that*, he thought, and went and got his binoculars. You passed by on your way to a destination, you didn't walk around in the same place like those two were doing. They looked like they were searching for something.

He didn't recognize either of them, but he'd been able to figure out which car was theirs after watching them for a while. A simple Internet search told him it belonged to a certain Fabian Risk, who worked as a homicide investigator at the National Bureau of Criminal Investigation in Stockholm. The pregnant woman was certainly a colleague and yet another of Herman Edelman's subjects.

In a way he was not the least bit surprised. He knew that they would eventually creep out of their holes and show their disgusting mugs, he simply hadn't expected it to happen so fast. But here they were. Fucking cops.

The question was how it had happened. As soon as he'd been set free, he'd done everything to lie low. He not only changed his surname to his mother's maiden name, he hadn't even put it up on the door of the apartment he rented second-hand – or was it third-hand? He'd turned the temperature down as low as he could and bided his time in the hope that one day he would be completely rid of his former self, just as his therapist had promised.

But it hadn't worked. Even though he'd done exactly what he was told and went through all the exercises, the fire burned inside him. He had done what the therapist had expected of him. But deep down, after a year or two in treatment, he'd already come to the realization that it would never go away. Whatever he did, the hunger would always be there.

He took another look in the binoculars and saw the two police officers disappear under the scaffolding. Was it really possible that they'd already found him? And who gave them the right to persecute him by knocking down the door and stomping in? Who said they could push him down on the floor, put handcuffs on him and search his home?

It may be that his thoughts were forbidden and out of control. Maybe he and his therapist had worked hard for years to quiet them down without success. He knew that it was best for the community to not have them, but he no longer cared. For the first time in many years, he relished every single one of his forbidden thoughts.

If those disgusting pieces of shit came and knocked on his door, he would be prepared. He would sink his teeth into them and tear them to pieces. He had nothing to lose anyway.

16

IF ONLY THIS DAY would end soon, thought Dunja Hougaard, imagining how she would creep under the covers and fall asleep before Carsten got home. But it had just started, and even though she'd drunk at least two litres of water and taken several spoonfuls of oral rehydration salts, she still felt like a wreck.

She poured a cup of black coffee and sat down in her place at the conference table across from Jan Hesk, who still seemed convinced that she'd gone behind his back and had something going with Kim Sleizner. Kjeld Richter sat at one end and tried to find somewhere to fix his gaze. None of them said anything, which made the silence more awkward with every passing minute.

Finally, the door opened and Sleizner came in, quickly scanning the room. He was dressed in a shirt with cufflinks and tie. His make-up from the press conference was still visible. Dunja didn't know any other man in police headquarters who put on make-up before a press conference, but then again, Sleizner also loved his press conferences more than anyone and announced them all the time. No one was better than him at standing in front of the cameras making something out of nothing.

'Did any of you see the press conference?' He walked up to the Nespresso machine.

Hesk, Richter and Dunja all shook their heads.

'Don't ask me how, but I managed to convince everyone that we know what the hell we're dealing with, so now it's up to you all to ensure that I haven't promised too much.' He pushed in the coffee cartridge and left the rest to the machine.

And he never paid for it, Dunja noted, even though he was the first person to complain when there was no money left in the coffee fund. She never used the machine herself, not just to avoid Sleizner's sermons, but mostly because she didn't think it tasted as great as everyone else did. It was a mystery to her how more or less the entire Western world subscribed to the idea that you had to buy your coffee at an exclusive store and pay three times more than you needed to. She couldn't even bear to think about the environmental impact of it all.

'Okay, let's hear what you have. What scenario are you working from?'

Hesk cleared his throat and stood up. 'As I said, we're still in the first phase of the investigation and have tons of unanswered questions. But based on the leads that Kjeld and his men have found, it's now absolutely clear that a third person was involved.'

Hesk insisted on standing up whenever Sleizner was in the room and Dunja could never understand why. If there was anyone who despised Sleizner and everything he stood for, it was Jan Hesk. However, he was probably just smart and did what was required to give his career an extra push.

The more she thought about it, the more Hesk's constant fawning over those who were a few ladder rungs above him irritated her. If Sleizner pulled down his fly, Hesk surely wouldn't hesitate if it would mean some personal gain.

'She's been distracted the whole day.'

It took several seconds before Dunja realized that Hesk was referring to her.

'Sorry, but what are you—'

'So is that how you see it too?' asked Sleizner, turning to look at her.

'The scenario,' Richter clarified. 'You know. Neuman comes

home from his TV show, finds his wife in bed with Mr Big, and runs amok with the axe.'

'Excuse me if I seem a little absent. But...' Dunja had no idea how to proceed without stepping on Hesk's toes.

'But what?' said Hesk.

'I don't know. However you slice it, I have a hard time imagining that Aksel Neuman would do something even remotely close to this.' She picked up one of the pictures that showed Karen Neuman's violated body and looked at it.

'I've been in contact with the staff at Karriere Bar, and evidently a number of gin and tonics were consumed,' said Hesk.

'Besides, it's happened more than once that he's knocked down people at the bar,' said Richter.

'Yes. But still.' Dunja fumbled for a continuation. 'It might sound trite, but Aksel and Karen were actually one of those couples who after all the years seemed to be genuinely in love.'

'Dunja, we're police officers investigating a crime, not scriptwriters for a new soap opera,' said Hesk, rolling his eyes.

'But that's a good idea,' said Richter, picking up his ringing cell phone. 'There are plenty of plot twists here. Yes, this is Richter.' He stood up and left the room.

'All I can say is that I don't think it's him,' said Dunja.

'Is anyone interested in what you *think*?' said Hesk. 'And if he's as innocent as you maintain, why has he disappeared?'

'I don't know. Hopefully he'll have a good answer when we find him. But if he came home earlier than planned, perhaps the perpetrator was still in the house and he took up chase. That would be more like him, especially if he was drunk.'

'Exactly. That's along the lines of what Kjeld was getting at,' said Sleizner, nodding in agreement.

'And then there's one more thing I've wondered—'

'Perhaps we can discuss that at the coffee break afterwards?' Hesk interrupted. 'If we're going to catch him before he gets too far we have to—'

'Please, let her finish talking.' Sleizner indicated that Hesk should sit down.

Dunja could sense that Hesk was about to implode, but she had no choice other than to continue. 'Jan, I don't understand why you're so angry at me.'

'No?'

'The only thing I'm trying to do is to move the investigation forward. And sure, I may be completely wrong, but it feels as if there's something that doesn't add up. Just take the murder weapon, which according to Pedersen is probably a big axe. From what I could see, there was no wood or fireplace in the house, which suggests there wouldn't be an axe there. Where did it come from? Did Aksel have it with him in the car in case he needed to murder someone?'

Hesk thought about it and shrugged.

'So what are you really saying?' said Sleizner without looking in Hesk's direction.

Dunja held up one of the pictures, which showed Karen Neuman on the bloody bed. 'Just look at how much blood there is here. Yet there wasn't a single trace of blood on the floor or in the hall, which suggests that the perpetrator was well prepared and had rolled out plastic, or something along those lines.' She dropped the picture down on top of the pile. 'Whoever did this has killed before.'

'That, undeniably, does sound more logical,' said Sleizner, just as Richter came back.

'The analysis of the third tyre track is complete,' he said, sitting down at his place. 'And there is a rather interesting detail.' He made a dramatic pause that was too brief for anyone to notice. 'Everything indicates that we're looking for a sports car with studded tyres.'

'Studded tyres?' said Dunja. 'Who drives around with studded tyres these days?'

'That's just what I'm wondering, too.'

'Swedes. They're crazy about studded tyres,' said Hesk. 'When we drive up to Småland to celebrate Christmas every Emil is driving around with studded tyres on his Volvo.'

'So we're dealing with a Swedish perpetrator,' said Sleizner. 'This just keeps getting better and better.'

'I'm still leaning toward Aksel Neuman, but at the same time I don't want to close any doors. For that reason, I think we should put out a search for him while we follow up with the Swedish lead,' said Hesk.

Dunja nodded, relieved that Hesk was starting to regain his normal facial colour. 'We can ask Scandlines if they had a sports car with Swedish plates on board last night. If it is a Swedish perp, it's conceivable he took the ferry over to Helsingborg.'

'Well thought out, Dunja.' Sleizner stood up. 'From here on, you will all report to Dunja, who as of now is responsible for the investigation and will report directly to me. Questions about that?'

No one said anything and Sleizner immediately left the room.

The anxiety descended like a thick, sticky fog. Dunja felt the lump in her throat growing bigger and bigger, making it hard to breathe. Besides, her nausea was about to turn the little she'd managed to eat at lunch inside out. She didn't know where to look or what to say. She desperately wanted a sinkhole to open up beneath her.

But all she could do was stay seated while her thoughts raced: was this her fault? Had she crossed the line and taken up too much space, pressing too hard for her own opinions? Or had it been Sleizner's plan from the very start? Was that why he'd called her and not Hesk out at the murder scene? And in that case, why? What was he really after, because there had to be something? Of that she was certain.

'Okay,' said Richter in an exhalation, breaking the silence. 'Is there anyone who gets what all that was about?'

'I have no idea. I don't understand a thing,' Dunja said, turning towards Hesk, only now noticing that he was shaking with fury.

He could get angry, she knew that. He had told her how he'd thrown things on the floor and kicked holes in the wall during the worst years with small children but she'd never seen him this angry.

'Jan, you have to believe me. I understand just as little as you do. This is your investigation, and I... I—'

Hesk interrupted her with a snort and fixed his gaze on hers. 'You don't need to sit here and try to—'

'I'm not trying anything. I'm just saying that it—'

'Shut up, you fucking cunt!' He stood up so that the chair overturned behind him. 'Do you think I don't get what you're up to? Huh?'

Dunja wanted to stand up and show him that she had nothing to be ashamed of. She wanted to let *her* chair overturn, hold up a threatening finger and tell him to go to hell if he didn't want to listen to her. But her legs would never hold, and for some reason the force of gravity felt extra strong right where she was sitting. 'I understand that you're upset. But can't we try to talk about this like adults? If we're going to work together we'll have to be able to put this behind us, and—'

'Behind us?' Hesk laughed and went around the table. 'And how the hell is that going to happen?' He placed himself right in front of her and looked down at her. 'You clearly haven't understood a thing. You strut around here like an absent-minded fucking whore, but I can tell you one thing: this is just the very beginning of your little hell. So go ahead and enjoy it because you're never going to feel as good as you feel right now ever again.' Hesk left the room.

And Dunja sat there, still unable to stand up.

17

ALTHOUGH THE BUILDING AT the corner of Östgötagatan and Blekingegatan was in the heart of one of Stockholm's most popular areas, it had been abandoned midway through the renovation. Torn pieces of protective netting swayed in the scaffolding where joined iron pipes creaked and screeched in ominous complaint. There was no problem passing along the sidewalk, yet the majority of pedestrians chose to take the detour out on to the street. It was a telling reminder of the aftermath of the financial crisis.

Fabian and Malin searched the area around the building, but didn't find the minister's secret cell phone. Now they were at the entry to Östgötagatan 46. As expected, it was locked, but with the help of an iron rod from the scaffolding Fabian broke one of the six windows in the door, reached his arm in and turned the lock from inside. The entrance was filled with construction waste and dust. Dried flakes of paint were hanging from walls and ceiling. A dozen old toilets were lined up along one wall, with bathtubs and refrigerators along the other.

'That's pretty much how it looks at our house,' said Malin, walking up to the row of toilets, while something dark and four-legged disappeared up the stairs. 'On closer inspection, this is probably a trifle cleaner.'

'It's perfect if you want to be left alone,' said Fabian, following the footsteps in the dust up to the elevator.

'Okay, how should we proceed? We could search here for days or even years. Are you sure you got all the numbers right? All it takes is one wrong digit for us to end up in Haparanda or Kuala Lumpur.'

'I'm sure. However, just because the digits add up doesn't mean the cell phone is still here. After all, if you had just kidnapped the minister of justice, you might have the sense to get rid of his cell phone pretty damn quickly.' Fabian opened the elevator door and looked in.

'There is no way I am setting foot in there.'

'But the footprints lead in that direction.'

'Not mine.' Malin started walking up the staircase where the construction dust created a thick carpet across the stone floor. There were no shoeprints. However, the tracks of rat feet exploded in all directions.

As soon as humans turn their backs, nature takes over, thought Fabian, following Malin up, floor by floor. They didn't find human footprints until they reached the fifth floor. There were clear tracks from heavy boots that passed between the elevator and an apartment door at the far right. The construction dust outside the other doors was untouched.

Malin took out her cell phone and took a few close-up shots of the shoeprints, while Fabian went up to the unmarked apartment door. He put one hand over the peephole and carefully opened the mail slot with the other.

It was too dark for him to see in and he couldn't hear a sound. He signalled to Malin to come over and keep her hand over the peephole while he shone a light into the mail slot with his phone. There was a worn doormat in front of the door and a roll of plastic protective film propped up against the wall.

'Shouldn't we call the special response team and let them go in first?'

'It's not possible, as long as SePo is officially leading the investigation.' Fabian carefully closed the mail slot and felt the door handle; it was locked. He went over to the neighbouring apartment door, which turned out to be unlocked. 'Wait here.'

'Am I just supposed to stand here and—' She interrupted herself with a sigh.

IT WAS DIRTY AND run down and looked exactly how you would expect a condemned apartment to be. In some places the floor was broken up and bare electrical wires were hanging from the ceiling. There was no furniture, besides a mattress that seemed to have been used a lot. Fabian went up to the only window in the room, opened it and climbed out on to the scaffolding.

It would be an exaggeration to say he suffered from vertigo, but he'd never liked heights, and he still hadn't used the balloon ride he'd got from his associates as a fortieth birthday present. For the first two years they'd asked if he ever intended to redeem his gift card; he always gave vague responses until he realized that the only way to get them to stop asking was to lie about what an amazingly powerful experience it had been. He told them he had taken his camera with him, but was so captivated by the view that he completely forgot to take pictures.

Now he had no choice other than to hope that the icy scaffolding would hold. Looking down would be no help, and it was better to direct his gaze forward and focus on firmly holding on to something with at least one hand so that he didn't slip.

Three windows later he was outside the locked apartment: Östgötagatan 46. The blinds were pulled down so it wasn't possible to see in. He looked around for something to help him get in, but when he couldn't find anything, he decided to try kicking in the window, which was considerably firmer than he'd expected. *If anyone was inside the apartment they would have plenty of time to prepare themselves*, he thought, as he wriggled through the broken window frame.

Once on the floor he looked around and could see that the room was about twenty square metres. In contrast to the first apartment, the floor was swept more or less clean. There was a pantry with a hot plate, a sink and a refrigerator along one wall.

A porcelain doll with long curly hair and wearing a dress and matching hat, looked down at him from on top of the fridge.

He continued into the adjacent room, which was so dark that his eyes struggled to adjust to his surroundings. He groped along the wall and finally found the light switch. The light was so bright that he was forced to look away.

After a few moments, he gradually turned his gaze back towards a plastic-covered table with a hole in the middle and some loose straps hanging down the sides.

18

IT HAD NOW BEEN almost half an hour since Kjeld Richter wished Dunja luck and left her alone in the conference room. But she was still sitting there, trying to gather enough energy to walk out into the department with her head held high.

The nausea had finally passed, only to be replaced by a piercing headache. If she didn't get some fluid in her soon her head would burst. And if that wasn't enough, she also badly needed to use the bathroom.

She'd thought through the possibilities and realized that she was completely alone – besides Sleizner, whom she didn't want to touch with a ten-foot pole. Hesk was too good a police officer to leave the investigation to chance, but she had no doubt he would do everything he could to thwart her.

Richter was the only real question mark. She hadn't been able to read his 'good luck' as either obvious sarcasm or consideration. He probably had no idea where he stood either, but if Dunja understood him correctly, he would choose the path that created the fewest problems at the coffee maker.

Clearly, this would be an uphill battle. No one expected her to be able to manage this by herself, presumably not even Sleizner. But simply giving up was not an option. There was no easy escape route. Her only alternative was to shoulder the responsibility, finish the investigation, arrest the guilty party and show everyone that she was a force to be reckoned with. Though, unfortunately, she didn't even believe that herself.

She took a little red cloth from the bottom of the fruit bowl and wiped the sweat off her forehead. Then she closed her eyes and took a few deep breaths before she put her hands on the table and carefully stood up.

Both her legs and hands were shaking, and her heart was pounding through her chest. She needed to get used to it. Hesk was almost certainly right – this was just the beginning of her little hell.

19

AFTER UNLOCKING THE DOOR and letting Malin into the condemned apartment, Fabian returned to the rectangular table in the middle of the larger of the two rooms. It was screwed down into the floor with angle iron and clad in transparent plastic, which had been attached on the underside with a staple gun. There was a funnel under the hole with a thick hose leading down into a can. But the can was empty and the funnel appeared to be clean, just like the plastic and the dangling straps. Fabian could see no traces of either blood or excrement.

In contrast to the rest of the room, the table looked new and immaculate. The screw heads holding the straps in place were shiny, and there wasn't even a speck of dust on the lamp hanging down from the ceiling. Either someone had cleaned up extremely carefully or the table had not yet been used.

He went over to the windows, which were carefully covered in plasterboard. It kept out all the light and prevented anyone from seeing in. There was another roll of protective plastic film in one corner and a power screwdriver and a circular saw with a long extension cord in a pile on the floor.

The condemned apartment had clearly been prepared for something. The question was what. Torture? Surgery? Dismemberment?

Could it simply be a macabre set-up to hold someone in confinement? Who was behind it? And who was supposed to be strapped down? If it was intended for the Minister for Justice, why wasn't he here? His secret cell phone had evidently been in the building. But where was it at this point? And above all: where was the minister now? The questions kept piling up on top of each other and then collapsing into a shapeless heap.

Fabian sighed. 'Malin, what do you say about having an early lunch? My treat.' He needed a break to clear his thoughts before he could continue.

'Already?' Malin called out from the hall. 'Can't we finish in here first?'

'Okay.' Fabian went into the room adjacent to the pantry. It was the only thing left to go through before he completed his search.

Like the rest of the apartment, it looked more or less cleaned out. There was an unplugged electric kettle, an upside-down glass and a coffee cup on the counter. Someone had been there for a few hours, at most a full day.

He turned on the tap, which coughed out some air, before unleashing a steady stream of clean water. No brown clumps came out. There was air, but no rust. Someone had been here between a week or two ago, probably to prepare. If someone had been there during the past twenty-four hours they definitely hadn't run the water. He turned off the tap and opened the refrigerator. To his surprise, it was turned on and contained some loaves of rye bread, a package of liver sausage and a glass jar with Hayward's pickled onions, which was almost empty.

There were two frosted resealable bags in the freezer. He took out one of them, squeezed it, and wiped off the ice. He initially thought it was a tapeworm coiled up in a white pile. He'd actually never seen one before, but knew that they could be up to twenty metres long. Then he saw *sausage casings* written on the label and realized that it was hog intestines to stuff your own sausage. The other bag looked like it contained the inner organs from a hog, or maybe some chickens.

Fabian had never been particularly fond of offal, even though he had a cookbook from the 1930s that contained a number of recipes for the inner organs of animals, including grilled cow brains, a South American delicacy. But who ate that sort of thing these days? And above all, what did it have to do with the disappearance of the minister of justice?

'Fabian! Come here. Look at this!' Malin called.

Fabian went back out into the larger room and was on his way to the hall when he noticed it. He hadn't spotted it before, presumably because he'd been standing with his back turned, focusing on the rectangular table. He might have reacted because he'd already seen something similar on top of the refrigerator in the other room. Here was another porcelain doll with blonde curls and blue eyes looking right at him from the top of the fuse box.

He took it down and inspected it. He'd never liked dolls, especially not the porcelain kind. Even though they were generally quite small, their faces were so uncomfortably realistic. When he was young, he'd got one as a Christmas present from his grandmother. He still shuddered when he thought about the doll sitting on the shelf among the other toys, staring at him all night long. It didn't take long before he started having nightmares and sleeping badly. He hid it in a cupboard and covered it with a blanket. He even threw it away once. But his mother kept putting it back on the shelf, emphasizing how nice and expensive it was.

One afternoon, when he was home alone, he mustered up the courage to put it into his backpack and went to the cement factory behind Kojak, the high hill on Dalhem that was north of Helsingborg. Like so many times before, he climbed over the fence with the many *Prohibited for unauthorized persons* signs and threw the doll down into one of the big mixing tanks. He stood there for quite a while, watching the doll slowly sink into the viscous cement mixture and disappear – out of his life, anyway. Perhaps it was encased in a wall somewhere, still staring at someone.

'Fabian! What are you doing?'

He went into the bathroom, where Malin was now standing in the bathtub shining a flashlight into a hole in the wall. 'Check this out.' She stepped to the side and handed the flashlight over to him.

'Do you see what I see?'

Fabian nodded. A broad-brimmed hat and a black coat with a fur collar had got stuck a metre or so down the narrow service duct.

'Aren't those Grimås' clothes?'

'Sure, but…'

'But what?'

'I can't put the pieces together.' He turned toward Malin. 'To be honest, I don't understand a thing.'

'What don't you understand? Grimås was here and—'

'But why? Was he here of his own accord, or was he brought here by someone else?'

'If it wasn't for the torture table in there, I would have guessed he came here on his own. Maybe he knows the owner of the building and knew he could change here undisturbed, before heading off elsewhere.'

'But—'

'I'm now leaning more towards the idea that someone brought him.'

'Then why isn't there anyone here still?'

'I think they brought him here and undressed him, but don't ask me why. Maybe they needed him to change clothes? And then, in the middle of everything, they found his secret cell phone and realized that it was only a matter of time before we arrived, so they left as quickly as possible and – voilà.'

'So you think he left the parliament building alone, and was then abducted by the quay?'

'Maybe he got an ultimatum before he left – after all he was twenty minutes late. I don't know.' She sighed and held out a mop to Fabian. 'I'm just trying to get it to fit together.'

Fabian took the mop, guided it down into the duct and pulled up the clothes and the minister's briefcase, which had got stuck crosswise.

They both stepped out of the bath. Fabian took care of the briefcase, while Malin went through the clothes. The briefcase contained a half-empty tin of Läkerol, three ballpoint pens, a Filofax personal organizer and a folder with a document, which, after a quick review, seemed to concern a number of reports and studies about the outcome of last year's law changes. The Filofax proved to be even more interesting. Most people had switched to electronic calendars, but not Grimås. He belonged to the old school, where every address and phone number was handwritten and could be read without passwords. The pages were also filled with scheduled meetings and handwritten reminders, such as, *When will it occur to the Green Party members that there actually is a reason to wear deodorant? ... That socialist bitch still doesn't know what she's talking about. Maybe good in bed? ... Don't forget to schedule appointment at IA*. And so forth.

It wasn't the content that made Fabian's pulse rise, but the handwriting itself. It was so unusual to find these kinds of items as evidence; Fabian could count the occasions on one hand. But the reward was usually big enough that it was worth the struggle to get it, like a tidy goal in soccer after one frustrating drawn-out match after the other. An impossible puzzle piece was about to find its place.

'And here we have it. Just as I said.' Malin held out the cell phone. 'Hello? Earth to Fabian.'

Fabian looked up and met her gaze.

'What is it? Did you find something?' she asked.

'I don't think he's been here.'

'Who? Grimås? Of course he's been here. Lookie lookie.' She waved Grimås' phone in front of him.

'I'll have to see the surveillance video from yesterday again, before I'm completely sure.'

'Wait, I don't understand. How can you—' She realized that there was no point and gave up.

Fabian had already left the bathroom and was on his way out of the apartment.

20

SOFIE LEANDER REALIZED THAT she must have slept soundly for once. She usually woke up immediately when she heard steps or voices approaching. Every muscle in her body tensed to breaking point, and she kept repeatedly visualizing, in excruciating detail, what was going to happen to her, like a scene in a horror movie.

But every time the steps walked past her, she knew she had a bit more time – until now.

This time everything was different. She wasn't wakened by steps or a voice, but by the sound of the electric motor and the creaking gate. Her body now stayed calm and relaxed, as if it had been on tenterhooks so long that it could no longer be afraid.

But Sofie was scared – scared to death.

She could hear the louvre gate lower once again and the clasps on a hard case clicked up. Then there was a clink on the metal table right behind her. *It was probably the scalpels and the tongs*, she thought, trying to stop the scene of her being opened up from playing over and over again in her head.

She tried to twist her head to see if it was the doctor who had brought her there, but gave up when the strap around her throat cut too deep into the wound. It didn't matter any more – the waiting was over and it was time to end it.

The devices around her were turned on and she could hear them emit different sounds. The strap around her left wrist was loosened and she could feel cold scissors press against her lower arm while the sleeve on her blouse was cut open. She felt a prick in the crook of her arm and started to lose consciousness.

The wait felt almost like eternity. She'd hoped that the tape would be released from over her mouth, so that she could at least express how sorry she was and try to explain how she'd been aware of how wrong it had been all along, but didn't feel she had any choice. She wanted the chance to say that even though she was afraid, she accepted her punishment, and in a way felt that it was appropriate. But she didn't get that opportunity.

21

'FIVE MINUTES, THEN YOU have to go,' the security guard said, double-clicking on the video file. 'Okay?'

Fabian and Malin nodded. While they waited for the uniformed man to leave them alone, they took a look outside, where a SePo team was dragging for Grimås' body in the bay right outside Kanslikajen.

They were in the small staff room behind the guard box in the parliament building. It had been quite a struggle to get access to the surveillance video that showed the Minister for Justice leaving the building. Not only had SePo classified the video as top secret, they had also alerted the security supervisor that someone from the National Bureau might come and ask questions.

What they hadn't counted on was Malin and her mood swings, which, when she didn't get her way, were enough to make anyone give in.

Fabian started the video, which showed the empty entranceway with its double glass security doors. The same sequence of Carl-Eric Grimås entering the frame had been played for him the night before. The minister walked alone with the briefcase in his left hand, pulled his pass card through the reader with his right, pushed the first door open, then the second and disappeared out into the snowstorm.

The solution had been right before his eyes the whole time – just as Fabian had suspected. They simply hadn't known what to look for. Only a right-handed person would carry his briefcase in his left hand and pull the pass card through with the other.

But the incline of the handwriting in his Filofax revealed that, like his own wife, Sonja, Carl-Eric Grimås was left-handed.

Fabian turned towards Malin. 'Do you notice anything? This guy is right-handed.'

'So that isn't the Minister for Justice, but someone who's dressed like him.'

Fabian nodded. 'It's probably the perpetrator.' He played the video again from the beginning and walked through it frame by frame. 'Look closely, he knows exactly where the camera is located and how he should move to avoid showing his face.'

'But even if that is the perpetrator, where is the minister?'

Fabian looked Malin right in the eye. 'I don't know. But if he hasn't left the building through any of the other doors, we can't rule out that he's still here.'

22

Nanna Madsen, age 21, 5 December 2005, dumpster in Herlev

Heavy bleeding from bite marks across large portions of her back and chest as well as genitalia. Analysis of teeth impressions show bites from both perpetrator and dog, probably Doberman Pinscher. Secured traces from perpetrator lacking.

Kimie Colding, age 17, 23 April 2007, Peblinge Lake

Injuries around genitalia after rough penetration. Both rows of teeth broken and several open fractures in the skull indicate forceful battery to the head, probably from a blow with a hammer. Water in lungs indicates she was alive when she was dumped in the lake. Secured traces from perpetrator lacking.

Mette Bruun, age 37, 7 September 2008, Amager Fælled

Mutilated anal opening and large intestine. Severe internal injuries from the genitalia all the way to the stomach, which probably occurred after penetration with thick branch or spiked club. Secured traces from perpetrator lacking.

Dunja Hougaard dropped the folder on the table, leaned back on the couch and closed her eyes. She needed a break from all the images of penetrated female bodies that begged and pleaded for redress but would never get it.

Instead Kim Sleizner appeared in her thoughts. She had hardly sat down at her desk before he came to say hello and asked her to stop by his office after work. The penny finally dropped. A cold shiver went through her body as she finally realized what he was really after. The last thing this was about was her competence.

In retrospect, she couldn't understand how she could have missed it, given that it was evidently obvious to everyone else. It felt like a bad practical joke, and the only thing she could do was prove everyone wrong.

She was working at home on the couch, even though the workday was officially over. She had brought all the very roughest unsolved rape cases from recent years with her. Mikael Rønning at the IT department had helped her filter the cases, even though he didn't have police authorization. But she needed an ally, someone who didn't have the slightest connection to her department.

Like a steer in a pasture, he threw himself into the search with full energy. But his mood declined as the printer spat out case after case, each worse than the last. He finally declared that his faith in humanity had been depleted.

Dunja hadn't been the least bit surprised by the brutal violence or the fact that the perpetrator in almost all cases was a man and the victim a woman. The only thing that surprised her was how many investigations in Copenhagen remained unsolved, and how simple the decision seemed to be to choke off resources and let the cases fizzle out.

The list of dormant rape investigations seemed to go on and on. Even though she'd asked Rønning to only include those with a fatal outcome, she'd taken away over a dozen investigations from the past four years – and those were just from the coastal strip from Køge up to Helsingør.

There were three cases per year where innocent women had been forced to suffer pain so severe that death must have felt like the final rescue; three investigations per year that had routinely been shut down, even though the perpetrator was still at large.

Dunja looked out the window at the dark-grey clouds moving across the sky. They looked as if they were forming into yet another storm and carrying away what little daylight was left. The images of Karen Neuman's hacked-up body would not leave her in peace. In several ways it was the same insane but also studied violence as the older cases, and just as she'd said at the meeting, this was not the work of a beginner. Whoever it was, he'd done it before. Karen Neuman was not just another random victim.

But as she went through the files, she couldn't find connections to any of the older investigations. She'd tried everything. She sorted them according to various criteria, read the detailed injury descriptions more than once, and studied every image of the tortured bodies under a magnifying glass. But nothing stood out as a possible link.

She'd been able to put seven of the cases aside right away. Four of them had so many similarities that they formed a group of their own. There had also been a strong suspect for those crimes, but unfortunately he managed to kill himself before he was convicted.

Three of them also belonged together without a doubt. In those cases, the perpetrator had taken part of each victim's scalp as a trophy. According to Oscar Pedersen's report, the profuse flow of blood from the severed scalps indicated that the all the victims were still alive during the process. And whoever was behind these bestial acts was still free.

But he wasn't the person she was searching for now, even if she promised herself that she would breathe life into the investigation as soon as she had time and capture that bastard.

Five investigations were still on the table; five cases that were still officially open, but in reality had gone cold.

All showed such brutal, studied violence, evident in what happened to Karen Neuman, that it couldn't possibly be the work of a beginner. At the same time, all five differed markedly from each other. There was nothing that seemed to connect them. The victims not only had different ages and appearances, but the crime scenes were widely dispersed and the killer used various methods to kill his victims.

Each case seemed unique. A perpetrator who, on a single occasion, crossed the line and raped and tortured his victim to death in the most hideous of ways, only to return to his normal life, without leaving any traces or binding evidence behind. It was impossible. There had to be a common denominator somewhere – she was sure of that.

Her cell phone ring interrupted her thoughts. It was Kjeld Richter, so she tried to sound as professional as she could, even though she was actually relieved that he was calling her instead of Hesk. According to Scandlines, which ran the ferry between Helsingør–Helsingborg, two cars had run down a gate when they were leaving the harbour's terminal area last night, which was what Richter had been sent to investigate.

'Hi, Kjeld. Are you still in Helsingør?'

'Dunja, I like you. But I want to make one thing damned clear: you have so much water over your head you risk drowning. And whenever that happens, don't count on me.'

'Kjeld, listen to me now. This is Sleizner's idea. I understand just as little as—'

'I'm not getting involved. I intend to do my job, but I just want you to know where I stand.'

'Sure. I hear what you're saying,' said Dunja, taking a deep breath. 'I assume you didn't just call to tell me that you're another hen in the chicken coop. I hope you've got some information for me, too.'

'Huh?'

'You heard me,' said Dunja, impressed at how she managed to assert herself. 'Well? Have you found anything? If not, I want—'

'I've already reported to Jan, and only wanted to tell you that I'm going home now.'

'But you were supposed to report to me. Sleizner couldn't have been more clear on that point.'

'The last thing I want to do is to end up in the middle of some fucking power struggle between—'

'Kjeld, you said you were going to do your job. If you do, then everyone will be happy.'

There was silence on the other end of the phone and Dunja could tell that Richter was weighing the pros and cons.

'I don't remember which of you brought it up, but there is no doubt that the Swedish car with the spiked wheels and Neuman's BMW had been inside the ferry terminal and forced the gate into Helsingør Harbour.'

Dunja got up from the couch. 'And then what happened? Where do the tracks go?'

'Right out on to Færgevej, but it's been driven on since and was ploughed a while ago.'

Dunja went up to the window and noticed that the snow had started falling outside. Usually she loved snow, especially the first snowfall of winter that nestled everything in a clean white blanket and forced everyone to take it a little easier – but not today. Now the storm meant nothing more than a battle against the clock. Every additional snowflake contributed to removal of the tracks and the possibility of finding out what had happened in Helsingør Harbour.

'Just so you know, I've secured everything that I possibly could and now I have to go.'

'Kjeld, wait. Has it started snowing where you are yet?'

'Yes, it's really coming down, so if I don't leave soon I won't pick up the kids on time.'

'But I want you to stay and—'

'What do you mean, "stay"? Thursdays are my only pick-up day. If I miss that Susanne isn't going to talk to me all weekend.'

'That's too bad. I want you to finish working first.'

'I am done, dammit! Are you hard of hearing?'

'You're not done until I say you are.'

Richter let out a long, heavy sigh and then collected himself. 'Do you think I don't see what the hell you—'

'Who's leading this investigation? You or me? Do as I say now, before it's too late!'

She was met with complete silence and Dunja realized that Richter was probably just as shocked by her outburst as she was. She had never gone after anyone that hard, not even when she'd been so mad at Carsten.

'Before you go home, I want you to continue north along Færgevej and see if you can find tracks that continue along the edge of the road, or if they turn off on to a smaller street.'

'What's the point? They could have driven anywhere.'

'Just do as I say, instead of—'

'I've already started.'

'Okay. How far have you got?' She hurried over to her desk under the bookshelf in the corner, turned on her computer and zoomed in on Helsingør Harbour.

'I'm at Stationspladsen, turning right on to Havnegade. Then I'll continue north along the harbour basin.'

'You can probably see where all the buildings are on the left side, no?'

'What the hell do you think? It's like looking for a needle in a haystack – a needle made of hay. There are quite a few new tracks, because the snow is pouring down like... I don't know what. But—'

'Where are you now?'

'I've more or less passed the harbour. Pretty soon it turns into Nordre Strandvej.'

'Turn around and drive back in the other direction.'

'Huh? Why would I do that? The only thing there is the harbour pier.'

'Just do as I say, before it's snowed over completely! If you keep stalling your kids are going to have to spend the night in daycare.'

Dunja expected some form of protest. She'd indicated that she was joking, but Kjeld Richter was notorious for not perceiving sarcasm or having any sense of humour at all. The others at the department called him the Swede, but he couldn't even laugh at that. Instead he went to the HR manager and filed a harassment report, and everyone had been called in to an emergency meeting.

'Kjeld, that last thing I said was just a joke. Of course they won't have to—'

'Dammit, I think I've found... Wait.'

'What? What have you found? Kjeld, talk to me. Where are you exactly?'

'Do you see the railway tracks that run along Havnegade?'

Dunja zoomed in to the railway line that passed between the road and the pier. 'Yes, is that where you are?'

'I'm right where you can drive across the tracks out to the pier. I'm just going to—' She heard the car door open and the ferocious sound of gusty winds. 'Jesus Christ, this weather.'

Despite the elements, Dunja wished she was there. 'Have you found the tracks?'

'It can't be anything else. There's one with studs and one with... It looks like they've skidded out on to the pier and...'

'What? What is it? Kjeld? Have you found something?'

'Yes. Pieces of plastic from a tail light. But, what the hell...'

The frustration was making her scalp itch, and Dunja wanted to shout at him to describe what he saw, but she managed to restrain herself. Neither of them said anything for a few long seconds.

'So, it seems like Neuman followed the car with the studded tyres out on to the pier and it drove right into... Wait, I'll just... Yes, dammit. It can't have happened any other way.'

'Kjeld? What happened?'

'It went down into the water.'

'You think the Swedish car is at the bottom of the harbour?'

'I'm as good as certain.'

'Does that mean that the perpetrator is down there, too?'

'It's possible, but I'm not sure. There are some footprints here, but there's already too much snow to see whether it's from one person or several.'

'Okay, secure as much as possible. I'll talk to you tomorrow.' She ended the call and went back to lie down on the couch to collect her thoughts.

If Richter had read the tracks in the snow correctly, Aksel Neuman had chased the perpetrator after coming home and finding his wife murdered in bed. As far as they could tell right now, Neuman had shadowed the Swedish car all the way up to the ferry terminal in Helsingør, at which point the perpetrator must have spotted him. Then it turned into a car chase that ended abruptly on the pier.

But where Aksel Neuman and his BMW had gone was still a question mark.

He could be lying low because he risked being charged with the murder of the perpetrator. The perpetrator could have also managed to swim out of the car. Or perhaps he wasn't even in the car when it went over the edge, but was hiding somewhere, and had overpowered Neuman and taken both his life and his car.

It was a plausible scenario, but whether it was sufficiently probable was another question. If Dunja was asked to give an answer herself, it would be an unhesitating no. It wasn't even close to being probable. But something told her that the last thing this investigation would be about was what was probable or not.

14 June 1998

I don't know where you are, or if you even exist, but this letter is to you and no one else.

I used to see you almost every day on the other side of the checkpoint and the barbed-wire fence. But that was a year ago. You would sit there for hours. Maybe you were passing by, or maybe you came just to look. I don't know. In the camp there were rumours about Palestinian women who met Israeli soldiers in secret and maybe you came for my sake. I would stand at the boom, hoping.

I knew that women from the Nablus mountains could have blue eyes, but I'd never seen them before you. You were the most beautiful person in the world. I didn't understand it at first, but my heart started to beat twice as fast when I saw you. It still does, just thinking about you, as if it refuses to accept that it's too late and will all soon be over.

I can't stop going over our last night together. Do you remember it? How it was starting to get dark and you stayed longer than usual. My shift was done and I figured it was now or never. I walked along the barricade and saw you move in my direction. I almost screamed with joy.

I would have turned my back if I knew what would happen next, warned you about being too close to the border – even threatened you and forced you back. I would have never stood by that fence and let my eyes meet yours, so you wouldn't have come all the way up and put your palms against mine. Your lips...

I can't keep going much longer. There's not much blood left now.

How long did we stand there in silence? A few minutes, or was it a whole hour? There was so much I wanted to say, ask, but didn't dare. I was so afraid of disturbing the moment by trying to put my thoughts into words. How you were the most beautiful woman I'd ever seen. How your eyes could be so blue. How I loved you already, even though we'd only ever met with a fence between us. I didn't even get your name. All I could do was turn on my portable radio. Do you remember? They were playing Etta James. No one could say it better than her anyway. I pinched myself hard on the arm to be sure it wasn't a dream, so hard that I still have a scar.

I don't know who took you away or if that's why you never showed up again. Was it your father or someone in your village? Are you even alive? Maybe it was all just a dream anyway and for a while I thought it would be enough.

The scar, and the idea of you, kept it all alive.

23

PARLIAMENT ACTUALLY CONSISTED OF seven different buildings: the East and West Houses of Parliament on Helgeandsholmen and the parliament building, Brandkontoret, Neptunus, Cephalus and Mercurius in Old Town. All the buildings were linked by underground tunnels and guarded by a hundred-odd cameras, which was a lot for just two guards stationed in the security centre to monitor. Considering the combined square metres of the buildings and the number of high-profile politicians who went in and out of them daily, the area was virtually unguarded. If you knew where the cameras were located, it was not hard to make yourself invisible.

After almost two straight hours of looking at various surveillance videos Fabian, Malin, and one of the guards managed to identify the minister for justice as he came out of the assembly hall through door four at 2:42 p.m. Grimås stopped to put on his fur-collared coat before continuing towards the escalator.

'Did you see that? He's holding the briefcase in his right hand and the hat in his left.' Fabian pointed towards the monitor where the minister disappeared down the escalator. Malin nodded.

The next time the minister was caught on camera, he was walking resolutely through the big hall of the Swedish Central Bank, which it was still called even though the official Central Bank moved to Brunkebergstorg many years ago. The briefcase was still in his right hand, and he was using his left to put on his hat.

'And this is the most direct route to get to the parliament building?' Malin said and the guard nodded.

'He seems prepared to go out, anyway,' said Fabian, who noticed that nothing in the minister's body language seemed to indicate that this was anything other than an ordinary day.

Fabian noticed similar behaviour as they watched him go through the 'gutter', the name given to the first part of the underground tunnel to the government buildings in the Old Town. The minister didn't seem nervous or hesitant as he looked out the windows at Riddarfjärden – where his first cell phone would later be found – or when he greeted other members of parliament as they walked by him. He was likely completely ignorant of what was coming.

Seconds later, it happened. The time stamp showed 2:45 p.m. In the underground hall right after the gutter, the minister stopped mid-step and turned around as if someone was calling his name.

'Play that again and zoom in,' said Fabian. The sequence replayed, zeroing in on the minister. Even with a considerably grainier image, Grimås' puzzled expression could not be missed.

'There's no other angle we can look at to see who's calling him?' asked Malin.

'We only have cameras at the doors. Politicians are not particularly thrilled about being under surveillance. But let me see what I can do.' The guard switched between a number of different camera angles. 'Here. I think I've got it,' the guard said, pressing play.

The video showed a guard with a moustache and ample waist yell and wave to the minister, who was on his way in the opposite direction. The minister turned around and walked over to the guard, leaning in to hear him speak. The guard was at least a head shorter than him.

'Are there any microphones down there?' said Fabian.

'Unfortunately not.' The guard zoomed in on the frame of the minister listening attentively.

'Do you recognize that guard?' said Malin.

'No, but everyone is supposed to have an ID number on their uniform. It's hidden by the minister here.'

Grimås nodded again and then followed the guard off camera.

'Where did they go?' said Fabian.

'I'm not sure, but it looks like they continued straight ahead toward Brandkontoret or Neptunus, instead of turning right towards the parliament building. However—'

'Change to another camera. We can't lose them.'

'Fabian, this isn't live,' said Malin. 'Everything should be recorded, isn't that right?' She turned to the guard, who nodded with an exaggerated smile.

But Fabian didn't feel any calmer. It happened right then. In front of their eyes, the minister had disappeared.

'I don't understand,' said the guard, switching back and forth between various videos, some of which were completely black. 'It seems as if some of the cameras were... sprayed, or something? I get sabotage alarms if someone cuts the cable.'

'Go back to the sequence where they were last seen and then fast-forward to three twenty.'

The guard clicked a little ahead on the timeline and about half a minute later the minister came back into the frame. 'There he is. I almost got a little worried.'

'If it's actually him,' said Fabian.

24

DUNJA TRIED TO THINK about something else, but she couldn't shake the images of all the mutilated female bodies with their shredded genitalia, slashed throats and lifeless gazes that looked like they had been thrown like garbage on the floor of a slaughterhouse. She had analysed the pictures down to the smallest detail in an increasingly desperate attempt to find a link to Karen Neuman.

But after far too many hours on the couch she had reached a dead end and decided to go to bed. Her brain, on the other hand, refused to rest and continued to review the facts on its own. When she heard Carsten returning from his Christmas dinner, she lay completely still and hoped that if she acted asleep, she would finally get there for real.

Maybe she should have been upfront and told him that there was no point in trying because her mind was preoccupied with sequences of one woman after another being raped, sawed or hacked to pieces. But instead she tried to pretend and left the field open, something Carsten did not wait long to exploit.

Once he'd made up his mind, arguments like fatigue and headache were irrelevant. Her low libido didn't hinder him either. On the contrary, he was convinced that simply rubbing her clitoris a little harder would remedy everything. She finally relented, hoping her brain would get a much-needed break. Unfortunately, it wasn't working.

But somewhere deep down, she really wanted to sleep with Carsten. For that reason, she let him pump in a rhythm as even as a metronome, even moaning once or twice when he panted in her ear and asked if she liked it.

'By the way, there's something I forgot to tell you.'

'Why now? Can't it wait?' asked Dunja, trying to ignore the image of what a spiked wooden club could do to a woman.

'No, otherwise I might forget. I have to go to Stockholm this weekend and won't be home until Tuesday.' The tip of his tongue worked its way further into her ear and Dunja wondered whether he was aware of how loud it sounded. 'I think it's a seminar on a new way to calculate a company's credit rating after a merger.'

Dunja nodded and let him continue thrusting. Could there really be five widely divergent perpetrators – six, including Karen Neuman's? How could there be six different men who attacked an innocent victim with such studied evil, only to return to their daily lives.

'Sorry I wasn't in the mood yesterday. I promise to make up for it now.'

Dunja nodded and tried to ignore the fact that she had got so dry, it had started to sting. Instead, she thought about all the great sex they'd had when they met. They had done it everywhere, several times a day. Everything revolved around their lovemaking. She walked around feeling constantly horny, and they'd tested every possible and impossible position.

Now she didn't know what to call what they were doing. It wasn't sex in any event. She'd always heard that sex got deeper and more intimate the longer you were together. In their case, it had only got worse and monotonous to the point that anything but the missionary position felt criminal.

She wished he could just surprise her once in a while with something unexpected – anything would be better than this monotonous bumping and grinding. Even if he just moved a little more irregularly, or better yet pulled out completely and started licking her. Or he could flip her over on to all fours and take her…

Wait, that's exactly how it all fits together. Suddenly she saw it so clearly that she couldn't understand why she hadn't thought of it before.

'What is it?' Carsten stopped in mid-motion.

'Nothing. Just keep going.'

The discrepancies were the common denominator. How could everyone have missed it, herself included? Obviously it was the same perpetrator. He simply didn't want to do the same thing twice. If he was going to get a high, he needed to execute more sadistic methods each time.

Dunja faked to finish it. Two minutes later Carsten rolled over on his side, satisfied at his performance. Finally, she could get out of bed.

'Honey, I'll be right back. I just have to do one thing.'

'I promise not to go anywhere. I'm just getting started here,' said Carsten, taking hold of his tired erection.

'I promise to hurry back,' said Dunja as she pulled on her kimono and left the room, well aware that he would have fallen asleep long before she was finished.

25

'BRANDKONTORET AND NEPTUNUS ARE the two smallest buildings,' said the burly, out-of-breath guard as he hurried through the underground passage that went straight through the old city wall while directing the rest of the force through his radio. 'And if he did in fact go this way we should find him soon.'

Fabian and Malin followed the guard to the last place where the minister and the mysterious security guard had been spotted by the surveillance cameras. They hurried through a labyrinth of passages, old cellar arches and narrow stairs that led up to the two government buildings. The feeling that they were getting closer to their goal was intensifying. The guard had force split up between the two buildings and started searching room by room.

But after almost six straight hours of searching, they hadn't made any progress. They hadn't even managed to find so much as a trace of what had happened to the minister for justice. Their energy was running out, and their theories about what happened had multiplied. Maybe the minister had simply left through another door dressed as someone else? Or perhaps it was him on the surveillance video after all?

Fabian had increasing difficulty justifying a continued search, and after another hour, as the time approached midnight, the effort was called off. According to the guard responsible, the minister was absolutely not there. They had meticulously combed through both buildings and the cellar vaults – two, even three times – and there was nothing to suggest that he would suddenly appear on the fourth. Besides, it was almost midnight.

Fabian was about to question whether they really had searched everywhere, but he was stopped by Malin, who took him aside.

'Fabian, I know this isn't your style, but have you given any thought to the possibility that there might be something to what they are suggesting? Perhaps, wait now, they're even right?'

'So you don't think he's here either?'

Malin shrugged. 'I have no idea. Something definitely happened between the minister and that guard, but that doesn't mean he's still here. If the guard did go out in Grimås' clothes, then Grimås himself may have gone somewhere in the guard's clothes, don't you think? That's not something we'll discover now, no matter how many surveillance videos we watch.'

'Well, first of all, his uniform would be much too small.'

Malin sighed and shook her head.

'Malin, I agree with you. If Grimås was involved, we could have stopped the search hours ago. But he wasn't. You saw for yourself how the guard suddenly called to him as he was on his way to his transport. Until then he had no idea what was waiting. Besides, there's not a single unguarded door here, so whether he left any of the buildings, voluntarily or involuntarily, has yet to be confirmed.'

'So what's your explanation?'

Fabian shrugged. 'I don't know. They must not have searched everywhere.'

'Yes, they have – three times.'

Fabian didn't say anything. There was no point. If he didn't go along with ending the search, he would have both SePo and the police commissioner on him. But he couldn't shake the feeling of being so close. He had no doubt that the minister was the victim of a crime. And the more he thought about it, the more significant the location of the offence became. How ironic was it that the Minister for Justice was least protected in the parliament buildings? During the few hours between question time and exiting the building, SePo had made the fatal mistake of skimping on his personal protection.

A security guard had called for the minister's attention, taken him to one of the camera's blind spots, and returned a little more than half an hour later in the minister's own clothes. That much was certain; what happened after that was still unclear.

Either the minister was still in one of the parliament buildings, or someone had managed to get him out without being caught on any of the surveillance cameras. The perpetrator's risk of being discovered was enough to suggest that the minister was likely still inside. But where?

There must be some space they had overlooked, somewhere that was never used.

'Well, then, I guess we'll say thanks and wish you luck,' the guard said, showing them to the door.

They shook hands.

'It's very possible that we'll be contacting you again,' said Malin, as she began walking out the door.

If he was to hide someone in police headquarters, Fabian knew exactly which room he would have chosen, the room that all major workplaces were forced to have by law, but was never used.

'Fabian? Hello? We're leaving now,' said Malin.

Fabian nodded and followed Malin out, but stopped again, and turned towards the guard. 'Have you looked in the nap room?'

'Nap room? We don't have one of those here,' the guard said with a snort.

'Are you quite sure?'

'I know every nook and cranny in these buildings. Despite what people may think about politicians, they don't take naps.'

'It was just an idea,' said Fabian, turning to leave.

'Wait a second. Behind all the old overhead projectors in the arch under Brandkontoret…' The guard's face turned pale. 'Why didn't I think of that?'

'About what?' asked Fabian, but got no response.

The guard had already hurried off at such high speed that Fabian and Malin had a hard time keeping up.

26

'You're joking! Do you know how late it is!?' Mikael Rønning's voice was shrieking through the phone.

'Yes, I am aware. And, no, I'm not joking,' said Dunja, curling up on the couch with her phone. 'But you're the only one who can help me. Where are you? Far from the office?'

'No, Ben had a conflict. And I mean conflict in quotation marks. I know we have an open relationship and yada yada yada, but you have to agree that's in poor taste.'

'Absolutely. But where are you?'

'I'm still here playing the Sims.'

'You're at the office?'

'Yes, but I was just about to head out to Cosy Bar. Do you know what I'm going to do there?'

'No, but I can imagine. Can you help me before you leave to get revenge on Ben? By the way, is his name really Ben?'

'Yes, but most people call him Big Ben.'

'But not you.'

'In that case it would be Big-But-Not-Bigger-Than-Me Ben. But forget about that fucking fairy now. What do you want help with?'

'I think some of the cases you pulled for me have the same perpetrator.'

'How could that be? Besides the extreme violence they have nothing in common.'

'I know. And that's just the point. He gets bored. So to get the same thrill, he has to reinvent the wheel every time. Do you follow?'

'And what do you want me to do for you?'

'A new search that goes further back in time.'

'How far?'

'Ten or fifteen years. And it doesn't have to result in a fatal outcome. Rape is sufficient, or even attempted rape. He must have had a first time.'

'There are going to be a lot of hits.'

'Please, can you just do this for me?'

'Your wish is my command.'

'Sorry, it wasn't my intention to—'

'It's okay. But if, God forbid, we were to end up in bed together, like at a Christmas party or something, I'll be the one holding the whip, okay?'

'Sure, I promise,' said Dunja with a laugh. 'Call me as soon as you're finished. I can't sleep.'

'That won't be necessary. I have them pulled up now.'

'Okay, how many are there?'

'Like I said: there are a lot.'

'As in triple digit?'

'Oh, yeah.'

Dunja held the phone away from her mouth so that Rønning couldn't hear her sigh. He had been right. It was disgusting how frequent rape or attempted rape had become in Denmark. They needed something that distinguished her perpetrator from all the others, some little detail that was both searchable and could connect with one of the later cases.

She sat up on the couch and looked at the five investigations sitting next to each other on the coffee table, something she'd done more times than she could count.

'Hello? Are you still there?'

'Hmm...' she said, finally realizing how tired she was. She really ought to set Rønning loose on Cosy Bar and go back to bed; Carsten had surely fallen asleep by now. But she was on the trail of something that refused to let go and she wouldn't get a wink of sleep until she made some headway. Her gaze fastened on the investigation of Nanna Madsen, who had been found in a Herlev dumpster with severe bleeding from deep bite marks. 'Listen, what if you include a dog in the search field?'

'A dog? What kind of dog?'

'Try "Doberman Pinscher", "fighting dog", or simply "dog".' Dunja could hear the tapping keys as Rønning entered the new search.

'Bingo. On 14 June 2004, a Maiken Brandt reported an attempted rape where the perpetrator, among other heinous acts, is alleged to have set an aggressive dog on her. According to her testimony it was a Doberman Pinscher.'

'Could she identify him?'

'Yes, she'd seen him in the area several times and could identify him. She even testified against him in court.'

'And?'

'His name is Benny Willumsen, age thirty-six. He was sentenced to two years, but was released after one.'

'Can you see exactly when he was released?' Dunja picked up Nanna Madsen's file. She was murdered on 5 December 2005.

'He was discharged on 17 July 2005.'

'So, six months later, he was at it again.'

'What happened six months later?'

'I want you to do the same search you just did, but only focus on the days between 17 July and 5 December 2005.'

'Okay, there are three different incidents on 15 August, 23 October and 4 November. The last two were complete rapes, but all three investigations were closed due to lack of evidence.'

'And on 5 December he goes even further and kills his victim. It's him. It must be him. Do a search and see where he lives.'

'I've already done that, but he doesn't seem to be registered anywhere in Denmark.'

'Have you tried looking up another Willumsen? Maybe his parents or other relatives?'

'He didn't have any siblings and both parents are deceased. He may have moved abroad.'

'I hadn't thought of that. Can you try Sweden?'

Dunja heard his fingers racing across the keys again, but for some reason she already felt calm. When Rønning started speaking she wasn't the least bit surprised.

'He lives on Konsultgatan 29 in Malmö, third floor.'

27

'TAKE IT EASY, DON'T forget I'm pregnant,' said Malin, who had a hard time keeping up with Fabian and the guard who, despite his size, navigated his way around the underground passages like an eager bloodhound. After passing several closed washroom doors, they turned left, and followed an offshoot of the corridor that came to a dead end. The guard finally stopped, caught his breath, and pointed towards dozens of old overhead projectors stacked on top of one another like a monument to the advances of technology.

'Behind all of that there should be a door.'

Fabian and the guard moved the projectors one by one, but soon realized that some were strategically placed so they could easily be rolled aside, revealing a narrow passage that led to a closed door with a sign showing the image of a bed: the obligatory nap room that no one ever used. *Not until now, anyway*, Fabian thought, pushing down the handle.

Other than the metallic odour of blood, there was nothing obviously surprising about the room that contained only a cot, small table and floor lamp. The Minister for Justice was lying face-up on the cot with his eyes closed, covered by a blanket. Despite the smell, there was no blood anywhere, Fabian noted as he turned on his phone and aimed the light at the neutral wall-to-wall carpet that covered the floor.

'Is he alive?' said Malin, squeezing in beside Fabian.

Fabian pressed his fingers against the minister's carotid artery and shook his head. The body was cold and rigor mortis had almost completely subsided, suggesting he'd been dead about twenty-four hours.

'Do you smell the same thing I do?' Malin closed the door so that the guard wouldn't enter.

Fabian nodded. His suspicions were confirmed when he pulled back the blanket from the naked body. There was a large, gaping hole covering the whole abdomen.

'Good Lord, what's happened?' Malin went up and stood beside Fabian, who was shining his light down into the opening that was several inches wide and completely scooped out.

'He's been emptied of all his inner organs,' said Fabian. 'The intestines, liver, kidneys. As far as I can tell, it's all gone.'

'I don't get it. This must have required an incredible amount of planning. Do you know what all this is about?'

Fabian didn't answer, even though he had just realized the true contents of the freezer bags in the condemned apartment.

'First Palme, then Lindh and now Grimås,' Malin continued, shaking her head. 'This is just sick. If assassination of our ministers continues like this, we won't have any politicians left.'

'Are you okay?' said Fabian.

'How the hell could I be okay, Fabian? The Swedish Minister for Justice has just been murdered. Do you understand what's coming? We're going to have every reporter in Sweden after us! Edelman's not going to be able to do anything other than hold press conferences where he won't be able to say much more than we're working with several parallel leads. But...' She sighed heavily with her hands resting on her protruding belly. 'At least we can be happy that there's no longer any doubt that a crime has been committed and that, as of now, the investigation is officially with us.'

Fabian nodded in agreement, even though he hadn't heard a single word she'd said. He was completely preoccupied with connecting the cut-up body in front of him with the contents he'd found in the freezer of the condemned apartment. He doubted those pouches were filled with sausage casings or sweet meats from a hog.

'What do you think?'

Fabian held up his hand to shush her and directed the beam of light toward the minister's face. If his theory was correct, those weren't pickled onions swimming around in the Hayward's glass jar.

Once he leaned forward he saw the sunken eyelids.

'What is it? Have you found something?' said Malin.

Fabian nodded, took hold of one eyelid with the help of some tweezers, and lifted it up.

And just like the abdomen, the eye socket too gaped empty.

28

Fabian,

I don't know what time you'll be coming home or if you're even coming home. I don't want to get involved in what you're up to, but I would really like you to call for the children's sake, especially Matilda's. She can't let go of the thought that we'll separate. What have you said to her? She asked me if we had already split up and I didn't know what to say. Have we?

Theodor is a whole other story. I have no idea what he's doing in the evenings, but I'm sure it's nothing good. Regardless of what our future looks like that's something we have to deal with – together.

There are leftovers in the fridge if you're hungry.

Sonja

P.S. I'll be at the studio all weekend.

She'd given up, thought Fabian, picking up the handwritten letter from the kitchen table and hiding it in the cupboard among the pill containers. He could understand her point of view and was prepared to agree that it was probably the right decision. But however right it seemed at the moment, he couldn't make himself take the step towards separation. He would never forgive himself if it turned out to be a wrong decision in retrospect. Maybe they were just in an unusually long rough patch that they were struggling to leave.

He took the food container out of the refrigerator and opened it. Inside was mushroom risotto, which was one of his favourite things. No one made risotto as well as Sonja. He took a fork and ate it cold right out of the container in case the noise of the microwave woke the others. He decided not to let it be over until they'd made a final, concerted attempt to save their marriage.

When he had finished, he pushed the container into the overflowing dishwasher, turned off the light and went into the bathroom, where he took a shower, brushed his teeth and started the usual activity of flossing. His dentist had been after him more aggressively recently and threatened loose teeth if he didn't start flossing soon. Considering how much his gums were bleeding, those were anything but idle threats.

Sonja was asleep in the bedroom. There was really nothing quite like the sound of her sleeping. Her heavy, irregular breathing was interspersed with light snores, which were so unique that not even she was able to imitate them when she tried to pretend to be asleep.

He set the alarm for seven o'clock and crawled under the covers. Every part of him was in desperate need of a few hours' rest. Their crime scene investigator, Hillevi Stubbs, was combing the nap room in the parliament building and the condemned apartment for clues, while the forensic team was examining Grimås' body. Malin had got a second wind and returned to the parliament building. She had wanted to study the surveillance videos in more detail so that she could try and identify the mystery guard.

She'd wanted him to come along, but he declined, well aware that this was the calm before the storm and likely his last chance to get some sleep. Within the next thirty minutes, the news of the minister's death would be public and, even if Edelman withheld the worst details, the media would inevitably find out, nosing their way from headline to headline, each worse than the last.

But right now none of that mattered. He couldn't stop thinking about Sonja's letter and the possibility that she had thrown in the towel. They had spent so many amazing years together, he couldn't accept that their relationship was about to expire silently, like sand in an hourglass.

The least they could do was talk to each other. Sonja had proposed more than once that they go into therapy and explored options about where they could go. But he'd opposed every suggestion and thought she was exaggerating the problems. He thought they should be able to sit down and talk about their issues alone, without some money-hungry stranger watching them. But the truth was, he didn't dare.

He rolled over on to Sonja's side and burrowed himself under her blanket. She was warm and her hair smelled faintly of oil paint, even though she'd just showered. She was sleeping too deeply to notice his presence and didn't even react when he said her name. *Perhaps she was listening subconsciously*, he thought, leaning down towards her ear. 'Sonja, I love you. Just so you know, I love you more than anything,' he whispered. 'And I promise you that I haven't given up, not by a long shot. Do you hear me? If you want us to go into therapy, then let's do it. Okay?'

'Mmm.'

Whether that was an answer or only a sound was impossible to say.

'Sonja, I love you,' he whispered one more time. 'Fabian loves you.'

'Love you too,' she said in an exhalation so low that it was almost inaudible. But for Fabian it was more than enough.

29

IT WAS ONLY ELEVEN minutes to six in the morning when Fabian and Malin stepped into the faintly illuminated stairwell at Hornsgatan 107. In several respects it was a perfect location on Södermalm, a stone's throw from the Årstaviken green space, but judging by how it looked up close it might as well have been any run-down suburb, thought Fabian.

Malin had called twenty minutes earlier to report how she had managed to decipher the guard's nametag on one of the surveillance videos from the parliament buildings. The guard who went off with the minister was named Joakim Holmberg. He was thirty-seven years old, lived alone and had worked as a guard for the past five years.

'Sixth floor,' Malin said, pulling open the elevator door.

'Let's take the stairs,' said Fabian, making to leave.

'Easy for you to say. You don't have a whole family to drag along,' said Malin, hurrying behind him. 'I asked Wojtan to look him up. Do you want to hear what he found?'

Wojtek Novak had replaced Niva Ekenhielm when she quit two years ago. He refused to be called 'sci-fi cop', and insisted on being addressed as an 'information technology criminal investigator'. Most people called him 'Wojtan' or 'Cyber-Wojtan'. After spending a year getting up to speed, there was no longer any doubt that he was an asset, even if he would never be anywhere close to Niva's level.

'Absolutely. Let's hear it,' said Fabian, losing the struggle against a yawn.

'As I said, he's thirty-seven years old and lived with his mother until she died of breast cancer two-and-a-half years ago. Cosy, right? And I don't mean the breast cancer. Now he's taken over the lease.'

A loner who had never moved away from home. *It couldn't get much worse*, thought Fabian, and waited for Malin, whose face was starting to get red from the exertion of walking up the stairs. 'Anything else?'

'Oh, yes. I'm just getting started. On Facebook he likes both Swedish Democrats and the blog *Politically Incorrect*. And every week on Flashback, he contributes to various different gun threads.'

'No other types of threads?' Fabian continued up the last staircase.

'Such as?'

'Hunting, dismemberment, human anatomy and so on.'

'No idea. If he did, he wrote it using a pseudonym. But listen to this: from 1997 to 2000 he applied to the Police Academy every year without being accepted. The explanation…' She climbed up on to the last step, took out her phone and read out loud: '"The applicant suffers from such powerful social phobias that we consider the police profession to be completely unsuitable."'

'But working as a security guard at the parliament buildings was evidently not a problem.'

'Or maybe that's how he got scared of the dark. Hold on, this is where it starts to get really interesting. Do you know who was rector at the Police Academy during that period?'

Fabian thought, but finally shook his head.

'Carl-Eric Grimås.'

'Really?'

Malin nodded.

'You think that could be a motive,' said Fabian, holding out the door to the access balcony.

'Why not? In 1995 he quit as head of the National Bureau and became rector at the Police Academy for a few years before going into politics.'

'But that was almost ten years ago,' said Fabian. 'Seems like a very long time to hold a grudge.'

'Maybe he couldn't execute his plan until his mother died.'

They continued along the access balcony from which they could see right into the residents' kitchens. The first two apartments were vacant; five people were playing cards in the third; and the fourth belonged to Joakim Holmberg. His lights were off.

Fabian curved his hands around his face and looked into the kitchen, which did not appear to have been cleaned since Mum had died. The counter was full of crusty dishes and the floor was covered with old pizza boxes and McDonald's bags. But the Coca-Cola cans were most striking of all. They were stacked by the hundreds and formed various high towers.

'Shit, it's open,' said Malin, while Fabian turned around. 'What do you say? Should we go in or wait for the response team?'

Fabian nodded and stepped carefully into the hall. Behind him, Malin took out her pistol, chambered a round, then followed him in and closed the door. The air was thick and stuffy and the only sound was from the traffic on Hornsgatan.

'Isn't it a little strange to leave your door unlocked?' Malin whispered. 'Even if you're at home you lock the door, especially when you have an access balcony.'

Fabian signalled for to her to be quiet and opened one of the doors in the hall with his foot.

'You don't think he's home, do you?'

Fabian shrugged and looked into the bedroom, which appeared to be in the same need of sanitization as the kitchen. There was an unmade bed and dirty clothes tossed in piles on the floor. More stacks of Coca-Cola cans covered large parts of one wall.

'Talk about dependency,' said Malin, entering the room.

Fabian continued through the hall, which opened up into a larger room. In contrast to the kitchen and bedroom, it was pitch dark. Once he finally managed to find the light switch, he realized that in this room was the key to Joakim Holmberg. He had put his soul in here and had built up a world in which he avoided confronting other people, a world where he alone was in the centre.

Just like in the condemned apartment on Östgötagatan, the windows were covered and couldn't let more light in even if it was a sunny summer day. All light came from the spotlights in the ceiling, which were aimed at a dozen mannequins, each dressed in a different costume, including a monk's cowl, a bikini, a nurse's uniform and bondage gear.

Some of them sat on the leather couch, as if they were talking to each other, and had wine glasses set out on the smoke-coloured glass coffee table in front of them. Others stood or were lying on the floor in various obscene positions.

There was a swivel armchair with cup holders raised up on a small podium in the middle of the room that faced a shelf containing a big-screen TV, PlayStation, Xbox, desktop computer and a surround-sound system. A box of Kleenex and a tube of softening cream sat atop a small round table beside the armchair.

Fabian approached the armchair, climbed up and sat down, discovering immediately that all the mannequins were turned towards him in one way or another, as if he was the centre of the party and the natural focus of everyone's attention.

Joakim Holmberg clearly liked to be alone so he could pretend he was the centre of attention. He was an expert on weapons, sympathized with the far right, and, unsurprisingly, had not been accepted to the Police Academy. Fabian went over everything in his head. He sensed they were still missing the key piece that would make everything fit together.

He got out of the chair, walked around one of the mannequins that was spread out on the floor and went into the bathroom, where he turned on the light.

The tile and the porcelain in the sink and toilet, which had obviously once been white, now leaned more towards yellow. There was a can of baby powder on a shelf alongside a neat pile of adult nappies. A distant flushing interrupted his thoughts about an article he'd read on an adult daycare in England where elderly men used nappies and baby bottles. The next moment he could hear the water running through the drainpipes.

He was about to open the mirror-covered door to the medicine cabinet to see whether there were any medications, when he noticed, reflected in the mirror, a knee hanging out over the edge of the bath beneath a drawn shower curtain. Why did he have a mannequin in the bathtub? Or did he...

Fabian turned around and pulled back the curtain.

The man was dressed only in underwear and undershirt. His hands were joined with heavy tape. His eyes were shut and his mouth wide open. A dog collar was clasped around his throat with rivets that disappeared down behind his back. Fabian had only seen him on a grainy surveillance video, but the short, corpulent body, and the moustached face could only belong to Joakim Holmberg.

Had he committed suicide? Fabian carefully pressed his fingers under his ear against the carotid artery. Joakim had a pulse and suddenly lurched forward in shock in an attempt to sit up, only to be pulled back down by the collar.

30

'I DON'T KNOW,' SAID Joakim Holmberg, scratching the raw skin around his throat from where the dog collar had been.

'Don't know, as in you don't remember, or do you actually not know? Or do you not feel like answering?' said Fabian, who was sitting across from him with Malin, his skin crawling with irritation.

'I don't know.' Holmberg finished a can of Coke and set it on the table alongside the other empty cans.

They'd been sitting closed up in the interview room for over two hours struggling with Holmberg, whose answer to almost every question was 'I don't know'. The room was stuffy, and the air they were breathing had been recycled so many times that Fabian didn't even want to think about it.

It didn't help that he'd had no more than three hours' sleep and was still waiting for Sonja to call. She would probably be in a terrible mood as soon as she realized he'd already left and would probably be gone all weekend. He didn't count on her understanding the explanation he'd left on his nightstand.

'You don't seem to know much,' said Fabian, trying to ignore the fact that Holmberg quite unselfconsciously had an index finger stuck far up one nostril. 'What do you know? Can you tell me your name? Do you know that?'

Joakim Holmberg kept his eyes on the table as he pulled out a booger and held it up in the air between his thumb and index finger. 'Where can I get rid of this?'

Fabian exchanged a look with Malin, who was as visibly disgusted by the man on the other side of the table as him. 'I don't know. Does that sound familiar?' He got up and started walking around the increasingly claustrophobic room. 'I don't know. I don't know. I don't know. But the difference between you and me, or to be more exact, one of the millions of differences, is that I'm telling the truth. Because I have no fucking idea what people like you do with your disgusting slimy piles of snot, and I'm not sure I want to know either.' He stood behind Holmberg and leaned on the back of his chair. 'Malin, what do you say? Do you have any idea?'

Malin shrugged and shook her head without changing her expression.

Fabian could see that she was not following at all. He was surely about to cross a line, but he couldn't resist any longer.

'We had this one in class, a real creep,' he continued. 'You'd probably like him. He used to eat them. And not just his own, but others' too. He said he thought they tasted good. So maybe there's something to that? What do you say?'

Holmberg ignored Fabian and wiped the snot on one of the empty Coke cans. Then he reached for another one.

'No, you can forget about that. There'll be no more Coke going forward.' Fabian grabbed the can. 'Not until you've told us what the hell happened.'

'I have. I was sitting on my throne—'

'You mean armchair.'

'Yes, and then—'

'Stroking yourself. We've understood that much.'

'No, I was going to do that, but I never got that far.'

'Fabian, can I have a word with you?' Malin motioned for him to follow her out and closed the door behind him. 'What the hell's going on with you? What are you doing?'

Fabian looked towards the TV hanging from the ceiling, which was showing the live police press conference. Herman Edelman was sitting to the left of Police Commissioner Bertil Crimson behind a cluster of microphones. Anders Furhage from SePo sat to his right explaining that the minister's death couldn't be ruled out as a terrorist act. Personal security had been increased for the majority of politicians, and the country's threat level had been raised from two to three on the five-point scale.

'Fabian? Has something happened?' Malin tried to make eye contact with him.

His initial impulse was to play dumb, but he could tell from both the tone of her voice and the look she gave him that she wouldn't give up until he gave in and confessed. 'I don't know. Sorry. I'm...' He closed his eyes and started massaging his temples. 'Sonja and I are going through a bit of a rough patch right now and, to be honest, I don't know how things will end up. And last night I didn't get a wink of sleep.'

'You think I did?'

Fabian felt as if someone had just emptied a bucket of cold water over him.

'Besides the fact that I stayed up all night working to identify that creep in there, these two pests have made sure that the only sleep I've had the past few weeks is when I blink a little slower. But that doesn't give me the right to stomp in there and behave like shit.'

'No, you're completely right.' Fabian could only agree. 'But I just can't take him. There's something, I don't know, about his whole—'

'Yes, he's a slimy creep who does strange things you'd rather not hear about. But he's no murderer. He's not the one who carved up the minister. That's not even him on the surveillance video.'

'I know. But why is he withholding information and refusing to talk?'

'He's not. *You're* the one who's not listening.'

'Listening to what? The only thing he's saying is that he doesn't know anything, over and over again.'

'You're asking the wrong questions. I'm taking over as of now.'

They went back into the interview room, where Holmberg was once again sitting with one index finger up his nose.

'Okay, Joakim, let's take this from the beginning,' said Malin, closing the door behind Fabian. 'You had just sat down on your throne and were going to have a little fun with yourself.' She opened a can of Coke and handed it over to him. 'But then something happened.'

Holmberg chugged a little more than half the can, let out a loud belch and nodded. 'But I don't know what,' he said, going quiet. Malin did nothing to break the silence in the room. 'I thought I heard something from the hall, but I wasn't quite sure,' he continued. 'I'd just connected the surround sound and put on a movie.'

'So you turned off the movie?'

'Yes, and I went out to see what it was.'

'And what did you find?'

'I don't know.' Holmberg finished the can and started squeezing it.

Stillness filled the room again, while Fabian exchanged a look with Malin. She could always read him like an open book and signalled to him to stay calm and wait, but a few minutes later he could tell that the silence was also starting to get on her nerves.

'It was, like, just white.'

The sentence came out of nowhere, and both Fabian and Malin looked as if they were unsure they'd heard right.

'What do you mean, "white"?' Malin moved her chair closer to him.

'I don't know. White.'

'And then?'

'I woke up tied up in the bathtub wearing a dog collar.'

'So you have no memory at all of how you ended up there?'

Holmberg shook his head.

'But everything was white. Did you hear anything?'

'I don't know. Well, yes, actually. It sounded like Darth Vader.' Holmberg laughed and reached for another Coke.

'Darth Vader from *Star Wars*? He came in and stole your clothes and passcode?'

Holmberg nodded, opened the can and drank. 'It was kinda like this.' He demonstrated by putting one hand in front of his mouth and nose and started to breathe exaggeratedly, like he was wearing a gas mask.

Malin turned towards Fabian. 'Are you thinking the same thing I am?'

Fabian didn't understand what she was talking about, and a moment later Malin was on her way out of the interview room.

THE VIDEO ON MALIN'S computer screen was divided into four squares of equal size. The top two panels showed different angles of various cars approaching a lowered peppermint-striped boom, which went up after the driver stuck a hand out and took a ticket from the machine. The two lower panels showed cars driving out in a steady stream.

'What's this?' said Fabian over Malin's shoulder.

'This is what you missed because you were in such a hurry to leave the morning meeting yesterday.'

Fabian thought back to the meeting and remembered Tomas Persson and Jarmo Päivinen describing their breakthrough in the investigation of Adam Fischer, which after eight days had been categorized as a kidnapping. 'Is that the Slussen car park?'

'You guessed right,' said Malin, nodding. 'Adam Fischer, who lives up by Mosebacke, rents a parking space there.'

'And what does this have to do with Carl-Eric Grimås?'

'You'll see,' said Malin, trying to pinpoint the right spot on the timeline at the very bottom of the screen. 'Here he is.' She paused the video.

Fabian saw the licence plate number of the SUV in the upper-left square, and Adam Fischer sitting alone behind the steering wheel in the right-hand one. 'I get that this is the last time he was seen before he disappeared, but I still don't understand the connection—'

'His facial expression seems completely relaxed.' Malin interrupted, pointing towards the screen. 'Just like Grimås. He doesn't have a clue about what's coming,' she continued, dragging along the time marker. 'A little more than eleven minutes later his SUV left the garage. And here is what I wanted to show you.' She froze the frame just as the boom went up and the car was about to drive out.

The two lower squares showed the SUV leaving the garage. But Adam Fischer was no longer sitting behind the steering wheel.

The driver was wearing dark, heavy clothing with a gas mask covering the face.

31

THE SNOW HAD POURED down all through the night, burying major portions of Copenhagen. News reporters were talking about a record-breaking winter and people were warned not to go out on the roads unless it was absolutely necessary. Dunja Hougaard's first thought when she woke up on the couch and looked out the window had been to work from home. But when Carsten called to her from the bedroom, saying that they should continue where they left off, she decided to drive in to the station.

When she stepped outside Blågårdsgade 4 an hour later, she quickly realized that the reports had grossly understated the conditions. Her bicycle wasn't visible under the huge mass of snow and her car would take an hour to dig out. Instead, she decided to walk the whole way, which seemed to be the only way to get anywhere. All public transport had stopped more or less, and not even the subway was operating.

But the state of emergency put Dunja in a good mood. The otherwise busy streets were free of cars for once. Pedestrians, who had abandoned the sidewalk, ignored the traffic lights, and it felt as if they'd all taken back the city and never intended to return it.

She was cutting across Peblinge Lake, which had frozen over, when the security supervisor at Scandlines called her to confirm that Aksel Neuman's BMW had crossed to Helsingborg on the ferry that left Helsingør Harbour at 1:00 a.m. Wednesday night. Unfortunately, they only registered licence plates, and didn't use security cameras, so they couldn't confirm whether it was Aksel Neuman, Benny Willumsen, or someone else entirely behind the wheel.

She attempted to contact the criminal investigation department in Helsingborg as she walked past Rådhuspladsen on H. C. Andersens Boulevard. Astrid Tuvesson, the head of the department, had already left for the Christmas holidays, so she was transferred to Sverker Holm, who naturally didn't answer. *Wasn't there anybody working on the Swedish side?* she asked herself. She left him a voicemail introducing herself and explained that she needed help locating a BMW X3 with Danish plates that belonged to TV host Aksel Neuman.

When she finally got to the department at the police station neither Jan Hesk nor Kjeld Richter was there. She didn't know whether it was due to the inclement weather or if they'd called in sick in protest. Even if part of her wanted to call and demand a doctor's note, she thought it was satisfying to be able to work in peace and quiet.

She barely had time to set her coffee down on the desk, turn on the lamp and start up the computer, before her cell phone started vibrating.

'Yes, this is Dunja Hougaard.'

'Hi. How's it going? This is Klippan. I heard you needed a little help.'

'Excuse me? Do you work for the Helsingborg police?'

'Sverker Holm's the name, but people call me Klippan – you know, like the Rock, but don't ask me why. I just got your message.'

'My call concerned a Danish BMW—'

'Yes, I heard that in your message. I've already searched for it and managed to locate a photo for you.'

'Really? Can you see who's driving?'

'Unfortunately not. It was from a traffic camera on E6 south, and they don't include any faces.'

'What time was the photo taken?'

'Wednesday night at 1:33 a.m.'

Dunja repeated the time again in her mind. It tallied fairly well with the ferry that left Helsingør Harbour at one o'clock and took twenty minutes to get to Helsingborg. If the car proceeded on E6 south it was, in all likelihood, en route to Malmö and perhaps all the way home to her suspect Benny Willumsen at Konsultgatan 29. 'Thanks a lot. That was exactly what I needed.'

'Sorry, there was one more thing, out of pure curiosity.'

'Yes?'

'I assume that this concerns the brutal murder of Karen Neuman in Tibberup.'

'Yes, that's right. But unfortunately I have to—'

'You can't miss it in the papers. We worked on a similar case here in Rydebäck just over two years ago that showed the same loathsome brutality.'

'You have to wonder where all this evil comes from. It was really nice talking with you and have a nice weekend.'

'It turned out that the Rydebäck perpetrator was actually Danish.'

Dunja, who was just about to hang up, brought the phone back to her ear again.

'He actually lives here in Sweden. In Malmö to be exact,' Klippan continued.

'Is his name Benny Willumsen?'

'You've got it.'

'But how can he still be at large? Did you ever arrest him?'

'Yes, we arrested him, and it went all the way to trial. We had witnesses, circumstantial evidence – the whole nine yards. The case fell apart when he was accused of the brutal murder of a woman who was found after her body floated up on the Ven shoreline. I don't know if there was anything about that in the Danish newspapers.'

'Why did the case fall apart?'

'The thing was he had a watertight alibi, so everything collapsed like a house of cards. Personally, I didn't really believe he committed that particular murder, but we weren't really in agreement here at the station. I'll never forget when the verdict was announced and he was released. It was like a blow to the face.'

'And you worked on it?'

'Yes, along with the rest of the team here. It's the biggest investigation we've ever done. So what I'm trying to say is that if there's anything I can do to help out, anything at all, just speak up.'

'It would be really helpful if you could send me all the material you have on the case.'

'Absolutely. No problem, and remember, I'm just a call away.'

'Okay, thanks a million.' Dunja ended the call, leaned back and put her feet up on the desk.

She now had even more ammo supporting her theory that Benny Willumsen was behind the murder of Karen Neuman. Unfortunately, she lacked exactly what her Swedish colleagues had: technical evidence strong enough to connect him to the case. Circumstantial evidence, witnesses and any similarities with previous cases wouldn't be enough to convict.

She raised her coffee cup to take a sip when a hand gripped her shoulder.

'You're working all alone.'

She jerked forward and managed to spill most of the coffee on her jeans.

'Goodness. I hope that wasn't my fault.'

'No. I just didn't hear you come in.' She turned around towards Kim Sleizner, who stood smiling right behind her.

'You never stopped by my office yesterday.'

32

'IN ALL SERIOUSNESS, YOU think there could be a connection between the murder of the Minister for Justice and the kidnapping of Adam Fischer?' Herman Edelman poured a few drops of cream in his coffee.

'Yes,' said Malin, casting a quick glance over to Fabian as if to reassure herself that he was with her. 'That's exactly what I think.'

'Malin, for one thing—'

'Who's the person who's always telling us about the importance of having an open mind and thinking outside the box?' Malin interrupted him, crossing her arms over her protruding belly.

'Agreed, but in this case I'm not so sure. Maybe I'm blind, but I honestly see nothing that connects these two cases.' Edelman put a lump of sugar in his mouth and raised his cup.

'If you would let me finish what I'm saying, maybe you would get your vision back and see that there's not only a connection, but that it actually seems to be the same perpetrator.'

Edelman set his cup down again, the lump of sugar still between his teeth. *It's lucky she's pregnant*, thought Fabian. Neither he nor any of the others would have got away with that tone, especially not after a press conference, which, nine times out of ten, made Edelman extra touchy.

'What do you think, Fabian?' Malin gave him a look that suggested his very survival depended on his agreement.

Fabian nodded, even if he really didn't know what to think. As Malin was saying, there certainly were things that suggested they were dealing with the same perpetrator, but he couldn't understand how, and in a way he felt just as blind as Edelman. He'd tried getting in touch with Hillevi Stubbs to see if she'd discovered any technical leads that might reinforce their theory, but she had her phone turned off, which she often did when there was a lot going on,

'Here's an image from the surveillance video at the Slussen car park,' Malin continued, holding up the image of the kidnapper driving out of the car park in Adam Fischer's car with a gas mask on their face. 'Fischer is probably drugged in the car, which explains the gas mask.'

'Isn't it conceivable that he didn't want to be identified?' asked Tomas Persson.

'Uh… Yes, but?' Malin turned towards Fabian and gave him a look begging him to step in.

'Sure, it could be,' said Fabian. 'But there are considerably easier ways to disguise yourself other than by wearing a gas mask.'

'The point is that the exact same thing happened to Joakim Holmberg, one of the guards in the parliament buildings, in his own home.' Malin held up a picture of the guard and fastened it to the whiteboard. 'On Tuesday night, he heard a sound out in the hall. He went out to investigate and could see only white.'

'I don't follow.'

'White smoke,' said Fabian. 'Our theory is that the perpetrator dropped some form of gas vial through the mail slot. If you study the image from the Slussen car park more thoroughly, you'll see that there are also traces of smoke inside the car.'

'And the last thing Holmberg heard, before he woke up in his own bathtub without his uniform or pass card, was someone breathing through a gas mask,' said Malin.

'Not to be the party-pooper here,' said Tomas Persson, setting aside his protein shake. 'But just so we're clear: your guy didn't see anything, but he just *heard* something that reminded him of a gas mask, something that could just have been a draught through the mail slot or tinnitus.'

'True,' said Malin. 'But—'

'Wait, I'm not done. Just because there's a gas mask or some other similarity doesn't mean it's the same perpetrator. It might just be a coincidence.'

Malin sighed and rolled her eyes. Fabian could tell that she was trying her best to stay calm. 'Sure, it may be an unfortunate coincidence, but let's investigate it first before we start shouting too loud.'

'What are you suggesting?' Edelman threw back some more coffee.

'I think we should combine the investigations into one led by me and Fabian.'

'Uh, excuse me here,' said Tomas, holding up one hand. 'Was that a joke? Jarmo, have you heard a single argument for why they should take over our investigation?'

Jarmo Päivinen shook his head.

'Does it look like I'm joking?'

'Wow, she's really on fire today.' Tomas grinned, thrusting forward his chest muscles that were clearly outlined under his overly tight T-shirt.

'For your sake, I'll choose to ignore that. Herman, you're always talking about the importance of cross-fertilizing investigations.'

'Absolutely. But in this case I have to agree with Tomas. A sound that is reminiscent of someone breathing through a gas mask isn't much to write home about. Other than that, is there anything that suggests the cases belong together?' said Edelman.

'Not that we know right now,' said Fabian.

'What do we have to lose by giving this a chance?' Malin turned towards Tomas and Jarmo. 'And if we're going to be completely honest, your investigation is not exactly rushing ahead.'

'Listen, we've actually—'

'Seen the car on a surveillance video. Tomas, I know. But what has that amounted to, other than a picture of the perpetrator in a gas mask? Why not try throwing ideas out and seeing what sticks? The perpetrator's motive, for one. Maybe he's not in it for the money. After all, the Fischer family has offered a reward and he hasn't taken it. Maybe he's after something else entirely.'

'Such as what?' said Jarmo.

'I don't know.' Malin shrugged as she took a Danish cookie. 'Grimås lost both his eyes and his guts.'

'Maybe he was just hungry?' Tomas said with a laugh.

Malin rolled her eyes and gave Fabian a meaningful look indicating it was his turn to take over. But he was too busy trying to understand the significance of what Tomas had just said.

Suddenly the door opened and Hillevi Stubbs came marching in with a metal case in one hand. Her hair was pulled into a tight bun on the top of her head. It gave the impression that she was at least four inches taller than the five feet it said on her passport, according to rumour. Her nostrils were flared, which meant she was in an extremely bad mood. The best thing to do was to keep as far away from the line of fire as possible.

'You'll have to excuse me, but I actually don't have all day.' Stubbs set the case on the table. 'And to be quite frank, I don't understand what you're doing.'

Fabian saw that Malin was just as perplexed as he was.

'Yes, I'm talking to the two of you,' she continued. 'What happened to we find a crime scene, then we investigate and then we move on to another scene? How can you find three crime scenes at more or less the same time? The condemned apartment in Östgötagatan on its own would have been quite enough, let alone the nap room in the ministry *and* the filthy apartment of that disgusting guard. Do you think I can clone myself?'

'Hillevi,' said Edelman. 'I understand if it's too much. But—'

'"Too much" isn't even the start of it. This afternoon was my only chance to do any Christmas shopping. Do you think my grandchildren will accept a hollowed-out government minister as an explanation for no presents this year?'

'If you want I can look into borrowing some resources from the Stockholm—'

'You mean Petrén and his guys. Thanks, but no thanks. With that man on the scene you can forget about this being wrapped up any time before Christmas.'

'We don't have all the time in the world either, so could you stick to the essentials instead, such as why you're here. Have you found anything?' asked Malin, whose irritated tone matched Hillevi's.

Fabian was sure that Stubbs would have cut him to shreds if he'd come even close to giving that kind of attitude.

She turned her gaze toward Malin. 'Absolutely.' She clicked open the clasps on the case, opened the lid, pulled on a pair of white gloves and picked up a black cloth bag. She set it down on the table, loosened the knot and took out a glass jar. 'This was in the refrigerator in the condemned apartment on Östgötagatan.'

'What do you mean, "condemned apartment"?' said Jarmo.

'The last known location of Carl-Eric Grimås' second cell phone,' said Malin, showing a picture of the plastic-covered table. 'As you see it's clearly prepared for—'

'Maybe you can deal with that after I'm done,' Stubbs interrupted with a stiff smile. 'I thought this might be of interest.' She held up the jar in the air so that everyone could see.

Fabian immediately recognized it as the Haywards jar. And, just as he'd suspected since they found the minister, it didn't contain pickled onions at all. Four eyeballs bobbed around in the dark fluid.

'This must be sent to Thåström at forensics as soon as possible. But no one should be surprised if two of them turn out to belong to the Minister for Justice,' Stubbs continued.

'And the other two?' said Malin.

'That's where the two of you come in to the picture. You might be of some use after all.'

Fabian wondered why Malin had even bothered asking. He couldn't tell if she was really curious or if she just wanted to be nice. He had no doubt whatsoever about where the eyes had come from.

'Can I see?' said Tomas.

'Look, but don't touch.' Stubbs set the glass jar down on the table in front of Tomas, who leaned down and studied the four eyeballs swimming around with severed optic nerves as tails. Two of them had blue irises, the third was green, and the fourth brown.

Tomas looked up, turned toward Jarmo with a tense expression and nodded.

'Are you sure?' asked Jarmo.

Tomas nodded again. 'With one green and one brown, they must be Fischer's.'

33

IT WAS TOMAS PERSSON'S joke about the perpetrator being hungry that gave him the idea. In a way it would have been easier to do a computer search, but Fabian didn't want to tell anyone until he knew for sure – the theory was still too fragile. And it would definitely be shot down immediately, given the mood of the group now the two investigations had been combined. He left the meeting room first and made his way down to the archive on the ground floor of the police station. He searched back among the sliding walls to the second quarter of 1993.

He'd been twenty-seven years old and was in his last year at the Police Academy. Summer had started early and most people in his class were looking forward to a nice vacation before they started work. But not Fabian. All he'd been able to think about was the homicide investigation that was splashed all over the tabloids and got almost daily features. It was somewhat of an anomaly: a serial killer was wreaking havoc in Stockholm. It was the kind of case you only read about, and which never really happened, especially not in a country like Sweden.

But he still remembered how it had stirred up emotion all over the country, primarily because of the extreme, brutal nature of the crimes and the suffering experienced by the victims, but also because of the conviction: the perpetrator was sentenced to closed psychiatric care instead of life imprisonment.

He couldn't even remember the name of the assailant, only that it was something unusual. On the other hand, he did recall that seven victims had been found, all of whom had been confined to different places for several weeks before they'd been subjected to...

He'd reached the files he was looking. He pulled out the first of the five bulging folders. Here it was: the investigation he wished he'd been able to work on. Once he opened it up, and saw the name in print, everything came flooding back as if it was yesterday: the images the police had released of the various victims, whose eyes had been poked out; the fear that anyone could be the next victim; the headlines that competed to reveal all the details about Ossian Kremph – Sweden's first real cannibal.

'OKAY, THIS IS HOW I see it,' said Tomas, keeping pace with Malin through the corridor.

'Anyone see where Fabian went off to?' asked Malin. Jarmo shrugged. 'He's not here either,' she continued when she walked into their office.

'Maybe he's just in the john,' said Jarmo.

'Excuse me, but I was about to say something,' said Tomas.

'Just keep talking.' Malin set her bag down on the desk and started rooting around in it.

'Okay, Jarmo and me, we've worked on this for over—'

'I can't bear to hear your whining. Besides, I feel sick as a pig and I'm going to throw up soon if I don't find... Who took my... Oh, wait, here they are.' She tore open a packet of Marie biscuits and put two in her mouth at one time. She chewed and swallowed as fast as she could, before sitting down and exhaling. 'Shit, that was close.'

'Are you done?' asked Tomas, walking towards Malin, who nodded and stuffed another biscuit into her mouth. 'Good. Then maybe you can explain to me what you mean by "whining". Dammit, we have to decide how we're going to—'

'No, the only thing we have to do is get to work,' said Malin, swallowing. 'And if you can't manage that, I suggest you go and sulk elsewhere.'

Tomas was about to argue, but Jarmo sent him a look that made him calm down and clench his teeth. 'What the hell are you waiting for then?'

'Good. Excellent! This is going to be really great, I promise.' Malin stood up. 'I suggest that we start by investigating whether Carl-Eric Grimås and Adam Fischer have anything in common. A motive could emerge in the connection.'

Jarmo nodded, while Tomas stood still and didn't speak.

'We know quite a bit about the Minister for Justice,' Malin continued. 'But what do we know about Adam Fischer? And why do I seem to think I've seen him in the gossip magazines?'

'Adam Fischer is thirty-three years old, the son of a diplomat, and his life goal seems to be to never grow up,' said Jarmo. 'He likes spending Daddy's money, drives around in expensive cars and goes to gala premieres. You don't need much more than that to get into the gossip magazines.'

'And his father? Is he familiar to anyone?'

'Yes, to Jarmo and me anyway,' said Tomas. 'His name is Rafael Fischer and he was the Israeli ambassador here in Stockholm for most of the nineties.'

'Israeli ambassador?' Malin repeated.

'Here he is,' said Jarmo, pointing at a black-and-white picture on the whiteboard.

The picture looked like it was from a holiday celebration and showed an older man with chalk-white hair, wearing a dark suit and sitting at a decorated table along with two other men.

'Is Adam the younger man to the left?' said Malin.

'Yes. We believe this was taken at his sister's wedding. When was that again?' Jarmo turned towards Tomas.

'August of 1998,' said Tomas. 'The old man died three months later.'

'Why is Adam holding the cane and not him?' asked Malin. 'Doesn't Adam look a little pale and skinny?'

Jarmo pulled the picture down to get a closer look. Sure enough, Adam was sitting with a cane in one hand, looking very feeble. 'You're definitely right about that. We had assumed he was just borrowing his father's.'

'Let me see.' Tomas grabbed the picture.

'Who's the guy on the other side?' Malin pointed to the man sitting to the right of the ambassador, leaning towards him as if he was about to say something in confidence.

'Good question,' said Jarmo. 'We've tried to find out, but haven't succeeded.'

'Here he is again, but with the current ambassador.' Tomas pointed at a colour photo taken years later of the same man getting out of a car with the current ambassador and another man.

'And who's the third guy?' said Malin.

'Israel's ambassador in Copenhagen,' said Jarmo.

'So he knows everyone. Have you been in contact with people at the embassy and questioned them?'

Jarmo and Tomas shook their heads.

'I think we'll start by... There you are. Where've you been hiding?' Malin asked Fabian, who was walking in with the archive folders in his arms.

'I was in the archive investigating a suspect.' Fabian dropped the pile of folders on his desk.

Tomas grabbed one of them and opened it. 'Ossian Kremph? Who the hell is that?'

'It's funny you're the one who's asking because you were the person who made me think of him.'

'Wasn't he that cannibal?' said Jarmo, and Fabian nodded. 'It was before my time here at the bureau, but I was in a patrol car and there was a lot of talk about it.'

'Does anyone feel like telling me what you two are talking about?' said Malin.

'This,' Tomas said, laying out a double-page spread with pictures of mutilated victims with their eyes poked out.

'Nice,' said Malin. 'Why just the eyes?'

'I'm not quite sure,' said Fabian. 'But from what I recall, he maintained that he was only obeying the voices that ordered him to collect various "chosen souls".'

'Oh, no, not another crazy. And he's been released?'

'He's been out for three years and four months.'

'So he's been declared competent?' asked Malin, shaking her head. 'As if a little medicine and therapy can help anyone who's capable of these crimes.'

'As if,' said Tomas. 'The rest of the medical world accepts that a paralysed lower body will always be paralysed, but psychology is different. Everyone can get healthy with a little treatment, regardless of how disabled they are.'

Malin looked at Tomas with a surprised expression. 'Did you think of that yourself, or did you read a newspaper for the first time?'

Tomas answered her with a smile and reached for the package of Marie biscuits.

'Help yourself. I've lost my appetite anyway,' said Malin, browsing further into the old investigation. 'Is there any connection between the victims, or were they simply chosen at random?'

'From what I remember, the victims were both men and women. And I think one was somewhat of a celebrity,' said Jarmo.

'You're thinking about that radio voice who read the sea reports,' said Fabian.

'Yes, exactly! And Fischer and Grimås are kind of semi-famous.'

'Maybe he chooses people who get him worked up,' said Tomas.

'At any rate, we can definitely identify one person who

almost certainly worked him up,' said Malin, looking up from the folder. 'Do you know who was head of this investigation?'

The others shook their heads.

'Carl-Eric Grimås.'

34

DUNJA HOUGAARD SAT IN Kim Sleizner's visitor's chair, trying to make herself as small as possible. She really should have been sitting proud and stretched with her legs spread, just like Jan Hesk surely would have done in her situation. Against all odds, she'd managed to identify a strong prime suspect in less than twenty-four hours. If everything worked out, Benny Willumsen would get the conviction he deserved, and three older investigations would finally be closed – four, if you counted the Swedish case.

But the mere thought of being alone in a room with Sleizner was enough to make her want to jump up and run away. She forced herself to breathe calmly, lowered her eyes, and looked at the dried coffee stain on her jeans that made it look as if she'd peed her pants.

It was so quiet she could hear the air running in and out of his congested nostrils from the other side of the desk while he skimmed through the old case files and her draft of a report. She wondered if he was dragging it out just to prolong her agony. She only looked up once she

heard the document folder being closed. Sleizner was looking at her, smiling.

'I knew you were the right man for the job,' he said, removing his reading glasses. 'And just so you know, I've had a good feeling about you since the first time I saw you.'

Dunja didn't know what to say, so she emitted an affected laugh.

'It's nothing to laugh about – it's the truth. So enjoy it while it lasts. Tomorrow it may be over. No, I'm kidding. On a more serious note.' He held the folder up. 'This is completely brilliant. I don't know how you made the connections between a dog-bitten girl found in a dumpster in 2005 and Karen Neuman being hacked to death in Tibberup, but the important thing is that this Benny Willumsen will be put away for life. It's always fun to rap those Swedish bastards on their knuckles on their home turf. I dare say, Dunja, I'm going to live on this for a long time.'

Dunja forced a smile and nodded.

'First and foremost, I'd like to hold a press conference, where I intend to let you get all the attention you deserve.'

'Press conference? When were you thinking about holding it? Shouldn't we arrest—'

'Relax – of course he'll be arrested before we give out any information. But as you know, I like to be the first to the punch, and I want you to feel assured that I don't intend to let anyone else take credit for your work. Do you understand me?'

Dunja nodded.

Sleizner sighed. 'You look like you've just lost your best friend, and it's all my fault.'

'That's not it at all. I feel as if there's work left to do before we can declare victory. Just like our Swedish colleagues, we lack sufficient evidence to get him convicted. We should recover the car in Helsingør Harbour as soon as possible so we can prove that the perpetrator ditched his own car and took Aksel Neuman's. Who knows, maybe Aksel is down at the bottom of the harbour too.'

'You're quite right, but everything has to be done in the right order. Naturally, we need to arrest him before anyone else is subjected to his ingenuity. With a little luck we'll find enough technical evidence in his apartment to keep the dredging costs off our budget. You should be aware that scouring a harbour in the kind of winter we're having is not exactly a cheap operation.'

'Right, but did you read through the entire Swedish case file? They didn't find anything of value in his—'

Sleizner interrupted her with a laugh and shook his head. 'I've read enough to know that I have more experience with this sort of thing than you do. Dunja, it will work out. If we don't find anything in the apartment, we'll definitely pull up the car.' He got up, rounded the desk, and stood behind her. 'I hope you understand what a boost this is going to be for your future career. Before you know it, you'll be sitting in my chair. I promise you.'

The moment his hands landed on her shoulders, she felt as if she was being penetrated by a cold poker. Was this what it felt like to be violated? The thought came from nowhere and was gone just as quickly.

'Dunja, you can't walk around with this much tension. You're as hard as a rock.' He started massaging her in calm, soft movements. 'Try to relax. Not to brag, but if there's anything I can do, it's massage.' He took hold of her shoulders and pulled them back so that her breasts stuck out. 'You ought to think a little more about your posture. It doesn't look professional to sit at a press conference looking like a sack of potatoes. If you don't already have neck pain, you'll get it in the future.' He moved her hair to the side and started kneading the back of her neck. 'It came out of nowhere as soon as I started here. If Henrik Hammersten hadn't insisted I go for a massage session, I'd certainly be in a wheelchair today. I've gone twice a week ever since and haven't had so much as a hint of a problem.' His fingertips worked their way up and started massaging her scalp and behind her ears.

'Oh, and I forgot to mention, I've arranged for you to sit at the management table at the Christmas party. Not only do we get served, so you don't have to rub elbows with the others, we get unlimited schnapps. Nice, huh? We'll get an opportunity to get to know each other a little better.'

Dunja was no longer listening to what he was saying. Her racing heartbeat drowned out the sound of everything else. She wanted nothing more than to get up, turn around and slap him as hard as she could, but her body was paralysed. She couldn't even ask him to take his hands off her. All she could do was sit there and feel every muscle in her body grow more and more tense.

35

WHEN BENNY WILLUMSEN WOKE up, he had no idea where he was. Was he even still in Sweden? The light from the lamp right above him made it hard to see anything. Only once he had managed to loosen the tape that stretched over his jaw and forehead could he twist his head and grasp his position. He was taped down naked on his own kitchen table in his Malmö apartment.

The picture of his beloved Jessie, which he'd framed and hung the day she passed away, dispersed any doubt. She had died almost seventeen months ago, and every day still felt like an uphill battle. He'd thought about getting a new dog, but decided it would never be the same.

Slowly and hesitantly, his memory finally started to come back to him. He'd taken his regular evening walk. Even though it had snowed heavily, he had chosen the long route, which took almost two hours. He'd felt calm, without the slightest sense of worry.

It was the opposite of how he'd felt after his conquest in one of the houses down by Fortuna Beach in Rydebäck two years ago. The act of raping and stabbing the woman to death on the beach while her husband was just fifty metres away watching the late news had always made him feel calm and warm. But the day after, worry had started to creep in. He realized he had committed a mortal sin by missing an insignificant little detail: the fucking unpaid parking tickets that had whirled out of his car when he had opened the door to drive away. He could have sworn he'd picked them all up, but he heard on the news that the police had found a lead that would take them to the killer. He had lain awake for a whole week before the Helsingborg police finally tracked him down and arrested him.

If they hadn't also mistakenly accused him of the murder of the bolted-down woman who landed at Ven, he would almost certainly have been convicted. Now he was out, he promised himself to never, ever again miss a detail, regardless of how small and insignificant it might appear. And so far he hadn't done that either.

After he returned from his walk, he relaxed by devoting the rest of the evening to exercise. He did three sets of dips, push-ups, double arm lifts, angled dumb-bell presses and Romanian Deadlifts. He'd hit his max and his chest was pounding when he finished.

Then it happened.

He'd heard something fall through the mail slot, but by the time he got to the kitchen to investigate, the room was already filled with white smoke.

He'd tried to get out, but he couldn't crawl or pull himself forward. The last thing he remembered was someone entering through the front door, walking up to him and leaning down; someone in dark, heavy clothes, wearing a gas mask over their face.

And now he was taped down on his own kitchen table without any idea of what was coming. He had his suspicions. He'd immediately dismissed the police as being a complete improbability. And during the few minutes he'd been awake, he'd gone through every one of all his old conquests in detail.

He'd initially been convinced it was one of his very first failures, someone who was still alive and was now out for revenge. But, on second thoughts, he decided that none of them had what it took to subject him to this manipulation. Instead, he wondered whether it might be one of the relatives of the Rydebäck victim, but finally rejected that idea.

He heard someone get up from the couch in the living room, which confirmed he wasn't alone. He tried to twist his head to see who was walking into the kitchen, but he couldn't move. Then he felt a blindfold being placed over his head, and for the first time in years, he was afraid. Not much, but enough to feel the unfamiliar tickling sensation creeping up from his toes. To be honest, he kind of liked it.

Now it's starting, he thought. Whatever was coming was about to begin.

36

FABIAN RISK GROPED ALONG the wall with one hand while the ring tone sounded in his headset. It was pitch black and he couldn't see anything until he managed to find the switch and turn on the lights. He wondered what he would do if she didn't answer, or if she would ever answer again. Maybe it would all be for the best, anyway.

'I was just starting to wonder what happened to you.' As usual Niva's voice had a playful undertone that suggested everything was just a game. 'I thought maybe you'd been told off at home and crawled back into your shell.'

'Can you help me?'

'That depends.'

'I need to locate an address for a certain Ossian Kremph.'

'Like I said. It depends.'

'The thing is, he's an ex-convict who doesn't live at his registered address. We're treating him as the prime suspect in the deaths and dismemberment of Adam Fischer and Carl-Eric Grimås. We're sure he sublets elsewhere.' Fabian waited for a reaction, but he didn't get one. 'Niva? Are you there?' he continued, pretending that he didn't hear her breathing.

He understood exactly what this was about and couldn't help thinking she was right. He had made a promise and just needed to get it over with. After all, it shouldn't feel like anything more than a reunion with an old colleague. 'How about tomorrow night?'

The silence that followed was just long enough to make him regret it.

'Let's meet at nine at Lydmar. Do you have his personal identity number?' she finally replied.

Fabian read out loud from his notes. '540613–5532,' and could hear her fingers immediately go to work on the keyboard.

'He's registered in Norsborg.'

'Yes, but as I mentioned, we have information that he's subletting elsewhere.'

'Let's see where he banks... He's with Nordea and he has a regular debit card linked to his personal account.'

'Is he working? What money is coming in?'

'No, he's not. He just has various subsidies and presumably has rental income from the place in Norsborg.'

'Does he have any other accounts?'

'He must, but this debit card has enough transactions that it ought to work.' Fabian could hear her fingers working their way across the keys once again.

He sat down on the toilet seat and wondered what he should say to Sonja – if anything at all. Maybe she didn't even expect him to come home, and would assume that he would be working all night. She must have heard about what had happened on the news, and would likely anticipate that there would be a number of late nights. Was that why she didn't react to his attempt at an explanation?

'He uses three ATMs regularly: one in the Ringen shopping centre at Skanstull, one outside the Konsum store on Gotlandsgatan, and the last at the Nordea branch on Bondegatan. I would guess that he lives somewhere between Ringvägen and Bondegatan around Götgatan.'

'That could be several thousand apartments. If he's renting second- or maybe even third-hand, his name might not even be on the door at all.'

'I wonder about his time in prison. Could he have met someone there?' asked Niva. Fabian could already hear her steering new searches.

'But he was in confined psychiatric care, so there wouldn't have been many—'

'I know, but in 1996, he was clearly considered healthy enough to be moved over to Kumla, where he served his final ten years with medication and regular therapy.'

'Yes, and now he seems to be healthy as a squirrel,' said Fabian, who, like the others on the team, couldn't understand how you could declare someone healthy who had mutilated, tortured and poked out the eyes of his victims. 'What about the prisoners? Are you getting any matches?'

'It doesn't look like it. In any case not among the prisoners he spent six months or more with. One of them is registered on Lindvallsgatan at Hornstull and another on Tantogatan, but no one in this three-block radius.'

'Try reducing six months to three.'

'I'm doing it as we speak, but there are suddenly a lot of names to go through.'

'Try the therapist instead,' said Fabian.

'The therapist?'

'Yes, he must have seen one more or less daily.'

Fabian could hear Niva working in front of the computer.

'Unfortunately, he lives in Gamla Enskede, on the same street as your colleague Malin Rehnberg actually. Maybe she knows him and walks over in her crocs to borrow sugar, discuss noise levels and the need for more speed bumps.'

'I don't know if crocs are exactly her style,' said Fabian. He could feel Niva's bitterness at still being single run out of the phone like a yellow, viscous sludge.

'I heard she went and got pregnant.'

'With twins.'

'How sweet.'

'Not if you ask her. Right now she seems prepared to offer them to the lowest bidder.'

'The daughter—'

'I don't know if they've found out the gender yet... Wait, actually it's two boys.'

'Not Malin's. The therapist's.'

Fabian didn't understand what she was talking about.

'The therapist's daughter is registered at an apartment at Blekingegatan 67B, but is studying down in Lund. We're talking about a long shot, but it may be worth a try.'

'Absolutely. I don't know how I can thank you.'

'You know how. I'll see you tomorrow night.'

There was a click, and Fabian got up from the toilet and put the phone back in his pocket.

If it turned out to be true, he wasn't sure if the therapist had broken the law or if it violated their professional regulations. But regardless of the outcome, he had clearly crossed some ethical boundary.

'FABIAN, WHAT HAVE YOU been doing?' Malin came walking straight towards him as soon as he unlocked and opened the bathroom door.

The question was purely rhetorical. She had undoubtedly already figured it out, a talent she'd always had as far as he was concerned. *You're just as predictable as Donald Duck on Christmas Eve*, she liked to say. He hadn't managed to keep a single secret from her the entire time they'd been working together, yet he still went on the defensive like a stubborn mule. 'What, a person can't go to the bathroom?'

She snorted and stuck her head into the bathroom. 'I see you've started putting down the toilet seat after you. And you haven't even bothered to get the sink wet. Is it Niva?'

Fabian sighed and was about to confess, but couldn't get a word in edgewise.

'Fabian, I know exactly what you're thinking. But I can promise you, she's bad news. Niva Ekenhielm is a living catastrophe who goes around on two skinny legs and sets her teeth into anything that doesn't get enough on the home front.'

Fabian tried to look as expressionless as possible.

'Don't stand there looking like a fool. You know exactly what I'm talking about.'

'No, I really don't.' Fabian couldn't believe how pathetic he sounded. Fortunately, he didn't need to dig himself any deeper into humiliation because Tomas and Jarmo joined them.

'There you are. Are you coming with us?' asked Tomas, who had put on his shoulder holster.

'Where are you going?' said Malin.

'Cyber-Wojtan can't pin down another address, so we thought we'd drive out to the apartment in Norsborg where he was last registered,' said Jarmo, pulling on his leather jacket. 'With a little luck, we'll find a lead.'

'Let's go here instead.' Fabian held open his notebook. 'I have more confidence in this address.'

'Let's see.' Malin grabbed the book. 'How did you get this? Let me rephrase: how did Niva find this?'

'Niva?' Tomas turned toward Fabian. 'As in Niva Ekenhielm?'

'It's a long shot. But a number of factors indicate that Ossian Kremph sublets an apartment from the daughter of his therapist, who, by the way, lives on the same street as you out in Enskede,' said Fabian, feeling like he was getting the boat on an even keel again.

But Malin didn't hear what he was saying. Instead she was just staring at the address. 'Blekingegatan 67B. I may be wrong, but isn't that…' She looked up and met their gazes. 'Isn't that in the very same block as the condemned apartment on Östgötagatan?'

37

BENNY WILLUMSEN DIDN'T KNOW how he should react, his thoughts and emotions were swirling in all directions. On the one hand, he felt a growing anxiety about the almost probable imminent pain, but on the other, he had no doubt he deserved some form of punishment. Maybe it was one of his previous victims – or failures as he chose to see them – after all? Although he was surprised that it had taken so long for one them to take the law into their own hands.

He was not ready to die. It hurt to think about how much more he wanted to accomplish. His notebook was filled with drawings of simple constructions that would take his actions a step further. Like the whip with razorblades, or the boiling-water shower. Every one of his designs shared one very simple goal: to make the victim suffer as much and as long as possible. Now he might never be able to try out his new inventions. Yet, despite this, he couldn't help but enjoy the hands that weightlessly hovered over his bare skin, making him shudder with pleasure with every feather-light touch. They glided gently over his chest that was still hard and pumped-up after the latest workout session, and further across his six-pack abs – his great pride.

Even though he was over forty, he was in the best shape of his life. His body was as close to perfect as it could be. Not only did he have muscles, he was perfectly proportioned and very flexible, thanks to a few years of yoga. In addition, his subcutaneous fat was as good as gone, so all his veins and tendons were exposed.

If there was any time he should be observed and touched by a stranger, it was now.

He'd never found himself in a similar situation – naked and taped down on his own table with eyes blindfolded – and never in his wildest fantasy would he have suspected that it was something that would give him any pleasure. But it did. Though he was scared, he was forced to admit that the uncertainty turned him on. Being powerless certainly contrasted to all the times when he'd been the active party, the person planning, acting and executing.

It wasn't that he didn't like being in charge – he loved it. He enjoyed holding the rudder alone. Having power over someone else's life was a feeling that topped almost anything, even seeing the look of fear in their eyes when it occurred to them that they were stuck under his control. There was a possibility for enjoyment at every stage in the process. If you rushed, there was great risk that you would miss out on the small nuances, like when fear turned into terror as soon as they realized that he not only had the power but also intended to exercise it.

Each stage was a new feeling and once they'd experienced it, they could no longer get their innocence back. Over the years, he'd got better at milking every last drop of fear from them, keeping them at a specific stage for as long as he wanted, before taking them further along the path that he led all his conquests down.

He'd gone after terror in the first few years, but now hope had taken over as his favourite expectation. It always appeared after terror and made their gazes light up again. Sometimes he got a smile or even an almost natural laugh. At that moment, he liked nothing better than to lull them into a false sense of security and let their hope grow so big and strong that they believed it completely. He liked convincing them that if they simply obeyed and didn't fight back, everything would be fine. Then, but only then, would they survive.

The longer he could draw this out, the greater his reward. He loved watching them realize that there was no point holding out hope. No matter how much they begged and pleaded, there was only one way it could end. They still breathed in air and their hearts continued pumping blood as if nothing was happening, but their eyes knew better. They knew exactly what was coming. There was nothing more beautiful than when a gaze softened and gave up.

The careful hands lightly grazed his groin and continued down along his legs. For the first time he could do nothing other than wait and receive. Even though he knew how it would end, he couldn't help enjoying his final moments.

His breathing got deeper and his member had also come to life. He could feel the blood pumping, making it bigger and harder as the light hands approached.

He'd initially thought they were a woman's hands, but now he wasn't so sure. Unlike so many others, he'd never brooded over whether he might be homosexual, or bisexual for that matter. He'd been completely sure that he was hetero his whole life and would get turned off as soon as a man touched him.

But apparently his body didn't have a preference, because his erection had now risen to its full size and was so pumped-up and bursting with blood he could feel it moving in time with his pulse. He was sure that the person playing with him was impressed. With a length of twenty-nine centimetres and a circumference of eighteen-and-a-half, it was bigger than most.

Then they finally touched it, with light, barely noticeable strokes, from the base along the underside all the way up to the tip. He couldn't be certain, but he was pretty sure that the tip of a tongue was playing around his throbbing glans.

He didn't really know what he'd expected, but he definitely did not think that he would be kept alive for such a long time. He could only say thanks and enjoy it for as long as it lasted. At any moment it could be over. He could feel how his body was getting prepared to die. Every single muscle was tense, and he had started to sweat like a baby trapped in a hot car. One well-aimed slash with the sharpened meat cleaver he kept in the kitchen and he would bleed to death in fifteen minutes.

Instead the hands grasped the rock-hard base and angled his member so that it pointed straight up. A warm, moist mouth worked its way deeper down the glans. He could still not tell whether it was a man or a woman, but the longer the hand and mouth worked in perfect interplay, the less he cared.

Normally he masturbated at least twice a week because it helped him stay more or less calm. But during the past few weeks he hadn't even touched himself, putting all of his focus into his workouts, letting the pressure build up. If he were to come now it would be a commanding bullet.

He didn't want it to end now, not before he was finished. They could do whatever they wanted with him later, anything at all. As long as he was just able to—

He felt his balls contract and his rock-hard erection prepare itself. Right after the first load shot out, his member continued pumping the white semen as if it would never ever end.

Only when he was completely drained did the hands release their grip and he could relax and let his body get heavy. He was about to fall asleep and could feel himself sinking down through the table, heading deeper and deeper towards the darkness.

Whatever was coming, he was ready to take his punishment.

38

FABIAN COULDN'T UNDERSTAND HOW the others could seem so sure of themselves when they rang the apartment doorbell and stood with their guns drawn, as if they knew exactly what was waiting on the other side. Or maybe they were just more confident that their weapons would protect them. Despite his twenty years on the force, Fabian had still never fired his gun anywhere other than the shooting range. He couldn't imagine putting a bullet through somebody, though he told himself that when the moment came, he would be ready. The question was whether this was the moment. Whether they would run into a white fog, be anaesthetized, and have their eyes plucked out by Ossian Kremph. Or perhaps it would turn out that he wasn't home, or didn't even live there.

After ringing the doorbell a number of times with no response, Tomas insisted on picking the lock with his skeleton key. Half an hour later they'd been forced to call in a real locksmith, who opened the door in ten minutes, which was considerably longer than the thirty seconds it normally took. They finally got in and discovered tons of extra locks on the inside of the door, explaining why it had taken so long to enter.

A new text prevented Fabian from going in with the others. It was from Sonja, who wrote that she didn't know when she would be getting home from the studio that evening. She'd made arrangements with their teenage neighbour, who could pick Matilda up from school and babysit until six thirty – she already had plans to see a movie. Fabian responded that he would be sure to be home before that and wished her good luck with the paintings.

He didn't need to take more than a step into the hall to see that Niva's long shot had actually turned out to be true against all odds. There was no way a healthy person lived in this apartment.

'Holy fucking shit,' said Tomas, pushing his gun down into his shoulder holster.

'And I thought it was messy at our house,' said Malin, looking around the living room, which was crowded with so many gadgets and trash that it would take an eternity for Hillevi Stubbs and her men to go through it all.

'This is roughly what it looks like at Jarmo's since his divorce. Although you have a bigger stack of porn magazines,' said Tomas with a sneer, patting the two-metre-high stack of free newspapers.

'Shut up and make yourself useful instead,' Jarmo muttered, continuing towards the bedroom.

'I suggest we split up and each take a room,' Tomas continued, taking one of the newspapers from the pile.

'Isn't that what we're already doing?' asked Malin, starting to go through the contents of a number of black garbage bags.

'Aren't we a little sensitive today,' said Tomas. 'At least, there's no doubt that we've come to the right place anyway.' He held up a newspaper, where the eyes of every person on the page had been carefully cut out. 'Check this out. He's been at it with a scalpel on every fucking page of this paper.'

Fabian connected his earphones to his iPod and put on Kashmir's *No Balance Palace*, his favourite Danish band, in an attempt to shut out the others and let the apartment speak for itself.

It was a corner apartment and faced both Blekingegatan and Östgötagatan. A kitchen table stood by a window in the rounded corner furthest away from him. The apartment layout looked familiar, but he couldn't place it. He glanced out of the window and then it hit him. The last time he'd seen this view was in the condemned apartment in Östgötagatan where they had found Fischer's and Grimås' eyes in the refrigerator. The condemned apartment wasn't too far from here. It didn't take a huge leap of imagination to assume that Kremph used one apartment for living in and another for killing his victims. He turned around and noted the old wallpaper and peeling paint hanging down from the ceiling. Kremph's building was in need of a major renovation. Perhaps that was the reason he was able to rent it.

He'd filled every shelf and cupboard with various objects. There wasn't a vacant space in the whole apartment. As soon as he'd stepped into it, Fabian, like the others, had thought it was messier than an over flowing bin room. But now he could see that it actually wasn't that messy at all. Yes, a number of things had been carelessly tossed on the floor, but most of it was in neat piles, stacked up and categorized with what appeared to be great care. Ossian Kremph was evidently a collector.

Fabian continued into the innermost room and looked around. It appeared to be used as a study and had an old wooden desk along one wall with a chair in front of it. In contrast to the rest of the apartment the desktop was completely empty.

He went up and sat down in the office chair, which creaked as he leaned back. The desk had three horizontal drawers directly under the desktop. There were no handles, only gaping keyholes, but they were unlocked, so he was able to nudge them out from below.

The right-hand drawer contained scissors, a scalpel and a roll of tape. An album filled with clippings of newspaper pictures of Carl-Eric Grimås and Adam Fischer lay in the middle compartment. The pictures, all taken at different times and in various environments, had one thing in common – the eyes were missing, just like in the newspapers that Tomas had found earlier. Fabian was struck by how much personality was found in the eyes, and how, without them, both Grimås and Fischer looked more like zombies than themselves.

The left-hand drawer also contained pictures, but they weren't neatly pasted into an album or cut out from newspapers. It looked like Kremph had probably been holding the camera. There were thirty-odd pictures, all of which had been taken at some distance from inside a bus. They showed various passengers reading, conversing with the person beside them, or looking out the window daydreaming. And from what Fabian could tell, none of the subjects was in more than one photo – except one woman who was in every single one.

A woman with her eyes cut out.

Was there yet another victim? Was that why Kremph wasn't home?

He set the pictures out on the desk to study them more thoroughly, but was interrupted by shrieking voices that drowned out David Bowie's 'The Cynic'. He pulled the earplugs out and hurried out to the others, who stood with their guns drawn, shouting at the same time.

'Get down on your stomach!' yelled Tomas, who stood with his gun in both hands. 'Down, I said!'

Fabian almost couldn't believe his eyes. Ossian Kremph was standing like a statue in the middle of the room with a grocery bag in one hand, among piles of newspapers. It was almost as if he had materialized out of nowhere and he looked just as surprised as the police.

'But, this isn't right. You can't just—' he said, shaking his head.

'You damn well better believe we can!' said Tomas. 'Get down, dammit!'

'No, this isn't right. Not right—'

'It's probably best if you do as we say,' said Jarmo, who had also drawn his weapon.

Fabian was surprised at how small and different Kremph looked in real life, compared to the surveillance video of him dressed as a guard with a beard and a considerably bigger waist. Were all his surgical tools hidden under his clothes?

'No... This isn't good, not good at all.' Kremph shook his head harder and harder, letting go of the grocery bag and waving his arms. 'You have to leave now! Get out of here!'

'Shut up and lie down!' said Tomas.

'Ossian, listen to me now,' said Malin, with her gun in one hand and ID in the other. 'We're police officers and I think you know why we're here. The best thing you can do is to just stay calm and do exactly as we say.'

Ossian Kremph relaxed a little and nodded.

'Very good. Now hold your hands above your head and get down slowly on your knees.'

Kremph held up his hands and made an effort to lower himself. But then, without warning, he turned around and disappeared out towards the hall.

'Stop!' Tomas and Jarmo shouted at the same time.

But it was too late – Kremph was already out of the apartment and down the stairs, judging by the echo.

'What the hell are we doing? He's getting away, dammit!' Tomas shouted on his way out.

OSSIAN KREMPH RUSHED OUT of the front door on Blekingegatan and ran as fast as he could towards Götgatan. He knew he was faster than most – he always had been – and whatever happened he didn't intend to let himself be arrested. Not again. He just needed to get down in the subway to be safe. He had his paths, and could easily disappear right before their eyes – fucking cops.

How could he have been so naïve? It wasn't at all like him. And he'd seen them wandering down the street just a few days ago. He'd promised himself to be prepared if they came and rang his doorbell, and yet he walked right into their trap.

There wasn't far to go now. He just had to cross Götgatan and then head down into the underworld. He knew exactly how to navigate his way through the subway entry in the most efficient way possible, which meant having to force your way past all the bastards who didn't know that you should stand on the right side.

He could hear the shrieking voices of the police behind, ordering him to stop and raise his hands above his head. They could scream all they wanted. He was done obeying orders and playing nice.

Once he was down on the platform, he jumped quickly on to the tracks, and continued running right into the darkness. He would soon reach his goal: a place they would never find him.

He'd been lucky. There was no train in the station and all was quiet on the tracks. He heard something behind him that sounded like a car tyre bursting. But there obviously weren't any cars here. He didn't even realize what it was until his left leg gave way, making him fall headlong and strike his head on the rails.

It was the sound that made him come to and recognize what was about to happen. The characteristic track shaking that indicated a train was on its way.

39

THIS WAS EXACTLY WHAT her father had warned her about, thought Katja Skov, who had no idea where she was or how she'd ended up here. He had poured hundreds of thousands into various security systems and told her that under no circumstances should she leave the house in Snekkersten unless it was planned in advance with the bodyguards. She hated it. It felt like she was under house arrest, while her friends were all out partying in Copenhagen. The past few years he'd talked about almost nothing other than how softer targets were becoming more common as traditional thefts got harder to pull off.

But now it was a fact – she was living her father's worst nightmare.

She'd been abducted and carried off like a victim in a bad movie that you knew would end happily, except this was no movie.

She tried to estimate how long she'd been there, but gave up. Considering how much she'd consumed yesterday, her sense of time was the last thing she could rely on. And it was dark, so dark that she couldn't see a few centimetres in front of her, even though her eyes should have grown accustomed long ago.

She was definitely confined in a cramped space. She tried to scratch her nose, but there wasn't enough room. She was wrapped up in something hard, maybe a rug, and could hear a rustling and there was the smell of plastic around her. She certainly ought to be afraid, but she didn't have the energy to really care. It would surely work out.

She closed her eyes in an attempt to focus on what had really happened, but it didn't take long before everything started spinning and a sense of weightlessness took over. She was still high, and if she didn't come down soon she wouldn't be able to say which way was up or down.

She assumed they were trying to scare her and they wanted her to pound and scream as loud as she could. But she didn't intend to treat them to that. Instead she would stay so quiet and calm that in the end, they would be the ones who were worried. And when they finally came to take her out into the light, she would play dead, just like you should do if you fall down into a bear's den.

She couldn't imagine what their reaction would be when they discovered their plan to make millions was now worthless.

She thought about the party. It was supposed to be a quiet gathering but it had degenerated into a shameless orgy with people snorting up almost her whole supply and fucking in every corner. But that's how it almost always went: the most fun and successful parties were the unplanned.

And when Niels suggested that they should go to Helsingør and make the rounds like real Swedes – actually, it wasn't Niels but that girl someone had dragged along – she couldn't say no. Leaving without telling her father or any of the guards made her jump for joy.

The group consisted of her closest friends and a few more whose names she didn't know. They'd left the house through the window in the bathroom and managed to get over the wall by using a protruding branch from a tree.

The taxis had been waiting for them on Strandvejen, and before she knew it they were sitting on the Swedish ferry on their way to Helsingborg. Everyone had agreed they should keep partying and always stay away from the boring old everyday – which was pretty much how she'd been living her life for the past ten years anyway.

Her father had done everything in his power to get her to calm down and to start taking care of herself. And God knows she'd tried everything, from working at one of his many companies, to therapy, physical activity and medication. But nothing could get rid of the feeling that she had nothing left to lose and that it could all be over at any moment. No matter how you looked at it, she was living on borrowed time, so why shouldn't she make the most of it? Suck the marrow out of every day as if it were her last – *carpe fucking diem*.

Of course, that wasn't what her father had imagined when she had initially got her diagnosis. He'd started pulling all the strings he could. If it was up to him, she would have had a thriving career and worked at least sixty hours a week. But what was the point? They already had more money than they could ever spend.

It wasn't that she couldn't understand his disappointment, especially in the first few years, but now more than ten years had passed and his disappointment still coloured their whole relationship. He tried to hide it for the most part, but bitterness almost always shone through in his eyes and, reading between the lines of the things he said to her, it seemed that sometimes he regretted having helped her at all.

She felt a vibration and could hear a motor starting. She couldn't tell if she had only just started to feel afraid because she realized she was in the trunk of a car or because she was moving. But she was scared now – no, terrified. Only now did it occur to her that this was real and it wasn't just a bad joke. She suddenly remembered that poor woman she had seen on the news. Karen Neuman – that was it. But hadn't the police announced that they had caught her murderer? Terror ran through her body like a high-voltage charge. Every one of her muscles tensed as if in spasm and she screamed as loud as she could.

But the rug made such an effective muffler that she soon gave up. She could feel them start to slowly roll forward. They hit a few bumps, after which the surface smoothed out. *They were driving off the ferry*, she thought. But into Denmark or into Sweden she didn't know.

For the first time in a very long time, she realized how much she had to lose.

40

DUNJA TRIED TO SWALLOW the lump in her throat as she looked out over the journalists and photographers taking their seats in front of her. The more crowded it got, the more uncomfortable she felt.

It didn't surprise her that there was a lot of interest in the press conference. She'd been familiar with Aksel Neuman ever since he launched his radio programme, *Voices in the Night*, but he'd only become a national celebrity after his appearance on *Let's Dance* and subsequently got his own talk show. But she hadn't expected the interest to be so great that they'd have to move the press conference to the big hall so they could fit them all in. They were still streaming in, though, and it was unlikely they would have enough room for everyone.

If it had been up to her, she would have been with the operation at Benny Willumsen's apartment in Malmö instead. But Sleizner insisted that she sit beside him and emphasized how important it was for her career that she be seen by the media every now and then and didn't just work behind the scenes. *Considering how well things have worked out for him, even though he never did any real police work, he certainly knew what he was talking about*, she thought, feeling the sweat starting to bead on her upper lip.

It was the dress's fault. It was much too warm, made of some material that didn't breathe and left her feeling like a stuffed sausage. Carsten had given it to her as a Christmas present last year, but it was two sizes too small, which was the case whenever he gave her clothes. She was sure she'd lost over five pounds since then, but it didn't seem to make a difference.

She looked at Sleizner, who smiled at her, while taking out a handkerchief to dab at his upper lip. She'd hoped her own sweat wasn't visible and was afraid that her make-up would be ruined if she tried to wipe it off. *The cursed drops of sweat that persisted in making awkward appearances*, she swore to herself, dabbing as carefully as she could with her handkerchief.

'Are you okay?' asked Sleizner, and she gave him the most convincing smile she could. But evidently that wasn't persuasive enough, because he leaned towards her, placed his hand on her thigh and whispered in her ear, 'Just relax and let me steer the boat until we're in the port. Once we're there, I promise to treat you to something really good.'

She nodded again. Mostly because she didn't know how she should react. Actually, she did know, and the truth was that she didn't want to challenge him.

'I want to start by welcoming all of you here!' Sleizner removed his hand from her thigh and looked out over the assembly. 'My name is Kim Sleizner, and for those of you who don't know me, I'm head of the homicide unit here in Copenhagen. I have Dunja Hougaard with me, who will be a new face for most of you. This is the first time she's joined me up on stage, so I hope you'll be kind to her.'

Scattered laughter spread throughout the assembly and Dunja smiled as best she could.

'Dunja is responsible for the investigation of the murder of Karen Neuman. She has come to a number of interesting conclusions, to say the least. We've not only managed to identify a prime suspect, but it also appears we'll be able to close five older homicide investigations – cases that have dogged us for several years. And in addition,' he continued, holding a finger up, 'it looks like we're also going to be able to help our Swedish colleagues where they've faltered. But I'll turn the floor over to Dunja.' He turned towards her. 'Be my guest.'

'Thanks very much. Uh… Yes, just as Kim Sleizner was saying, we're dealing with a perpetrator who is active on both sides of the Sound,' said Dunja, feeling the sweat run down her back. 'Our prime suspect, who is still at large, is named—'

'Closer to the mic! Can't hear you!' someone was yelling.

'Sorry.' Dunja leaned toward the microphone. 'Is this better?'

'Yes, but it would be even better if you turn it on,' said Sleizner, once again getting a few chuckles.

Dunja also forced a laugh, while she fumbled for the little button on the microphone with shaky hands. Her laugh caught in her throat like a sticky mass that made her want to throw up and scream out loud to everyone that Kim Sleizner was a sexist, male chauvinist pig and that they could all go to hell. Suddenly, she felt as if something burst inside her.

It didn't hurt in the least. On the contrary, it calmed her. And when she raised her eyes and looked out over the laughing assembly, she had to bite back a laugh as it occurred to her that their low-pitched voices sounded like a herd of cows in rut. Her fingers stopped trembling and she calmly turned on the microphone.

'Can everyone hear me now? One-two. One-two,' she said, pulling the microphone out of its holder so that she could hold it. 'You too, Kim?'

Sleizner nodded, even though he looked anything but amused.

'Excellent! But now the fun is over,' she continued, pressing on the remote control that pulled up a portrait of Benny Willumsen. 'This is Benny Willumsen. He's a Danish citizen, but lives in Malmö. About two years ago, the Swedish police arrested him for this crime.' She pressed the button again, whereupon an image from the murder scene in Rydebäck was projected behind her: a woman was lying lifeless on a sandy beach. A white sheet, stained red in several places from all the blood that had leaked from the deep wounds, covered her body.

'Without going into specific details, we can confirm that there are a number of striking similarities between this case and the Karen Neuman investigation in Tibberup, even if he went a step further in the latter and...' Dunja trailed off and looked at her phone that was vibrating on the table in front of her. It was Sverker Holm from the Helsingborg police, or 'Klippan' as he was evidently called.

She shouldn't have had her phone out, much less had it turned on, even if it was on silent. And she knew that under no circumstances should she answer. Yet she went to pick it up.

'Dunja, perhaps you should put that away now,' Sleizner hissed with an irritated expression. Dunja refused the call and set down the phone.

'Sorry. Where were we?'

'The connection between the Swedish case in Rydebäck and the Karen Neuman case in Tibberup.'

'Right.'

The phone vibrated again. This time it was a text message: *Willumsen has struck again. Call as soon as you can.*

'Dunja. What are you doing?' Sleizner now looked really stressed.

Dunja read the message over again, and met Sleizner's perplexed look. 'He's struck again. You'll have to take over from here. I have work to do.' She got up and stepped down from the stage.

'I see,' said Sleizner, throwing out his hands. 'Unfortunately it looks as if you'll have to put up with me again. Where were we?'

Dunja dialled Klippan's number and left the room.

'Hi, Dunja.' Dunja could hear that Klippan was starting the engine of a car.

'Have you found a new victim?'

'No, not yet.'

'Is it a Swede this time?' She continued towards the elevators and passed a TV that was playing the ongoing press conference without sound.

'No, she's a Danish woman. Her name is Katja Skov. Maybe you've heard of her father, Ib Skov?'

'Yes, he's one of our biggest businessmen.' Dunja tried turning up the sound on the TV. 'I still don't know if I quite get what's going on,' she continued, failing to locate the right button and abandoning her attempt to hear the TV briefing in frustration.

'As I understand it, she had some sort of gathering or party in their house in Snekkersten. Early in the morning she and some of her friends took a taxi to Helsingør where they boarded the ferry to keep partying. You know, drink alcohol and ride back and forth any number of times on a single ticket.'

'I thought Swedes were the only people that did that.'

'That's what I thought, but evidently they also did it. There was quite a lot of drinking, and suddenly they realized that Katja Skov was missing.'

'And you're sure she's not just passed out in a lifeboat or something like that?'

'Personnel have searched the ferry twice. As soon as I heard about it, I contacted the guy at Scandlines – what's his name again?'

'Yes, I know who you mean.'

'I asked him to check the surveillance videos, and just as I'd suspected he'd been there with the same car again.'

'You mean Aksel Neuman's BMW with the Danish licence plate?'

'Exactly. He reportedly drove off the ferry in Helsingborg exactly twenty-two minutes past twelve today.'

Dunja looked at the clock. That was not much more than two hours ago – an eternity in these circumstances, but considerably better than nothing. 'Klippan, what do you think about me coming over to Sweden and us working on this together?'

'That's what I wanted to suggest. Call me as soon as you know what time you'll be arriving in Helsingborg and I'll see about picking you up at the station.'

They ended the call. Dunja took a few deep breaths in an attempt to lower her heart rate, but it was pointless. Her adrenaline was pumping as if she'd just thrown herself into a ravine with a thick rubber band around her ankles.

She looked over at the TV and watched Sleizner end the press conference and leave the stage. Considering how much he loved being the centre of attention, he looked unusually tense, which could only mean one thing – he was furious.

In a way she could understand it, but on the other hand, she didn't care.

41

'HI, MATILDA. WHAT'S ON your mind?' inquired Fabian on his way through the corridor towards the meeting room.

'When are you coming home? I've called Mum a bunch of times, but she's not answering.'

'She's at the studio, and I'm sure she has her phone turned off. Isn't Rebecka with you?'

'Yeah, but I don't like her very much. She's always out on the balcony talking on the phone and smoking. I want you to come home now.'

'But, pumpkin, you know that isn't going to happen right now. It's only one thirty and I have to work for a few more hours. But once I finish, I promise to come straight home, so we can watch TV and have a cosy Friday night. Does that sound good?'

There was no answer, but he could hear the babysitter asking Matilda if she wanted to play The Missing Diamond.

'Okay, Dad, see you later.' There was a click in Fabian's ear before he had time to respond, so he put the phone into his pocket and continued to the meeting room.

Tomas, Jarmo and Malin were already waiting. They were only missing Herman Edelman. The mood around the table was almost exhilarated. Fresh coffee was ready in a thermos and a tin of cookies was just waiting to be opened and passed around. Everyone would allow themselves one or two extra calorie bombs, but not yet.

In accordance with tradition, Edelman would arrive with a tray full of food and praise them all for their work that had led to the apprehension of yet another perpetrator. Then he would serve them each a shot and let them help themselves to his dishes, which over time everyone had learned to love: Finn Crisps with Kalle's caviar and finely chopped red onion.

'We also have to congratulate Tomas on acing that first shot with his six-shooter,' said Jarmo, imitating a little pistol with his fingers.

'You have to agree that it was nicely done. We're talking about fifteen metres in pitch-black after all,' said Tomas.

'Luck,' said Jarmo, sipping his coffee.

'Luck? I could do it again with a blindfold on.'

'Then you'd be even more lucky. Besides, you forgot to fire a warning shot.'

'You don't think I wanted to give him the opportunity to surrender? I got to bring that bastard down. Boom – right in the thigh! That's more than you've done your whole career.' Tomas patted Jarmo on the shoulder.

'You haven't started without me, have you?'

Everyone turned towards Edelman. He set down an overfilled tray of food in the middle of the table and they started applauding. Schnapps glasses were distributed and the frosty O.P. Anderson bottle was passed around.

'And what am I supposed to drink?' asked Malin.

'Lemon water or light beer,' said Edelman while he unscrewed the little red plastic cap from the tube of caviar and pressed a hole in the protective foil with the star-shaped tip. 'Or you can have a little one and pretend you're in Denmark again.'

Everyone laughed and helped themselves to the Finn Crisp–caviar sandwiches and then dipped them into the finely chopped red onion. Fabian took a bite, enjoying the strong taste of onion mixed with the saltiness of the caviar and the hard bread. It was really good, and today he couldn't understand why he'd initially been so sceptical.

After everyone had taken a few bites, Edelman wiped off his beard and raised his schnapps glass. 'I just want to take the opportunity to congratulate you all on an amazing job. Not only have we arrested the perpetrator, you've spared me lots of press conferences by doing it in record time!'

They threw back their drinks and Edelman passed the bottle around for a second round. 'Just so you know, Ossian Kremph was my first thought once I heard about what happened to Grimås.'

Fabian and the others exchanged glances.

'It's true, but I didn't say anything,' Edelman continued while he prepared another open-faced sandwich. 'Because I was convinced that it couldn't actually be him. I thought he was being kept away from the general public for ever. It didn't even occur to me that he might have served his sentence and was at large. Ossian Kremph was not only an unusually smart, studied perpetrator, but he was without a doubt the coldest offender I've encountered in all my years here; so cold that without blinking he tore the eyes out of his own defence attorney when he sensed the direction things were heading. And they let him out after only thirteen years.' Edelman shook his head and emptied the glass in one go. 'However, there are still a number of loose ends, and before we take off for Christmas and buy lingerie for our wives, we have to tie them up.'

'What threads are you referring to?' said Malin.

'We still don't know what he's done with Fischer,' said Jarmo.

'As one example,' said Edelman.

'Then we have this woman,' said Fabian, setting out some of the pictures of the woman with poked-out eyes from the bus.

'Who is that?' Edelman picked up and looked at one of the pictures.

'We don't know right now, but these photos were in his apartment along with similar images of Grimås and Fischer.'

'So there may be another victim who's locked up somewhere?' Edelman shook his head and sighed.

'Or else she'll be blissfully ignorant of the fact that she was next in line.'

'When can we question him?' asked Malin, preparing another Finn Crisp.

'I've just been in contact with Stockholm South General Hospital,' said Edelman. 'They're in the process of sewing him up right now.'

'So we should be able to go there in an hour or so.'

'Not so fast. Evidently he's not mentally stable after what happened.'

'And he was before?' said Tomas with a laugh.

'His therapist seems to think so and has now issued a ban on visitors.'

'What do you mean, "ban on visitors"?' said Jarmo. 'He can't just obstruct our investigation, can he?'

'Unfortunately that's exactly what he can do, as long as it concerns the suspect's health, and let's not forget that. However sure we may be of his guilt, he's only a suspect at the present time.'

'So when can we see him?' Fabian repeated, even though he already felt that it would be a while from now.

'They promised to get back to us after the weekend, but said we should count on waiting at least a week.'

'A week?' said Tomas, emptying the last of the schnapps. 'I shot him in the leg, for Christ's sake, not the mouth!'

'The question is whether it's even possible to have a fair interrogation,' said Malin.

A week or even two wouldn't work, thought Fabian. Fischer would most certainly be dead by then, so would the woman on the bus.

'What do we do now, besides sit here and twiddle our thumbs?' said Tomas.

'Obviously, no one's going to be twiddling their thumbs,' said

Edelman. 'Stubbs is already busy going through his apartment and she might find a good lead.'

'Okay, then we'll just have to cross our fingers,' said Tomas, dipping another Finn Crisp with caviar in the plate of red onions.

'I don't think we'll get much further right now.' Edelman stood up. 'Help yourselves to the food. I have a press conference to prepare for, which will hopefully be the last one related to this case.' He left the room.

Silence descended on the room. The happy mood from earlier had been extinguished.

'Unless something happens, I guess I'll see you Monday,' said Fabian, shoving back his chair.

'Absolutely. Have a nice weekend,' said Jarmo.

'Same to you.' Fabian left the room and could hear Malin hurrying after him.

'You're going home?'

'Yes, but not to my place. I'm actually heading to your street.'

'Huh? I don't understand—'

'And you're coming along to pay a visit to one of your neighbours.'

42

IT WAS A RACE against time. Willumsen's more than two-hour head start had to be made up at any price, every precious second. Unfortunately, a lot of valuable time had been spent getting her dress off. The zipper on the skirt stuck, and after trying it gently both up and down Dunja finally pulled on it in sheer frustration, so that it split and ended up in the wastebasket. It took two packets of tissues to wipe the sweat off her body.

Fortunately, the last people from the department had already gone home, so she could change right in front of her desk. The moment she pulled on her jeans and polo shirt she felt like herself again. She gathered up the files of old investigations and turned off her computer.

'So, this is where you've been hiding.'

Dunja turned around and saw Sleizner walking towards her.

'What happened in there?' He threw out his arms. 'It must have been something incredibly important for you to just leave in the middle of a press conference.'

She nodded and put the files in her bag. 'It was the Helsingborg police. Willumsen has struck again. He abducted a young woman off the ferry to Sweden, so I have to get out there as soon as possible. I'll be in touch and explain more when I'm on the train.' She slung her bag over her shoulder and turned around to leave.

'Not so fast.' Sleizner took hold of her arm so that the bag fell to the floor. 'Let's take it a little easier.'

'Kim, I'm sorry, but I really don't have time to—'

The grip on her arm hardened while he pressed his index finger from his other hand against her mouth. 'Now you listen to me. Is that understood?'

Dunja nodded and Sleizner loosened the grip on her arm.

'Do you have any idea what you just subjected me to out there?' He started to walk around her. 'I gave you an investigation that some people in this building would give their right arm for. I let you sit up on stage with me. I rolled out a wide, long and newly minted red fucking carpet for your sake! And what do I get in return?'

Sleizner was standing right behind her with his face so close to her that she could feel his breath against her earlobe. It smelled of a stubborn cold and she had to force herself not to lean away. It wasn't Sleizner's first outburst. On the contrary, it was normal that he chewed out his employees right and left. But this was the first time she'd been in the line of fire herself. When Hesk and all the others had been in this situation they'd stayed calm and simply taken it until he was finished.

'Yes, I'm going to tell you,' Sleizner walking in circles around her and then stopping to face her.

But she didn't have the time. Every second that passed gave Willumsen a longer head start.

'A big fucking middle finger right in front of the cameras!' He held up his middle finger so that it grazed her nose. 'I sat there like a fucking fool and had no idea—'

'Kim, you have to excuse me.' Dunja removed his hand from her face. 'But I really don't have time for this right now.'

'Time? I tell you what you have time for! And right now that's to stand here and listen to me. Did you simply think you could leave now?'

Dunja nodded and Sleizner looked shocked.

'I'm sorry if it got a little ridiculous out there. I truly am. But you assigned me to lead this investigation and that's exactly what I intend to do.' She picked up the bag from the floor and went towards the exit.

'Dunja, wait—'

She turned around and saw him walking towards her. 'Yes?'

He let out a long, heavy sigh. 'I'm sorry. That wasn't how I intended this to go.' He stopped in front of her again and looked her directly in the eyes. 'It felt like you pulled my trousers down out there. I know that you're only trying to take responsibility for this investigation, but that wasn't the right way to go about it. Even you have to agree with that.'

Dunja nodded. 'Yes, and I'm really sorry about it. But I have to—'

'I am too – sorry, that is. And we were having such a nice time before all this happened.' He took her hands in his. 'I'm prepared to wipe the slate clean and start over from scratch. What do you say?'

'Okay,' said Dunja, making another effort to leave. She just needed to get away from here, but Sleizner persisted in holding on to her hands and gazing into her eyes.

'Sure?'

She nodded again, and he broke into a smile.

'Good. Then we know where we stand with each other.' He kissed her hand and let her go.

43

ONLY AFTER THE THIRD ring did Malin's neighbour finally answer the door, looking back and forth between her and Fabian with a bewildered expression. He was dressed in beige corduroy trousers, a white shirt and leather waistcoat. With his small round glasses and greying, shoulder-length hair, he looked more like a fiddler from the northern Swedish forests than a psychoanalyst of some of Sweden's most violent offenders.

'Hi, how's it going?' Malin shook hands with the man, who looked even more confused, if that were possible. 'Don't you recognize me? We met at the barbecue last autumn. My husband burned all the hot dogs, so we had to order pizza instead. I live just a few doors up the street.'

'I'm sorry, but I have a client who's sitting and—'

'No problem, this will take no time at all. May we come in?'

'Uh, no. It's not convenient.'

'Great! I wouldn't say no to a chair to sit on. When you're this pregnant, certain positions completely take everything out of you. By the way, this is my colleague Fabian Risk from the National Bureau of Criminal Investigation.' Malin rolled her eyes at Fabian as she squeezed into the foyer and found a chair to sit down on. 'Ah, just what I needed.'

'Excuse me, but what is this about?'

'Ossian Kremph. Does that name sound familiar?'

'So you were the people who chased him on to the subway tracks and shot him.'

'Actually, that was a different officer. But we do need to see him – as soon as possible.'

'Out of the question.' The therapist shook his head. 'Haven't you done enough damage? Ossian has served his time and deserves a life in peace. I can't think of any of my clients who have worked as hard on themselves as he has. Then you come in and turn his whole life upside down.'

'What are you so worried about?' said Fabian. 'That you won't get your rent?'

The therapist turned towards Fabian with a shrug. 'I have the association's permission for that and I report the amount for tax purposes if that's what you're referring to. There's nothing at all illegal about—'

'Who said anything about illegal? I'm thinking more about professional ethics that say you shouldn't cross the line and get too personally involved with your clients.'

'Have you?' said Malin.

'What?'

'Crossed the line.'

'Not really.' The therapist adjusted his small eyeglasses with a shaking hand. 'On the other hand, I'm back to square one where his rehabilitation is concerned. And that's nobody's fault but yours.'

'I'm sorry to hear that, but you're forgetting one small detail.' Malin showed some of the pictures of Carl-Eric Grimås and his empty eye sockets.

'He didn't do that – it's impossible.' The therapist handed back the pictures with a snort, pushing some of his grey curls behind one ear.

'And why is it so unlikely?'

'Don't you think I can tell what you think about my work? That it's just an expensive pastime for people who feel sorry for themselves and don't know what to do with their money. Or, in Ossian's case, the taxpayers' money. I can assure you that it's a science, a rather exact one. Ossian and I managed to work all the way down to his innermost core and establish the root cause of his illness.'

'And what was that?'

'You lack the right tools to even come close to understanding. Ossian is aware of the consequences of his actions. And along with the medication he is on now, I'm completely convinced of his innocence.' He crossed his arms in front of him.

'And what would happen if he says he's taken his medication, but in reality hasn't done so for several months?' asked Fabian.

'That's a hypothetical question. Ossian would never lie to me.'

'No?'

'Look at these.' Malin got up from the chair and showed him the images of the victims from the sixteen-year-old investigation. 'Do you see similarities?'

The therapist reluctantly looked down.

'We suspect that he has two more victims hidden somewhere,' said Fabian. 'The trust-fund playboy Adam Fischer, whom you've surely heard about on the news, and then this woman.' He showed one of the photos of the woman with the poked-out eyes on the bus.

'Oh, good lord.' The therapist covered his mouth.

'Do you recognize her?'

He shook his head. 'No, but this is exactly what he did when he was sick. He couldn't stop it. At its worst, he could empty every single page in the newspaper of eyes.' The therapist sat down on a chair and his face suddenly looked very pale.

'Shall I get you a glass of water?' said Malin.

The therapist nodded and put his head in his hands.

44

THE MAN WAS LYING on the table in front of him, naked and strapped down. He'd been tube-fed for ten days to allow enough time for the toxins to leave his body. His body was clean, shaved and disinfected, and two empty bloody holes gaped where eyes should have been. The anaesthetic had worked the way it was supposed to, and the man only gasped and moaned a little while he was pulling out the eyeballs, which he then dropped into the viscous fluid. Now his breathing was back to normal again.

The man was ready to contribute his body to satisfy his desire. But he would keep him alive and draw it out for as long as possible. Only when it was time for his inner organs to be prepared would he finally be terminated and the major parts cut away and put in the pan.

Until then, he would confine himself to little bite-size pieces from various parts of the body. It was like combining the appetizer with foreplay, something he had recently started to appreciate more. He could now drag it out for days. Just letting the newly sharpened knife penetrate into the flesh all the way down to the bone made him shiver with pleasure and he'd even ejaculated before he'd had a taste on occasion.

Normally, he would cut loose bite-size pieces with the small knife, but he had taken it a step further and had his teeth sharpened to a point. It was painful, and he had to go all the way to Poland to find a dentist willing to perform the procedure, but he still thought it was worth it many times over.

He took out both his upper and lower dentures and felt the razor-sharp row of teeth with his fingers while he circled the man on the table. After two rounds, he settled on the left thigh. He leaned over, opened his mouth, and let his teeth slowly work their way into the flesh. The warm blood streamed out immediately, filling his mouth and overflowing down his chin.

He chewed the raw meat, swallowed, and leaned over for yet another bite. All of a sudden, the man's hand came out of nowhere and hit him in the face. How could that happen? The man was tied down and was staring right at him, even though his red eye sockets were empty. The man mumbled something. He leaned forward to hear better.

'He's waking up now.'

Ossian Kremph looked around and realized that there were another three people in the room. He'd seen two of them only briefly, but the third – the man with the small round eyeglasses and curly grey hair – he recognized all too well.

Several seconds later it occurred to him that he'd been dreaming. In reality he was at Stockholm South General Hospital where he was the person shackled to the bed. Just to be safe, he glided his tongue along his teeth and could tell that they were definitely not sharp. Part of him let out a sigh of relief, but another part of him, somewhere deep inside, was disappointed.

'Ossian,' said the grey-haired man. 'There are some people here who want to have a few words with you.'

'Not now... I don't want to... Can't... You have to leave.' He tried to get away from the man who always smelled of too much cologne, but the handcuffs held him tightly in the bed.

'The best thing you can do is answer their questions.'

And why should he do that? He didn't want to. 'Leave!'

'This is exactly what I mean,' his number-one object of hatred said to the others.

'Is it possible to give him something so that he calms down?' the pregnant woman said.

'Then he'll fall asleep right away.'

The other man leaned forward. 'Hi, Ossian. My name is Fabian Risk. I only have three questions for you.' He held up three fingers in front of his face. 'Three simple little questions, then we promise to leave you alone again.'

'I haven't done anything. You're the ones who are intruding, not me.' He didn't like this. He didn't like it at all. 'Tell them to go now!' he screamed. 'Get out!'

'We will as soon as you've answered my questions. One: what have you done with Adam Fischer?'

Ossian shook his head, and tried to hold his hands in front of his eyes, but the chains of the handcuffs were much too short.

'Ossian, answer now,' said the one who claimed to be his friend. 'Where did you hide him?'

'I already told you that you can't be here. I want you to leave now.'

'Okay, then we'll skip to the next question for now,' the policeman continued. 'Do you have any other victims? What about this woman, for example?' He showed him a picture of a woman with poked-out eyes on a bus.

Like hungry vultures they were hacking at him with their questions.

'Fischer.'

But he couldn't answer.

'More victims?'

He wanted to speak, but he couldn't get the words out.

'And finally: where are you keeping them hidden?'

He closed his eyes and shook his head as hard as he could to get them to disappear, but they refused. Instead they just came closer with their hacking beaks.

'Ossian, I'm not here to harm you,' the policeman lied. 'I just want to understand how this all fits together.'

'Understand?' He couldn't help but laugh. 'That's good – really good. Who doesn't want that? I do anyway.'

'Sorry, but what do you mean?'

'Mean? How should I know? I don't know anything. I don't even get to have a radio, even though I haven't done anything. They just say no, no, no.'

'Ossian, try to listen to the police now.'

'How can I listen to the sea report without a radio? Huh? It's impossible. Now it's time to leave. Visits are no good.'

'Fabian, can I talk to you outside?' the fat one said. In the corner of his eye he saw them pass a cleaning woman as they left.

Finally.

'THERE'S NO POINT,' SAID Malin, starting to massage her hips.

'So we should just give up?' Fabian took a thermos of coffee from the food cart and filled a cup.

'He's been diagnosed with severe dissociative identity disorder, so there is actually a risk that he doesn't remember anything that he's done.'

Fabian nodded. Malin was presumably right, but waiting for him to get healthy was not an option. They would have to take a different route.

'Do you believe me now?' The therapist closed the door to the examination room behind him.

'Of course. We have this whole time,' said Malin.

'I hope you're aware how much this will negatively affect his confidence in me. This relationship took me years to develop and it just went up in smoke.'

'We appreciate that and we're very sorry,' said Malin. 'But as I'm sure you'll understand, we have no other choice than to try all possible—'

'We need to show him the crime scene,' Fabian interrupted, turning towards the therapist. 'Preferably as soon as possible.'

'Sorry, but... I don't know what you mean.'

'We need to bring him to one of the crime scenes and see if that activates his memory.'

The therapist gave Fabian a quizzical look. 'Were we just in the same room? Can't you see how badly he's doing?'

'Yes, but presumably that's nothing compared to how badly his victims are doing right now. You'll have to excuse me if my sympathies aren't with you or your patient.'

'I couldn't care less where your sympathies lie. Any visit to a crime scene is out of the question.'

'I think you should lower your voice a bit,' said Malin, standing in front of Fabian. 'Regardless of what happens, Kremph is certainly going to be convicted. We are just trying to do everything in our power to save the lives of any further victims, and clear up a number of question marks in the investigation. You can think about it anyway.'

The therapist nodded, but didn't say anything. Then he turned around and went back into Kremph's room.

45

THE SMELL REMINDED DUNJA of her grandfather's old auto repair shop in Kolding. They used to go four times a year when her parents were still married, but after the divorce it increased to as often as one weekend a month. Every time they visited, she would sneak down into the garage after hours, lie down amongthe tools on the dirty concrete floor, close her eyes and enjoy that special smell. It was one of her favourite things, and even today she still caught herself taking an extra deep breath as soon as she was in a garage or gas station.

But she wasn't in Kolding today, she was in Helsingborg, trying to locate and arrest a serial killer. She looked around and noted that the Helsingborg police lab for technical forensic investigation looked quite different from Kjeld Richter's office in Copenhagen – it was the exact opposite of a white and clinical set-up. The floor and walls were concrete and fluorescent light fixtures hung from the ceiling, illuminating a number of different workstations.

She took out her phone and saw that it was five to five. Benny Willumsen, presumably with Katja Skov tied up in his car, had now had over a four-and-a-half-hour head start, an eternity in her mind. He would have no problem hiding far outside their range, assuming he kept his pace up. If, on the other hand, he was convinced that the police were busy searching his apartment for non-existent evidence, there was a good chance he would slow down, meaning his time advantage could just as well be rounded down to zero.

She turned to Klippan. 'Should we get going? I think it's—'

Klippan shushed her. 'He doesn't like to be disturbed when he's this focused,' he whispered, closing the door as quietly as possible behind her.

'It doesn't matter. This is going to hell anyway,' a voice said from inside the room.

Only now did she realize that there was a man in a white coat sitting inside the room staring at a large computer. The man turned towards them, putting his chin to his chest to look over his reading glasses.

'This is Dunja Hougaard. The person I told you about,' said Klippan, continuing into the room. 'From the Copenhagen police.'

'Yes, I don't have Alzheimer's,' said the man, turning back to face his computer screen, which was filled with long columns of letters and digits in various combinations.

'At any rate, this is our forensic technician Ingvar Molander. I can attest that he's normally in a considerably better mood.'

'Are you having problems?' asked Dunja, walking towards Molander.

'If you define a problem as a perpetrator who's disappeared into thin air then the answer is without a doubt yes.' Molander started playing a surveillance video of Aksel Neuman's BMW with the tinted windows driving off the ferry. 'As you see, he got off the ferry in Helsingborg at 12:22 p.m. today. He should have appeared on one of the speed cameras outside the city, but over four hours have passed and he still hasn't been seen on a single one in all of Skåne.'

'But what if he wasn't driving fast?'

Molander exchanged a look with Klippan.

'I don't know how far you've got with this technology in Denmark, but Malmö is test-driving ANPR here. Tuvesson managed to get the okay for us to make use of their data just for this case – don't ask me how,' Klippan said.

'They were just as shattered as we were when Willumsen was released,' said Molander.

'She must have pulled a few strings that went pretty far up because it's fairly controversial.'

'What's ANPR?'

'Automatic Number Plate Recognition,' said Molander. 'Speed cameras are directly connected to a server that registers all the cars that pass in real time, regardless of what speed they're driving.'

'Are you really allowed to do that in Sweden?'

'Not yet. They don't count on all the clauses being in place for another two years. So it's not something we can make use of as evidence,' said Klippan.

'It doesn't matter anyway because we're not getting any hits,' said Molander with a sigh.

'Maybe there's a bug in the system?' suggested Klippan.

'No, it's more likely that he has deliberately chosen side roads where there aren't any cameras. I'm in the process of gathering more data from all monitored garages and gas stations. With a little luck—'

'Or else he just changed a letter or number on the licence plate,' said Dunja, setting aside her winter coat and scarf on an empty chair.

'That's not a dumb idea, actually,' said Klippan, nodding insistently. 'In principle, a little black electrical tape is probably enough. What do you think?' He turned toward Molander, but the question lingered in the air unanswered because Molander was already busy searching alternate registration numbers.

In the meantime, Dunja caught sight of a folder with the title 'The Ven Case: August 2007'. 'What's this?'

'That's what I was telling you about on the phone. It's the whole reason that Willumsen is still free. I didn't include it in the email to you because I'm sure he's not the perpetrator. But Ingvar insisted that you should be able to make your own assessment,' said Klippan.

'Of course, I believe it was him,' said Molander with a sigh. 'Who else could it be?'

'That's a good question. In any case, I believe it's not Willumsen. His alibi was watertight. But there's no reason to continue debating it now,' said Klippan, turning towards Dunja. 'As you can tell, we're not quite in agreement.'

'What was his alibi?'

'He was at a gym in central Malmö where he'd been working out for almost eight whole hours.'

'Eight hours?'

'Yes, evidently he's a real exercise addict and strong as... I don't know what. He's not someone you want to meet alone in a dark alley.'

Dunja opened the folder and skimmed through the two-and-a-half-year-old investigation. There were photos of a naked woman on all fours attached to a freight pallet that had floated to the shore near Sankt Ibb on the north side of Ven.

'Is she fastened to it?'

'Yes, she was screwed down with ten-gauge self-drilling screws.' Klippan illustrated the length of the screws with his hands. 'It must have been terrifying. Ingvar knew her.'

'That might be an overstatement. Depends on how you define "know",' said Molander from in front of the computer.

'Well, they lived on the same block. By the way, how's her husband doing? Is he still living there?'

'No, he sold the house a year and a half ago.'

'Didn't he start drinking and gamble away all his money on Internet poker?'

'Yes, but if I'm going to have any chance at all to be done with this before the holidays, you'll have to keep your—'

'Absolutely. I'm sorry, we'll leave you alone.' Klippan turned to Dunja. 'He's always this touchy when there's something exciting going on.'

'Can you tell me more about this case?'

Klippan nodded and led Dunja away from Molander. 'It's a frightful story. Her name was Inga Dahlberg and she was out jogging in Ramlösa Park when she was attacked and abducted from the scene. Unfortunately, there were no witnesses, but we secured traces of blood from the jogging trail. As you can see here, she was struck in the face by something hard.' He browsed ahead in the investigation file to some photographs that showed the victim's battered face. 'It was probably a spade or something similar. We secured more evidence from an out-of-the-way place among the trees by the river.'

'And what did you find there?'

'Primarily more blood, but also her jogging clothes and some of those unusually long self-drilling screws.'

'So that was where he took her clothes off?'

'Yes, and screwed her on to the pallet on all fours. She must have woken up after the blow with the spade and somehow believed that she would survive if she obeyed him. He made use of washers, so the screw heads wouldn't go through her hands and shins.' Klippan stopped talking and shook his head.

'Then what happened?'

'He raped her and sent her out on to the river. According to the medical examiner, her lungs were filled with salt water, so she must have miraculously survived all the way out into the Sound before she tipped over.'

In many ways, it was a typical Willumsen murder. He was undoubtedly a thrill-seeker who needed to push himself further every time, and, if this had happened today, Dunja would have been completely convinced that it was him. But the set-up was far too elaborate for the other crimes he'd been committing two-and-a-half years ago, with the help of a Doberman Pinscher and a spiked club. Even without the strong alibi, she didn't think it could have been him.

Her thoughts were interrupted when Molander called to them.

'Have you found him?' said Klippan.

'You're more damned impatient than my grandchildren on Christmas Eve. Check this out.'

Dunja stood beside Molander, who showed them notes on his paper.

'This is Aksel Neuman's registration number.' He pointed to AF 543 89. 'If we proceed from Dunja's theory that Willumsen stole the car from Aksel and then changed the licence plate with a little electrical tape, it would be easy to turn an F to an E, and nine to an eight, which would give us three new numbers.' He showed them AE 543 89, AF 543 88 and AE 543 88. 'Or, the five could become a six, which gives us another four variants,' he continued, showing another four numbers: AF 643 89, AF 643 88, AE 643 89 and AE 643 88.

'Shouldn't we see if they get any hits?' said Klippan.

'And what do you think I've been doing? Jesus!'

'How long will this take?' said Dunja, regretting her question immediately when she saw Molander's face.

'I don't know how fast the computers are in Denmark, but—'

'Wait a moment, what's this?' Klippan pointed at a blinking registration number AE 643 89 on the screen. 'Is that what I think it is?'

Molander looked at the blinking number and nodded. A few commands later and they had a map with a number of different markings on it.

'Do those dots indicate the route he's taken?' Klippan pointed at the screen.

'Yes, but can you please not touch the screen?' Molander sighed and removed Klippan's hand. 'As you can see here, he drove along route 17 between Landskrona and Eslöv.'

'Is it possible to see at what time?' said Dunja, feeling that they were finally starting to reduce his head start.

Molander zoomed in on the map and clicked on one of the markings. 'At about quarter to two, which would make sense if he drove off the ferry at twenty past one.'

'It looks like he's on his way to Eslöv,' said Klippan.

'No, then he would have been recorded on more cameras. Somewhere between Teckomatorp and Marieholm, he turned on to a back road.'

'Where there aren't any cameras,' said Klippan.

'You guessed right.'

Dunja studied the map and noted that there was only one road that Willumsen could have turned on to from route 17, which was route 108 that led straight down to Kävlinge. 'Maybe he's on his way to Kävlinge?'

'Yes, he could be,' said Klippan. 'I suggest we send the registration number out to all the gas stations around Skåne. There's a chance he stopped to fill up.'

Molander nodded. 'Okay, but it will probably be tomorrow before we get an answer.'

'Then I say we call it a day. It's already five thirty. Dunja, I've booked a room for you at Mollberg's. I can drive you there,' said Klippan.

'No, thanks, I can walk. I need a little fresh air.'

'Sure, but I'll pick you up there a little later, because tonight you're coming to my place for dinner. I've already asked Berit to make her lamb stew. And I can promise you, there's nothing better.'

Dunja nodded, while she wondered how to get out of the situation. The last thing she had time for now was more socializing.

46

SOFIE LEANDER WAS CONFUSED. The last thing she'd expected when the doctor stuck the needle in her arm was that she would ever wake up again. She'd been quite certain what was coming, so certain that she'd accepted her fate.

Now she no longer knew. She wasn't even sure if she was still alive.

She felt as if she'd ended up on loop because she was still tied down on the plastic-covered table in the middle of the room, looking right up at the ceiling, just as she'd been for the past few days.

Or maybe that wasn't what she was doing at all. Perhaps this was what it felt like to die, old memories played one last time before they were erased and flowed out into eternity. But the fact that she didn't float up towards the ceiling and couldn't look down at herself suggested that she was still alive. Besides, the pain in the wound was getting worse and worse, which indicated that the anaesthetic was starting to wear off.

But why?

What was the point of all this planning, and the work that must have gone into it, if she wasn't here to die? She tried, but couldn't think of a reasonable explanation. Instead, she reviewed what had happened, but could only remember how she'd heard the louvre gate open and the surgical instruments being set out on the metal table. Then a needle was guided into the crook of her left arm and she faded away, quite convinced that she'd reached her end.

She thought about her husband and wondered how far he'd got in his search for her. He'd obviously contacted the police long ago, but it was impossible to say what leads they had produced. They must have started by going through the surveillance tapes from Stockholm South General Hospital and seen how she was rolled out of the ward and into the elevators, but how much they had to go on after that was even more uncertain.

The police had undoubtedly released her photograph to the newspapers and asked the general public for leads. But what if no leads had come in? What happened then? How long would she be their highest priority if they didn't make any progress? Maybe she wasn't even in the headlines any more. Maybe the police had already started prioritizing other cases, and put her in the growing pile of forgotten fates.

One of the machines beside her started making a sound. It was out of view, but she had no problem figuring out what it was: it was the exact same bubbling sound that she'd been forced to endure four times a week during all the years that she couldn't do anything other than wait for the opportunity that might never come. How she hated that sound, so much so that she'd at last decided to give up waiting and take matters into her own hands.

But here it was again. The difference was that now she had no idea what she was waiting for.

47

ALL HE COULD SEE were the empty holes staring back at him. Fabian had lost control over his own gaze and couldn't look anywhere other than at the carved-out holes that looked as if they were made of dark material with an infinite gravitational force. There should have been eyes there – eyes that looked, blinked, wondered, and reflected personality and the soul. Now there was nothing.

He couldn't help the feeling of discomfort that crept beneath his skin as he studied the photographs that had been taken surreptitiously on the bus. It was almost as if he could feel the blade of the scalpel penetrating into the tear duct and pressing all the way behind the eyeball, severing the optic nerve and popping out the eye.

'God, it's hard to see what she looks like when the eyes aren't there,' said Malin, who was leaning over the images spread out on Fabian's desk. 'Besides that she has long, brown hair and appears to be about fifty.'

Fabian nodded and took out a magnifying glass that could help him focus on details other than the cut-out eyes. He noticed a reddish-brown hair clip, a crying child, the hands on a watch displaying a quarter past five, building exteriors in various colours, a kiosk, the gold chain around her neck with a hexagram and an iPod with white earphones.

'They're wearing coats and jackets but no hats, so I would guess that this was taken in the autumn or last spring,' Malin continued.

'Why not last autumn?'

'Wait, do you mean that—' She stopped herself and took hold of her belly.

'What is it? Are you okay?'

Malin nodded with eyes closed and took a few calming breaths. 'It's just the Karate Kid here who can't stop kicking me under the ribs, even though I've threatened to disinherit him. Have you found anything?'

'Look at the billboards at a kiosk.' Fabian put his eyes against the magnifier and searched for it again. '"Carola Losing Her Voice" was *Expressen*'s headline.'

'And *Aftonbladet*'s?'

'"Swedish TV's Order to Jury Can Stop Carola".'

'It must have been before the Melody Festival final.'

'The question is when: Carola's been in the final almost every year.'

'No, far from it. She's actually only been in it four times – five, if you count 2005 when she performed "Through It All".'

'Hello? How could you forget 2006? She went on cortisone because she'd lost her voice during rehearsals.'

Fabian shook his head and wondered who was the bigger fan: him or Malin?

'It wasn't certain whether she could even finish the competition,' Malin continued. 'And then she went on to win it. It's unbelievable, when you think about it. Isn't it?'

Fabian nodded, and leaned back in his chair. 'Spring of 2006 – that means the photos were taken over three-and-a-half years ago.'

'Talk about meticulous planning. Can I take a look?'

Fabian handed one of the photos over to Malin. 'It's not the impression I get of Kremph. Do you?'

'I agree. But if he is extremely methodical, maybe part of his plan is to give a false impression of himself?' said Malin while she studied the picture.

'You mean he's just pretending to be mentally ill?'

Malin shrugged. 'Why not? This kiosk.' She looked up and met Fabian's gaze. 'Isn't this on Mariatorget?'

Fabian took back the photo and looked. 'Yes, you're right. What buses go by there?'

'The 43 for sure. I always took it when Anders and I lived at Tanto—' Malin took hold of her belly again. 'Oh, now they're having a little kickboxing match.' She sat down on her chair and took a few deep breaths. 'By the way, have I ever said how much I hate this?'

'Hmm,' said Fabian without looking up from the magnifying glass.

'There isn't a single part of my body that likes being pregnant.' She turned on her computer and pulled up an SL map on the screen. 'Now let's see: the 43 and 55, plus a number of night buses seem to go by there.'

'And this is definitely Norrmalmstorg,' said Fabian, holding up one of the other photographs.

'In that case it's the 55, because the 43 continues north on Regeringsgatan.'

'Where does the 55 go after that?'

'Stureplan and then out toward Hjorthagen.'

'On a completely different note, have you noticed that the weather is different in several of the pictures?'

'You don't think they were taken on the same day?'

Fabian nodded.

'So she takes the same route every day on her way to work,' Malin continued. 'Is the time of day indicated anywhere?'

'Yes, at Mariatorget it's quarter past five.'

'She must work late, unless she's on her way home.'

'Doesn't the 55 start in Sofia?'

'Yes, and it's almost only apartment buildings in that area. If we assume she lives there and works in the city—'

'Check how long it takes to get from Sofia to Mariatorget by bus.'

'That's just what I'm doing,' said Malin. 'Here it is – twenty-seven minutes to Slussen, which is the next stop.'

'So it starts at quarter to five from Sofia?'

'Well, four forty-seven p.m. to be exact.'

'What time is it now?'

Malin looked at the clock. 'Four thirty-three.'

They exchanged glances and immediately hurried off.

48

HILLEVI STUBBS ALMOST NEVER had any major problems interpreting a crime scene or a perpetrator's residence. Mostly the places spoke for themselves, and usually it took no more than an hour or so before she had worked through what had happened and who was involved.

Ossian Kremph's apartment on Blekingegatan was different.

Yes, it had spoken to her, even if she didn't understand what it was saying. Or maybe she did, in a way at times. But however she tried, she couldn't make it fit together. Each time she had an idea she found something that shot it to the ground, like a bar of soap in the shower that kept slipping out of your hands just as you got hold of it.

Finally, she asked her assistants to leave the apartment and take a coffee break. She had never done that before, and both of them looked as if a UFO had just landed in front of them. But she needed to be alone and let her thoughts operate completely undisturbed. Not until she heard the front door close behind them could she relax and start working for real.

Ever since she had first stepped into the apartment, she felt like there was something that just didn't add up, although she couldn't put her finger on it. The apartment was so overloaded with garbage that it looked like a storage space that had never been emptied, but at the same time it was relatively tidy and pedantically organized in several places. Someone with an enormous need for control lived here, a person who was constantly fighting against the chaos.

For example, the newspapers, where every single eye in the pictures had been carefully cut out, were in neat piles so high that they almost reached the ceiling. The shirts were arranged by colour in the closet, and almost everything that had a label was in alphabetical order, such as the books on the shelf, the spices in the kitchen and the row of pill containers in the bathroom.

Yet there was a layer of chaos over everything. Clothes had been carelessly tossed here and there. There were leftovers and unwashed dishes in the kitchen. And foul-smelling black garbage bags were starting to leak on to the floor. They'd made the majority of finds in this chaos, including a roll of the same type of protective plastic that had lined the table in the condemned apartment; the scalpel that had not even been washed clean among the kitchen knives; and the container of hexane gas that had possibly been used to put Adam Fischer to sleep in his car.

It almost appeared as if he hadn't even tried to conceal his tracks. Or had he simply not anticipated that they would find him this quickly? He had fairly carelessly run right into the arms of Risk and the others, whereas the execution of his crimes was so thoroughly calculated.

Now that she was finally alone she could lie down on the floor, close her eyes and find the key to how this whole thing fitted together.

When she opened her eyes again and looked at the clock, she discovered that she had slept for more than eighteen minutes, which was a much more effective energy kick than all the coffee in the world. She sat up and waited for her blood pressure to normalize, before standing and looking around the apartment. It didn't take long before she realized the obvious explanation for everything.

Ossian Kremph's entire home replicated his schizophrenia: part of him sought structure and order, and another chaos. And so far they had only found the secrets of the careless side. With any luck, she would now discover the stickler's.

It wouldn't be as easy. He had devoted a good deal of thought and energy to identifying places where nobody other than him would think of searching. But they were there somewhere, she had no doubt whatsoever. She started with the most obvious spots, such as behind the books on the shelf, on the underside of the desk, inside the ventilation grate in the bathroom and in the binders behind the pasted-in newspaper clippings. But she didn't find anything, not even in the water tank in the toilet.

It was only once she opened the door to the broom closet that she got her first bite, written in faded red ink on the underside of the loose linoleum mat: *Högdalen Corridor D 6895*. To her own great surprise, she knew immediately what it was because she'd also had one for many years. It had started as a temporary solution following her separation from Gert-Ove, but a few years ago she had reluctantly accepted that it was something she would be forced to pay dearly for every month for the rest of her life. Hers, however, was in Solna not in Högdalen.

She searched the information on her phone and immediately got a hit. It was not only accessible by car and had a large covered unloading area, but also had twenty-four-hour access.

49

IT HADN'T TAKEN DUNJA Hougaard much more than five minutes to navigate her way through the pedestrian and bike tunnels to the Statoil station where she could rent a car. No GPS was available, so she bought a road map of Skåne, some chocolate bars and two bottles of Christmas sweet cider, which she understood was as Swedish as *surströmming*. Sales of Coke dramatically decreased in the country every year around Christmas.

She was fully aware that it was against all the rules to drive there alone and she knew there wasn't much more they could do until Molander got the information from the gas stations. But she couldn't just sit and wait in her hotel room.

Even though Klippan seemed really nice, and his wife no doubt was too, she couldn't spend hours in their company while Willumsen's head start got longer and longer. She was certain she was right and Willumsen had stolen Aksel's car and changed the licence plate. He could be heading anywhere with Katja Skov bound up in his car – if she was even still alive. Besides, she didn't eat lamb. It didn't matter how good everyone said it was, the very smell of it cooking made her sick to her stomach.

She thought about suggesting that she and Klippan drive together, but decided they had far too little to go on for him to sacrifice his Friday night. If he knew what she was doing now, he would never have agreed to let her loose. For that reason, she was now sitting alone behind the wheel, forcing down a few gulps of the sickly-sweet, seriously overrated soft drink as she passed the speed camera right after Teckomatorp on route 17 toward Eslöv – Benny Willumsen's last recorded spot from about quarter to two that day. It was now quarter past six, which meant he was four-and-a-half hours ahead of her. And according to Molander, he had probably turned off somewhere before Marieholm to conceal himself from the cameras.

But she didn't think he stayed on the back roads to avoid speed cameras. He probably wasn't even aware that they could record all traffic in real time and likely would have chosen a completely different route starting in Helsingborg as a result. On the other hand, there was a chance he had business in Kävlinge and would spend the night somewhere in the area.

She turned right on to route 108, the only possible road he could have taken down to Kävlinge. It had already crept down to minus twelve degrees Celsius. She scanned the open landscape on both sides. It was dark and she couldn't see much more than scattered groves of trees and fields so frozen and snow-covered that it was impossible to believe that rape seed would be in full bloom in only six months. She didn't see any houses with their lights on or an abandoned BMW, and there were no roads that appeared to lead to anything worth checking.

The longer she drove in the darkness, the more she realized what a long shot this was. The chance of choosing seven correct lottery numbers was surely considerably greater than the possibility of finding anything of interest. But she had nothing to lose by at least trying.

She came to a roundabout where she turned left on to route 104 towards Kävlinge. She had no idea whether she was in a small village or a bigger town. All she knew with certainty was that if Benny Willumsen really had stopped he would likely be indoors somewhere. Besides, Mikael Rønning hadn't found anything registered to him other than the apartment in Malmö, so he had either borrowed a house from a friend or had broken into an unoccupied summer cottage. Or else...

Dunja stopped the car on the hard shoulder and looked towards the industrial building on the other side of the road. Did something blink in one of the small windows or was it just the reflection from the streetlights? She couldn't be sure. But a large, illuminated banner in the middle of the long wall facing the road indicated there were 780 vacant square metres to rent. Only two of the five spotlights still worked and it looked very worn, so she estimated the space had been abandoned for a long time.

She opted to take a look, and drove further until she could turn left at a tyre shop. A smaller road led her around the back of the building, and she drove into the empty parking lot behind the grey sheet-metal building with its small, grated windows a hundred or so metres apart.

She braked and turned off the engine, her eyes glued to the tyre tracks in the snow in front of her – they led all the way up to the building and then disappeared around the corner.

50

EVEN THOUGH FABIAN AND Malin had run through the corridor, taken the stairs all the way down to the garage instead of waiting for the elevator – which had a habit of not showing up when you most needed it – thrown themselves into Fabian's car and driven from Kungsholmen all the way to Tengdahlsgatan in Sofia in less than fourteen minutes, they had still managed to miss the bus.

'Dammit, he saw us! I'm sure he saw us,' said Malin as she caught her breath and looked at the clock. 'Besides, it's only 4:46. That bastard left early.'

'We'll get it at the next stop,' said Fabian, starting to run after the bus.

'Are you out of your mind? Over my pregnant body,' Malin called after him, a bit too late.

Fabian had already rounded the corner at Tegelviksgatan and was running as fast as he could without slipping in the snow. No one was waiting at the next stop, which compelled him to continue all the way down to Barnängsbryggan by Hammarby Lake where he managed to get on board and hold the bus for Malin, who looked more dead than alive when she finally sank down into one of the seats for the disabled.

'God, I'm worn out.' She unbuttoned her coat. 'I think I just beat the record for the three hundred metres with twins.'

Fabian nodded, even if all his attention was directed towards the other passengers on the bus. There were five of them, and none of them remotely resembled the woman they'd seen in the photographs. Only a few passengers boarded at the stops after the pier along the Hammarby Canal.

However, once they reached Skanstull across from Åhléns so many people poured in through all the doors that it felt as if the bus was being invaded. Fabian and Malin split up so that they didn't miss anything, working their way through the bus before it stopped at South Station and opened the doors. Several of the passengers got off, but a new horde squeezed in, and suddenly it was impossible to move.

Fabian forced his way up to Malin. 'We'll stand at each exit. It's the only way.' But he got no response. Only now did he notice that she was completely pale and her face was sweaty. 'Hey, what's going on? Are you okay?' He tried to make eye contact with her, and she looked at him with a glassy gaze and barely noticeably shook her head.

'Are you sick? Do you have pain somewhere?'

She looked lost in her gaze.

'Malin, can you answer me? Malin? Hello?'

She moved her mouth but no words came out.

Fabian turned towards an elderly woman who was sitting in a seat. 'Excuse me, but could you please stand up so that she can sit down?'

The woman, who was dressed in beige sports clothing and wearing hiking shoes, looked at him as if that was one of the stupidest things she'd ever heard. 'Listen, I'm actually seventy years old, and I've worked my whole—'

'Yes, and she's very pregnant,' Fabian interrupted. An ornery retiree was the last thing he had patience for right now. 'So stand up now, dammit.'

The woman snorted and looked away.

'Get up, I said.' Fabian took hold of the woman's arm to pull her up.

'Wait, you can have my place instead,' said the woman in the seat ahead of them, who was wearing a flowery red shawl over her coat. She stood up and squeezed out into the aisle.

Fabian thanked her and helped Malin sit down.

'You ought to be ashamed,' the older woman hissed behind them.

Fabian ignored her and directed his attention to Malin. 'Just take it easy now and breathe.' He took off her scarf and set it on her lap.

'This country is going downhill because of people like you,' the woman behind them continued as they passed Mariatorget and continued toward Slussen and Old Town, where she got off along with several other passengers.

'Finally,' said Malin, shaking her head. 'What a fucking bitch.'

Fabian nodded and, to his great relief, he could see she was starting to recover some of the colour in her face.

'I wish I could see to it that she has to take paratransit services for the rest of her life.'

Fabian laughed, but was struck by the fact that there was something familiar about the woman who had given up her seat. Maybe she had a new haircut, or was wearing different clothing because it was winter. He turned around, but couldn't see her anywhere.

'What is it? Did you find her?' said Malin.

Fabian shrugged and took out one of Ossian Kremph's pictures from the bus where the woman was seen more or less clearly. Then he realized what it was he had noticed.

The hexagram.

The flowery shawl had been attached to the coat with a brooch of the exact same hexagram she had worn around her neck in several of the pictures. It couldn't be anyone else.

'I think it's the woman with the flowery shawl,' he said, looking around for her.

The bus stopped at Kungsträdgården, where several of the passengers got off and new ones poured in.

'There is a technical problem on the bus ahead of us, which has been taken out of service. It's going to be more crowded as a result. We apologize and thank you for your patience,' the bus driver informed them.

Fabian forced his way towards the doors in the middle of the bus as quickly as he could, but didn't get there before they closed and the bus drove on. It was impossible to tell whether the woman had got off or was still on the bus. It was so full again that he couldn't see anyone other than those standing right next to him, and forcing his way ahead risked triggering the scuffle that he could feel brewing.

Someone started to complain about standing and waiting for an eternity; another chimed in that this wasn't the first time. But at Norrmalmstorg the pressure alleviated enough so that Fabian could move again.

Then he caught sight of her – right after the bus had stopped at a red light. She had taken off the flowery shawl and was standing by the rear door.

Without warning she turned around and looked at him. He didn't know what he should do. If he averted his gaze too quickly it would seem suspicious, but it would be just as suspicious if he kept on looking right at her. Instead, he tried to look past her, while he took out his phone and called Malin.

'Have you found her?'

'She's standing at the exit in the back.'

'God, it's nice to know that he didn't get her.'

Malin was right, of course. He had been preoccupied with wondering why Kremph had been interested in her at all, and what she had in common with Adam Fischer and Carl-Eric Grimås.

The bus stopped at Stureplan. The doors opened and the woman got off.

'We have to get off. She's left the bus.' Fabian jumped down on the sidewalk and watched the woman, who was walking quickly towards the mushroom-shaped concrete rain shelter. 'Malin, where are you? We can't lose her.'

'Take it easy, I'm on my way,' said Malin, joining Fabian. 'God, I'm completely wiped out.'

Fabian nodded, his eyes directed toward the Mushroom where the woman was now standing with another woman. Judging by their body language, they were discussing something that upset them both. She turned around and once again met his gaze. Immediately after that the other woman looked at him too.

'I think she's figured out that we're following her. Come on, let's go and talk to them.' He made an effort to leave.

'Wait,' said Malin. 'To be honest I don't know if I can handle any more right now.'

'Are you okay?' He turned towards her. 'Can I help you—'

'No, it's fine. I think I'll just take a taxi home and lie down on the couch for a bit.'

'You sure?'

'Yes, I'm just a little... pregnant. Forget about me now and get to work.' She hailed a taxi, which pulled over and stopped.

Fabian nodded and watched her walk to the taxi. Then he turned back to the Mushroom, only to discover that the two women were gone.

He ran over to assure himself that they weren't hidden behind the central pillar. Then he climbed up on the wave-shaped wall that faced Birger Jarlsgatan and looked across the square. They were nowhere to be seen.

His phone started ringing. It was Hillevi Stubbs. 'Listen, can I call you back? I'm in the middle of something,' he said as he jumped down from the wall and jogged towards the entrance of the Sture Galleria.

'Of course you can. But just so you know I'm not going to answer,' said Stubbs, emphasizing what a bad idea she thought that was.

'Okay, what's this about?' Fabian stopped with a sigh.

'I don't have time to explain now. It's better if we meet there.'

'And where's "there"?' He couldn't help but be irritated by Stubbs' insistence on keeping him on tenterhooks.

'I found something in Ossian Kremph's broom closet. The passcode to a storage unit in Shurgard out in Högdalen.'

51

THE BUILDING WAS ONLY one storey tall and almost 800 square metres. It looked like it had been hastily constructed with no consideration whatsoever for the surroundings. But why would that bother Benny Willumsen? It was considerably more important to him that the parking lot was behind the building and the view from the road as good as non-existent, which made it the perfect refuge for anyone who wanted to be left alone.

Dunja Hougaard grabbed her bag from the passenger seat and took out her service pistol. She put in a magazine, well aware that she was outside the borders of Denmark, but there was no chance she would leave the car and follow the tyre tracks in the snow up to the building unarmed.

Winter was having a hard time deciding if it should melt the snow or freeze it to ice, which made it impossible to see whether the tracks came from Aksel Neuman's BMW. All she could say for sure was that they had driven only in one direction. She continued around the building, where the tracks continued for a few more metres until they disappeared into the building under a lowered garage door.

There were no windows to look in through and no handle or knob to open either. Then she heard a sound, a dull rumble that was difficult to locate, as if a truck was idling somewhere nearby. She pressed her ear against the garage door; it was coming from inside the building.

Nonetheless she didn't give contacting Klippan a second thought. Car tracks outside a vacant industrial building in the middle of nowhere and a rumbling sound that could have come from a ventilation system simply weren't enough to interrupt his Friday night. She would need considerably more proof before she could call for back-up.

She made her way to the back of the building again and found a door. It was locked. She went over to the window alongside, turned on her small flashlight and looked in. The only things visible behind the drawn curtains were some office furniture and a number of removal boxes. The window had also been equipped with both a protective grate and burglar alarm, even if it was almost certainly non-functional.

She tried walking around the building from the other direction and continued to the front, which faced the road some twenty metres away. The snow was deep and when she tramped through the frozen crust she sank down several inches.

The little window where she'd seen the light blinking was too high for her to look in, but the upper part of a fire escape was hanging down from the gutter at the far end of the building. Normally it would be impossible to reach without a fire ladder, ensuring that people couldn't climb up and get on to the roof.

Normally.

The wind had created a high wall of snow right under the fire escape, so Dunja simply had to make her way up on all fours as carefully as possible so that she didn't sink down through the crust. Once she was on top she managed to get hold of the lowest part of the fire escape. She tried to heave herself up, but had far too little muscle strength to get the whole way.

It wasn't the first time she'd promised herself to start working out seriously. She'd bought exercise clothes and an annual gym pass, and used it twice, maybe three times. But this year she would keep her New Year's resolution – it would be her top priority.

She tried to twirl around so that she could hang upside down, like a child on a jungle gym, and finally she was able to get her feet up so that her knees were resting on the bottom rung. After that it was simply a matter of crouching up and taking hold of the next rung.

Once she was on the roof she was damp with sweat, even though the icy cold was cutting straight to her bones. Friends and acquaintances who had vacationed on the Scanian plains told her that the westerly onshore wind was both colder and harder than the offshore wind on the Danish side. But this was the first time she'd experienced it for herself, and if she didn't get into a warm place soon, she risked freezing solid and cracking into thousands of pieces.

She made her way along the horizontal ladder on all fours towards the roof ridge, which ended after a few metres. She pushed away the snow, revealing a skylight. A few well-aimed kicks later and she'd made a hole big enough to fit through.

But it was so dark it was impossible to see what was in the room below her when she let go.

52

SOFIE LEANDER HAD GIVEN up trying to figure out what was happening. For a while she'd thought she understood. She'd thought that everything that had happened to her was somehow logical, and a reasonable consequence of her actions. But when she woke up and realized that she was still being kept alive, uncertainty had returned and gained the upper hand. And, contrary to human nature, she was neither relieved nor reassured. She had long since given up hope that this was something she could survive.

Then, a few minutes ago, she had heard a big gate opening somewhere in the building. It wasn't the first time she'd heard the characteristic creaking that cut through the thin metal walls – her heart rate always increased and she tried to summon the person's attention any way she could. But each time they continued about their business, and slowly but surely she paid less and less attention to the sound.

This time wasn't like all the others, even if she could hear that same penetrating creak. It was the other sounds she heard that gave her hope again: not one but several cars driving in and braking so that the tyres screeched against the surface; car doors opening and slamming shut; loud voices echoing in the space; and the beeping and static of walkie-talkies.

It couldn't be anyone other than the police.

Finally, they'd managed to find her. She wasn't forgotten after all. She'd never really believed that anyway, but only now did it occur to her that there were people working specifically on her case and maybe even working in shifts to find her. And if she knew her husband, he hadn't given them a quiet moment until they started making progress.

Once again, she imagined her face on every billboard and how her mysterious disappearance must have been the major topic of conversation around every water cooler all over Sweden. Maybe at this very moment reporters were crowding around outside, just waiting to rush in and interview her as she was rolled out towards the waiting ambulance.

She let her thoughts run wild, even though she was fully aware that these were nothing but idle speculations. She really had no idea how much interest there was in her case, or whether the police had even chosen to report on their progress. It was actually more likely that they were keeping a low profile to keep the doctor in the dark about how close they were to locating the building.

The only thing she knew for certain was that they were right outside, preparing to come in at any moment to rescue her. She heard hard, heavy cases being set down on the ground and opened, and tools being taken out and plugged in. Everything filled her with such warmth and energy that it no longer mattered that she didn't understand why this had all transpired in the first place. Whatever the reason, the police got there first.

She hoped that her husband would be there, too, ready to receive her. After all, he was the person who'd contacted the police. So, in a way, he'd rescued her – again. Her heart started beating faster as soon as he came into her thoughts.

She already knew that she loved him, but this could mean nothing other than that he still loved her. She had doubted it, she really had, but now she knew for sure.

An angle grinder started up right outside, and the sharp, malevolent sound was like music to her ears.

She had probably never been this happy.

53

THE BLINKING BLUE LIGHTS were obvious from far away in the darkness and made the GPS instructions superfluous. They're asking for attention, thought Fabian, as he turned off Huddingevägen and continued south on Magelungsvägen. He couldn't understand why so many police kept their blue lights on after they'd parked their cars.

He tried to call home again, but neither Matilda nor Theodor answered this time either. Theodor probably wasn't home yet because it was only twenty to seven. Matilda, on the other hand, was probably upset, which he completely understood. He had promised to come home with Friday treats before the babysitter had to leave, but now found himself well south of the city. He wanted to put on the brakes, make a U-turn and drive home, but it wasn't possible. Not after his conversation with Stubbs.

He turned into the parking lot outside Shurgard and stopped by the ambulance and police cars. Some of the uniformed police officers were starting to cordon off the area outside the entrance and others directed him to park next to Aziza Thåström, his favourite medical examiner.

She'd come to Sweden as a teenage refugee. Only a year or two later she spoke nearly fluent Swedish and had married her teacher. Now, at the age of thirty-five, she was without a doubt one of Stockholm's best, most sought-after medical examiners. Whatever Stubbs had found, Edelman had given it the highest priority.

'There you are.' One of Hillevi Stubbs' assistants came up to meet him. 'We were almost starting to get worried.'

'Worried? Stubbs called me half an hour ago,' said Fabian, following past the response team that was packing up.

'It's not your style to be last to the ball. And you know how the Stub can get when she's found something.'

Fabian knew exactly what mood the assistant was highlighting. Hillevi Stubbs was one of the most impatient people he knew. Once she'd discovered a lead and made a decision on how to proceed, nothing could move quickly enough. 'What's she got?'

'You should probably see it with your own eyes.' The assistant held up the barricade tape and showed Fabian in through the open garage doors.

Stubbs was standing by her van a little inside the building, dressed in blue protective overalls with the hood pulled down and going through the pictures on her camera. 'You're late,' she said without raising her eyes from the camera screen.

'What have you found?'

'Put these on.' She took a pair of folded-up protective overalls from a crate and threw them over to Fabian, who pulled them on as quickly as he could, before they went in.

The storage room was about forty metres ahead of them. A bright light flooded out through the sawed-out opening in the louvre door and extended a good way out on to the concrete floor outside. Stubbs disappeared into the room and Fabian followed her. The air inside was several degrees warmer because of the strong searchlights. Once his eyes adjusted to the light, he realized that the storage room was bigger than he'd expected, almost thirty square metres and probably one of the largest in the facility. But Thåström and Stubbs covered most of his field of vision: he couldn't see much more than a pair of bare feet at one end of a plastic-covered table that looked like the one in the condemned apartment. There were a number of different devices and gauges with cords and hoses that coiled like snakes on the floor and under the table.

Only once he went around his colleagues and stood on the other side of the table was he able to completely see the naked body that was tied down to the table with a number of straps, pulled through drilled-out holes in the tabletop. The legs, torso, arms and throat were all so tightly lashed that several of the straps scraped off skin and penetrated into the flesh. And just like the Minister for Justice, there were two empty, bloody holes where the eyes should have been. Fabian noted some kind of dried pink porridge-like substance had bubbled out of the taped-up mouth, down across the throat and on to the floor.

'What's that?' Fabian pointed towards the pink sludge.

'Food,' said Stubbs. 'As you can see, he's been tube-fed through this hose.' She pointed at a tube that disappeared into his mouth. 'I haven't taken any samples yet, but my guess is it contains some laxatives to cleanse the body of various toxins and waste products. This is not unusual in cannibalism.'

'So he was being kept alive. For how long, do you think? When did he die?' Fabian couldn't help thinking about how much pain Adam Fischer must have gone through before he finally passed away.

'I'll need to examine the body more thoroughly to give you an exact answer,' said Thåström. 'But if I was to make a rough estimate, I would say he died about three days ago.'

So he'd been lying here, strapped down, for more than a week, hovering in total ignorance of what was to come, wondering if the police would find him in time – or if they were even searching. Fabian speculated how long he would have faith in a similar situation and how long it would take before he started hoping for death instead.

'I guess that he died in connection with this incision.' Thåström pointed towards the left part of his chest where there was a large, carved-out hole, just like Carl-Eric Grimås' abdomen. It was round and a few inches in size, and looked as if an enormous printing press had punched out part of his body.

'Why the heart?' Fabian turned towards Stubbs and Thåström.

'I guess he had to start somewhere,' said Stubbs, shrugging.

'Was there a heart in the freezer in the condemned apartment, where we found Grimås' inner organs?'

'No.' Stubbs shook her head. 'And it wasn't in the freezer in his own apartment for that matter.'

'Maybe he'd already eaten it,' said Thåström.

'It's possible,' said Stubbs. 'But there's nothing that suggests that here, in his apartment or in the condemned apartment.'

The silence removed even more oxygen from the already warm, stuffy room. Fabian couldn't bear to stay much longer, but somewhere deep down in the confusion of his subconscious, a thought had started to take shape: a thought so small and fragile that it risked disappearing for ever if he released it.

First Grimås' organs and now Fischer's heart: maybe it wasn't even about the eyes – they had already found those in the glass jar, but the heart, on the other hand, was missing. The question was whether it was in the freezer of the condemned apartment. He couldn't quite figure out the connection just yet.

'Those inner organs from the condemned apartment,' Fabian said in an attempt to make it sound like an off-the-cuff comment. 'Have you had time to examine them?'

'I had just thawed them and was getting started when this came up,' said Thåström. 'Is there something in particular you're wondering about?'

'I think we can be pretty certain that they come from Grimås,' said Stubbs.

'It's not that. I just want to know if he is missing anything else.'

54

DUNJA COULDN'T FEEL ANY immediate pain, but she didn't know whether that was bad or good. The best thing to do was to stay as still as possible and wait for help. But she couldn't help wondering if she should try to move, well aware of how common it was to be more injured than you think after an accident.

If she could even move.

The light from the street lamps above her streamed down through the broken skylight along with the sound from the occasional car. She estimated that she fell about four or five metres, and recognized that the outcome might have been quite different had it not been for all the empty boxes from stereo equipment that were in a large pile on the floor.

She carefully turned on to her stomach and pushed herself up on all fours on the cardboard. So far she couldn't feel much more than a pulsing soreness in her body. It wasn't until she had moved on to the floor and tried to stand up that the pain in her left foot became so great that she was forced to breathe very quickly so as not to scream out loud. She had presumably sprained it and she could feel it starting to swell.

As soon as the pain subsided a bit, she took out her phone to see if she had service and noticed that it had a serious crack in the screen. She'd just had it replaced after dropping it on the bathroom floor at home. It had still been possible to use, even if she'd cut her fingertips several times, but now it didn't matter how many times she pressed the power button and tried to start it, it still wouldn't work.

She gave up and tried disconnecting an extension tube from a vacuum cleaner, so that she could use it as a crutch to make her way to the flashlight that was glowing weakly on the floor. She turned off the light and stuffed it into her jeans' pocket. Then she heard the rumbling sound again. She stopped and listened. It seemed to be mixed with an angry howling now. She turned around completely, but couldn't identify the source or location of the noise in the building. Then it stopped.

She limped out into the increasingly dark corridor. Soon she was forced to grope her way along the wall in front of her with her free hand. Twice she bumped into framed posters, and after another few metres, a large hole opened up in the wall. She stopped and used her hand to feel along the edge. It was a doorway.

She stepped in using the vacuum cleaner tube as a support, taking deep breaths in and out. She tried to think about something other than the intense pain in her foot, which was now so swollen that she would never be able to get her boot off. The sound had stopped, and there was dead silence apart from her own breath.

She kept walking in the darkness with her one hand holding tightly on to the vacuum cleaner extension and the other stretched in front of her. After about ten metres she reached a wall covered in a soft, sound-absorbent material. The wall ended a few metres on the left, and she continued around a corner over to the other side of the room, where she could finally see something. A faint light ahead gave the impression of an open door.

Then she heard the sound again. This time it sounded like a distant tractor engine that roared and rumbled on idle. But why would anyone be driving a tractor around indoors? It was only once the furious, howling began again that she realized this wasn't the first time she'd heard something like this. It was a familiar part of her visit to her grandparent's car repair shop.

Her grandfather had told her it was called a tiger saw, explaining that the teeth of the saw were like a tiger's and could bite through basically anything.

She took out her pistol, chambered a round, and hurried as quickly as she could towards the sound, despite the searing pain in her foot. On the way, she stumbled over a microphone stand, but was quickly on her feet again. Then she saw it.

Aksel Neuman's BMW.

Benny Willumsen was here, just as she'd suspected all along.

The hatch was open and there were some tied-up garbage bags in the baggage compartment on rolled-out protective plastic that hung over the edge like a tail. A gas-powered electrical generator was rumbling close to the car and an electric cable disappeared along the floor. She followed it with her pistol in one hand and the vacuum cleaner extension in the other, moving closer to the sound that brought forth images she didn't want to see.

The cable disappeared through a crack in the door, which Dunja realized was the source of the faint light. She pressed her ear against the wall. The roaring sound was intermittently working its way down into something so close that she instinctively recoiled.

Thoughts about what she should do and what was waiting on the other side of the door rushed through her mind like an aggressive spring flood. But her body had a mind of its own and she started running her hand across the door. She couldn't find a handle so she stuck her fingers into the crack and pulled on it.

She should have closed her eyes. She should have turned around and run away. But it was too late. What she saw would be etched in her memory fore ver.

He stood with his back to her in the middle of the vacated sound studio, glowing in the light from the single bulb hanging down from the ceiling. At last, the man who had got away with raping and torturing a series of innocent women to death.

He had earplugs in and was wearing a gas mask that was pulled back on his head, as if he were staring at her. He looked smaller than she'd imagined, and on top of his heavy, dark clothing he was wearing a transparent plastic apron that took the worst of the blood spray.

He was holding the tiger saw in both hands. The sound cut through the air as the toothed-saw blade worked its way through the groin of the naked body on the plastic-covered table. Dunja wanted to scream as loud as she could to make him stop – and make it go away – but all she could do was stare.

At the groin that opened up as the saw penetrated deeper.

At the neck, where there should have been a head.

At the leg that fell to the floor with a thud.

At the blood that sprayed.

At her.

At Katja Skov.

Everywhere.

55

ON THE WAY HOME from the Shurgard storage facility in Högdalen, Fabian stopped at a McDonald's on Folkungagatan and bought a McFeast with mineral water for himself, a Big Mac with a Coke for Theodor and a Happy Meal for Matilda. Even though he was so tired that his whole body ached and he couldn't shake the image of Adam Fischer's mutilated body, he intended to keep his promise to Matilda about Friday treats. He also hurried by the 7-Eleven store on the corner of Ölandsgatan and bought a big bottle of Christmas cider, rustic potato chips with garlic dip and a tub of Ben & Jerry's Cookie Dough ice cream.

It was already nine when he stuck the key in the door twenty minutes later, which meant that the kids had been alone for two and a half hours. It wasn't ideal, but not a catastrophe either. Besides, he could hear a Christmas special on the TV, so it clearly wasn't that bad.

He hung up his coat, went into the kitchen and set the hamburgers on real plates, before putting the ice cream in the freezer. He noticed that every lamp in the apartment was on. 'Matilda! Theodor! I'm home. Now we can eat,' he called without getting an answer. He walked into the living room where a Coca-Cola commercial was streaming out of the TV in a desperate attempt to compete against Christmas cider. He went around the sofa and saw Matilda lying all alone, sleeping with her red teddy bear close beside her.

He couldn't remember the last time he'd cried. He might have shed a few tears when he saw a sad movie like *Steel Magnolias*, but otherwise he almost never wept. It wasn't that he didn't want to – sometimes he really tried to let his feelings come loose, but it usually amounted to little more than a lump in his throat.

He was quite unprepared for the tears that suddenly started dripping from his eyes on to the floor. Matilda lying alone in a foetal position on the couch with her teddy bear was one of the most beautiful things he'd ever seen – and also the saddest. He dried his face with the back of one hand and pinched his eyes shut, but the tears continued to flow and he realized that his whole body was shaking.

It couldn't go on like this with his job, which consumed everything in its path, and Sonja, who was more or less living in the studio. They needed to talk. He just didn't know what he should say or if he even wanted it to work out any more.

He called for Theodor, but didn't expect an answer. It wasn't much past nine, but he was only thirteen and shouldn't be running around town all night, or whatever he was doing. He tried phoning him, but it went to the voicemail message where Theodor tried to pretend that he answered before the beep. Instead he sent a text message asking his son to come home as soon as possible. Then he turned off the TV, took a few deep breaths, then sat down on the couch with Matilda and tried to wake her. But even though he enticed her with McDonald's, chips and ice cream she didn't want to get up.

He finally gave up and carried her to her room, where he tucked her in under the blanket, kissed her on the forehead and whispered an apology in her ear. Then he sat down in the kitchen to eat the cold, tasteless hamburger while he wondered whether he should call Sonja.

He decided to wait and threw away the sad leftovers. He walked around turning off all the lights while brushing his teeth, then went to bed. His body was pounding with fatigue and it felt like he hadn't slept for a whole week. He adjusted the pillows, lay down and let gravity lower his eyelids. But he couldn't fall asleep.

Instead, the events of the past few days replayed over and over in his mind. He couldn't stop wondering what the woman from the bus had been talking so enthusiastically about with the other woman under the Mushroom at Stureplan, and what connection she might have with Grimås' organs and Fischer's missing heart – if there even was a connection.

An hour or two later, he gave up and went over to Matilda's room, picked her up along with her teddy bear and carried her over to his own bed, where he could hold her in his arms, feel her warmth and hear her calm, deep breaths.

He managed to count three of them.

56

THE CHURCH BELL STARTED to reverberate over Katarina cemetery and the surrounding blocks, sounding all the way down Östgötagatan, southwards and past Fabian, who was locking his car in front of a charming design office that highlighted its many framed distinctions on the inside wall.

It was Saturday, and even though it was only three o'clock in the afternoon, it was starting to get dark. At ten o'clock that morning Malin had called him and explained that she'd managed to convince the therapist to grant Ossian Kremph a crime-scene visit. Five hours later, all the papers and permits had been signed, which was fairly quick, considering how many people had to sign off on it.

But for Fabian it had felt like an eternity. The ten straight hours of sleep had done him good. The fleeting thought that had emerged in the Shurgard storage space had developed overnight into a concrete theory. He was on the trail of something, and hopefully Kremph's crime-scene visit would indicate if he was on the right path.

He still hadn't said anything to the others, not even Malin, which was unusual. A good theory wasn't enough to get them involved at this point. There couldn't be any doubt – the consequences were much too great if it turned out he was wrong.

He hadn't been completely idle at home, however. While waiting for the green light he'd had time to play a game of Monopoly with Matilda and Theodor. He'd contacted Aziza Thåström and managed to convince her to interrupt her Christmas preparations to resume the examination of Grimås' inner organs. And, just as he'd suspected, one of the organs was missing: the liver.

Maybe Ossian Kremph had prepared and eaten his liver. In most species, the organ was a delicacy. Together with Fischer's missing heart, he might have made a real feast. Unless there was something other than hunger behind the murders, something that would put the whole investigation in a new light and make everyone realize that it was a long way from being over.

He waved to Malin, who had turned the corner on to Blekingegatan and was desperately looking for an empty parking space. Tomas and Jarmo came walking from Katarina Bangata, each carrying a pitta wrap, and the riot squad's bus was already parked in front of the container outside the entrance.

They had certainly not skimped on security. The force was made up of six men, all armed with automatic weapons, bulletproof vests and helmets with lowered visors. Two of the men stood on either side of the bus and scanned the area, before another two quickly disappeared into the condemned building on Östgötagatan.

They would have preferred to take him to the Shurgard facility in Högdalen where they had recently found Adam Fischer, but Stubbs was still working in full swing, and the nap room in the parliament building would have drawn too much attention. That left the condemned building – still a well-kept secret from the general public. They hadn't been able to find traces of any dismemberment there yet, but they had no doubt that the plastic-covered table was set up with only that in mind.

Now it was time to hear from Ossian Kremph, who was helped out of the bus by the last two riot police. Both his hands and feet were shackled, like a prisoner condemned to death. Kremph's head was lowered and the half-metre-long chain from the shackles scraped against the icy asphalt as he was led past the container and under the scaffolding.

'God, I don't understand how you cope with living in the city,' said Malin, stopping to catch her breath. 'I had to search all the way up to All Saints Church before I found a—' She was interrupted by a shrill whistle; Tomas was waving for them to come over.

OSSIAN KREMPH WAS LED into the room with the bright lamp over the plastic-covered table. His gaze was still lowered and he limped on his injured leg. After a few metres the two police escorts released him and stood on either side of the doorway.

Kremph looked curiously around as if he'd never been there before. He wouldn't look at Fabian, who was standing by the far wall, or Tomas, who was squeezed into the corner right behind him, filming everything. But when he caught sight of Jarmo, who was strapped down on the table as the victim wearing only underwear, his eyes were transformed and he started shaking his head while he backed out towards the hall.

They had two hours with him. If you subtracted the time for transport and security preparations, there wasn't much more than an hour left. It wasn't much time to put someone in the right mood so that their most repressed, shameful memories would come to the surface.

Edelman had managed to ward off the therapist's demands to be involved, so at least they had Kremph to themselves.

'Hi, Ossian.' Malin stopped him. 'Do you recognize me?'

Kremph shook his head, without taking his eyes off Jarmo's body.

'You've been here before, right?'

He shook his head again. 'I don't like this at all. Can we go back now?'

'Not quite yet. Soon. First we're going to look and then talk a little. Can you come with me?' She tried to coax him towards the table.

'I don't want to – not here. Now let's go.'

'Ossian, this is completely safe. All you have to do is look around and see if you remember something that you've forgotten. After that we can go back, okay?' She extended one hand to him.

Only after looking back and forth for over a minute between Malin's outstretched hand, the porcelain doll on the bookshelf and Jarmo on the plastic-covered table did Kremph finally go along with her. Fabian noted that his breathing was getting more and more jerky with every step he took towards the table. And by the time they were close to Jarmo, who was lying completely still, Kremph appeared to be on the verge of a breakdown.

'Is this how you strap down your victims?' said Malin, pointing at one of the straps that was holding Jarmo's neck down on the tabletop.

'Not me,' said Kremph as his eyes wandered over Jarmo's body. 'I only want to listen to the radio.'

'Perhaps it's the other Ossian?'

Kremph shook his head. 'The sea report is really good.'

'Ossian, now I want you to listen to me. We know you did it. We have a lot of technical evidence against you. Now we're just trying to understand *how* it happened. Did you pluck out the eyes before or after you started cutting?'

'Not me, I'm telling you! I haven't done anything!' He started to violently shake his head.

'I can understand this may be difficult, but try to take it—'

'I've always done the same thing, and there was never a problem. I know that. No one ever complained.'

'What do you mean? They could protest while they're tied down and being slashed?'

'And the sea report, always the sea report,' Kremph said without taking his eyes off Jarmo. 'Every morning. It's the only thing, just the sea report and Sudoku. But I don't have a radio at the hospital. I don't know why, but I don't. They say I can't have one,' he continued, more and more manically. 'Why can't I have one? Answer me! Why aren't you answering?'

Malin turned towards Fabian, who signalled to her to continue, even though he could see that she didn't want to. She really hadn't wanted to lead the interrogation, but it had been one of the therapist's stipulations.

'Why?' Kremph continued.

'Ossian, I honestly don't know why you can't have a radio. But now I want you to tell us in detail how—'

'How can I listen to the sea report then? I have to, because I do it every morning.'

'Ossian, instead can you tell us how you—'

'And the medications. I have to take them, too. I do it every day: morning, noon and night. They're in the red tin. They're always in the red tin in the medicine cabinet, so I won't forget, especially two o'clock. That's when... There's always so much going on then, and time... it just disappears, and suddenly I've forgotten, although of course I don't know it right then.' He started scratching his neck with both hands.

'No, of course not.'

'But that's not good at all. It's very bad. It doesn't work, then everything goes wrong.' He was speaking faster and faster with the saliva running out of his mouth. 'Everything has to be right, and if it's not everything starts twirling round and round, and I get so tired. All of a sudden he's there, the weird guy, although I'm the only one of course.' He swallowed and continued scratching until a scab loosened and blood started running down his neck. 'He has the keys and he's there anyway. He fixes and helps out. He doesn't think I know, but I do, and then everything gets so dark and heavy, and then it's like I just go away.'

'Ossian, try to take it easy and concentrate on the body that's lying here.'

'I lock up every day and I've even replaced the bolts. Lock,

lock and then I check whether it's locked – always. Otherwise you can't be completely sure.'

'Ossian?'

'I can't stand it. It's so awful. Really awful.' He held his head in his hand and caught his breath. 'I'm so tired, so tired. I can't take any more now.'

'Ossian, we don't have much time left. Try to—'

'Have to rest and just close my eyes a little, but it's not possible. As soon as I close my eyes I'm there again, back to…' He trailed off and collapsed, out of breath and drained of energy.

'Back to what? Ossian, tell us what it is you come back to.'

Without any warning at all, Kremph started screaming and threw himself right at Malin, who lost her balance and fell to the floor. She yelled to the others while she tried to kick and claw her way out of his grip.

Fabian, Tomas and the two riot officers were already on their way over, but the seconds dragged on and Kremph calmly lowered his head toward her throat and hissed something into her ear before he was torn off her and dragged into the adjoining room.

Fabian helped Malin up. 'Are you okay?'

Malin nodded and started straightening her hair. 'But that really scared me. I thought he would…' She fell silent to catch her breath. 'That he was about to…' She broke down and started crying. Fabian hugged her and let her rest her head on his shoulder.

'There, there, Malin. It's over now.'

Malin nodded and tried to calm down.

'He said something to you, didn't he?' asked Fabian.

Malin pulled out of his arms and looked him in the eye. 'He asked when he was going to get his radio back.' She broke into a smile and laughed. 'Isn't that just sick. After all of this, the only thing he can think about is his radio with the sea report. Oh, God. How do I look right now? Has the make-up run completely?'

'You're fine.'

'I'm going down to the station with this now,' said Tomas, holding up the video camera. 'It doesn't look like much more is going to happen here.'

'Perhaps someone can be so kind as to undo me,' said Jarmo.

'You seem to be comfortable where you are, if you ask me,' said Tomas, disappearing with the camera.

'Fabian, how many years have we worked together?' Malin opened a compact mirror and looked at herself.

Fabian shrugged. 'Five or six years?'

'Seven-and-a-half. For seven-and-a-half years we've spent more time with each other than with our significant others.' She took out a tissue and dried her eyes. 'And this is the first time you've ever given me a hug.'

'And let's hope it never happens again.'

Malin laughed and took out a mascara wand to freshen up, but immediately dropped them both and fell down on the floor.

'Malin! Malin!' Fabian quickly dropped to his knees and tried to wake her. 'Malin, do you hear me?' But he got no reaction.

'What the hell's going on?' asked Jarmo.

'I don't know. She just fell all of a sudden—' He stopped when he saw a pool of blood spreading out on the floor below her. 'Hello! Can someone call an ambulance?!'

Two police officers came hurrying in from the adjacent room.

'What the hell are you waiting for? Call, dammit! She's about to have a miscarriage! And Anders – we have to call Anders, her husband.' Fabian fumbled for his phone and tried to keep his fingers steady enough to enter her home number.

'The ambulance is on its way,' said one of the riot officers.

'Good,' said Fabian while he listened to the ringing phone. 'Answer already.'

'Hello, you've reached the Rehnberg family. We can't come to the phone right now, but please leave a message after the beep.'

'Hello, this is Fabian Risk. Anders, call me as soon as—' He was interrupted by a loud sound that he couldn't initially interpret, even though it was loud and clear. His brain was already so overloaded that it couldn't put together the sound of breaking glass with any real event. He wanted to continue describing what had happened to the answering machine, but he couldn't even do that, and soon he was up on his feet and on his way into the other room.

It was empty. He walked towards the broken window, followed by two riot officers arguing about who'd had responsibility for Kremph. A real snowstorm had started brewing outside and snowflakes were already whirling in the room.

He'd had a gut feeling the past few days, but his brain needed to catch up with him. Now he knew for sure.

Ossian Kremph was innocent.

PART II

19–24 December 2009

My love for you makes me move mountains. It makes me do the impossible, and the most awful, but absolutely necessary. And a little more.

After you disappeared from the barracks that day, I tried to sustain myself with the idea of you. I listened to Etta James and I touched my palm to the fence and imagined your blue eyes. But it was not enough. I had to find you. I left the barracks at night and left the camp through the hole in the fence. I could only hope that God would be there and show me the way. I'd seen the white cloth sticking out from under your coat and thought that maybe you worked as a nurse at the hospital in Urik a few kilometres away.

I didn't make it further than the alleys when loud sirens started howling and voices shouted through megaphones to wake everyone up. I knew about our nocturnal stress raids, but I'd never experienced one myself. Not until then.

They thought I was one of you, so I ran as fast as I could in no particular direction. They were driving around humiliating people and setting examples. Then the world exploded. The windows above rained down over me and my ears rang. I got lost in the white cloud that stung my eyes and kept getting bigger and bigger.

I should have given up right there and accepted that it would never work, but I couldn't let go of even just the possibility of seeing you and the hope that we would never be separated again. I kept running, but stumbled and fell headlong.

My eyes stung as if someone had stuck them with needles. I tried to get up, but it was hopeless. They were coming closer and closer in the corrosive fog. I recognized their voices. Their laughter in their gas masks seemed to foreshadow the fun that would soon begin.

I tried to resist, but didn't have the strength. I let them take hold of my arms and drag me across the asphalt.

So tired now... Must rest a little... Just a little... Don't know how much more I'll be able to write, but so much left to say. So little strength...

57

SHARDS OF GLASS WERE still stuck in his hands and forearms, revealing that Ossian Kremph had used his handcuffs to break the windowpane. He had then wriggled his way through the hole in the glass and jumped off the scaffolding. The fall was from a height of about fifteen metres – a certain death if it hadn't been for the container below filled with heavy waste.

But Kremph died immediately anyway. His head struck the edge of the container so hard that everything above the root of his nose spattered in a radius of several metres.

It was not the most satisfactory conclusion to such a complex investigation, argued Edelman, even if he quickly added that it was a conclusion nonetheless. For Fabian, Ossian Kremph's death meant anything but closure. There were still too many unanswered questions.

On the surface, the investigation had always seemed to be moving forward: new discoveries had been made, pictures were taken and notes written. Clues were discovered, labelled, put in bags and categorized. Everyone had worked double shifts and went through every possibility. Eventually connections had been made and judgements reached.

It all fitted together perfectly. Ossian Kremph, with his dissociative identity disorder and previous convictions, was almost the ideal perpetrator. The victims' eyes had been removed – his signature – and he also had a motive for revenge against Carl-Eric Grimås, who had been in charge of the investigation that had convicted him all those years ago. The fact that Kremph had memory gaps and refused to talk about the crimes didn't help either.

While Fabian's colleagues were convinced that Kremph was the common thread that finally guided them to a resolution, he couldn't shake the growing feeling that it had been too simple – that they were fumbling blindly without the slightest clue of what this was really about.

Only now was he starting to understand why.

There wasn't a common thread at all. It looked like one, but in reality it was nothing more than a marked trail, a studied plan that must have been extremely complicated to set up. One that most would think was so far-fetched it went beyond what could be considered credible. But credibility was not the same as truth.

Fabian was convinced that under no circumstances was Ossian Kremph capable of planning and executing the kidnapping and custody of Adam Fischer, much less the murder of Carl-Eric Grimås. On the other hand, he did constitute the perfect false lead.

With Kremph out of the way and the case officially closed, Fabian could start searching for the real perpetrator.

HE FOUND AN EMPTY parking space outside Rival at Mariatorget, and hurried towards the 7-Eleven on the corner on foot. It had been dark for several hours and he realized that he had no idea whether the sun had come up at all today. He'd never liked the winter up in Stockholm, but it was getting worse with every passing year. He felt like he was living in a constant state of darkness that lasted from November to the end of February. He repeated his promise to never move so much as one metre further north as he walked past the latest tabloid billboards.

Cannibal Man Dead After Jump from Fifth Storey, screamed

one headline. *Serial Murderer and Rapist Willumsen Still at Large in Denmark!* yelled another.

Fabian would have preferred to stay at the station in peace and quiet and gone through all the collected material from the case so far. Everyone else had left for the weekend, even Edelman, which meant that he would be alone. Desk lamps would be turned off, doors closed and the air freed of distant conversations, ringing phones and rumbling printers.

And it was only there in total solitude that he could go down deep enough and think a thought through to its end.

But it wasn't happening tonight.

He was so far out of Sonja's good graces that she hadn't even bothered to answer when he called to say that he was on his way home, which is why he had taken the opportunity to get two lattes with an extra shot and a Tosca square. Nothing could improve Sonja's mood like a Tosca square almond pastry from the 7-Eleven.

Personally, he preferred the princess cake, but he'd made a solemn oath to himself to cut down on calories and resisted the urge to stop by the bakery café at the corner of Swedenborgsgatan. It's not that he was fat – far from it. For as long as he could remember he'd weighed 164 pounds, but in the past two years he'd noticed an obvious change and was now up to 168, on his way to 170. If he continued at this same rate he would weigh 220 pounds by retirement.

He tried to get hold of Malin on his walk back to the car, but got no answer. So he made another attempt on her home number.

'Hello, Fabian.' He could not mistake Anders Rehnberg's drawling voice.

Fabian had met Malin's husband a number of times, but had never really spoken with him. It wasn't that he hadn't tried. He'd actively approached him at dinners and various events with significant others in an attempt to find common ground, but every interaction had left him with a bad aftertaste. One laboured topic of conversation after the other had fallen flat, and blunders jumped out of his mouth that he always bitterly regretted the next day. At their housewarming party in Enskede, for example, Fabian had babbled on about how Anders didn't need to worry because Malin wasn't his type anyway.

Since then they hadn't spoken. Anders and Sonja, on the other hand, had taken a liking to each other and seemed to have quite a lot to discuss at the party. On the way home that night, he'd almost brought it up, but restrained himself, asking the driver to turn up the radio, which was playing 'Forbidden Colours' by David Sylvian.

'I wanted to see how Malin is doing.' He tried to sound as neutral as possible.

'She's feeling about as good as she can be, considering her job.'

Fabian held back and remained silent.

'Was there anything else?' he asked.

'Yes, I was wondering if I might be able to speak with her quickly.'

'Listen, I don't think that's a good idea. Her pre-eclampsia is so serious and advanced that she's been hospitalized. She'll need treatment all the way until delivery. If it gets really bad they'll be forced to induce labour, even though she has a full two months left of her pregnancy.'

'I'm sorry, I had no idea it was so serious.'

'No? According to the doctor she must have shown clear signs that she wasn't feeling well. If she hadn't been pressed so hard on the job, it wouldn't have got this bad.'

'Anders, I'm truly sorry. I understand you're upset. But—'

'Fabian, she needs peace and quiet, so you shouldn't call her or come to visit. The only thing you should do is stay as far away from her as possible, okay?'

'Okay, but can you tell her I called?' said Fabian, but Anders had already hung up.

When he got home he found Theodor in his room, sitting in

front of the computer. Matilda was on the couch watching *The Lion King* on full blast. It was so loud the neighbours must have been able to hear Timon and Pumbaa's 'Hakuna matata'. 'Hi, Matilda. Isn't Mum here?' he said getting no response. He picked up the remote control and lowered the volume.

'No, stop it! I can't hear what they're—'

'Matilda, I asked you a question. Do you know where—' He stopped abruptly when he caught sight of the girl standing out on the balcony smoking, her cell phone glued to her ear. He opened the balcony door and noticed that she was using his indoor shoes and had already managed to fill one corner of the flowerbox with butts. 'You must be Rebecka.'

She turned around. 'Listen, I have to go now.' She hung up the phone, pushed it down into her overly tight jeans and held her hand out in greeting. 'Hi, there.'

'I thought my wife would be home, but—'

'No, she had to work, and said something about an opening the week after Christmas.' She put out her cigarette and immediately took out the pack to get another. 'Would you like one?'

'No, and I would appreciate it if you could do something besides stand out here and smoke all the time. I assume that my wife is paying you.'

'I'm not the one who doesn't have time to take care of my own kids.'

'No, you're quite right. And speaking of which, you can leave now.'

'Sonja said I could count on being paid for the whole night because she didn't know when you would show up.'

'I'll pay you for the whole night, if you just leave right now,' said Fabian, exerting all his willpower not to drag her off the balcony by force.

A thousand kronor later he took out a Post-it pad and started to write.

Dearest Sonja,

I understand that you're stressed, but everyone needs a break now and then.

Fabian

He attached the Post-it to the latte, and set it down beside the bag with the Tosca square and a CD he'd made with Prince's 'I Would Die 4 U' on nineteen times in a row – one for every year they'd been together. It was the first song they'd danced to together, and it had been their own ever since.

He remembered it like it was yesterday. He'd managed to borrow a membership card to Lido – a nightclub housed in a former porn theatre on Hornsgatan, whose members were mostly authors, musicians and actors.

Once inside, he'd been nervous that someone would discover that he didn't write or play in a band or – worst of all – that he was from Skåne, so he avoided everyone and hung out by the side of the dance floor, a beer in his hand. After a few hours he finally admitted to himself that it wasn't that cool and went to coat check to retrieve his jacket.

As he was heading for the door, the DJ put on that Prince song, and his life changed for ever. He'd turned back and ventured out on to the dance floor for the first time, even though he had no rhythm and never danced. But it hadn't mattered because suddenly she appeared out of nowhere. It's possible she'd been there the whole time, but without thinking he forced his way further into the crowd and started dancing with her.

In Sonja's version she was the one who'd caught sight of him, but that didn't change anything. He'd found home, and even today he could remember how he'd felt high on happiness the moment she took his hand.

Two minutes and fifty-nine seconds.

It didn't take a moment longer for both of them to understand.

That it was them and no one else.

Then the song ended.

How much time would they need now? he thought on his way down the front steps to the taxi waiting to drive the bag of treats over to Sonja's studio in Old Town.

58

DUNJA HOUGAARD WOKE UP abruptly from a dreamless sleep, as if someone had just plugged her in and turned on the power. She initially thought someone was trying to suffocate her by pressing plastic wrap over her face. No matter how hard she gasped for breath, she couldn't get air, until she managed to twist her face to the side.

Then she thought that she was at home in her own bed and had just ended up with her head under the covers. But even though it was midwinter and Carsten had swapped the lemon-yellow blinds to dark brown ones, it never got this dark in the bedroom. Besides, everything was shaking and careening around her.

She must be in a car. But how had she ended up here and why was she folded up in a foetal position, unable to move? What had really happened? She tried to remember, but she couldn't. The past few days, or maybe it had only been hours, were still an unwritten page waiting to be filled with memories and experiences.

Once they came flooding in, she wished herself back into ignorance and liberating forgetfulness, but now it was too late. They were spreading like manure, dirtying all of her thoughts. The images from the investigations of the raped women who'd been tortured to death had etched themselves permanently in her mind and would never leave her again, just like the vision of the abandoned industrial building before everything went black.

She tried to straighten her aching body, but it was too cramped. One foot still hurt from the sprain and the other had bumped into something hard. She felt pressure from every direction, as if the goal was to squeeze all the air out of her.

She struggled against the desire to give up and tried to summon enough energy to turn on to her back, pull up both arms and push away whatever was rustling right above her face. Five minutes later she'd managed to create a little pocket of air and could finally take a few real breaths.

Then she remembered the flashlight. She pulled it out of her jeans' pocket and pressed the little button at the end of the shaft. The light was so weak it looked like it might go out at any moment, but she managed to determine that the rustling was coming from exactly what she'd suspected: black garbage bags.

She put the flashlight in her mouth and poked one index finger through the plastic and made a proper hole in the bag right above her.

First there were a few drops.

Then it started running.

Right down in her face.

The corrosive stench struck her like a chemical weapon. She tried to scream so loud during those few seconds the viscous fluid entered her open mouth. Then she quickly fell silent and turned her face away from the hole, while the car braked and turned sharply.

It was blood. But the horrific smell indicated that the blood was mixed with purge fluid. She felt nauseous and tried to vomit, but nothing came out other than a few clumps of mucous. It reminded her of getting her tonsils removed as a teenager, when one of the wounds in her throat wouldn't heal. After a few days she'd vomited up so much coagulated blood that had collected in her stomach that she had to be taken to the ER by ambulance to have her throat cauterized.

Until now that was the worst thing she'd experienced.

She tried to regain a sense of calm, even though she could feel the fluid running down her neck and continuing under her blouse across her left breast. All she could do to keep panic at bay was try to think about something else, such as the first thing she would do when she got home. She wanted to take a nice hot bath and ask Carsten to order takeout from Pizza Mira, even though he thought it was unhealthy. She knew exactly what she wanted: number fifteen with tomato, cheese, onion, spinach, potato and feta cheese, with garlic sauce on the side.

If she did ever go home again.

After the last drop hit her face she looked back into the hole again with the flashlight and was met by dead eyes staring back at her. She wasn't surprised. She had simply assumed they would belong to Katja Skov and not Aksel Neuman.

So this was where he'd been the whole time: cut up and stuffed into garbage bags, just like Katja Skov, who was presumably also in the trunk.

For some reason the perpetrator had spared her. Or had he run out of time and was on his way to another location where he could continue working in peace and quiet? No, now they were definitely stopping. She heard the engine turning off and then a car door opening and closing. She imagined the trunk opening and him pulling her out. He had probably saved her for last and had thought out something extra special to draw out her death for as long as possible. She tried to stay calm by taking a deep breath, but the air stuck in her throat. She was close to panic, and she knew if she didn't get control of herself soon she would start screaming and never stop.

She managed to take in a small breath and then made another attempt to stretch her legs, while she heard something being dragged across the roof of the car, but her legs wouldn't move. Instead she started pushing aside one of the garbage bags that was below her. It felt like it contained two feet. She was finally able to stretch out her arms behind her head and further along the floor past the garbage bags. At last she could feel a rough, carpet-like wall. She groped up along the slit in the middle of the wall until she found what she was looking for: a loop that clicked when she pulled on it and lowered the seats.

Now she could finally drag herself out of the trunk to the back seat of the car. She still couldn't move her legs, even if the feeling was on its way back, and dragged herself to the right-side back door and tried to open it. This was her only chance to get out of the car and run away from there before he was back. But no matter how hard she pulled and tore at the handle it was impossible to open. Desperation took hold and she could no longer stop herself from screaming and banging against the windowpane until the last of her energy was consumed. Then she collapsed in tears.

Only once she'd calmed down and opened her eyes did she catch sight of the shaft sticking under the passenger seat.

The axe – the murder weapon Kjeld Richter and his men had never found.

Richter would presumably be furious, but she had no other choice. She nudged it forward, picked up the axe and smashed it against the window with all the force she could muster. The axe bounced back as if it were a film on rewind. Then she hit it again, and again, and again. Ten strikes later she could finally see a crack and after twenty the glass shattered completely. She ran the blade along the edges of the window to remove the remaining shards of glass and squeezed out through the hole. Her head knocked against some kind of covering and she fell down on a cold, hard floor.

Get away from there, she repeated to herself. Wherever she was, she had to get away as quickly as possible before he came back for her.

She crawled under the covering and squinted from the bright lights. She slid across the rough floor, scraping the skin on her forearms. There was a large white arrow under her and hundreds of light fixtures above that lit up endless rows of cars. There were no people in sight. Had he really just left her?

The blood had finally started to work its way into her legs, so she gathered her strength and carefully stood up on her healthy foot. Her leg was shaking and it didn't take long before her whole body was trembling too. She was cold and missed her winter coat. Maybe it was still in the car. It didn't matter. Nothing would get her to turn back now.

She limped forward, revealing row after row of cars. Then she finally saw the sign she'd hoped to find. The glass doors moved silently to each side and she walked in. It felt several degrees warmer in here, maybe even a few notches above freezing. She noticed a spiral staircase that went in both directions, but she made her way to the row of elevators and pressed the button.

Almost immediately she heard a ping in the elevator furthest away from her. Even though she hobbled there as fast as she could, the doors struck the side of her already sore body as they closed. Once inside she pressed the green button, and waited for the elevator to take her up or down. She turned to face the mirror. When she saw her reflection staring back at her she realized that she didn't understand anything.

Not one thing.

59

'SO WHAT SHOULD WE DO?' asked Matilda, who was still sulking because he'd turned off *The Lion King*.

'I guess we can start by doing a little grocery shopping and making a nice dinner.' Fabian turned towards Theodor, who had agreed to leave his computer for once and come out of his room.

'Can we get candy too? Pleeease,' Matilda whined.

Fabian thought about the ban on candy that Sonja had introduced at the end of summer when she'd started to worry about Matilda's weight. He'd never shared her concern, and her extra few summer pounds had already melted away anyway. 'Okay,' he said at last. 'Just don't say anything to Mum.'

'And Christmas cider because we're already out!'

'Sure. And then I thought we could rent a movie that we haven't already seen a hundred times. Does that sound good?'

'Yes!' Matilda shouted, starting to clap her hands.

'And what about you, Theo? What do you say?'

Theodor shrugged and looked right past Fabian. 'Sure, I guess that sounds okay. But I can't.'

'And why can't you, may I ask?'

'I have other plans.'

'I see, what kind of plans?'

Theodor shrugged again. 'Nothing special. Just going out and seeing some buddies.'

'Which "buddies"?' Fabian felt like a stuck record.

'Nobody you know.'

'And what are you and your "buddies" going to do?' said Matilda, crossing her arms.

'Matilda, you don't need to play cop. I'm the parent here. Not—'

'I was just asking.'

'You don't have a damn thing to do with this! Okay?' shouted Theodor.

'I actually do,' said Fabian. 'If you haven't decided on anything other than wandering around town, why don't you stay here and have crisps and watch a movie with us?'

Theodor rolled his eyes and got up from the chair. 'You don't understand a damn thing.'

'Listen! We don't use that kind of language here!'

'Other than when you and Mum argue, you mean.' Theodor turned his back on them and disappeared into his room.

He'd walked right into the jab and was down for the count, and the worst thing about it was that his son was correct. They were both fully aware that it was wrong to fight in front of the kids, but he and Sonja did it anyway, using cruder and cruder language each time.

'Nice,' said Matilda, putting on a stiff smile while she started drumming on the table with her fingers.

He didn't know if it was Matilda's sarcasm, or simply a pathetic attempt to set limits, but suddenly he was standing in the middle of Theodor's room, pumping fury. 'I don't know what kind of attitude you think is appropriate around this house, but I've got just one thing to say to you: it's not okay. So if I were in your shoes I would drop it right now. Do you get that?'

'Whatever,' said Theodor, who had already settled down in front of the computer.

'No, it's not at all "whatever"!' Fabian went over and ripped out the cord to the computer, which turned off.

'What the hell are you doing? You can't just—'

'Yes, don't forget that I can! I'm the one who paid for it and I'm the one who pays the electric bill!'

'You're too fucking—'

'Now, you listen to me! You're only thirteen years old, and however hard it seems, it's Mum and I who decide what's best for you, which will continue to be the case for another five whole years. And right now, I've decided that you're staying home tonight! Is that understood?'

'Forget it.' said Theodor, reaching for the cable.

'Forget it? You know what you can forget? Huh? Look at me when I'm talking to you!' Fabian was now so angry that his whole body was shaking.

Theodor sighed and met his gaze.

'You can forget sitting here in front of the computer! As of now you'll be out there with me and Matilda making this into a nice evening!'

'Life is too short for this. Decide whatever the hell you want. I'm leaving now anyway.' Theodor got up from the chair.

'The hell you are!' Fabian screamed, pressing him back on the chair.

'You're fucking sick in the head!'

'What did you say?'

'I said that you were—' He got no further.

The slap came out of nowhere and surprised Theodor as much as Fabian. He had never hit either of his kids before – had never even come close to it. But now he had crossed the line, and however hard he tried, he would never, ever be able to undo it.

Theodor held his cheek and looked down at the floor. Neither of them said anything for several minutes. He tried, but he couldn't think of anything that would even remotely repair the damage he had just caused.

As a kid he sometimes used to get really angry, but he couldn't remember it happening as an adult. Not until now, at least. Once it was wakened to life, the blind fury couldn't be stopped. Was he really that stressed? After another few silent minutes he crouched down in front of his son. 'Theo, I'm so sorry. I just got so angry. That's no excuse, but... It was a really dumb thing to do and it's unforgiveable in every way.'

'It's okay,' said Theodor with his eyes nailed to the floor.

'No, it's not okay at all. What I did is actually criminal, so you can report me if you want.'

'Knock it off. I said it's fine.'

'Listen, what do you say about starting this evening over again?'

'Okay,' said Theodor, nodding. 'I think I'll stay home.'

'I'm glad,' said Fabian, clinging firmly to the vague hope that perhaps the evening wasn't lost completely.

Theodor raised his head and looked him in the eyes. 'But I would really like you to leave my room now.'

'Sure. Of course.' Fabian got up, patted Theodor awkwardly on the head, and left.

60

BENNY WILLUMSEN GOT OFF the train at Central Station in Copenhagen, even though he could have stayed on for another two stops before Nørreport. He'd decided to change to the S train because the woman across from him was reading Ekstra Bladet. She had got on at Copenhagen Airport and would likely realize at any moment that his face adorned the cover.

'*Wanted – Now Being Hunted in Sweden*.'

The picture under the headline had been taken at the trial, and he remembered how he'd tried to smile and look as friendly and innocent as possible.

Unfortunately, the S train was also full of people browsing *Berlingske Tidende*, *Politiken*, and *Urban*, the free newspaper: '*Still No Traces of Katja Skov – Swedish Police Fear the Worst*'.

They didn't know shit, he thought as he got off at Vesterport Station. They think they understand, but they have no fucking idea. He pushed his hat down with one hand so that the wind wouldn't blow it away, and then hurried up the stairs, before continuing along Kampmannsgade. Then he jumped down on the ice and crossed Sankt Jørgen Lake.

He shouldn't be surprised. The fact that he was a suspect was no more sensational than his train initially being delayed in Malmö. Given the similarities between these crimes and his own activities it was only a matter of time before he would end up at the top of the suspect list. And, after his little adventure on the kitchen table, it was even more astonishing that he was still alive.

After having been drained of his orgasm, he'd been quite sure that his last hour was upon him. He'd almost felt ready. It would have been rather appropriate because the orgasm itself was almost worth dying for. But when he woke up on the kitchen table again to the sound of loud banging from outside, the tape that had held him in place was gone and he quickly realized the police were busy forcing open his door.

He had no time to consider what had just happened. His reptile brain leapt into action. He jumped down from the table and made his way out on to the balcony naked. He navigated the sleet and climbed over the railing, swinging down to the balcony below. Fortunately, the balcony door to the neighbour's apartment was unlocked, and he'd been able to pull together a pair of underwear, socks, trousers with suspenders and an aged yellowed shirt without waking the sleeping old man.

Out in the hallway, where the walls were adorned with decorative plates, he'd found shoes, a coat and hat. Then he walked out through the stairwell and down the stairs, facing a stream of uniformed and plain-clothes officers who asked him to get out of the way.

He'd done exactly that ever since. The first few days he'd been in constant motion so that he didn't attract attention, but when he found an unlocked yacht – a Maxi 95 – in its cradle up on land in Limhamn he was finally able to lie down in the cabin and relax.

And then, somewhere in the stage between sleeping and waking, he realized how everything fitted together: the striking similarities between Karen Neuman's murder and his little exercise at Fortuna Beach in Rydebäck two years ago; why he was still alive; and what the erotic session in his apartment had really been about.

At that moment, he realized he didn't stand a chance. There was only one way this could end. He'd made sure not to leave any traces, and never, ever repeat himself. He was the one who, despite all odds, managed to escape unscathed through a trial.

Now it was over.

He was a wanted man, likely far beyond both Sweden and Denmark. It was just a matter of time before that Danish policewoman, who the newspapers reported was now after him, would get him sentenced to life with technical evidence so strong that no defence lawyer in the world would be able to get past it. And he was not ready to get locked up, not by a long shot. He still had so many untested ideas left.

It was in that sense of frustration that the idea came to him, the little piece of candy that would stay behind in his memory long enough to gild all the years of imprisonment he had ahead of him. It was so simple that he couldn't help but laugh as he walked across the last few metres of ice. Instead of hiding himself, he should try to find her first.

He climbed up on the edge of the pier, crossed Rosenørns Allé and continued past the Bethlehem Church. It had been several years since he'd been in Nørrebro, but it felt like yesterday. He would have no problems finding the way to Blågårdsgade 4.

61

HALF AN HOUR INTO *Harry Potter and the Half-Blood Prince* Fabian had stopped concentrating and struggled to keep his eyes open. One more Quidditch match and he would fall asleep for ever. If he'd been able to choose the film, they would have rented *The Hangover* instead. Malin said it was one of the funniest movies she'd seen in years, and she recommended he see it with Theodor. But Matilda had been unrelenting and insisted on *Harry Potter*, even though she'd already seen it twice at the cinema in the summer.

They'd still had a nice evening, managing to fit in some karaoke and a game of Monopoly, which Matilda won after only an hour and a half – she had been quick to put hotels on Centrum and Norrmalmstorg.

On the other hand, he'd heard nothing from Sonja, even though it had been several hours since he'd sent over the bag of treats. He'd tried not to let it bother him, but he couldn't hold back the creeping sense of irritation as the evening went on. There was no doubt that they were both really busy, but he was at least trying to show that he cared. Sonja couldn't even be bothered to send a short thank-you text.

'I'll go clean up,' he said, getting up from the couch.

'Should I pause it?' Matilda reached for the remote control.

'No, that's okay. Just keep watching.'

On his way to the kitchen he stopped outside Theodor's closed door and raised his hand to knock, but stopped himself. He couldn't do more tonight. He could say I'm sorry and regret it any number of times, but it wouldn't change a thing. Theodor would have to take the next step, and aside from grabbing food, he hadn't set foot outside his room all evening. And if Fabian knew his son, it might continue this way for quite some time.

It was a trait he'd inherited from his mother. No one could utilize silence as effectively as Sonja. It was a corrosive silence that had, over the years, made his existence miserable and often forced him to apologize after a fight, even if she was the one who'd been in the wrong.

On one occasion, he'd fought fire with fire and refused to take the blame after a fight on a family holiday. For a two-week-long road trip in France and Italy, they hadn't said more than what was absolutely necessary to each other. After a few days, the mood had rubbed off on the kids, who got restless and started squabbling. In a wordless agreement they'd each taken a child and went out on their own as soon as they had the chance. To this day it was still one of the worst things he'd ever experienced, even though he couldn't remember what the fight had been about.

He tried to shake the memory while he took out his phone to check that he hadn't missed a text or call. Then he walked to the kitchen and turned on the stereo. Broken Social Scene's self-titled album started up as he cleared the table. For the past six months he hadn't been able to play any other CD because the stereo's output mechanism was broken. Fortunately, the album was so multifaceted that he still hadn't got tired of listening to it.

The phone pinged in the middle of 'Hotel'. *Finally*, he thought, opening the message. He was surprised how disappointed he was when he realized that it wasn't from Sonja.

Just got out of the bath. I'll be ready in an hour. Timing still good on your end? I'll meet you at Lydmar. N

He'd completely forgotten that he'd promised to treat Niva to a drink this evening – or else he'd repressed it. He typed in a reply explaining that unfortunately he had to cancel because he was home alone with the kids.

Too bad. I had planned to bring you a little present. One I know you'd appreciate.

Two-and-a-half hours later Theodor had yet to emerge from his room, Matilda was asleep in her bed, and Sonja still hadn't given any signs of life.

And Fabian was in a taxi on his way to Lydmar.

62

DUNJA HOUGAARD'S FIRST THOUGHT was that she couldn't be the person staring back at her in the elevator mirror. There had to be someone who'd been rooting around in her closet and put on her black jeans and light beige blouse, which was actually too nice to wear for every day, but that she'd chosen anyway because she was going to meet her colleagues on the other side of the Sound.

Now it was torn and soiled with blood, just like her jeans.

Her hair had clumped together in thick, sticky tangles.

But most of all it was her face.

Even if she could admit to herself that she wasn't looking at some other woman for a few seconds, her face made her doubtful. The blood and various other dried bodily fluids were one thing, but the scrapes across her forehead, not to mention the bruises and swelling, were much worse.

Whatever Benny Willumsen had done with her, he hadn't been very careful.

The elevator doors opened and Dunja took her eyes off the mirror and limped out into the night. The ice-cold winds breezed through her, as if her body was perforated. A steady stream of taxis drove by, but she made no effort to try to stop one. Considering how she looked, she wouldn't have even picked herself up.

She walked along a narrow, icy sidewalk for about thirty metres. Then she heard a booming rumble. When she looked up towards the starless night and saw navigation lights guiding a landing, she realized that she was right outside Copenhagen Airport.

Was he about to flee the country? Was that why he'd left the car there? she wondered as she boarded the driverless Metro train, ignoring the other travellers' terrified looks. Willumsen was a fugitive and as long as he hadn't changed his appearance and arranged a fake passport he would never make it through security.

At Nørreport Station she gave up trying to piece it all together, and got off. The thought of home gave her enough energy to defy the pain in her foot and hurry all the way along Frederiksborggade and across Dronning Louises Bridge. Once she got to her building, she pressed the button beside the illuminated little sign of her and Carsten's surnames; but there was no crackling on the loudspeaker or buzzing in the lock.

In a way it was typical Carsten. As long as he wasn't expecting a visit he never bothered to pick up the phone that was all the way in the hall. *Either it's a burglar or someone's distributing flyers* was his usual excuse. But it could also be someone who'd faced a serial killer and lost their keys and cell phone and was well on her way to getting frostbite.

She tried again, holding down the button long past the limit of what could be considered reasonable, even if she knew it wouldn't work on Carsten. On the contrary, it just gave him yet another argument for why he shouldn't get up. *Why let someone in who's already put me in a bad mood?* But shouldn't he have realized it was her by now? She'd been away at least twenty-four hours so he must be curious about her whereabouts. She took a few steps back out on to the street and looked up at the apartment. No lights were on. Wasn't he at home? This was getting really strange.

She returned to the door again and aggressively tried ringing all the other residents. She needed to get warm. Finally, a neighbour let her in, but she couldn't help thinking that something didn't add up. Without turning on the light in the stairwell she made her way up to the fourth floor, where she straightened the yucca plant that looked like it was about to fall over. She peeked into the mail slot and saw that the hallway lights were off. But the door was unlocked, which was even more puzzling. She went in and carefully closed the door behind her.

It was quiet, apart from a muffled Madonna song coming from the neighbour's apartment. So Carsten wasn't home. Yet the apartment had been unlocked. She walked in without turning on the lights, and groped her way along the walls to the bedroom.

The bed was made with the cover stretched just so, as only Carsten could. Normally that would irritate her because he always complained about how she made the bed, but this time it calmed her. Somehow it made him feel more present. There was probably a rational explanation for his absence anyway.

She continued to the kitchen, and found the explanation in the form of a handwritten note.

Hi honey,

I tried to reach you. I'll miss the flight if I wait any longer. See you Tuesday evening.

Carsten

She had completely forgotten he was going to Stockholm for a seminar. He'd wondered where she was hiding and tried to get hold of her until he was about to miss his flight. She sighed at her own forgetfulness while she turned on the ceiling light and rinsed her hands and face under hot water. She was going to take a bath, but first she needed to get some food in her before she fainted.

Unfortunately, the kitchen was 'Carsten-clean'. In other words, not a single thing was in the wrong place, and the kitchen counter was so shiny smooth it could also serve as a mirror. The fruit bowl was in the dish rack and the breadbasket was empty. He'd thrown out all the perishable food because he didn't know when she would be coming home. The refrigerator had suffered the same fate. All she could find was a jar of orange marmalade, a few cans of herring they'd bought several years ago when they'd been in Malmö, and a tube of Kalle's Caviar, which Carsten insisted on buying at IKEA and had refused to touch ever since.

She decided to fish some apples out of the garbage can and rinsed off the coffee grounds and other detritus. Every bite was sheer enjoyment, and she could feel her body sucking up all the energy from the sweet juice long before it reached her stomach.

She went back out into the hall, turned on the light and opened the bathroom door. She groped along the wall to the switch and pushed it several times, but it wouldn't turn on. Instead she lit the block candles that were lined up along the inside edge of the tub and started running the water.

She threw her clothes in a pile on the floor, sat on the toilet and peed while she studied her tender foot, which was seriously swollen. Then she climbed into the steaming bath. The heat from the water stung her skin and it almost felt like she was getting a first-degree burn. But it was a lovely pain, and she leaned back and let the warmth thaw her out.

She closed her eyes and was about to doze off when an idea made her sit up. Why hadn't she thought about it before? No one knew where she was and what had happened. She stepped out of the water, wrapped a towel around her, and hurried through the hall, dripping all over the living room until she reached the phone.

She could see a young couple having dinner with friends in the building opposite. It could have been her and Carsten. Two windows down money changed hands and new cards were dealt, and in the adjacent apartment someone was having a party with lots of colourful drinks. Everyone seemed happy and indifferent to what went on in the darkness outside their little bubble.

Until the day they were affected.

She picked up the phone and dialled directory assistance. First she would contact Klippan. Then she would have to call Sleizner and ask him to send Richter out to the airport garage. She would take care of Carsten last, so that they could talk while she bathed.

But there was no signal. She pressed the dial button several times, but the line was dead. They had already spoken about cancelling the landline service and switching over to cell phones completely, but they hadn't made a final decision. Besides, Carsten was against it.

Then she felt along the cord from the base and realized the line had been severed.

63

HE'D HAD TIME TO change his mind several times during the taxi ride to Blasieholmen. At one point in Old Town he even asked the driver to turn around and drive him to Sonja's studio instead. When he finally stepped into the hotel restaurant and saw Niva waiting on a barstool, he'd veered off into the washroom, splashed his face with water, and asked himself what the hell he was doing.

Before he left the washroom he checked his phone one last time and saw that Sonja had still not broken the silence. He decided to give her one last chance and dialled her number. If she answered, he would leave right away and take the first taxi home.

As the ring tone sounded, he pictured her looking at the phone, seeing that it was him, and then setting it back down again.

'You've reached Sonja Risk. Unfortunately, I can't take your call right now.'

'Hi, it's just me,' he said, as two boisterous men entered and stood at the urinals. 'I just wanted to check in and see how the Tosca square tasted. I thought you might want to take a little break from the brushes and grab a drink. We could meet at Mårten Trotzig, so you don't have far to go to get back to the studio. Kiss kiss.' He hung up and regretted it immediately. Once again she was the one making him crawl, even though he had nothing to be ashamed of.

Niva was still sitting at the bar at the back of the restaurant. She was picking up an olive from a martini glass with a toothpick while she busied herself with her cell phone. She always looked good. There was something about her long, narrow body in combination with her short, almost boyish haircut that had made most men – and women – at the police station turn to get a second look.

Today, if possible, she looked even better. Her lips were dark red and a silver necklace with coloured stones that matched her bracelet was hanging around her neck. The short, tight skirt revealed most of her crossed legs. She'd started working out. Her shoulders and arms were considerably more defined than Fabian remembered and her posture was almost perfect.

The cell phone vibrated in his pocket. He took it out and looked at it.

If the mountain doesn't come to Muhammad, I guess Muhammad comes to the mountain.

He read the message again, but he still didn't get it. The sender's number was anonymous.

'A Hendrick's and tonic.'

Fabian looked up from the phone and saw a waiter standing in front of him with a full highball glass on a serving tray.

'Ordered by the lady over there.' The waiter handed over the drink and nodded towards Niva, who waved back.

Fabian took a deep breath and walked towards her.

'I was starting to doubt that you would ever show up.'

'Me too,' said Fabian, taking the stool beside her. 'But who could resist a promised present?'

Niva answered with a smile. 'A drink first.' She raised her glass without releasing his gaze. 'To not letting doubt stand in the way.'

Fabian raised his glass and took a sip. It was one of the best drinks he'd ever had. It was still very carbonated and the bubbles shot up over the surface and spread the aroma of sprinkled lemon, while the perfectly balanced ratio of gin and tonic washed down his throat. It was so good that he had to take another sip before setting the glass down on the marble countertop.

'So, how's the investigation going?' Niva set down her phone.

'I assume you know that the perpetrator, Ossian Kremph, was arrested and is now dead.'

'In other words, it's over.'

Fabian wondered whether he should tell her what he really thought, but decided to nod instead. 'Niva,' he looked her in the eyes. 'To be honest, I don't know what I'm doing here, besides getting that promised present, of course.'

Niva laughed and smiled. 'You never change. You're still just as bad at lying as you used to be. I think you know exactly why you're here, which is why you're scared.'

'Scared? What should I be afraid of?'

'Don't ask me.' She shrugged. 'I'm not the one who goes and hides in the washroom or asks the taxi driver to turn around.'

Fabian didn't know what to say. How could she know about that? But before he had time to answer she leaned over and kissed him. He didn't want to, or rather, he wanted to, but it wasn't a good idea. Yet he couldn't resist the light breath against his cheek, the soft lips and coiled tongue that tasted of gin and vermouth, and the heat from someone else's body.

Fabian couldn't remember the last time he and Sonja had been so close – much less when they'd last kissed. He dismissed the thoughts of leaving. Instead he let his body's needs take over and let their tongues play. However much he wanted to, he had passed the point where he could say no.

He put his hand on her leg and felt the heat radiate up through his palm and waken parts of him that had been dormant for far too long. Her thigh was one of the smoothest he'd ever touched. His hand continued upward and he noted her breathing deepened. She parted her legs slightly as if to accentuate the obvious.

His hand danced along her thigh and continued under her dress. 'We could get a room here,' he whispered in her ear. 'If there are any vacancies.' The words came automatically, and there was nothing he could do to stop them.

'There are.' She emptied her glass and nodded to the bartender for another. 'But maybe you should answer first.'

Fabian didn't know what she was talking about until she waved her phone at him.

'Who knows, maybe it's important,' she said.

'Who knows, maybe I've already gone to bed and I'm sound asleep.'

'Maybe.' She fished out his vibrating phone from the inside pocket of his jacket and looked at the display with an inscrutable smile.

'Who is it?' He reached for the phone.

'Haven't you gone to bed?' She held up the phone in the air so he couldn't reach it and only gave in after it had stopped ringing. Then she took a sip from the fresh dry martini the bartender had just put in front of her.

The missed call was from Malin, who had probably heard the news about Kremph's suicide. In any event, she was likely feeling well enough to watch TV, even though she was under observation at Stockholm South General Hospital.

'Come now,' said Niva, placing her hand over his fly.

Fabian set down the phone, resumed the kiss, and let her hand continue. But he couldn't shake the feeling that he really should call Malin and tell her his suspicions about Kremph's innocence, even though he'd promised her husband to stay away.

So when his cell phone started vibrating again he took the call. 'Hi, I just saw that you'd called and was about to—'

'What are you talking about? I didn't call you.' To Fabian's surprise it wasn't Malin on the other end, but Sonja. He felt like he had just made a hazardous U-turn in the middle of the freeway right over the median and could only pray that he survived.

'Sorry, I'd just fallen asleep and must have been dreaming.'

Niva rolled her eyes and focused on her drink.

'Oh, I didn't mean to wake you. I just read your message now and really wanted to thank you for the coffee and Tosca.'

'It was nothing. I hope it was good.'

'It was perfect. And evidently it was just what I needed because since then I've got a lot done.'

'That's good.' Fabian exchanged a glance with Niva. 'But listen, I don't want to disturb—'

'You're not – and I need a break anyway. So if your offer still stands...'

'Ah, that would have been really nice, but I don't know now.' He thought feverishly about how he should continue. 'I'd hoped that Matilda would be asleep, but she's woken up several times and been really worried.' He turned his gaze towards Niva, who put her hand to her mouth and mimed a yawn.

'Worried about what?'

'About us – that we're going to separate. Right now that seems to be all she thinks about.'

'Do you want me to come home?'

'No, it's okay. Keep on working. I'll take care of it.'

'I've been thinking about that actually: we have to stop fighting in front of the kids.'

'We should stop fighting altogether.'

He could hear her sigh on the other end. 'Can I talk to her?'

'Uh... Sorry?'

'Matilda. Can I talk to her?'

'Honey, she just fell back asleep.'

'Okay, but you can call when she wakes up.'

'Absolutely.' He looked at Niva, who was tapping her watch and throwing out her arms. 'Listen, I hope your inspiration continues. I'll see you when you come home.' He ended the call and took a big gulp of his drink. But it was already just as flat as he felt.

Niva looked him in the eyes. He wanted to explain and try to put his confused emotions into words, but she got there first.

'Fabian, it's okay. I can wait.'

'Wait for what?'

Niva cracked a smile and ran her fingers through her hair.

'Niva, if you think it's going to be the two of us—'

She put her finger over his mouth and hushed him. 'You're still so full of ideals. It's lovely, almost a little sweet, but most of all it's naïve. Although it doesn't matter. You've kept your promise and treated me to a drink, and now I intend to keep mine.'

Fabian didn't understand what she was talking about.

'That was why you came here, have you forgotten? I promised you a present. You'll find it in your phone.' She stepped down from the barstool, put her middle finger between her legs, then pressed it against his lips. 'Don't call me again until you're ready.'

64

THE REALIZATION RAN THROUGH Dunja like a cold wave of sweat. Her legs were about to collapse, even though her body felt stiff as a board. Nausea was overpowering her and the pieces of the apple she'd just eaten were on their way up. She just wanted to run and hide under the covers.

Someone had been in her apartment and severed the phone cord, which also explained why the front door was unlocked and the yucca palm out in the stairwell, with the extra key hidden under the pot, was crooked. But who? And above all, why? Benny Willumsen had already had his chance with her in Kävlinge.

Then she remembered the light in the bathroom that didn't work and that the shower curtain had been completely closed. She'd noticed it, but hadn't been able to think about anything other than sinking down into the steaming water. It was nothing unusual per se, except that Carsten was always on at her to leave it halfway open after she'd showered, so that the tile would dry properly and wouldn't start to get mouldy in the corners.

She set the cordless phone down on the couch, tightened the towel around her body and went back into the hall, where she skilfully stepped in places where she knew the old wooden floor wouldn't creak. Once she was in the kitchen, she picked up the meat cleaver from the magnetic knife strip, and went back out into the hall and stopped outside the bathroom.

She hesitated; perhaps she should leave the apartment and ask a neighbour to use their phone. But she wasn't wearing any clothes and she hadn't heard anyone other than herself since she came home. If someone was after her, he had already had half an hour to do something.

No, she thought, whoever it was, he was surely far away by now.

She went into the bathroom, and moved towards the drawn shower curtain, her heart pounding adrenaline into her blood. With the meat cleaver in one hand, she took a deep breath and tore the curtain to the side with the other.

It was empty and besides her razor on the floor, everything looked normal. She leaned down to pick it up, wondering when she'd last changed the blades. Suddenly a cord was pulled around her neck stopping the supply of oxygen and forcing her to drop the razor and the cleaver, which landed only a few millimetres from her left big toe.

She'd already imagined this situation and had reviewed the different possibilities over and over again in her mind, but she hadn't envisioned it happening right now. In some ways she was surprised that she hadn't had her fair share of life-threatening experiences yet as a police officer, even though she had anticipated it the moment she submitted her application to the Academy. She'd wondered how she would react, what would go through her mind and how it would feel.

Nothing came close to what she'd imagined. Strangely, she wasn't afraid or nervous. Even though she might only be moments away from death she did not give it a second thought. She wasn't even surprised that someone was actually in her home. She still had no idea who it was, and truthfully she didn't care right now. She could only think about one thing: surviving – at any cost.

She needed the meat cleaver. She moved at lightning speed to get two fingers from both her right and left hand in between her neck and the cord. Now she had at least bought herself a few seconds and could keep it from cutting into her neck, but she still couldn't get any air.

All of a sudden, she felt a jerk and fell backwards. But she didn't hit the tile floor, instead she was being dragged on her back, her hands holding the cord. She tried to see what the intruder looked like, but didn't have time before she was pulled up and then down again into warm water.

The sound of her heart was much louder now and it pumped oxygen-deficient blood around with increasing desperation. She could see his head like a dark, hovering shadow outside the tub, too far for her to reach with kicking legs, unlike the candles that fell down and went out one by one.

If she didn't get air soon it would all be over. Her body had started to give up and was shutting down one bodily function after the other from her head all the way to her feet. Soon her arms wouldn't function either.

She made an impulsive decision to remove her fingers from underneath the cord. Now, more than ever, time was of the essence. She grabbed one of the block candles that was still flickering on the edge of the tub and held it up towards the dark shadow. Her strength was gone, and the rules of physiology dictated that she should have dropped the candle – but she didn't.

Then she watched the light from the fire spread across the shadow and grow in strength. Finally, the cord was released from around her throat and she could raise her head out of the water and get closer to the fire that now illuminated the whole bathroom.

She filled her lungs with air, coughed, and took a few more quick breaths, before she realized that it was Benny Willumsen who was on fire, not the room. She had no idea what was going on, but crawled out of the bathtub as fast as she could, and crept out of the bathroom, away from his screams.

One way or another she had to get out of the apartment, but the security gate was locked. It had cost over ten thousand kroner, and according to Carsten, it was more important than the last-minute trip to Rhodes she had wanted to take so badly.

From the hall she could see Willumsen leaning over the bathtub with his head under the water. She could have easily slipped into the room, grabbed the meat cleaver that was still in the shower, and chopped into his back with as much force as possible. But she couldn't move. It might have been because of her lack of oxygen or maybe she still couldn't understand how it could be him.

She didn't even react when he turned towards her, stood up, and carefully felt his burned scalp. Only once he grasped the cleaver did the paralysis release its hold. She pulled the key out of the bathroom door, slammed it shut and locked it from the outside right before the meat cleaver penetrated the wood as if it were made of papier mâché. She fled into the living room, and started turning the lights off and on over and over again, so that someone in one of the buildings opposite would catch sight of her.

She could hear the bathroom door beginning to lose its fight against the cleaver, so she forcefully kept flickering – on, off, on, off.

Finally, the couple with dinner guests reacted. She waved and gesticulated to try to indicate that she was in danger, but was met only by laughter and applause. Then she heard a loud crash from the hall as the bathroom door gave way. Without thinking, she overturned the jade plant in the big floor pot that had survived months without either light or water, and opened the window right above it.

Cold air immediately filled the room and gave her bare skin goosebumps. She grabbed the phone from the couch and hurried to the bedroom and, leaving the door ajar, she went into the closet.

In total darkness, she raised her healthy foot as high as she could and stuck it into one of the shoe holder compartments that was hanging on the inside of the door. To her surprise it held, and she managed to climb up into the piles of old knitting projects that had never been completed and forgotten clothes filled with holes from hungry carpet beetles.

She could hear Willumsen entering the living room, and could only hope that the overturned pot and rattling window would catch his attention. She pressed the green button on the phone, and held it against her ear, hoping for a miracle. The silence felt endless, but at last it came: a lifeline in the form of a dial tone mixed with a lot of crackling and interference. Just as she'd hoped, the neighbours above them still had their base station in the bedroom.

She entered the first of the two phone numbers she knew by heart, but didn't need to hear more than 'You've' to be able to recite the rest in her mind: 'Reached Carsten Røhmer. Unfortunately, I can't talk right now.' Obviously he was out for dinner or something. What had she expected? Normally she didn't care when he didn't answer, but this time she just wanted to cry. She whispered a message telling him to ask her colleagues to break into their apartment as soon as possible.

The other number she mostly remembered because it was so hard to forget. She couldn't help it that it went to Jan Hesk of all people. She dialled his number as she heard Willumsen make his way into the bedroom.

'Yes, this is Hesk.'

'Hi, Jan, it's me,' she whispered as quietly as she could.

'Huh? Hello?'

'Jan, it's me, Dunja. I can't speak louder than—'

'Dunja, is that you?'

'Yes. You have to listen to me. I need your help,' she said, and listened to the sound of the meat cleaver dragging against the wall right outside the closet.

'The connection is really bad.'

'Jan, you have to help me.'

'What? I can't hear you. There's a hell of a lot of interference.'

'I need your help and it's urgent.'

'Help? You need help?'

'Yes, Benny Willumsen is in my home—'

'Hello? You're fading out. Do you hear me?'

'Yes, I'm here.'

'You should have thought about that before you stuck a knife in my back.'

'No, Jan, wait—'

There was a click in her ear. She pressed the green button to dial 112, but didn't have time before the door was torn open. She held her breath and tried to make her heartbeat quieter. It wasn't clear whether he'd seen or heard her, but she could clearly hear his slow breathing and smell the pungent odour of burned hair. The seconds dragged by until he finally closed the door again. She breathed out a sigh of relief.

The phone suddenly started ringing in her hand. Three devastating rings sounded before she managed to turn it off, but by two the door was torn open again.

'That's what I suspected.' She heard his voice as she tried to get away from his hands that were searching around on the shelf like two angry snake heads. But it was impossible, and soon they'd taken hold of her right shin.

Her legs had always been strong. Every year she had cycled no matter what the weather, and she'd always run between almost every class in school. But now her kicks were as useless as her screams for help. She was ripped down from the shelf and thrown over his shoulder like a freshly shot animal that would soon be slit open and butchered. She reached for something to hold on to, but couldn't grab anything other than clothes and unfinished knitting.

She tried to wriggle loose, hit and bit him on the back, but he held her as if she was in a vice. He didn't even seem to be exerting himself. Then he went over to the window and pulled the curtains. Only now did she realize that he too was naked, and judging by his back and butt muscles she didn't stand a chance. He could basically do whatever he wanted with her.

'And here I intended to make the suffering brief,' he said, moving towards the bed.

Dunja had never killed anyone. It had always been the absolute last resort in her mind, if that. For as long as she could remember, she had been convinced that there was always another way, a technique where communication replaced guns and violence.

Now she knew better.

RIGHT BEFORE BENNY WILLUMSEN got to the bed he staggered and dropped the meat cleaver to the floor, as if he was about to lose his balance. He tried to continue, but stopped mid-step to prevent himself from falling.

At that moment, he caught sight of the tip sticking right through his left chest. It must have penetrated both his lung and heart, which was still pumping. Blood was gushing down his well-exercised stomach.

DUNJA DIDN'T KNOW EXACTLY how much damage she'd inflicted, so she turned the knitting needle around to cause as much internal injury as possible. He was still standing, but he wasn't saying anything. She couldn't tell if he even understood what was happening. Only once she had shoved yet another knitting needle between his ribs on the other side of the spine, puncturing his right lung, did he slowly sink down, like a horse lying down to die.

'Why?' She looked him in the eyes. 'Why didn't you kill me in Kävlinge when you had the chance?'

She got no response.

But the look in his eyes right before they died said more than enough.

It wasn't him.

Whoever it was in Kävlinge it wasn't Benny Willumsen.

I woke up in a corridor. There were wounded people everywhere screaming in pain. I didn't understand what was going on. But when a nurse came by I realized that the hands in the mist did not belong to my old friends at all. Instead it was some of your people who had rescued me. I stopped the nurse and asked about you and described your blue eyes.

Her scream for help came out of nowhere. She must have recognized my Israeli accent, and soon her colleagues were there, spitting and hitting me. I wanted to explain, but I didn't get a chance. There was so much hate. I tried to get out of the bed to get away from there, but I fell. Or else someone pulled me down. I couldn't do anything other than curl up and pray to God that their blows and kicks would stop.

Then the doctor came. I think her name was Basimaa. She helped me get out through a back door. She said that she knew who you were and told me you had worked together at the same small hospital in Einabus. She knew your name and which village you lived in.

Aisha Shahin from Imatin, the most beautiful of names.

You exist, and you were so much more than just a dream.

65

'SÖDERLEDEN OR SKEPPSBRON?' THE taxi driver tried to make eye contact in the rear-view mirror.

'Skeppsbron,' Fabian answered from the back seat, his eyes locked on the phone. Somewhere in this device he would find Niva's so-called present. She hadn't wanted to reveal anything more than that.

'Just so you know, that's going to take longer.'

'I'm in no hurry,' said Fabian without taking his eyes off his cell phone screen.

'I see, you don't take the freeway on principle. In a way, I agree that it's ugly and should be buried – if money's not an issue, that is. Believe it or not, I actually protested against the third railway line. Although that was before I started driving. Now that I'm behind the wheel all day I can clearly see how politicians have literally run all of Stockholm's infrastructure into the shitter. Do you agree?'

Fabian didn't answer. Instead he asked the driver to turn up the radio, which coincidentally happened to be playing The National's 'Fake Empire' just as they were passing the palace. The driver stopped talking and turned up the volume so that Matt Berninger's baritone voice filled the cab. Fabian looked up from the phone and saw some teenagers running as if their life depended on it before disappearing into one of the alleys.

He thought about Theodor, perhaps because the teens were dressed in bomber jackets and hoodies similar to what he would wear. Theodor had been talking about hoodies ad nauseam the past year. Finally, he'd saved up enough to buy one for himself after Fabian and Sonja had said no, arguing that it was gang wear. No matter how fashionable, it was asking for trouble.

Sonja had started talking more and more about how Stockholm had become hard, and had expressed worry about whether it was the right place for their kids to grow up. It had definitely got worse compared to when he'd moved there in the late eighties. At that time skinheads were the biggest threat. But as long as you knew where they hung out, the most you ever had to do was make a detour. Today, dangers were lurking everywhere and if they did nothing there was a pretty high risk that Theodor would end up in just that kind of gang in only a few years.

He looked out over the frozen water towards the *af Chapman* – the illuminated ship that was docked at Skeppsholmen and was presumably the world's best-located youth hostel. Right after the drums in 'Fake Empire' started up, they passed the Slussen roundabout, and the driver turned down the volume and tried to make eye contact in the rear-view mirror again. 'I saw you looking at the ship at Skeppsholmen. Not all Stockholmers know that the *af Chapman* is actually a hostel. You know, there are showers at the bow of the boat, so you can stand there as God created you and wash yourself with a view of the royal palace. That's not bad at all, don't you think?'

Fabian didn't hear a word of what he was saying. He'd just found what he was looking for on his phone. It was an email link that had ended up in the trash because the sender was unknown. *I was wrong* was the subject line.

He pressed on the link, and a sound file started playing. He quickly put in his headphones.

'It's me. Do you have a moment?' Fabian could tell immediately that the voice belonged to Herman Edelman.

'Not really. I'll be sitting in question time in just a few hours and I haven't had time to prepare. Can I call you this afternoon

instead?' The other voice belonged to Carl-Eric Grimås. Only now did Fabian realize exactly what Niva's present really was.

'Preferably not.' A stressed sigh was heard. *'Carl, this is for your sake.'*

'I know, but—'

'It will be quick, and the more you know about what's happening, the better prepared you'll be to deal with it.'

'Let me shut the door.'

Just as Fabian had suspected. The NDRI had the Minister for Justice's cell phone under surveillance, and Niva had somehow managed to find the conversation he'd had with Herman Edelman hours before he was murdered.

'Don't tell me this is about that damned leak again.'

'Unfortunately it is.'

'In other words, the document is still missing.'

'No, but—'

'I knew it. This is exactly what I was worried about. I could feel it. I never would have agreed to go along—'

'But, Carl, listen now—'

'Dammit, all I've been doing is listening! I thought we were done with all of this.'

'I thought so, too. But the problem won't go away just because you've stuck your head in the sand.'

'I know, but what I don't understand is how it can be my problem at all. It's Gidon Hass who's violated his procedures, and therefore it's his job to resolve it.'

'It might seem that way, but if he doesn't succeed, it will end up with you whether you like it or not.'

Grimås emitted a demonstrative sigh.

'From what I understand, there's a lot to indicate that it's someone internal, who has access to keys and codes. The problem is that they haven't been able to find anyone without—'

'What do you mean, "internal"? Are you suggesting that someone on your own staff would—'

'Carl, I have no idea. The only thing I know is that the investigation is in full swing right now.'

'Okay, I'll call them.'

'That's the last thing you should do. Let them take care of it. I just wanted to keep you informed of everything. And if you haven't already done so, you should tell your chief of staff so that she can prepare some damage control in the event that the affair leaks out.'

'Damage control? You mean resign before the whole party is dragged down? As if that's going to help.'

'Let's not make too big a deal out of all of this. There is still a chance that—'

'Herman, you know just as well as I do that it's only a matter of time before this is on the front page of every paper. And when that happens, everything I've done for this country will end up in the trash. That's the plain truth. Now I have to go.'

'I'll be in touch if anything else comes up.'

'Okay. And listen, by the way... Thanks.'

'No problem.'

They both hung up, and the audio file ended. Fabian took out his headphones and tried to understand what the call had been about. Someone had got their hands on information they shouldn't have, that much was clear, something that put Grimås in such a bad light that it risked toppling the government. And only a minute or two after the conversation he'd phoned the Israeli Embassy. Was that what Edelman had advised against?

Fabian knew that about ten years ago, during the first few years after his wife died, Edelman had thought seriously about moving to Israel. At the time, he certainly had close contacts at the Israeli Embassy. Presumably, he must have known Rafael Fischer, Adam Fischer's late father and the ambassador to Israel. Was that a connection? Or just a coincidence? And who was Gidon Hass? Either way, it sounded like a document of some kind had gone missing from the Israeli Embassy. But what bearing could that have on the murder that happened just a few hours after the phone call? Fabian couldn't figure anything out, except that Herman Edelman, his own boss, obviously knew considerably more than he was letting on.

'We've arrived,' said the driver, stopping on Fatbursgatan outside the front door.

Fabian reached for his wallet, but stopped himself as he glanced up at the apartment with dark windows. He should be tired and longing to crawl into bed and close his eyes. The past two days had felt like a whole week. Not to mention, he'd been drinking. But that didn't matter right now. The driver was wrong.

They hadn't arrived at all.

66

SOFIE LEANDER HAD HAD no doubt whatsoever that the rescuers were in the building, even though she'd accepted three days ago that her chances of survival were zero. The police had located her and she would finally get an explanation for why she'd been kept waiting and alive for so long.

But she'd been wrong – so disastrously wrong.

The police hadn't found her. She bit her lip hard to try and stop the thoughts that were on an endless loop, trying to make sense of it all. But she didn't understand anything other than that her last hope of survival had been crushed. It was a naïve faith that she actually hadn't dared take seriously: the belief that it was over after all. She had hoped that once again she would be able to experience the warming rays of the sun against her face, taste a perfectly balanced cup of really good coffee and feel the security of curling up tightly in her husband's arms. But her hope relied on the presumption that her husband had been in contact with the police.

Now she knew better.

This acknowledgement had been one of the most painful experiences she'd ever had. It felt like a big, deep flesh wound just starting to heal was being torn open again. She'd recognized exactly how it would end the entire time, but there had been a small part of her that could not stop believing and hoping. Maybe her husband had been working so hard on his new project that he didn't realize that she was gone. Maybe he was talking to the police right now?

She'd always been a believer, but only now could she truly understand why religion was so popular and why it would never be possible to take it from people. It didn't matter how much logic or reason refuted it, a believer would never abandon their conviction – the pain was simply too great.

She wavered between two extremes: the belief in a rosy future where everything would work out in the end, and a longing to fade into nothing, to rot and treat the maggots to a feast. Both options were attractive, perhaps mostly because nothing could be worse than what she was being subjected to right now.

She needed to act and was less concerned with the repercussions. She couldn't keep on like this, but what were her choices? She'd heard about how people could lift cars to rescue their children, especially women whose desperation pumped so much adrenaline into their bodies that they had what could almost be described as superpowers. But she had no child and no car to crush it to death. All she had was desperation, which she had in limitless quantities.

The feeding tube started up again, ready to pump the sickly-sweet sludge into her mouth and down her oesophagus. She was being forced down on this table, somewhere in the middle of the hell between life and death.

She tried to turn her face away, but the hose followed and filled her mouth. She steeled herself against the pain from the straps and resisted with her whole body, first in one direction and then the other, while the sludge worked its way further down and stimulated her gag reflex.

Then she felt it. It might not have moved more than a millimetre or so. She couldn't say with certainty, but it was definitely something new, which was enough to give her the energy to continue tensing every muscle in her body to the left and then the right. Now she was sure: the table was moving. She swallowed a few gulps of the batter to get energy while she continued trying to rock the table.

A creaking grew louder in time with her movements, and she decided not to break until it stopped. She started counting every jolt and made it to 384 when the sound suddenly ceased and was replaced a moment later by a loud crash.

She didn't dare open her eyes for a while, but once she did, she realized that she was lying on the floor with the overturned table behind her. Some of the straps must have come loose, because she could now wriggle one arm out and move it freely. With a little luck she could reach all the way over to the scalpel that had fallen on the floor only a metre or so from her.

67

IT WOULD TAKE SOME time before Fabian fully understood the extent of the wiretapped call between Grimås and Edelman. His body's defences seemed to have switched on to keep the shock at bay. When the feeling had finally worked its way through, he got out of the taxi and took a few deep breaths in the winter night. His emotions were all over the place. Part of him couldn't believe what he'd just heard, but another pictured him throwing himself at his old mentor, pushing him down on the ground, and cuffing his hands behind his back.

He'd been on his way to Herman Edelman's apartment on Kaptensgatan to confront him about the recorded call, almost as if he subconsciously harboured a hope somewhere that there was still a sufficiently credible explanation that would allow him to get a good night's sleep, and the reassurance that everything would return to normal as soon as they'd put this behind them.

He realized now that there was no such explanation. Edelman knew much more than he had let on, and was involved in the death of the Minister for Justice in one way or another. When it came down to it, he would be forced to put his boss against the wall and demand an answer from him. But not yet. He still knew far too little, and needed to ask the right questions to get real answers.

He got back into the taxi and asked the driver to continue past Edelman's front door down towards Artillerigatan to the police station on Kungsholmen. Once he arrived, he swiped his pass card, entered the code and walked through the pitch-black corridor towards his and Malin's office.

He had planned to go through the investigation again with fresh eyes. He was convinced that the solution was somewhere among all the pictures, notes and strange coincidences.

But when he walked into the room, everything was gone. At first he thought he'd gone into the wrong room. But no, it was his and Malin's desks. He looked around in confusion. The whiteboard had been cleaned, the notes on the wall had been taken down and the piles of folders on the desks and floor had been tidied. The room was empty.

Yes, the investigation was officially closed and there would never be a trial, but it hadn't been more than seven hours since Kremph committed suicide. Technical evidence still needed to be secured and categorized, reports needed to be written and meetings conducted before anything was ready to be packed up.

He logged on to his computer and searched the archive, but couldn't find anything there either. Someone had removed all their evidence, and he didn't have a clue who it could be. In fact, it could be anyone from SePo to Edelman himself, or someone else entirely. He sunk down into his desk chair and rested his head in his hands. All he knew for sure was that it must be someone who, like him, was fully aware that the perpetrator was still at large.

He decided to go home and try to get a few hours' sleep, since he had no idea how to move forward. But just as he was turning off the computer, he noticed one of the two porcelain dolls they'd found in the condemned apartment. It was sitting on Malin's shelf alongside a pile of folders and two packets of Marie biscuits. He had no recollection of either of them taking the doll. Even if they had it should have ended up with Hillevi Stubbs. Was it the doll from the apartment or one just like it?

He took it down and studied the curly hair, embroidered dress and matching hat, and his thoughts quickly shifted to his childhood doll. But he didn't get much further than that before he realized that there was something off about the eyes, something that distinguished one from the other. When he looked closer he saw that the brown pupil was actually a hole.

With a growing sense of worry, he started to investigate the doll more thoroughly. He examined the hat, the unpleasantly realistic face, the hard arms and legs and under the skirt, which was attached with Velcro along the back.

At first it made no sense. Just like Carl-Eric Grimås' abdomen, the doll's back was hollowed out. A white, rectangular plastic box with a number of blinking diodes was squeezed into the little space. It said *Anbash* in the lower corner beside a little button, and a cable extended up one side through the neck towards the head. Fabian had never seen anything like it, but realized immediately that it had to be a battery-driven camera that was connected in some way to the cell phone network.

The moment he realized what was going on, he broke into a sweat and suddenly turned ice cold. The perpetrator had had the condemned apartment under surveillance, and their offices too, for the past few days. He had had access to all their thoughts and ideas and knew exactly where each of them was in the investigation, not only Malin, Tomas and Jarmo, but also himself.

In fact, the perpetrator could be looking at him right now.

68

DUNJA'S WHOLE BODY STILL hurt and she presumably looked like she'd been in a minor traffic accident, but she couldn't say for sure because she deliberately avoided all mirrors for the entire morning. After being examined in the hospital, she had spent the night at Hotel Nora around the corner on Nørrebrogade, while Kjeld Richter and his men examined her apartment. Sleizner promised to cover costs. A psychologist from the Crime Victims office had been recommended to her, but she declined. She didn't know why, but she hadn't been able to take in the events from last night at all. Maybe she was still in shock.

She'd decided to stay at the hotel as long as she could, and try to enjoy her Sunday. But when she finally managed to get out of bed, take a bath and order a room-service breakfast, restlessness took over. No more than an hour later she limped out of the elevator and down the corridor towards the department where she ascertained that a meeting was in full swing.

Given all of the events of last night, she knew she really shouldn't be there, but she couldn't help thinking that it was a bit rude. This was her investigation. She was the person who had discovered the leads and tied everything together. She was the one who had led her team to an abandoned car near Copenhagen Airport, containing the mutilated bodies of Aksel Neuman and Katja Skov. Regardless of the fact that her conclusions were ultimately wrong regarding Benny Willumsen, they should at least have asked if she wanted to be there.

The door to the meeting room was open and she heard scattered laughter: the sound of a complicated investigation ending and a feared perpetrator being neutralized. She could hear the exhilaration in the air. *They were eating up all the glory*, she thought, right before she knocked on the open door.

The laughter stopped and they turned towards her.

'Dunja? What are you doing here?' Sleizner stood up and came over to her.

'The question is, what are all of you doing here?' She held up a hand defensively. 'I thought I was the one leading the investigation.'

'Yes, but now it's over, thanks to you. It's just a matter of tying up—'

'Who said it's over?' Dunja asked. 'Not me, anyway.'

'No. But I did. After all, I'm still the one who makes the decisions in this department. Or have I missed something?' Sleizner started laughing and turned to the others, who immediately joined him.

Dunja didn't change her expression. The last thing she wanted was to join their little club.

'Dunja, I don't understand. What's the problem?' Sleizner continued. 'The perpetrator has been identified and is dead. Sure, the investigation into what happened at your place isn't finished, but that's not anything you should be worried about. Instead, take it easy and—'

'It wasn't him.'

'What do you mean it wasn't him?' Sleizner exchanged glances with the others. 'Are you suggesting, in all seriousness, that Benny Willumsen was innocent? For fuck's sake, the man broke into your flat and tried to kill you!'

'Yes, well, he's not guilty of the murders of Karen and Aksel Neuman, and Katja Skov, at least.' She limped into the room. Hesk looked so uncomfortable from her mere presence that he was squirming like an eel to avoid her gaze.

'Dunja,' Sleizner let out an exaggerated sigh. 'This is your first case, and it's not strange if you—'

'Kim, this isn't me—'

'Can you let me finish talking?'

'No, because I know exactly what you're going to say, and you're wrong.' Dunja fed a pod into the Nespresso machine and pressed start. 'So now you're the one who should let me finish talking.' She took the full espresso cup and was surprised to discover that she didn't feel obligated to put a five-kroner coin in the basket. 'For one thing, I've encountered the perpetrator – not Willumsen, but the real one. He's a much smaller man.'

'Was this in Sweden?' asked Richter, and Dunja nodded as she sat down.

'Yes. I had a hunch that he was travelling south towards Kävlinge. I followed him to a storage facility and caught him red-handed standing over the body of Katja Skov. It was horrible.' She shook the image of Katja's mutilated body from her mind.

'Did you see his face?' Hesk met her gaze for the first time.

'No, he was standing with his back to me. When he turned around he was wearing a gas mask. Then he anaesthetized me the same way he must have done with the others.'

'But he killed them.'

'Which is my next point: why would he let me live in Sweden, and then try to kill me in Denmark just a few hours later?'

She was met with silence and an exchange of glances.

'What's your explanation?' Sleizner said at last.

'Willumsen was basically after the thrill, but our perpetrator has a completely different motive. And I wasn't part of it.'

'And how does Willumsen come into the picture?' Sleizner went over to the coffee machine and conspicuously dropped a five-kroner piece into the basket. 'If he's suddenly so innocent, why would he break into your place and—'

'Who said he was innocent? Only the three most recent murders aren't Willumsen's, but they were carried out to look that way – with extreme violence and genital penetration.'

'You mean like a copycat?' said Richter.

'Yes, maybe. In any event, he must have understood that we were on his trail, and instead of fleeing—'

'No, I'm sorry, but this doesn't add up.' Sleizner threw out his arms. 'I have no doubt that this is Willumsen's work.' He nodded towards the whiteboard, which was filled with pictures and arrows that pointed to similarities between the old and new cases. 'I can't see a single point where we messed things up.'

'Are you blind?' Dunja exclaimed, slamming her palm on the table so that the espresso cup tipped over. 'The point is that a murderer is still running free out there!'

There was complete silence around the table once again. Gazes shifted and everyone expected some form of reaction from Sleizner. This was the first time anyone on the team had raised their voice at him. Dunja stood up, pushed another pod into the machine, let it fill a new cup and sat down again – without so much as an effort to pay.

'Dunja, I'm going to be completely sincere here,' Sleizner said at last. 'You've done an amazing job, there's no question about that. And I think I can speak for everyone around this table when I say that no one expected the investigation would move so quickly. So, congratulations.' He clapped his hands a few times in applause and started walking around. 'But your tone and attitude right now are completely unacceptable.' He stood right behind her. 'I'm sure it can be explained by what you've been through in the past twenty-four hours and the euphoria you now have from managing to stay alive. As far as this matter is concerned, I'm willing to overlook it – for the time being. As far as our suspects are concerned, I think you're on completely the wrong track. I'm convinced that you have no idea what you're talking about. But I don't want to be small-minded. I'll entertain the idea of this so-called other perpetrator, mostly just as a little game to see where it leads us.'

'How kind,' said Dunja. 'Then I suggest that we—'

'So then my first question is: Why pack you into the trunk with Neuman's and Skov's body parts and not simply leave you behind in Sweden? You led us to the car much faster and to a lot of evidence, one piece of which has just been sent for DNA analysis.'

'Evidence? What have you found?'

'Not us. Pedersen,' said Hesk, awaiting an okay from Sleizner before he continued. 'He's been working all night and has examined the body parts.' Hesk took out two photographs from a brown envelope and set them on the table in front of Dunja.

Both images were bird's-eye views: one showed Aksel Neuman's chopped-off body parts set up on an illuminated examination table in their anatomically correct places with a few centimetres in between each part. Dunja counted eleven parts, and could not help picturing a magician, failing to saw a woman in half. The other showed Katja Skov laid out in similar fashion on the table alongside.

'Where's her right breast?' Dunja looked more closely at the image. There was nothing where her right side should have been. Aksel Neuman, on the other hand, was cut down the middle.

'It's still missing, but here's the important part.' Hesk set out another image that was zoomed in on Skov's genitalia. 'Pedersen has secured traces of the perpetrator's sperm, which is exactly what's been missing all along to get Willumsen convicted.'

Dunja nodded. 'And what if it isn't his?'

'We'll find that out once we get the test results,' said Sleizner. 'But let's go back to my question: What's the point of keeping you in the car?'

'I've asked myself the exact same question and have decided that there's only one explanation.' She met the others' eyes. 'He wanted us to find the car and everything in it quickly.'

'You mean all the evidence?' said Richter. Dunja nodded.

'So the motive would be to get Willumsen convicted?' asked Hesk.

'That could be part of it, but likely more as a side effect. Keep in mind that we're dealing with someone who is prepared to kill innocent people and mutilate them. Willumsen must have been a diversion to point us away from what this is really about.'

'And what is that?' said Sleizner with barely restrained irritation.

'I don't know for sure, but the answer should be in the victims. Or, if you ask me, what's missing *from* the victims.' She tapped her finger against the picture of Katja Skov. 'Besides, we really should dredge up the car from the port at Helsingør, or at least have someone dive down and take a look. It's how the perpetrator got over here.'

Sleizner clenched his teeth and thought. 'Okay, as you wish, but as soon as the results from the DNA analysis arrive confirming it's Willumsen, this investigation goes to the archive. Is that understood?'

Everyone nodded.

Everyone except Dunja.

69

07:30–08:30 Breakfast

08:30–08:42 Clean up after breakfast

08:42–09:00 Shower

09:00–09:14 Get dressed & pack. Shave (Daddy)

09:14–09:15 Scrape the windows on the car

09:15–09:30 Drive to the water park

09:30–12:00 Water Park!

'COME ALONG NOW. I don't want us to be late.' Matilda yanked the handwritten schedule, illustrated with small, colourful drawings, out of Fabian's hands.

At thirteen minutes past seven, she'd turned on the overhead light, climbed up on the bed, sat on his stomach and showed him the plan for their Sunday together. He hadn't even got three hours of sleep, which was less than half of what he really needed to function.

Two double espressos later, he almost felt awake, and he promised himself that he would devote this Sunday entirely to being a dad. The investigation could wait. Anyway, he needed time to think about how he could move forward without Edelman's knowledge. Today he would let the kids decide. He even agreed to a visit to the water park, despite the fact he loathed it more than the subway at rush hour.

But first they would have a hearty breakfast. After he and Matilda had set out everything on the table and lit the Advent candle, he went into Theodor's room to wake him. Usually, when he went into his son's bedroom, the chaos and dust bunnies gave him an urgent desire to air out or, even better, decontaminate the room. But this time he felt something quite different, something that had nothing to do with the piles of clothes on the floor. It could best be described as a hard punch in the stomach.

Theodor was sleeping on his back, and Fabian was reminded of his own behaviour from last night. What he had done was not only a punishable offence, but a mortal sin. He had struck his son. His patience had run out, which had resulted in a hard slap right to his face.

Now it was not only red and blue, but also severely swollen around the right eye and the upper lip, where the blood was congealing into a scab. His stomach twisted and his appetite for everything waiting on the breakfast table disappeared. He sank down on the edge of the bed, put his head in one hand, and patted Theodor's head carefully with the other. Had he really hit him that hard? How could he ever forgive himself?

The dirty jeans in the pile on the floor provided the explanation; or rather, the melted snow in a little pool on the floor beneath them did.

Theodor had been out last night, even though Fabian had explicitly said no. He had promised to stay home, but had gone out instead. Fabian wanted to wake him and call him out. But to what end? The damage was already done, and the best he could do was to let him sleep and bring it up with Sonja when all the other stuff had calmed down.

'BUT DADDY, HOW LONG is this going to take?' said Matilda from the back seat while Fabian turned into the parking lot at Stockholm South General Hospital.

'Not long at all. Half an hour at most.'

'But then we won't make it to the water park. It opens at nine thirty. Daddy, you promised,' Matilda continued as she reached for the plastic bag on the other side of the back seat that was wrapped several times around its contents.

'But I couldn't know that Malin would call and be so angry that I haven't been to visit her. We'll have time for everything, except maybe swimming,' said Fabian, finally finding a parking spot. 'The movie, McDonald's, the whole rest of the programme – I promise.'

'But then I want candy.' Matilda got hold of the bag and pulled it towards her.

'Today? But it's Sunday.'

'Yes. Sunday candy. And I want it now.'

Fabian took the order from the back seat with a mute nod and got out of the car, while Matilda opened the bag and looked down at the porcelain doll with big eyes.

MALIN WAS IN A ward with five other patients. She was asleep. Her face was as pale as the sheets on the bed and patches of unruly hair were plastered to her sweaty forehead. One arm was connected to a drip and the half-unbuttoned hospital gown exposed far too much for his liking. Fabian put a bunch of flowers into a stainless steel vase on the wheeled table as quietly as he could.

'Is she dead?' Matilda whispered while he wrote a greeting on the card with the flowers.

'No, she's just tired. Come along, let's go.' Fabian took Matilda by the hand and went towards the door.

'And where do you think you two are going?'

Fabian turned and saw that Malin had opened her eyes. 'I thought you were asleep, and didn't want to…'

'I see. Sit down and tell me about it instead. And, hi, Matilda. How nice of you to stop by, too. There's another chair over there.'

Matilda went over to get the chair.

'Tell you about what?' said Fabian.

Malin rolled her eyes. 'I have pre-eclampsia. I didn't get a lobotomy!'

Fabian pulled up a chair and sat down. 'Malin, there isn't much to tell other than what I'm sure you already know. After you passed out, Kremph managed to jump out of a window.'

'That much I know. But then what happened?'

'Not much since then. The investigation is closed and everyone is happy.' He underscored it all with a smile, as he heard Matilda opening the bag of candy.

'Did Anders tell you to act like this?'

'What do you mean, "act"? I haven't even spoken to Anders. Malin, I don't understand what—'

'Knock it off, before I get paralysed for real. Don't come here and tell me that it's all over. Do you think I can't see from the frown on your face how much you're struggling with the fact that it's Sunday and you want nothing more than to work?'

Fabian went through his options, even though he'd already decided what to say, and sighed. 'I don't think it was Kremph. I think he was only a decoy and that the perpetrator is someone else altogether.' He expected the usual strong opposition and explanations that shot his ideas to the ground, but he got nothing – not even an eye roll. He couldn't tell if she hadn't heard him or if she was just too tired to react. 'Malin?' He waved one hand in front of her face. 'Did you hear what I said?'

'Yes, I heard. And, no, I'm not brain dead yet. I actually already suspected the exact same thing.'

'You did? Since when?'

'Some time after I woke up at the hospital. Right when it happened I thought he was just talking about his "other self", but that's not what he was doing at all.'

'Yes?' Fabian leaned closer to her.

'In the middle of the visit to the crime scene, don't you remember that he said something about someone who had suddenly appeared?'

Fabian shook his head. He'd been so preoccupied with tending to Malin that he almost hadn't heard a word of what Kremph had said. 'And unfortunately the videotape is gone.'

'What do you mean, "gone"?'

'I was at the department last night because I wanted to go through all the investigation material, including Tomas' video from the crime scene visit, but someone had already been there and cleaned up.'

'God, how strange. Who would—'

'SePo, if you ask me,' said Fabian, who had decided to keep the Edelman issue to himself for the time being. 'I don't know exactly how or why, but I have no doubt that this goes considerably higher up than our little department. I promise that it's not just you and me who've realized that Kremph was innocent.'

'It's really lucky that I didn't rely on Tomas and his film talents. Can you pass me the phone on that table?'

'Did you record it yourself?' Fabian asked, handing over the cell phone.

'It was mostly so I could listen to it right away when I got home.' She unlocked her cell and went to the audio files. 'Listen to this.'

'*But that's not good at all. It's very bad. It doesn't work, then everything goes wrong*,' Kremph's rambling voice was coming through the microphone. '*Everything has to be right, and if it's not everything starts twirling round and round, and I get so tired. All of a sudden he's there, the weird guy, although I'm the only one of course.*' Kremph swallowed and caught his breath. '*He has the keys and is there anyway. He fixes and helps out. He doesn't think I know, but I do, and then everything gets so dark and heavy, and then it's like I just go away.*'

'*Ossian, try to take it easy—*'

Malin paused the recording and met Fabian's gaze. 'Did you hear that?'

'Do you mean "the weird guy"? He's just referring to his other self there. He even says that.'

'I thought so too when I heard it the first time, but listen to it one more time.' She started the audio file again.

'Daddy, will you be done soon?' said Matilda in her whiniest voice.

'*Everything has to be right, and if it's not everything starts twirling round and round, and—*'

'But Daddy, this is boring.'

Fabian hushed her without turning around, and didn't see that she had the porcelain doll hidden inside her jacket, and was in the process of poking at the button on the back.

'*All of a sudden he's there, the weird guy, although I'm the only one of course. He has the keys and is there anyway. He fixes and helps out. He doesn't think I know, but I do, and then everything gets so dark and heavy.*'

'It's the keys he's referring to. "He has the keys and is there anyways. He fixes and helps out."'

Fabian nodded. Malin was right.

'Another thing,' Malin continued. 'He's not saying "weird", but *beard*, which means that it must be someone else he's talking about. Someone with a beard, who comes in, even though he doesn't have keys. Listen to this.' She started the recording again.

'*I lock up every day and I've even replaced the bolts. Lock, lock, and then I check whether it's locked – always. Otherwise you can't be completely sure.*'

'He's even changed the locks, yet the "beard guy" is still there, helping out.'

'You think it's the perpetrator?'

'Who else could it be?'

Fabian thought about what Malin had said. A cleaning woman pushed in her cart and started mopping the floor.

'Oh, how nice,' said Malin. 'As you can see, I spilled a little coffee last night.' She pointed to the light-brown spot on the floor beside the bed.

'There must be another way to get in to Kremph's apartment,' said Fabian, moving so that the cleaning woman could reach in.

'I was coming to that: the scaffolding.'

'No, there isn't any. The other entrance from Östgötagatan has some— Matilda?' Fabian hurried over to his daughter, who was playing with the doll. 'What are you doing?' He tore it out of her hands. 'Did I say you could play with this?' He searched for the tiny button in the back and turned it off as fast as he could. 'Huh? Did I?'

'I thought it was for me.' Matilda burst into tears. 'I thought it was a present because you've been gone so much.' Her eyes filled with tears that started running down her cheeks.

'Okay, then I understand,' Fabian said, patting her on the head.

'Are you really angry?'

'No, it's okay. You couldn't have known that only Dad gets to touch this before Christmas Eve.' He gave her a hug.

'Fabian. Can you explain what's going on?' said Malin.

He nodded. 'But first we have to see about getting you a different room.'

70

MAYBE MALIN WAS RIGHT when she accused him of being more paranoid than a private detective, but Fabian couldn't have cared less. Paranoid or not, he didn't feel relaxed until she'd been moved to another room, and the staff had agreed not to inform anyone other than the immediate family where she was under any circumstances.

Matilda had started the camera in the doll, and no one knew how long or how much it had transmitted to its unknown recipient before Fabian turned it off. In the best-case scenario it was nothing, but there was a risk that everything from pictures of them and the room to large parts of their conversation had been transferred.

He'd thought about destroying it, but decided that it was better to let Hillevi Stubbs look at it as planned. With a little luck there might be a way to find out what, if anything, had transmitted and maybe even to whom.

Stubbs didn't need to look at it for more than a few seconds before she could confirm his worst fears: Anbash Limited was a Chinese company that hadn't existed for much more than three years, but it had already released a number of products that could be described as advanced espionage equipment. And absolutely anyone could order them online.

The wireless camera was their latest creation. Just as Fabian suspected, it was equipped with a SIM card that used the 3G mobile network to transmit both images and audio as soon as the motion detector was triggered. Unfortunately, she had no idea how they could trace the recipient because the SIM card was from an anonymous prepaid phone. It was almost certainly connected to a proxy server that would allow the recipient to study the information without revealing his own IP address.

But, Fabian, there's one thing I don't understand, she suddenly said as he stuffed the doll back in the bag and asked her about the keys to Kremph's apartment. *Isn't this over? I mean, the perpetrator's dead, no?* He had nodded and said something about just wanting to tie up the final loose ends. *Just make sure so you don't fall*, she called to him as he returned to the car where Matilda was waiting.

Even though they'd deviated from the crammed schedule for most of the morning, Matilda was in a surprisingly good mood. The rest of the day, however, she governed with an iron fist and refused to agree to the slightest digression. The first stop was the SF cinema in Söderhallarna, where she insisted they see James Cameron's 3D epic *Avatar*, which had just opened. Even if both *Aliens* and *Terminator* were among Fabian's absolute favourite films, he did not have the slightest interest in seeing the 'blue man movie', as he chose to refer to it after seeing the trailer.

Unfortunately, his misgivings were warranted, and the only positive aspect of the two-hour-and-forty-minute-long 'walk in the woods' was that he could close his eyes behind the 3D glasses and get some much-needed rest.

Matilda, on the other hand, loved it, and thought it was the best film she'd ever seen – something she thought pretty much every time she went to the movies. This time she was prepared to go so far as to cancel the rest of the itinerary and go right back in and see it again. But hunger stepped in and they made a scheduled stop to the McDonald's on Folkungagatan. Afterwards they took the car to Mariatorget and bowled until they arrived at the last item on the programme.

7:15–8:00 Surprise Mum with coffee

Fabian had hoped that this idea would run into the sand, or that they would simply not have time: there was nothing Sonja liked less than surprises. In this case it would mean disturbing her in the middle of her final work before an exhibition, and at a time when she'd been more stressed than ever.

On the way to the car, which was parked further up on Hornsgatspuckeln, he tried to convince Matilda that they should just go and have coffee themselves instead, or call Theodor and see if he wanted to join them. But Matilda wouldn't budge an inch. It would be coffee with Sonja, and it would be a surprise. Half an hour later they were standing down on Munkbrogatan 6 buzzing up from the entrance.

'Why doesn't she answer?' said Matilda, with a steaming paper cup in each hand.

'I don't know. Maybe she's out buying more paint.'

'Now?'

'Or else she just doesn't want to be disturbed. You know how it is when she's stressed.' Fabian held down the button a little longer and waited. 'Matilda, let's go and sit down at the café, before your hot chocolate gets cold.'

Matilda shook her head. 'You'll just have to use your keys.'

'What keys?'

'Yours. You have a way in too.'

'No. Where did you get—'

'Daddy.' Matilda rolled her eyes.

Fabian actually did have a set of keys in case Sonja lost hers, or if he needed to get into the studio for some reason. But bursting in and surprising her was not what they were supposed to be used for, and the fact that Matilda even knew they existed made him wonder how much more she knew.

'Well, look at this, here they are.' He stuck one of the keys in the lock and turned it.

They took the elevator and walked up the last flight of stairs to the studio, where Matilda pressed the doorbell with one finger.

'Okay, unlock it,' she said after just a few seconds.

'Shouldn't we wait a little before—'

'Daddy, unlock it now.'

Fabian reluctantly opened the door. 'I'm going in first. You wait here.' To his surprise, Matilda actually nodded, so he went in alone and looked around.

He didn't know what he'd expected: Sonja lying in a foetal position shaking, totally incapable of filling all the empty canvases with new, meaningless underwater motifs, which was the theme of her last four exhibitions. Or what he encountered: Sonja wearing headphones, blasting 'Shout' by Tears for Fears on full volume, and singing along while she worked on several parallel stretched canvases.

Fabian exhaled, but felt a growing worry about what might happen as soon as she noticed him. *She would almost certainly lose her flow and rightly blame him*, he thought and decided that the best thing to do would be to sneak back out and convince Matilda that they should let her mother work in peace.

But just as he turned around, the light flicked on and off rapidly, which made Sonja turn around with a start and pull off the headphones. 'What are you two doing here?' The look on her face was just as cold and hard as he had expected. 'I thought I'd been perfectly clear about—'

'We're bringing you coffee,' Matilda interrupted, letting go of the light switch at the doorway.

Sonja stopped short and tried to smile.

'Sonja, I really tried, but you know how persistent Matilda can be.'

Sonja nodded and sighed. 'It's okay.'

'You sure?'

She nodded again and crouched down in front of Matilda. 'And what kind of goodies have you brought?'

'Coffee and Lucia buns.'

'Mmm, just what I'm hungry for.'

To Fabian's surprise, the coffee break far exceeded expectations. His premonition of trying silence and corrosive comments came to nothing.

Matilda had planned everything down to the slightest detail. Sonja was instructed to take out some fabric that could serve as a tablecloth in the middle of the floor, and he had to turn off the overhead light. Then he was told to light as many tea lights as he could find, and set them in a circle on the floor around the cloth. Matilda went over to the stereo and put on the CD he'd made with Prince's 'I Would Die For U' on it nineteen times in a row.

The coffee had cooled down long before and the Lucia buns had started to get dry, but that didn't matter. Matilda was enjoying herself immensely and steered the conversation through everything from what she wanted for Christmas to where they should go on vacation next summer. And like a piece of modern choreography, Fabian and Sonja helped to avoid the worst pitfalls.

Fabian found himself laughing several times, while he was struck by how Sonja's stiff smile seemed increasingly more relaxed and natural. The frown, hunched-up shoulders and tense mouth seeped away as he remembered how she had looked when they first got together, before the years with small children and performance anxiety in the studio, and before all the fights. If only it was that simple.

He noticed that it was well past eight. 'Matilda, we have to leave Mum alone so she can keep working,' he said, attempting to leave.

Matilda shook her head. 'Can I stay here instead?'

'No, how would that work?' Fabian reached for her hand. 'You know how much Mum has to do. Besides, the schedule says that we're supposed to leave here at eight o'clock, and it's almost eight-thirty.'

'Pleeeease.'

'No, let's go now.' He took hold of her arm and pulled her up.

'I said I don't want to!' she screamed, tearing herself out of his grasp.

'Fabian, it's fine,' said Sonja. 'She can stay. Christmas vacation starts tomorrow anyway.'

'Yay!' Matilda exclaimed, hugging Sonja. 'I promise not to bug you, even a little bit.'

Fabian looked Sonja in the eyes to see whether she really was okay with it.

'It's fine,' she repeated. 'These are the last ones anyway.' She pointed at the canvases set up around them. 'Ever.'

'But what are you going to paint after?' said Matilda.

Sonja shrugged and stood up. 'We'll cross that bridge when we get to it.' She followed Fabian to the door in silence and let him out. 'Listen.'

Fabian turned around. 'Yes?'

'I know we're not in the best place right now, and maybe it's just a phase that will blow over soon, like you said.' She sighed and lowered her eyes. 'Anyway, I've been thinking a little, and I don't know how long we can keep going like this.'

Fabian let the silence grow, well aware that it was his turn to say something. He knew that she wanted him to come out strongly and emphasize how much he loved her, and how much better everything would be soon, but this time he didn't. He had always been so sure that whatever happened they would stick together. Sure, he'd threatened divorce once or twice, but they had obviously been empty threats.

Now, he honestly didn't know any more. All he could do was nod, turn around and head back down the stairs.

71

SEMIRA ACKERMAN MADE A final round of the pool, picking up some towels and indoor shoes that had been left behind. The announcement informing people that the pool was about to close had already been made twice on the PA system, and most of the guests had dressed and were clearing out their lockers. But there was always someone who lingered behind, and tonight was no exception, she noted, when she heard one of the showers starting.

She didn't usually work on Sundays because she had managed to get the day off as part of her contract, unlike all of her colleagues. And each time the new head of human resources, whose age was a mockery of the rest of the staff, asked her to 'stand up for the team' when someone was sick, she'd said no. It was always that annoying 'team'.

As if anyone on the 'team' had ever stood up for her.

No, her Sundays were sacred. It was the only thing in her life that hadn't regressed and completely lost its meaning. Normally she spent it at home – or, more correctly, in the armchair with her legs on a footrest, a good book in her hands and a thermos of hot tea on the windowsill. She loved reading, and the only thing that could get her out of the chair was weather so beautiful that it would be a shame not to take a walk.

She usually tried to challenge herself and walk somewhere new. In the best-case scenario, she explored a different neighbourhood. But it almost always ended with her walking down towards the quay at Hammarby Lake, taking the Lotten over to the other side and wandering around all the buildings, which, even though they were newly constructed, were beautiful. It usually took a little over two hours, but sometimes it could take even longer if she sat down somewhere to read along the way.

But this particular Sunday she was working – by choice. When she had asked the head of HR if she could work, he looked at her as if she was pulling his leg. He quickly got serious and made it clear that she would not be getting overtime. She almost retracted her offer right then and there, but stopped herself at the last moment – she simply didn't dare be home alone for the whole day.

Nothing had been the same since that man, whom her sister thought was a cop, followed her on the bus. Although she'd managed to shake him off, she couldn't eat, sleep, read or even consider taking the bus again. Instead she'd started walking all the way to the subway at Medborgarplatsen and changing from the green line to the red line at Old Town to get to work. She felt infinitely more secure when she was out among other people and Sturebadet, where she worked, was such a place.

She was almost ready to close and would soon be on her way home, but she couldn't just yet because of the straggler in the women's changing room. Usually it was the men who lingered, often armed with a shameless proposition. Mostly she just shook her head and laughed, and asked the guest to get dressed before she called the guys at Securitas. If that didn't work, she always had the ice-cold spray of the water hose as back-up.

But women were almost never a problem, she thought on her way into the changing room, while she tried to convince herself that there was no reason whatsoever for worry.

Carnela had promised to keep her company that evening, and she intended to do everything in her power to convince her to sleep over. She would surely protest and bring up one excuse after the other, but sleeping over was the least she could do. In some ways, she was actually partly to blame for the whole thing.

Personally, Semira had been against the idea from the very beginning and had consistently refused to listen to her sister's argument about how simple and easy it was, not to mention safe. But as her condition worsened she'd started to waver in her conviction, and by the time she couldn't read a book without a magnifying glass, she was converted.

Afterwards, the worry manifested as a big lump in her chest and she'd had dreams so strange she didn't even want to tell her therapist. But as the years passed, the lump had shrunk and life returned to normal. She had finally felt that Carnela was right about how safe it was.

Until now.

The shower had stopped running so she started to look around the lockers, but couldn't find anyone. As far as she could tell, all the lockers were unlocked and empty, which was also a bit strange. She went into the shower room and noted that it too was empty. She was sure she'd heard someone showering less than a minute ago. She briefly glanced around the room and noticed one of the showers was still dripping.

She wondered whether she should call for help, but decided not to let worry get the better of her and continued towards the toilet stalls. Perhaps the person in question needed to make one final visit. But nobody was there. The last place left to check was the sauna. If it was also empty she would have to start over and search the whole facility one more time.

The door to the dry sauna was jammed, so she had to take hold of it with both hands to get it open. The wall of heat surprised her and reminded her how long it had been since she had taken advantage of the staff benefits and indulged in a few hours at the spa. As soon as this was over, she would make sure to use one of her Sundays off to make the most of it.

She went to pick up a towel that was up in the far corner, climbing up three rows of benches. The heat had changed from feeling like a warm, encompassing embrace to hard and aggressive. She reached for the towel and felt the sweat dripping down her body – and she almost never sweated. She would be soaked through before she knew it.

She climbed down again, and moved to open the door. It was jammed again and refused to budge, even though she pushed on it so hard that the sweat made her clothes cling to her body. On Monday she would have to inform the caretaker so that he could fix it right after closing. Only when she pressed her whole body against the door could she get it open.

On her way to the steam sauna she toyed with the idea of taking a shower before she turned everything off and went home, but there was no point because she didn't have a change of clothes. Besides, she'd decided on something else.

She didn't know how or why, she simply knew that it suddenly felt right. As soon as she got home she would contact the police and tell them everything she knew. Carnela would be furious, of course, but that wasn't her problem. It was the right thing to do.

The door to the steam sauna opened easily, and she stuck her head into the damp fog that made it almost impossible to see whether anyone was really inside.

'Hello? Is anyone here? We're closing now.' She wanted to sound as calm and neutral as possible, but as soon as she heard her own voice she realized that those were the last things she felt.

72

FABIAN TOOK THE FLASHLIGHT from the extra compartment in the trunk and closed the hatch. He pressed the automatic lock as he crossed Östgötagatan. On the way home from the studio he thought about what Sonja had said and tried to figure out where he stood. But somewhere by Slussen his thoughts wandered to Malin's idea that there was probably another way to get into Ossian Kremph's apartment – a way that didn't need a key. Malin was right. The perpetrator must have got into the apartment another way.

During the visit to the crime scene he had heard only confused babble about a radio, but despite her pregnancy and pre-eclampsia, Malin had had the presence of mind to actually listen to the words coming out of Kremph's mouth. He had flat-out admitted that a bearded man came to his place, even though he'd changed the locks himself. It was this kind of thing that made Malin a better police officer than everyone else in their department combined, himself included.

The decision to go there now instead of waiting until tomorrow was no more difficult than making a left turn and heading down to Söderleden instead of continuing straight on Hornsgatan.

On his way up the spiral staircase he thought about the recorded cell phone call between Grimås and Edelman. He hadn't mentioned anything about it to Malin, mostly because he still felt uncertain about how he should handle it. How much more did Edelman really know, and how would he react if he was confronted? The only thing Fabian felt sure of was that he wanted to avoid such a situation with his old mentor at any price. His best option would be to collect enough evidence to move the presumption of guilt away from Kremph and leave Edelman no other choice but to open the investigation again.

Once he arrived at the door, he unlocked it with the keys he'd got from Stubbs. He walked into the cluttered apartment and the flashlight beam floated along the walls. He wondered where he should start. The concealed entrance was actually only one of several reasons why he was there.

According to Hillevi Stubbs, Ossian Kremph's two personalities manifested themselves as two different layers in the apartment. One was extremely organized and methodical, and the other had a head full of memory gaps and spread everything around with no idea why. The theory sounded logical on paper, but in reality was quite inaccurate.

It had helped her quickly find the clue that led them to Adam Fischer in the Shurgard storage facility. But it wasn't, as Stubbs had assumed, the organized Kremph who had hidden the lead. He also didn't put the scalpel in the kitchen, leave behind the container of hexane gas, or cut the eyes out of all the pictures of the woman on the bus.

That was the perpetrator.

Someone had prepared the apartment, planted all the leads, and set up Kremph for the role as the perfect perpetrator. All Fabian needed to do now was find the evidence.

He decided to start with the bathroom, which looked like most bathrooms in need of a major renovation: the tub had an edge so yellow no cleanser in the world could scrub it clean; joints in the linoleum were black with mould; and the mirror of the medicine cabinet only reflected in a few places.

He opened the mirrored door and scanned the shelves inside. On the top row, there was a small pharmacy of containers with names like Atarax, Leponex, Zopiklon and Xanor. There were various types of creams for eczema on the middle shelf. But on the bottom shelf, next to a tube of toothpaste and a roll of floss, was what he was after: the red pill box that Kremph had mentioned at the visit to the crime scene. He picked it up and studied the plastic container that locked on top and had three small compartments for every day of the week: morning, noon and evening.

The compartments were empty from Monday morning until Saturday morning, which made sense because Kremph had been arrested just on Saturday. The remaining compartments were filled with different-coloured pills. He picked one out at random, put it in his mouth and chewed.

He should have taken the pill in for official analysis, even though he already had his suspicions. Kremph had been quite sure he'd taken his pills every day, which he had been doing, but judging by the taste he'd only consumed sugar. Fabian opened one of the bottles from the topmost shelf and tasted another pill – same thing.

Kremph had unknowingly gone without medication for some time. The question was, how long? If it was months, the perpetrator had had plenty of time to both control and exploit him during the period that his dissociative identity disorder reawakened.

He took the container with him out into the living room, set it on the table and looked around the room. There was one more thing he needed to find before he could start seriously searching for the entrance. He assumed that it was located centrally to cover an area as big as possible. His eyes fell on the shelves that were filled from edge to edge with books. It wasn't the first time he'd looked at it, but only now did it occur to him that there was something about it that didn't add up.

Among the titles were gardening and art books, Enid Blyton's old *Famous Five* series, and a lot of pink chick-lit. But not a single one of them could have conceivably interested Ossian so much that he would have put them on his nicest, most centrally located bookshelf. It could mean only one thing.

Someone else had put them there.

He started browsing through the books one by one. Once he came to the middle of the shelf, he pulled out *Can You Keep a Secret?* by Sophie Kinsella and found what he was looking for: the pages in the middle had been cut out so there was an empty space when the book was closed. A white, rectangular plastic box with blinking diodes, similar to the one hidden in the doll, was positioned in the space.

He turned it off with the little button, set it on the table beside the box of pills and turned his attention towards finding the concealed entrance. He was more certain than ever that this would have been how the 'beard man' got in after Kremph locked his doors. He started in the hall, but couldn't find anything behind the clothes hanging down from the coat hooks or behind the reddish-brown drapery that covered part of one wall.

He checked the two windows in the living room but saw no signs that they were broken. He opened one, leaned out and shone the flashlight along the exterior of the building. A dog's barking echoed between the façades and the Opel parked in front of his own car turned out and drove off along Blekingegatan. But he could see no signs on the façade to indicate that someone had come in that way.

Because none of the walls in the room bordered a neighbouring apartment, he continued by checking the floor: he picked up the rug and shone his flashlight under the couch. Then he aimed the beam of light towards the ceiling and searched for straight cracks at right angles. Aside from a number of spider webs and flakes in the yellowed ceiling paint, there was nothing resembling a concealed hatch. And there was nothing in the kitchen and bathroom.

He still had the bedroom to explore, but considering how much time Kremph seemed to have spent sleeping it was unlikely to be in there. The broom closet that was almost a direct connection to the kitchen and bathroom was considerably more interesting. If Kremph was sitting in the living room listening to the radio, the perpetrator could easily have made his way into the kitchen to plant the scalpel or to the bathroom to substitute medications.

He opened the door, which was covered in the same square-patterned wallpaper as the rest of the wall, and turned on the bare light bulb. The closet was about one-and-a-half square metres and was well organized, with everything in its place. On one shelf were all kinds of laundry detergent and cleansers, and on another one higher up were rolls of toilet paper and paper towels.

Fabian took out the vacuum cleaner, the two brooms and the bucket with the floor mop, and got down on his knees and started inspecting the old linoleum, which pulled up. A silverfish fled the light and disappeared into the cracks. But there was no trace of an opening there or anywhere else in the closet.

He put the vacuum cleaner and the other things back in and wondered whether there might be a completely different and obvious explanation that he couldn't see because he was too close. The beams of two flashlights out in the hall interrupted his musings.

Someone was on their way in, or perhaps there were two of them.

He backed into the bedroom as he heard someone mumbling something to another person out in the living room. He could not make out what was being said, but one of them seemed to be on their way into the bedroom. He quickly threw himself down on to the floor, pulled himself under the bed among the dust bunnies, and watched as a pair of heavy boots walked across the creaking floor.

They stopped a short distance from the bed and stood for what felt like several minutes. Fabian held his breath while the flashlight searched across the floor and a little way under the bed. He was not only unarmed, but he was also lying in such a way that the slightest movement risked emitting a sound loud enough to expose him. The only advantage he had was that this person was unaware of his presence. If the boots could only come a little closer...As if the intruder could read his mind, the boots started moving towards him. First it was just a step followed by an expectant pause, but then they took yet another step until they were standing right by the edge of the bed. He carefully reached out his left arm, past the side of one of the boots and around to the heel. All of a sudden, a whistle from the living room made the boots back up a few steps and turn away.

Fabian exhaled, even though he was fully aware that it was only a matter of time before they would be back to thoroughly search the room. He turned on the flashlight to see if there was anything he could use as a weapon, such as a rope or a dumbbell. But other than the dust there was only a pair of underpants, a few unmatched socks and a pile of newspapers in the room.

Then Fabian noticed a hole in the wall right under the bed. He had a similar one at home in the bathroom, but hadn't thought about it until water started running out of the little pipe that stuck out under it. The white-enamelled metal cover was an inspection hatch to get at the pipes and repair any leakage.

But there was no pipe here. Not to mention it was in the middle of the wall in the bedroom, a good distance from both the kitchen and bathroom, which was extremely strange. He wriggled up towards the wall, set the flashlight on the floor and pulled the cover loose from its spring bracket as carefully as he could.

He couldn't see any pipes, and from his viewpoint it just looked like a black hole. But once he shone the flashlight into the opening, he discovered that it was anything but a little hole. It was a shaft about two square metres in size that extended vertically through the building, from the top floor all the way down to the cellar.

He had nothing to lose and squeezed through the narrow gap holding the flashlight in his mouth. A sturdy bolt that stuck out from the wall right above the opening served as a handle so he could heave himself up and pull in his legs without falling into the shaft. He supported himself with one foot against the lower edge of the opening and found a number of thick electrical cables to use as passable foot support against the opposite wall. He stood up and examined the walls of the shaft.

A thick board rested against the wall a short distance below the opening and extended like a catwalk over to the opposite side of the chute, where there appeared to be a similar hole. The flashlight slipped out of his mouth as he moved one foot over the other to the catwalk, and a few seconds later it went out with an echoing crash.

The darkness became so dense that he was forced to straddle the board so that he didn't lose his balance. He felt along the wall with his hands and found that there was something blocking the opening. But it was no inspection hatch. It felt like twisted steel wire or some kind of thin grate. He tried to press it in, but was unable to move it. Only once he braced himself against the catwalk and pushed with both feet did it finally shift and he could make his way out through the opening.

At that moment he realized that he had been here before.

73

AFTER SHE CAME HOME Dunja barely had time to unpack her new phone and connect it to the computer to transfer all her contacts before it started ringing. She recognized Carsten's number immediately. Even if she had longed to hear his voice for the past twenty-four hours, she had no desire to answer right now, she had too much on her mind. Not once during the whole day had he tried to get in touch with her, or any of her colleagues for that matter. Only now, when the news about what she'd been through had reached all the way up to Stockholm, was it convenient.

But that wasn't why she didn't answer. She simply didn't have the time.

She had spent most of Sunday in the meeting room with Jan Hesk and Kjeld Richter, where they had turned every clue in the investigation upside down. They'd cleared the whiteboard and put everything up again in a new way to try and see it with fresh eyes. They were hoping to find a different motive where Benny Willumsen's only function was to act as a decoy.

Hesk had done everything he could to pretend that nothing had happened between them. He completely ignored the fact that she'd called him, desperately asking for help and pleading for her life, and acted like he hadn't turned his back on her when she needed him most. He hadn't even offered an apology or an attempt at an explanation. He seemed to believe it would be enough to just work through it.

They hadn't managed to come up with much more than a number of different ideas, all of which felt far-fetched.

All but one.

She'd been struck by it when she saw the pictures of Katja Skov's arranged body parts and noted that a large part of her chest was missing. Neither Hesk nor Richter thought it was strange and tried various explanations for how easy it was to lose a body part.

She was firmly convinced that they weren't chasing a perpetrator who went around losing things, so much so that she'd managed to convince Oscar Pedersen to skip the season finale of *The Killing* to go and examine the first victim, Karen Neuman, one more time.

Dunja let the ring tones from Carsten's phone call go to voicemail. Until he called for the third time.

'Dunja, is that you? What the hell happened? I heard on the news that—'

'Honey, I'm fine.'

'Fine? Isn't it true that—'

'Yes, but you don't need to worry. Everything's fine now.' She heard the beeping tone indicating that Pedersen was trying to get through. 'Listen, I don't have time to talk any more now. I have to hang up.'

'Huh? Wait a minute. I just—'

She ended the call and took Pedersen's. 'Hi. I'm sorry, I just had to finish another call. Have you found anything?'

'Yes.'

'And?'

'You were right. Her right kidney is missing.'

74

FABIAN STOOD UP, BRUSHED the dust off and shivered. He was standing in the condemned apartment and the gust from the window – still broken from Ossian Kremph's suicide – explained why it was so cold. He turned towards the refrigerator that he had just pushed to the side, and understood exactly how the perpetrator had been able to make his way in and out of Kremph's apartment unnoticed.

Two linked apartments in two different buildings: one with an address on Blekingegatan, the other around the corner on Östgötagatan. They were close enough that the police would suspect that the apartment with the plastic-covered table was Kremph's lair, but far enough away that they would never think the two were actually connected by a shaft in the wall.

He quickly took a few pictures of the hole in the wall and inside the shaft, and then pushed the refrigerator back in place and continued towards the door. Of all the times he'd been there, it was the first time that the door had been closed.

It took him all of two steps into the adjoining room to realize that the ceiling light was on, shining right on to the plastic-covered table, which was so wet it was dripping down on the floor and into a large tub that was filled two-thirds of the way with fluid.

Fabian's breath quickened. Someone had literally just been there to make use of the equipment. They must have missed each other by minutes. He hurried over, crouched by the tub, and studied the transparent fluid – rings spread out towards the edges with every drop that fell from the table. It looked like ordinary water. But when he leaned down to smell it, he sensed immediately that there was something about the odour that didn't add up. There was no doubt that it was water, but it was brackish. There was no way this had come from the taps in the apartment. But why would the killer want to carry a bucket of brackish water all the way here?

The next evening I knocked on your father's door. Your mother answered and started shouting. It didn't take long before your brothers were there. They pushed me up against a wall. I had brought disgrace to the family and your mother was forced to send you away. I was devastated. Everything was my fault. If I had just forced you to walk away from the fence that day, none of this would have happened. Now it was too late.

They tied me to a tree in the backyard and took turns hitting me while they waited for your father to return. I don't remember if your mother tried to get them to stop, I only remember that I was woken by a bucket of dirty water being thrown over me and tried to open my battered eyes. Your father's face was so close to mine.

How dare I set my dirty foot in your country, he shouted. I told him I was there to ask for your hand and that I was prepared to do everything I could to get his consent. I remember the wind, the flies, the leaves in the tree, even the dripping tap. Everything fell silent. Then he nodded and said that I should go with his sons on a mission.

Aisha, soon I won't have much energy left. There is blood everywhere, and your brothers have already fallen silent. I'm so sorry, but the convoy of settlers came just as we expected. We made our way out of the crevices and threw our stones.

The trucks stopped and I saw how our stones dented the metal. I thought it was strange that they didn't drive away. Your brothers screamed at me to continue. There was so much panic in their eyes. I did as they asked, but soon realized that something wasn't right.

They came out of their trucks with blinding searchlights, tactical vests and automatic weapons. Don't ask me how, but they knew about our ambush. The volleys of shots echoed against the rock wall, and we kept on throwing. I did too because I wanted to show your brothers where I stood and that I was a man of my word. But, Aisha, it just didn't work. One by one we fell, and the searchlights lit up parts of the rocks that were red with all the blood.

They laid us out in rows and studied our wounds. Zakwan on one side of me had been hit in the eye, but was still alive, and Wasim on the other side was coughing blood. I had been shot twice in the stomach and felt that I was bleeding to death. I could do nothing but look up at the black night sky, absent of stars. A storm was brewing.

I heard another truck drive up and stop. I recognized the voices from the camp and tried to turn my face away when they walked over and shone their flashlights. But no one recognized me, maybe because of all the blood. I was dragged away with the others and thrown into the van.

Aisha, it feels like you're here and reading every word over my shoulder. I don't want to stop writing, but strength has run out of my body. I must save my last bits so that I can fold this up, put it in the envelope and drop it in the night. I hope that God takes over and sees that one fine day it reaches you.

Wherever you are and whatever you are doing, I'll be thinking about that one fine day.

Efraim Yadin

75

SOFIE LEANDER'S FIRST THOUGHT had been to use the scalpel to cut her carotid artery and let the painful waiting slowly run out of her. The thought of just fading out into nothingness was almost as enticing as surviving and being released.

It was that *almost* that stopped her.

Just as she pressed the edge of the scalpel to her throat, it occurred to her that this tool, and the fact that she was no longer strapped down on the table, increased her chances of survival by several thousand per cent. True, there was no way for her to get out at the moment. She'd searched through the whole compartment, but hadn't found anything that could help her; not even the two small keys that were hanging on a hook inside one of the cabinets fitted anything. Not to mention that the motor for the louvre gate was outside the room and there didn't seem to be any way to control it from inside.

On the other hand, she could kick on the gate and scream for help, which would hopefully make someone passing by stop and realize that something wasn't right. But so far, no one had come.

Not until now.

With her ear pressed against the gate, she listened as the big door outside opened and a car drove in and stopped. Then she heard a car door open and close, and steps walking on the hard floor. She wanted to pound and hit and make as much noise as possible, but she hesitated. She still couldn't be completely sure who was on the other side and she wanted to wait until she could determine whether the steps were walking by her or stopping somewhere within her storage unit. The only thing she hoped they didn't do was to stop right outside her gate.

Her body was shaking from the exertion and she was struck by how little she cared that she was completely naked. It didn't matter if the person on the other side was a man or a woman, or whether they were old or young; she would ensure that they couldn't miss her. The steps came closer and closer, and in just a few seconds they would walk past to one of the units further in the building. As soon as she knew for sure she would start.

Instead, her worst fears were realized.

They stopped.

There was a brief silence and then the electric motor turned on and started rolling up the gate. It was not enough time for her to plan anything new, but she had prepared herself well and knew exactly how she should hide behind the cartons of the vomit-inducing dietary supplement and stand ready with the scalpel.

She had put the table back in place and set out pieces of cardboard and other material she'd found to try and make it look as if someone was lying there. It was far from convincing, but in the best-case scenario it would give her the extra second she needed to jump out and press the scalpel wherever she could reach, search through the pockets for the car key and then run without ever turning back.

The electric motor worked its way to the end. She crouched, motionless, and waited until she saw the person come in and walk to the table, just as she'd envisaged in her mind countless times. Only then did she leap out and strike with the scalpel.

A kick against her leg threw her off balance when she tried for a second time. Her head struck the concrete floor and she dropped the scalpel.

The last thing she wondered before the gas was sprayed in her face was why she hadn't followed through with her first idea.

*

WHEN SHE FINALLY WOKE up it was as if nothing had happened. It almost felt like a dream she'd just woken up from, or a subconscious game that was now over. She was once again strapped down on the plastic-covered table with the feeding tube taped to her mouth.

But she didn't have the energy to care any more. She had long since given up hope of being able to die soon. As of now she intended to let apathy take over. Most of all, she just wanted to check out and close down.

But however she tried, she couldn't help speculating about what was going on. Why was her hair wet and smelling of shampoo? Did she hear the sound of scissors? Was her hair being cut?

There was a damp towel over her face, so she couldn't see anything, but she could definitely hear scissors finishing up and being set down on a metal tray.

Her hair was surely in need of a wash – or two. But had she really been there so long that it needed to be cut? What did it matter if her hair got a little longer?

Evidently it did.

However much she resisted, she couldn't help having a little hope. What if she was to survive after all? Maybe she'd served her sentence and was now being prepared for release. Then soon she would be at home with her beloved husband again. She longed for him and his warm, calming embrace.

Something cold landed on her breasts, first one and then the other. Then some dropped down on to her stomach and over her legs. It was some kind of cream, which the hands started rubbing in.

It smelled good.

A little like coconut.

76

IT WAS ONLY FOUR thirty in the morning, and there were still several hours before it would be light outside. It was the shortest day of the year so maybe there wouldn't even be light, Dunja noted, as she got out of the car holding the cardboard tray with three coffee cups, feeling the cold, damp wind work its way through every tiny, invisible opening in her coat. Not even the Danish flag-pattern hat she'd got for Christmas from Carsten's mother, and normally refused to wear, seemed to have any warming effect.

She saw Kjeld Richter and Jan Hesk talking further ahead by the edge of the pier, but they fell silent as soon as they saw her. You didn't have to be Einstein to figure out that she was the topic of discussion. After less than a minute out in the cold, she was almost prepared to agree with Hesk and Richter's argument that conditions couldn't have been much worse.

The dark and the cold were bad enough, but the conditions in the water were horrible. The strong wind had stirred up the surface so that heavy blocks of ice pressed against each other like big teeth grinding everything in their path. And the harbour manager had demanded – several times – that they be finished by no later than six o'clock.

'Don't you look frisky and happy,' said Dunja without getting so much as a smile in response. 'Coffee?' She held out the tray until they were both forced to take a cup. 'How's he doing?'

'How do you think?' Hesk nodded towards the turbulent water. 'Do you have any desire to jump in?'

'No, but I'm not a diver. From what I can tell, it looks like he's already down there.'

'You can always get in…' Hesk sipped the coffee and clenched his teeth as if to mask how good he thought it was.

Richter's communication radio crackled: '*The car's here. Over.*'

'See if you can open the doors and get in. Over,' said Richter, moving away from them to talk on the radio undisturbed.

Dunja drank her coffee and stared over the edge of the pier, down into the black chunks of ice. But she couldn't make out any bubbles coming to the surface or see the glow from the searchlight. She looked beyond the wet dock and the boats that were moored along the quay opposite towards the back side of Kronborg Castle – the last outpost of the East.

She often reflected on this when she looked out over the Sound and saw Sweden towering up on the opposite side. Their neighbouring country was officially neutral and undoubtedly the Swedes leaned more toward the West in their basic values, but the sensibilities of the East had always been apparent with all their rules, state liquor stores and the like.

But her feelings were completely different this time. Instead of thinking the Swedes were hopelessly behind Denmark, she now thought they were further ahead. She didn't know if this shift was caused by meeting that very pregnant policewoman from Sweden, or the fact that she'd just set foot in the country for the first time only a couple of days ago. All she knew for sure was that, despite her experiences in Kävlinge, she felt an increasingly strong desire to go there again.

She turned to Hesk and asked whether the coffee was okay, but regretted it immediately. Why was it always her responsibility to break the silence? Hesk, for his part, had done nothing to alleviate the awkwardness. Instead he waited as long as possible before he shrugged and nodded almost imperceptibly. 'I guess it's okay.'

'Good,' said Dunja, feeling increasingly irritated.

He still hadn't so much as said a word about how he hung up on her when she was in grave danger. Nor had he even bothered to admit that she was right as far as Karen Neuman's missing kidney was concerned. If he thought he was going to get away with it by keeping quiet, he thought wrong.

'After we finish up here, I was thinking about stopping in to see Pedersen to hear what he has to say about that missing kidney,' she said, emphasizing the last two words.

'Okay.' Hesk took another sip of his coffee, his gaze directed out into nothingness.

Okay? Was that all he had to say? 'What are your thoughts about that? You weren't exactly enthusiastic about him examining the body again; luckily I stuck to my guns.' She regretted saying the last part, but it was too late now.

Hesk shrugged. 'As far as I can tell, it doesn't argue for or against Willumsen.'

'No?'

'No, I wouldn't describe it as a significant finding.'

'He didn't take any organs from a single one of his previous victims.' Dunja took a step towards him. 'Yes, he has raped, tortured and mutilated people, but the bodies were all found intact. Right now, we have a kidney missing from one victim and a lung from another. How the hell can you stand there and say this isn't a significant discovery?'

'It just means that he doesn't repeat himself, which, in my understanding, was his thing. He used to let the dog rip his victims apart, now he takes a trophy from them. Next time maybe he'll grind them up and use them as fertilizer on his lawn.' Hesk laughed and finished his coffee.

Dunja knew that she shouldn't take his bait, but she couldn't help it.

'I don't think there's any point in letting him continue down there much longer,' Richter shouted, and Dunja turned around. 'The car is evidently completely clean!'

'What a surprise,' said Hesk, shaking his head.

'Just make sure he gets the licence plate number!'

'He already has: HXN 674. It's Swedish, just as we suspected.'

Dunja did a thumbs up and forced a smile. Then she turned to Hesk and dropped the act. 'You're not taking this seriously at all, are you? This is just a game for you.'

Hesk shook his head.

'Admit it! You're like a bitter old bitch putting all your energy into working against me. You don't seem to care that there's a perpetrator still on the loose.'

'No, Dunja, it's not that way at all.'

'No? So how many more victims will it take for you to wake up? Three? Ten?'

'None, actually. There won't be any more victims because someone punctured both his lungs and heart.'

'But that's not—'

'Dunja! It was him, okay? No one – and by that I mean no one – in the whole fucking department believes in your ghost, except for you, of course! Everyone else is convinced that it was Willumsen. The only reason we're standing here freezing our asses off is because Sleizner thinks you're sexy and wants to screw you.'

Dunja didn't understand what'd she'd done until she'd heard the sound, but it was already too late to undo it. It came out of nowhere with almost infinite acceleration and surprised her as much as Hesk.

But that wasn't the worst part.

Her palm against his cheek.

The circulating blood that made it turn red.

The look that said everything.

The worst part was that he was right.

77

MALIN REHNBERG TURNED FROM one side to the other. It was a movement that normally wouldn't take more than a second or so, but with her very pregnant, pre-eclamptic belly from hell it took at least a minute and a half. She didn't know how many times she'd turned over, other than it was a depressing amount. She couldn't lie still for more than five minutes before she started imagining festering bedsores and maggots, and had to turn her carcass over once again.

But she couldn't complain about the new room that Fabian had insisted she be moved to. In many ways it was much better than the first one. Not only was it newly renovated with framed pictures, curtains and a TV, which, admittedly, wasn't plugged in, but it was a single room so she didn't have to share the toilet with anyone else – one of her absolute least favourite things on earth. She never went to the washroom at work, even after she was afflicted with acute pregnancy incontinence. If she could have had her way, she would have her own washroom, just like Ingmar Bergman had demanded.

The problem was that she was bored. She'd been woken to have her blood pressure checked at four o'clock and been lying awake ever since. Now, almost three hours later, she was so bored that she was unsure whether she could survive another five uneventful minutes. She could already picture the headline.

Pregnant Detective Inspector Dies of Boredom

It would have been so much better if she could at least go

home. There shouldn't be any reason why she couldn't lie at home with a drip and take her blood pressure herself every two hours.

'My love,' she got a kiss on the forehead. 'I'm here now.'

She looked at the man above her and realized that it was her husband, Anders. She must have fallen asleep. 'What time is it?'

'Almost eight thirty. How are you doing? Were you okay last night?' He sat down on the edge of the bed.

'Let's talk about something else instead. Did you bring the stuff I asked for?'

Anders held up her computer bag. 'I'll give it to you on one condition: you don't start working.'

'Yep, sure. Give it to me now.' She reached for the bag, but he held it away.

'My love, I'm serious. I spoke with the doctor yesterday, and he said that—'

'Anders, the investigation is over. I'm not going to work, I promise. I just want to read a few newspapers and Skype with Mum.'

He reluctantly set the computer bag down beside the bed. 'And has that Fabian been here to visit?'

'*That Fabian?*' She shook her head. 'I don't understand what you have against him. And, no, he hasn't been here. But if he had stopped by it would have been to see how I'm doing, not to work.' She met his sceptical gaze. 'Yes, that's actually how it is, so you can calm down.'

'I can't be calm until this is over.' He placed his hand on her stomach. 'And according to the doctor it's very important that you—'

'Rest. Anders, I know. All I'm doing is resting. I've rested so much that I'm tired of resting! By the way, don't you have to leave now?'

'Yes.' He looked at his watch and got up. 'But—'

'See you later.'

'Okay. Try to take it easy now, so—'

'Bye-bye, honey.' She waved to him, while he backed towards the door and left.

Malin was desperate to pull the bag up into the bed and get started immediately, but she knew her husband too well and waited until he had 'surprised' her by sticking his head in one last time before she tore out the computer, turned it on and connected her cell phone to a hotspot.

Finally, she could start working.

78

FABIAN SCRAPED THE LAST of the ice from the windshield, got in the car and waited for the engine to heat up. In the meantime, he tried to shake off the feeling that he was falling further and further down a steep hill. He had tried to unwind by taking a two-hour walk around Södermalm with The Cure's *Kiss Me Kiss Me Kiss Me* in his headphones, but it hadn't worked.

It felt like no matter what he did, everything was slipping out of his hands. At least Sonja seemed less agitated and had taken both of the kids out to stay with her sister Lisen on Värmdö where they would all celebrate Christmas in three days.

There was nothing Matilda liked more than going to see her cousins and her aunt, who was always at home and made sure there were freshly baked rolls and things to do. Fabian was sure that even if Matilda wouldn't admit it, she wanted nothing more than to exchange him and Sonja for Roland and Lisen.

Roland seemed to earn loads of money from his various companies, and Lisen had decided to give up her legal career to become a stay-at-home mum. No wonder the kids liked it. Even Theodor had gone along without protest. Everyone was there getting ready for Christmas, wrapping presents and hunting for a tree out in the forest.

Everyone except him. And he'd promised himself that he would never be a parent without time or energy who felt relief as soon as the kids were somewhere else and someone else's responsibility. He lowered the sun visor, opened the cover for the mirror and noted that he looked like one of those parents too.

On all levels he'd become like his father.

Sonja had given it a lot of consideration and decided that they should go their separate ways. She thought they both deserved something better than this seemingly never-ending rough patch. But he'd seen in her eyes that she didn't really mean it. He could tell that she wanted him to step up and convince her that they still had a future.

But his pockets were empty of reasons, and even though he'd lain awake almost all night and walked all the way around Södermalm, he still didn't know where he stood – where Sonja or Herman Edelman were concerned.

He had no idea how he could get his boss to agree to open up the investigation again without revealing too much. The only thing he was sure of was that he was in one of the most complex homicide investigations of his life with a perpetrator that everyone thought was identified and dead, but who was still at large, and did not show any signs of being finished.

PHOTOGRAPHS TAKEN BY A long-range lens were distributed around the table; they showed a dozen scantily clad women with shifting, worried gazes being dragged out of a truck and shoved in through a grey back door.

'These images were taken a little over two months ago outside the Black Cat. What you see here is a so-called "goods delivery" during which the women go through an initial screening,' Markus Höglund reported, and Jarmo Päivinen, Tomas Persson and Herman Edelman all nodded around the table.

'Does anyone know if Risk is on his way in?' asked Inger Carlén, who was standing beside Höglund and blowing her nose into a handkerchief that appeared to have passed its prime long ago.

'No, get started now,' said Edelman. 'I don't have all day.'

'All right,' said Carlén, suppressing a sneeze.

'Our sources tell us that the women are brought up on to a stage inside the club one by one where Diego Arcas "examines" each of them personally and decides which brothels they'll be taken to,' Höglund continued, taking the last Danish cookie from the tin.

'Examined how?' Tomas asked, even though he looked as if he already knew the answer.

'For understandable reasons we haven't been there and seen it with our own eyes,' said Carlén, 'but I'm pretty sure even you would feel sick if you saw it.'

'We've received information that another delivery should be coming any day now.' Höglund rinsed down the cookie with coffee. 'And that's when we'll strike.'

'So you don't know when exactly?' said Edelman, pulling on his beard.

'No, other than it will definitely be within the next few days. As of now, we'll have to work in shifts and have the response team ready.'

'Okay.' Edelman nodded. 'I'll let them know. How many officers do you need?'

'At least thirty-five,' said Carlén.

'Thirty-five?' Edelman looked up from his phone.

'We want to strike the club and the small brothels simultaneously,' said Höglund, just as Fabian opened the door and entered the room.

'Fabian.' Edelman turned towards him. 'We were just wondering where you were. Has something happened?'

'Do you have time to talk?' said Fabian without looking at the others. 'Preferably right away.'

'WHAT'S GOING ON?' ASKED Edelman, closing the door behind him.

Fabian looked at him. He had hoped to start calmly and

cushion his request with other news, but his late entry to the morning meeting had already ruined any such possibility. 'We have to reopen the investigation on Grimås and Fischer.'

Edelman looked as if he'd misheard him and took off his small round eyeglasses. 'And what makes you believe that? Sit down.'

'Herman, we've been on the wrong track. Ossian Kremph was nothing more than a decoy to lead us in the wrong direction,' Fabian said, sitting down on the worn leather couch.

'Do you think in all seriousness that Kremph is innocent?'

'And that the perpetrator is still loose. Yes, that's exactly what I believe.'

Edelman laughed, shook his head and took two beers out of the refrigerator, holding one up enquiringly.

'No, thanks. I'm fine,' said Fabian, even though it was just what he needed.

'I see. Well, speak up if you change your mind.' Herman opened one bottle, emptied it into a glass and sat down in the reading chair by the window. 'Fabian, this theory has come out of the blue. You know I think you're a good investigator – one of the best.' He sipped his beer, took out his pipe and started packing it. 'But to be completely frank, it sounds like you've lost your bearings.'

Fabian let him light the pipe and fill his lungs with the silver-coloured smoke before he continued. 'Do you remember that woman on the bus? The one whose eyes were cut out in all the pictures.'

'Yes, she was a possible victim.'

'Exactly. And now I suspect that she's dead.'

Edelman nodded and drank some beer with a sense of calm that was the opposite of what Fabian had expected.

'That is to say, I'm fairly convinced that she's dead,' he added, feeling that the whole conversation was about to derail.

'You're quite right about that.' Edelman treated him to a satisfied smile. 'Because dead is exactly what she is.'

'What do you mean, have you found her?' This wasn't going

remotely as planned. Instead of Edelman being surprised and unsettled, Fabian was the one who had to struggle with his balance.

'Her name is Semira Ackerman. The captain of the commuter ferry between Södermalm and Hammarby Sjöstad sounded the alarm last night, after discovering her floating between the blocks of ice. Evidently she decided to walk across the ice.'

'Who could possibly be so stupid as to try to walk over the ice there? That's right across the channel.'

'Maybe she wasn't planning on crossing, but just went out to have a little look, and unfortunately it ended badly.' Edelman shrugged and puffed on his pipe. 'It actually happens every other day this time of year. See for yourself – there's a photo on the desk.'

Fabian went over to the desk and picked up the image of the frozen woman being pulled up on deck. It was definitely the same woman, but this was no accident. At least now he had an explanation for the tub of brackish water.

'Fabian, how are you doing, really? You look very, how should I say—'

'Last night I searched through Kremph's apartment one more time,' Fabian interrupted him. 'And I found, among other things, a passageway that led directly over to the condemned apartment, which explains a good deal. And in—'

'Yes, that was probably his way of getting out to—'

'No, it was the perpetrator's way of getting *in* to his place.'

'And why would anyone want to—'

'To replace his medication with placebos. Herman, he's had Kremph under constant surveillance. In one of the books on the shelf…' Fabian stopped himself. He was about to lose control and say too much. He took a deep breath. 'Who is examining her in forensics? Thåström?'

'No, she doesn't do accidents. Fabian, her lungs were filled with water. It's no more complicated than that. I don't understand where you want to go with all this information. You think Kremph is innocent and that there might be someone else who... You'll have to excuse me, but it sounds bizarre.' Edelman sighed out the smoke.

'So you don't believe me?'

'It's not about what I believe. Every piece of evidence in this investigation, including the motive, points to Kremph – even that passageway you're talking about. You don't seem to have had a wink of sleep this whole week and then you stomp in here and maintain his innocence. I'm sure you understand that if I'm going to cast off the previous conclusion, I'll have to have something more specific from you.'

'Herman. The table was wet when I went into the condemned apartment. It was still dripping. Someone had just been there, and everything indicates it was where Semira drowned.'

'And what makes you so sure that it wasn't just some homeless person who dragged a lot of snow in and took a nap in a warm place?'

'Who also set a tub there and filled it with brackish water? I don't think so. And as far as this investigation is concerned, I'm convinced that there's sufficient evidence to support my theory. The problem is that it's missing.'

'What do you mean, "missing"?' For the first time during the meeting, Edelman looked sincerely surprised.

'Someone must have been here over the weekend and tidied up.'

'The investigation is over and because there's no talk of a trial, it must have been sent to the archives.' Edelman walked over to the desk and woke up his computer with his mouse.

'Not from what I could see. But perhaps you have another good explanation?'

'Excuse me?' Edelman met Fabian's gaze.

For the past few hours Fabian had been convinced that his boss knew considerably more than he let on. But now he suddenly felt uncertain. Perhaps Edelman still believed that Kremph was behind it all. Before he could go on, he had no choice but to paint his old mentor into a corner.

'Here it is, just as I thought.' Edelman looked up from the screen.

'What do you mean, you found a file number?'

'0912–305/H152 Scope: 0.4 shelf metres.'

'Oh, right,' said Fabian, without disclosing that there hadn't been a number assigned to it last night. 'I probably couldn't find it because I was too tired. Actually, maybe I should have that beer.'

'Please do, but you'll have to drink it up quick. I'm on my way to a budget meeting with Crimson.' Edelman turned off the computer and stuffed a few sticks of gum in his mouth, while Fabian opened the beer and drank.

'You're probably right. I'm likely just a little overworked.'

'Not that I've ever celebrated it,' Edelman adjusted his tie in front of a mirror, 'but I think the whole department is going to benefit from a little Christmas and time off.'

'Listen, by the way, that cell phone call you had with Grimås a few hours before he died.'

'Yes?'

'What did you talk about?'

'You've already asked me that.'

'Did I? And what was your answer?'

'Same as now: he wanted advice for the question time he was on his way to. Unfortunately, it was no more exciting than that,' said Edelman, tidying his beard.

All doubt disappeared. Edelman was lying right to his face, and even though Fabian wanted nothing more than to take out the phone and play the recorded call, he nodded and tried to look as satisfied with the answer as possible.

As of now, it was crucial to keep everything under wraps.

79

DUNJA NOTICED THAT OSCAR Pedersen looked frustrated, even though he was obviously trying to hide it when he met them at the Department of Forensic Medicine. For the first time during all his years as a medical examiner he'd missed what might turn out to be the most essential part of the whole investigation in the autopsy: namely, the motive for why Karen Neuman and then Katja Skov had been murdered. In the first case it was a missing kidney, and in the latter a lung.

The explanation for how he could have missed it was thin to say the least.

'As I said on the phone, there was no reason to continue my examination after the cause of death had been established.' Pedersen pulled his security card through the reader and opened the door so that Dunja and Jan Hesk could follow him into the morgue.

There was a variety of reasons why this was such serious negligence that Dunja could easily file a complaint to the National Police Board and have his licence suspended. But instead, she chose not to change her expression. Hesk, on the other hand, smiled and nodded as if to emphasize his agreement.

'It's not just my tax money, but yours too,' Pedersen continued, looking at Dunja. Then he opened the refrigeration box and pulled out Karen Neuman's body.

It had been almost a week since Dunja had been at the murder scene and seen the mutilated body for the first time. Seeing it for the second time, she could understand how Pedersen might have overlooked the missing kidney. 'As I said, she doesn't look so nice on the outside.' Pedersen nodded at the wounded torso. 'But that's nothing compared with how she looks on the inside. It looks like someone went wild with a blender in there,' he continued. 'And Dunja, if you hadn't stuck to your guns and explicitly told me to check if an organ was missing, I wouldn't even have discovered it.'

She wanted to brighten up and nod, show him how much she appreciated his praise, but she withstood the impulse and maintained her expressionless look. 'Did you find anything else?' she asked, not because she expected anything, but mostly to underscore that she was driving this part of the investigation.

Pedersen nodded. 'Yes, actually, now that you mention it,' he said, tugging on his moustache without saying more.

Dunja knew Pedersen far too well to fall into his trap and ask him what he'd found. He wasn't going to have it that easy.

'So, what have you discovered?' said Hesk, voluntarily placing himself at the bottom of the hierarchy.

'After Dunja contacted me, I took the liberty of going through the investigations on Willumsen's previous victims, and as far as the wounds are concerned, I could tell with the utmost certainty that he's left-handed. So I contacted my dear colleague Einar Greide in Helsingborg. Sure enough, it turned out that he'd arrived at the exact same conclusion in his investigations.'

'And why is that so important?' said Dunja, but wished immediately that she had kept silent. She could already see that Pedersen had grown at least five centimetres taller and was enjoying the attention.

'The cuts on Karen Neuman were made by a right-handed perpetrator. Of course, I need to do a more thorough examination to be one hundred per cent certain, but if you're content with ninety-five per cent positive, then the contact angle of the wound indicates that he was holding the axe like this.' He showed them with his hands in the air. 'With his right hand in front and the left hand back there. It is the most natural position for a right-handed person. And when he braced himself he raised the axe on the right side of his head, like this.' Pedersen chopped repeatedly with the air axe right towards Karen Neuman's mutilated abdomen.

'I think we get it,' said Dunja, and Pedersen stopped. 'So what you're really saying is this is yet another sign that indicates that this is not Willumsen's work.'

Pedersen hesitated, casting a glance at Hesk, before finally nodding. 'As I said, there is a certain margin of error, and there is a possibility that he struck like a right-handed person simply to confuse us.'

'But he must have really exerted himself since the wounds are so deep, which makes that explanation less likely.'

'You are correct.'

'Excellent. What do you say, Jan?' Dunja turned to Hesk and decided not to take her eyes off him until he answered.

'To be honest, I don't really know what to say. There is still too much evidence pointing to Willumsen for me to simply let go of him.'

'That's just my point. The murder has been carried out in such a way that suspicion will be directed towards him and away from the real perpetrator.'

'And what's the real motive?'

'Here it's the missing kidney, and with Katja Skov it's her lung.'

'Not to be nit-picky but, Dunja, those are organs not motives.'

Dunja rolled her eyes and turned to Pedersen. 'Is it possible for you to retrieve the victim's patient records?'

'It depends on what you mean by possible. Why should I—'

'Because I'm asking you to.'

Pedersen pulled on his moustache again, and exchanged a glance with Hesk, who gave him a shoulder shrug in response. 'Well, okay.' He went over to the computer in the corner and touched the mouse. 'But if we do find something of interest, the two of you have to clear it after the fact, okay?'

'Sure, sure, just get started.'

Pedersen clicked to the patient record archive and was about to enter his search when he noticed an email in his inbox. 'Oh, the DNA analysis is already done. That was quick.'

'The DNA analysis of the sperm sample? Shouldn't that take over a week?' said Dunja.

'That's what I thought too,' said Pedersen. 'I guess they wanted to clear their desks before Christmas. Anyway, here we have it.' He stopped talking to read it over.

'And?'

Pedersen turned toward Dunja and then to Hesk. 'It was Willumsen's.'

'Benny Willumsen?' Dunja repeated, and Pedersen nodded. She couldn't believe it. 'Just to be clear: we're talking about the semen sample you found in Katja Skov?'

'Both inside and a little around, to be exact.'

Dunja could picture the house of cards she was building crashing down. 'Okay, but can you retrieve those patient records now so I can look at them.'

'Dunja, that's enough now,' said Hesk. 'Sleizner gave us a deadline to continue until the analysis was done. And now it is.'

'Yes, but...' She turned to Pedersen. 'I need to see those records.'

'The investigation, from what I understand, is now closed, so I have to say no.'

'So all that talk about the perpetrator being right-handed doesn't mean anything to you any more?'

'As I said, there is a margin of error. And this time unfortunately it appears as if—'

'This is completely crazy. What the hell are you up to?'

'Dunja, we're just doing our jobs. Let's go so that Oscar can continue doing his.' Hesk turned around to leave.

'How on earth can you call this doing your job? Huh? I can see on your face that you also think there are enough interesting leads to explore.'

'You do?' Hesk turned towards her. 'Then why wouldn't I explore them?'

'Either you're just out to obstruct or you're just too cowardly to stand up to Sleizner, which is more likely. You know as well as I do that he doesn't give a damn if we have the wrong person, as long as the numbers look pretty.'

'You forgot the third alternative: it really was Benny Willumsen.' Hesk turned his back on Dunja and left the room.

80

WITH THE PHONE PRESSED against his ear, Fabian stepped out of the elevator three floors below ground and continued through the corridor to the archives. 'Hello? Can you still hear me?'

'Yes, and if you're the least bit interested in what I've found out about Gidon Hass you should listen now,' said Niva. 'You might think that if Grimås and Edelman were discussing him, he would be a public figure of some sort, but in fact, he's been almost impossible to track down.'

Fabian had promised himself that he would never see Niva again, but after the meeting with Edelman he could see no way other than to resume contact and tell her everything, from the events of the last few days to his own theories about how it all fitted together.

To his great relief, she believed his story, and she'd also agreed to help him without coercing him to drinks or dinner. Her only request was that the investigation remained officially closed as long as she was involved.

'Gidon Hass, or Gidon Ezra Hass, his full name, is a doctor and pathologist with a focus on – get this – organ transplants.'

'Okay,' said Fabian, feeling that things were finally coming together. 'Does he have a clinic somewhere?'

'He did, in the past tense: Israel's National Forensic Institute in Abu Kabir. Rumour has it that under his leadership they collected organs and tissues, and acted as a kind of co-ordinating centre. It was one of the largest single suppliers to the organ black market, which, until a year or so ago, was completely legal in Israel.'

'Legal?'

'Yes, because Jewish people prefer to be buried whole, the consequence is that voluntary organ donation is one of the lowest in the Western world.'

'So where did they get all the organs?' asked Fabian, walking along the rows of movable shelves, while trying to ensure he still had coverage.

'Primarily from so-called organ hunters who are prevalent in the former Soviet republics and in the poorest parts of Asia and South America. And if you believe the worst accusations, quite a few organs were also harvested from wounded Palestinians.'

'Nice.'

'It's true.'

'So he's no longer at the clinic in Abu Kabir?' said Fabian, finding his way to shelf number 152.

'No, when the new law went into effect he was fired and hasn't been heard from since.'

'Is he on the run?' Fabian cranked the shelf to the side, squeezed into the opening and found the archive folders numbered 0912–305 easily.

'As I said, he hasn't done anything illegal. Technically he has nothing to run away from.'

'But he's gone underground anyway.'

'It looks like it.'

The folders were filled with papers which, to the uninitiated, might resemble a case file: some copied documents here and a few pictures there that didn't have the slightest thing to do with the real investigation.

Just as he'd expected, the evidence was gone.

81

DUNJA HAD GONE TO the Copenhagen Police Department Christmas party for the first time two years ago. The shock of the event had continued well into spring, even though she'd heard all the rumours in advance about the flowing alcohol, the limbo dance where every failed attempt cost an item of clothing and the copy machines that collapsed under the pressure. She hadn't been prepared for the battlefield she encountered: colleagues who were normally quite level-headed behaved like lobotomized swine, to put it mildly.

She'd missed the following year because she was at home in bed with a flu that she couldn't shake until well into January. No one wanted to spill any details once she was back, but management's decision to hold the Christmas party on a Monday in the future said more than enough.

Dunja had decided not to go regardless, mostly because Sleizner had made sure to have her seated beside him, but also because she knew how hard it was for Carsten. No matter how much she stressed that she could never imagine being unfaithful, much less with any of her colleagues, Carsten was still after her like an interrogator, demanding a full account of every minute of the party.

But in the end, she'd decided to go, but not because she felt like it. She was the furthest thing from being in a party mood. The defeat with Pedersen still stung, and even if the DNA analysis of the sperm sample showed that it was from Benny Willumsen, she couldn't really believe that he was the person behind the murders. Not only had he been completely perplexed when she asked about the industrial space outside Kävlinge, he was a head taller and several sizes bigger than the man she'd caught red-handed mutilating Katja Skov.

She was quite sure that there was a completely different motive to explain the missing organs and she couldn't understand why Hesk, Pedersen and Richter were so uninterested in finding out. It was as if they were so intimidated by Sleizner that they didn't dare create conflict. Or maybe they just couldn't take any more right before Christmas.

She refused to let herself be dragged down to the level where people refused to take responsibility for themselves and didn't care about anything – least of all the truth. And that's where sitting next to Sleizner came into the picture.

She intended to make use of all her tricks and exploit the situation to her utmost advantage. She had to get him on her side so that he would let her continue with the investigation. She devoted both time and care to putting on more make-up than the usual mascara and eyeliner. She used power and concealer to hide the worst bruises, and after trying a few different lipsticks, she chose the reddest one she had, which matched her red dress perfectly. She swapped the small pearl earrings – a confirmation present from her mother – for two big gold hoops and wrapped a support bandage around her left ankle, which was already much better. Then she pulled on a pair of hold-up stockings and slipped her feet into her highest heels.

She was surprised how well she could stand in them and practised walking in the living room trying to pretend she wouldn't touch a pair of Converse with a ten-foot pole. After that she stood in front of the mirror in the bedroom, adjusted her hair to hide the scrape on her forehead and studied herself.

For the second time in recent memory she didn't recognize her own reflection. The dress, the make-up, the shoes: the whole look was as far from her as you could get, or at least the way she usually saw herself. But it wasn't about the clothes. They were nothing but a casing to wrap Sleizner around her finger. No, it was something else, something that was so much harder to grasp.

Something in her eyes.

82

'THIS CONCERNS A SUICIDE and isn't on my radar at all.' Medical examiner Aziza Thåström was normally one of the most amiable people that Fabian knew. She always had time for yet another question, and her patience was inexhaustible when you didn't understand something. Now, on the contrary, she sounded irritated. 'Besides, the investigation is closed.'

Fabian pulled open the heavy iron door and walked out into the car park, letting the silence do its work.

'Okay,' Thåström finally said with a sigh. 'What do you want me to look for?'

'I don't know. Preferably some organ that should be there but isn't.' He heard another heavy sigh in the phone.

'Fabian, we're dealing with a drowning accident. Besides water-filled lungs there are no visible injuries.'

'Yes, but something is missing – I'm sure of it. The eyes. Have you checked them?' said Fabian, who could tell by the altered room acoustics that Thåström was now inside the morgue and opening one of the refrigeration boxes.

'Yes and – surprise – the eyes are there. Do you seriously think that someone could have missed—'

'Aziza, can you examine them?'

'And why should I?'

'Just do it, please.'

He heard another heavy exhalation as he got into his car and turned on the ignition. He wasn't the least bit surprised with her response.

'I'll be damned, you were right. The cornea is missing in the right eye.'

'Thanks. That's all I wanted to know,' said Fabian, ending the call.

So that's what the perpetrator had done in the condemned apartment. After drowning Semira Ackerman, he had removed her right cornea, an intervention no one would discover as long as all focus was aimed at her water-filled lungs.

Fabian drove up to the garage door, which slowly started to let in the daylight. A shudder spread through his body and he shivered, even though he wasn't cold. His back got sweaty, while his heart rate increased. Something had happened. He just didn't understand what, until it occurred to him how close he'd actually been. If it hadn't been for the concealed camera in Ossian Kremph's bookcase, he almost certainly would have run right into the perpetrator.

Of course – that's how the perpetrator had seen him and understood that there was a risk he might imminently find the passage to the condemned apartment. Maybe he was even the person who drove off in the Opel that was parked right in front of his own car.

He drove out of the car park, leaving the police station behind him, with no idea where he was headed. He just needed to get away from the station, and away from Edelman and all the others. He turned right on Bergsgatan and then left towards Hantverkargatan, and felt his pulse slow down.

Even if only part of the information that Niva had uncovered turned out to be true, it was a scandal so serious that Israel's reputation would be spattered with blood for many years to come. The taped phone call between Grimås and Edelman made it clear that the Israeli Embassy was involved, but he didn't know to what extent or whether the horrific practice of illegal organ harvesting was sanctioned from higher up. As long as the investigation continued to be unofficial, he couldn't simply call in people for questioning, particularly those from an embassy.

His cell phone started ringing on the passenger seat as he passed Stadshuset. He could see that it was Malin Rehnberg and let it go to voicemail. When she tried calling again a second later, he realized that she wouldn't give up until he answered, like a stubborn mosquito with the scent of blood.

'Hi, I was just about to call and see how you're doing,' he said, continuing across Vasabron.

'Don't make me laugh.'

'Malin. I was actually just about to—'

'If you're so terribly interested, I can tell you that I've never been so bored in my whole life. I'm about to crawl out of my skin. And I promise you: if nothing happens soon, I'm going to go completely bananas. So tell me what's going on,'

'Not that much actually. I just had a meeting with Edelman, and we decided that I should start my Christmas vacation as of—'

'Ha. Ha. Ha.'

'What?'

'Knock it off. Who are you trying to fool? Yourself?'

'No, but maybe your husband,' said Fabian, giving up with a sigh. 'Are you aware that Anders has more or less forbidden me to talk with you?'

'Forget about Anders and tell me what the hell's happening!'

'Okay, but listen at your own risk,' said Fabian, who started to tell her about the passageway between Kremph's and the condemned apartment and how the perpetrator must have been there recently to drown the woman on the bus, whose body had just been found in Hammarby Lake. He also told her about the hidden camera he'd found in the bookcase, the recorded cell phone call between Grimås and Edelman, and how they'd mentioned someone named Gidon Hass.

'Wait a minute – we're not talking about Edelman as in Herman Edelman?'

'Yes.'

'Shit. Do you seriously think he might be involved?'

'He's lying about the call, anyway, and he refuses to open the investigation again. He must be hiding something.'

'And who is this Gidon Hass?'

'An Israeli pathologist and organ transplant expert.'

'Israel again. So that's how they're connected.'

'My thoughts exactly. And it accounts for the fact that all three victims had an organ removed: Adam Fischer's heart, Carl-Eric Grimås' liver and Semira Ackerman's cornea.' Fabian turned left on to Timmermansgatan and realized that he was on his way home, although he had no idea of what he would do there. 'Of course, we'll have to check their medical records before we can be completely certain, but I suspect that all three had been on a waiting list for new organs in Sweden and had finally chosen to buy one on the illegal market instead. Now someone is going around collecting those parts.'

'But why? Is it even possible to use them again? There must be some limit on how many times you can transplant an organ.'

'I'm sure there must be, but if he was only after fresh organs, there are considerably simpler victims than the Minister for Justice, for example.'

'Maybe he wants to punish the victims for their sins and teach them and everyone else considering an illegal organ a lesson?'

'No, I don't think so. Then he wouldn't put so much energy into hiding the traces and framing Ossian Kremph. Whatever it is, it's personal.'

'This pathologist, what was his name again? Do we know anything else about him?'

'His name is Gidon Hass and we don't know much more than that he went to ground after he was fired from the institute in Abu Kabir. I would really like to do a more advanced search, but I'm not sure how to go about it now that the investigation is officially closed.'

'Since when has that stopped you?'

She'd seen through him even before he knew his own intentions. Of course, he'd coldly calculated that Niva had already conducted the search on Hass.

'Don't you think I know that you're working together again?'

'Who are you talking about?'

'Stop it. Who else could have had access to that call between Edelman and Grimås? Just don't say that I didn't warn you.'

'You've already said that once.'

'And it warrants being said again. Speaking of that call, can you send the audio file over to me?'

'Absolutely, I'll do it as soon as I have a chance.'

'That may have sounded like a question – my apologies. I want you to do it now, as in right away.'

'Malin, I'm in the car and—'

'So pull over. Fabian, I'm serious. I'll go crazy if I don't have something to sink my teeth into soon.'

Fabian looked around for a parking space on Fatbursgatan, when a black Volvo came out ahead of him and turned right on Swedenborgsgatan, even though it was for buses only. 'Fine, but just so you know, I've listened to it several times and the only—'

'I'll go crazy for real.'

Fabian parked in an empty spot. 'Can I send it to your personal email address?'

'Use anders&malinsbrev@hotmail.com.'

'A joint account?'

'Yes, but he never uses it.'

Fabian found the email with the unknown sender and the 'I was wrong' in the subject line, and forwarded it to Malin. 'You should have it any second,' he said, before he ended the call, got out of the car, and walked up to the entrance to his building.

*

THE FIRST THING FABIAN noticed was that the little red diode didn't blink when he entered the code. Thinking he'd entered the wrong digits, he repeated the process three times before it occurred to him that the entry door was unlocked. This wasn't the first time the lock had got stuck: it was more the rule than the exception that it failed as soon as the temperature fell much below freezing.

He'd had a sense that something was off, but as soon as he got out of the elevator, all remaining doubt was gone. The door was ajar with the lock drilled out. He opened it carefully and went in.

It was clear from the hall that whoever had been for a visit was no longer there. They'd left a pile of chaos behind them – pulled-out drawers, turned-over furniture and piles of clothes – and it seemed likely that whoever had done this was the same person who'd removed the case files from the National Bureau of Investigation and searched through Ossian Kremph's apartment the previous night.

But what were they searching for? The porcelain doll?

He went through to the living room. From the light in the chandelier, he could tell that this room also looked like a minor battlefield. He went over to the couch, set it back in place and put the cushions on top. Then he sank down and looked out over the devastation, surprised that he and Sonja actually had enough belongings to create such massive chaos.

He didn't hear anything, but he felt the faintest change in the air pressure. Fabian looked up and rolled over behind the back of the couch in a single movement.

Now he could hear them. They were in the hall and on their way into the living room. So they had come back. He quickly went through his options, before deciding that he didn't have any other than confrontation. This time he didn't intend to let them get away.

'Holy fucking shit, this place looks—' one of them exclaimed.

Fabian recognized both the voice and the expression. But only after hearing the other person's voice did it all fall into place – and he was properly confused.

'Yeah, this is probably how your place looks.'

Fabian stood up. 'Excuse me, but may I ask what the hell you're doing in my apartment?'

Tomas turned around with a start and aimed his gun at Fabian.

'Take it easy, dammit. Can't you see it's Fabian.' Jarmo pushed down Tomas' arms.

'Yes, I see that now. Sorry. What the hell happened here? This place looks like...'

'That's exactly what I'm wondering, too.' Fabian walked over to the two of them. 'Apparently someone thinks I have something of value. I just don't understand what that would be. They've already confiscated the whole investigation from the Bureau.'

Tomas and Jarmo looked at each other. 'What investigation are you referring to?' asked Jarmo after a short silence.

Fabian was about to answer, but stopped himself. 'How about you tell me what you're doing here first? From what I can see it's not to wish me a Merry Christmas.'

Tomas and Jarmo exchanged another glance and nodded in silent agreement. They turned back to Fabian in unison, as if they'd been rehearsing in front of a mirror.

'We're here because we wanted to see you,' said Jarmo.

'Outside regular work hours,' Tomas added, pushing his pistol into the shoulder holster.

'It's about the Grimås and Fischer investigations.'

'And Semira Ackerman.'

'Semira Ackerman?' Fabian repeated.

'Yes, that woman on the bus who—'

'I know who she is,' Fabian interrupted.

'We don't think it was a drowning accident at all,' Jarmo explained.

'Or that Kremph was behind the murders,' Tomas continued.

First himself, then Malin. And now even Tomas and Jarmo.

'On what grounds?'

'If you go through the investigation from start to finish there are any number of threads that don't hang together,' said Tomas.

Fabian nodded dejectedly. 'Which explains why it's missing.'

'It so happens that it's not too far out of reach.'

'What do you mean, do you know who took it?'

Tomas nodded with a satisfied smile. 'Maybe you'd like to give us a helping hand?'

83

SOMEONE STARTED A DANISH drinking song and everyone raised their glass – even Dunja. She took only one sip before setting it down again, though. She'd already had too much, and if she was going to have the slightest chance of getting Sleizner where she wanted him she couldn't have one more drop. In any event, the dress had done its job and put him in a good mood again after their quarrel on Sunday.

'You're not fooling me.' Sleizner focused his gaze on her full schnapps glass. 'Around this table only one thing counts and that's bottoms up.'

'And here I thought we were going to control ourselves this year. Wasn't that why you moved it to a Monday?' said Dunja, forcing a smile.

'Listen, I was against that silliness from day one. I mean, come on, a Christmas party on a Monday? What the hell kind of idea is that? You'd almost start to suspect we've been occupied by Sweden.' Sleizner burst out laughing. 'Let's go show them who runs the show.' He filled his glass and raised it.

'Kim, I really shouldn't have—'

'Okay, let me make it a little simpler: in my role as your boss, I hereby order you to empty the contents of your glass.'

Dunja realized that she had no choice and gulped the cold alcohol, which burned all the way down her throat. The evening was about to slip out of her hands and she hadn't had a single opportunity to bring up the question of reopening the investigation without seeming too forced. Soon it would be too late.

'That wasn't so bad, now, was it? I'll fill her back up.' He replenished the glass to the point that it was almost spilling over.

'Kim, there's something I have to talk to you about.'

'Absolutely. No problem.'

'It's about the investigation.'

'You should know just how incredibly impressed I am with its quick resolution – not to mention proud. Not every police officer has that instinct, or whatever it is, in them, dammit. But you're clearly one of the few. Just jumped right in and – boom! –it's solved! It's unbelievable.'

'And that's just what I wanted to talk to you about. My instinct tells me that we should—'

'It's not just my department that's talking about you.' Sleizner chugged back some beer. 'I've taken the word higher up in the building, and believe me, if you continue like this you'll be going places. If I don't keep my eyes open, it'll be you pulling on the strings soon. Cheers.' He said, as he raised his schnapps glass. To avoid yet another kerfuffle about how important it was to keep drinking, Dunja drained hers too.

'Kim, I'm aware that the DNA analysis points towards Willumsen, but at the same time I'm convinced it's not him. There's something that doesn't add up.'

'Dunja, come here.' He motioned for her to move closer. 'This is not something we should discuss here,' he said, waving his index finger around.

'No, I know. But I would need an okay from you to continue as soon as—'

Sleizner put his finger against her mouth. 'There are too many curious ears here.' He pushed his chair back and stood up. 'Follow me. I know somewhere that's a bit more private.'

Dunja stood up a little too quickly and had to support herself against the back of the chair until her balance returned.

'Oh dear, do you need help?' Sleizner offered his arm.

'No, I'm okay,' said Dunja, even though she had to concentrate on every step to ensure she didn't trip on her way through the decorated room. The noise level attested to the fact that the majority had already forgotten that it was actually a Monday.

'Okay, tell me. I'm all yours,' said Sleizner, holding open the door to his office.

'Actually, there's not much to talk about,' said Dunja, following Sleizner in. 'I just want your okay to continue the investigation, preferably without Hesk. He's been working against me ever since you let me lead the investigation.' She waited for a reaction.

She should have seen it coming. She should have understood that this was what the entire preamble about competence and future had really been about. This was the price for getting her way.

Yet she was totally unprepared to feel his chapped lips against hers, so much so that it took her several seconds to sober up and realize what was about to happen. She pressed her hands against his chest and pushed him away from her.

Sleizner laughed and threw out his arms. 'Dunja, I know you want to. We can keep on pretending and play the game a little longer, but anyone could see this from a mile away. What's his name? Carsten? He must be giving you way too little – if any. Believe me, I see how you walk around and want nothing more than to be taken.' He clenched his fist. 'Every which way so that you feel like you're alive. Am I right?'

He leaned towards her, so close that she could smell his alcohol-loaded breath. She should have screamed as loud as she could, clawed him on the face and kneed him, but she did none of those things. Instead, as if she was under hypnosis, she let him press her down on the leather couch and bring his hand higher and higher up under her dress.

'And, I promise, you can be completely at ease,' he continued. 'Of course you'll get to continue with the investigation, if that's what you want.' He licked her ear while his eager fingers searched under the edge of her panties. 'As long as we have our little secret you can basically do whatever you want. Doesn't that sound good?'

He kissed her again and pressed his fleshy tongue into her mouth. Suddenly the fluorescent lights in the ceiling turned on and spread their cold, revealing glow. Sleizner only had a second to turn around before Hesk was tearing him off the couch. 'You fucking swine. You disgusting fucking swine!'

'Jan, I know this must be awkward for you, but we happen to be two consenting adults who know exactly what we're doing,' said Sleizner, pulling a hand through his hair.

'I doubt that, especially not after what she's just been through.'

'You can always ask her yourself.'

Hesk turned toward Dunja, who was straightening her dress. 'Dunja, is that true? Do you want this?'

Dunja tried to meet Hesk's gaze, but she couldn't. Somewhere she understood that she ought to be relieved – a minute or two later and it would have been too late – but all she could feel was shame.

'Dunja, just so you know, I have no problem with reporting him at once.' He picked up his phone and held it in front of him. 'But it's your call.'

She turned to Sleizner and looked him in the eyes. His gaze was not the least bit evasive or hesitant. Instead, behind the completely calm, expressionless face, she sensed a smile.

As if he already knew how she would answer.

84

'OKAY. AND LISTEN, BY the way... Thanks.'

'No problem.'

The call ended and the audio file was over. Malin Rehnberg had listened to the exchange between Herman Edelman and Carl-Eric Grimås so many times she'd lost count. But she didn't feel finished with it yet. After the first listen she'd been surprised by how little new information emerged and mostly saw it as confirmation of everything she already knew. If Fabian's theory was correct, they could simply be referring to Grimås' illegally transplanted liver and the Israeli Embassy.

But after the second listen, she started feeling more doubtful, and after the third and fourth it was clear to her that there was a lot left to discover. She felt as if the call was built up in several layers, and the only way to go all the way into the core was by listening through it, over and over again, layer by layer.

The first thing she flagged was that they both seemed to know exactly what they were talking about, and how Grimås even sounded exhausted by the subject, while at the same time they were both totally unaware of what lay ahead. Most of their worry revolved around the consequences of the truth leaking out, and how the Minister for Justice would be forced to resign. The possibility that someone would kill Grimås and then open him up and empty out his inner organs was something they'd not even been close to fearing.

The second was about the leak, or *that damned leak*, as Grimås referred to it. In reality, it wasn't a leak at all, but a perpetrator with a completely different agenda than gossiping to the press. But that wasn't what piqued her interest. She set the marker on the time counter she had finally memorized, and pressed the computer's space key.

'From what I understand, there's a lot to indicate that it's someone internal, who has access to keys and codes. The problem is that they haven't been able to find anyone without—'

'What do you mean, "internal"? Are you suggesting that someone on your own staff would—'

'Carl, I have no idea.'

She paused the recording. There were obviously strong suspicions that it was someone on the embassy's own staff. But what did Edelman mean by '*The problem is that they haven't been able to find anyone without…*'? What did someone not have?

The alternatives were almost endless and she had written a long list of possible continuations that more or less made sense. Finally, she'd decided on one word.

Alibi.

The full sentence became: *The problem is that they haven't been able to find anyone without an alibi.* It was completely logical. They'd suspected that it had been someone on the staff, but every one of them could prove their innocence, which either meant that one of them had a false alibi, or that it wasn't anyone internal at all, but someone distant enough to not appear on the personnel lists, but close enough to have access to the building.

Even though she'd turned off the sound on her phone, it started vibrating like a wound-up toy on the table next to her bed, disturbing her concentration right when she was finally getting somewhere. Now her thoughts scattered, and she didn't know if she could summon up enough energy to gather them again.

It was Anders – just what she needed. He'd tried to reach her so many times now that if she didn't pick up soon, he might legitimately start threatening divorce.

'Hi, honey,' she said, attempting to sound like she'd just woken up.

'Why aren't you answering?'

'Uh, wasn't that what I just did?'

'You're not working, are you?'

'I wouldn't dare, considering how much you've been after me. Was that why you called and woke me up?'

'Are you sure?'

Malin let out an exaggerated sigh. 'Do you think I'm lying right to your face?' she asked, realizing, to her own surprise, how good she was at being deceitful.

'No, but—'

'Good, because I'm half drugged, without a clue of what's happening outside the door. I haven't even had the energy to open the computer since you were here.'

'Okay, I'm sorry. I didn't mean to… I'm just so—'

'Worried. Honey, I know. But that doesn't help me right now. I just want this to be over. Was there anything else?'

'No – actually yes. Ursula was here yesterday. Did you tell her to put Christmas curtains up in the kitchen window?'

'No. Did she do that?'

'Yes, and they're… how should I put it?… really ugly. I can't even describe them. I know they're probably considered very beautiful in the backwaters of Poland, but I'm losing my appetite completely, and now I don't know what to do. I don't even want to touch them.'

Malin understood exactly what Anders was talking about. A year or two ago their cleaning woman started taking greater liberties in how their home was furnished. Suddenly, the worn footstool she'd inherited from her grandmother went down into a box in the cellar, to Anders' great delight. But when their white duvet cover was replaced by something synthetic with colourful flowers the following week, even he'd had enough. In united solidarity, they folded it up and put the white one back on.

Big mistake.

Ursula didn't say anything. Instead, she slowly but surely punished them by starting to clean less effectively. After a few weeks they'd tried to remind her with a discreet Post-it note of how dusty it was under the bed and that the inside of the refrigerator needed to be cleaned too. But it didn't get cleaned. Finally, they put the flowery bedspread – that gave them a shock every time they touched it – back on. By now she was used to it – and the garden gnome she got when she turned…

Out of nowhere, Malin was struck by a thought that was as unexpected as the fact that she'd fallen pregnant with twins only a few weeks after they'd decided to give up trying. It was so obvious, she couldn't believe she had missed it.

'Honey, are you still there?'

'Yes, I am, but—'

'What should I do then? She's going to flip out completely if I take them down.'

'Anders, I don't know. But I have to go. The doctor will be here any moment and I have to go to the toilet first.'

'Don't you think she'll get mad if I—'

'We'll talk later. Love you.' She hung up, leaned back in the bed, and closed her eyes to refocus as quickly as possible.

She wasn't certain, but the facts seemed to fit the idea that the perpetrator could be someone on the cleaning staff. Not only did they have access to keys and codes, they were also around when the rest of the employees had gone home. Besides, if they came from an outside cleaning company, they could be considered 'internal' even if they weren't part of the embassy's own staff.

There was only one way to find out.

85

DUNJA WOKE UP SUDDENLY and realized she must have fallen asleep. She was buckled in and everything around her was shaking. She didn't understand where she was or how she'd ended up there.

'We are now approaching Stockholm Airport. Please keep your seatbelt fastened until the aircraft has come to a complete stop and the seatbelt sign has been turned off,' a voice boomed over the loudspeaker.

As the plane braked, everything came rushing back: Sleizner's disgusting mouth against hers; Hesk, who risked his career and offered to file a complaint, even though he usually never talked back. She wondered if it was his way of asking for forgiveness. All she could do was shake her head and ask him to call her a taxi. She just wanted to get out of there and pretend that nothing had happened.

Blågårdsgade 4, she had said to the taxi driver. But as they passed the neon thermometer at Rådhuspladsen, which showed minus five degrees Celsius, she realized that Blågårdsgade was the last place she wanted to go. Why lie at home alone? If there was anyone who should comfort her after all that had happened, it was Carsten. Longing for him had struck her with such force and gave her no choice other than to go to Stockholm.

The driver shook his head, but agreed to make an illegal U-turn outside Hotel Alexandra and drove her to Copenhagen Airport. She was lucky and had managed to get a ticket on a flight that left fifty-five minutes later. Her mood improved as she passed through security and ordered a glass of white wine in the oyster bar.

And now, as she walked out of the revolving door into the Stockholm air, which was not nearly as trying as back home, it felt almost as if the incident in Sleizner's office had never happened. She laughed to herself at her impulse behaviour. Carsten would certainly be surprised. She liked nothing better than to be in control and prepped up to her ears, but she currently found herself anything but.

All she had with her was her wallet, her red, much too short dress, and her winter coat. Fortunately, she'd had the foresight to go to the Christmas party in a pair of boots and brought her high heels along in a bag, otherwise she would have had to use a wheelchair because her feet were in so much pain.

She signalled for a taxi and asked the driver to take her to Hotel Clarion at Skanstull in as clear Swedish as she could. This was her first visit to Stockholm and so far she wasn't particularly impressed. She hadn't seen much more than a jumble of roads and concrete viaducts.

It was only after they'd been through a long tunnel that she found that she hadn't been misled by the people who said that Stockholm was one of the most beautiful cities in the world. Because suddenly, the view opened up and she could look out over the frozen water surrounded by lights from an endless number of illuminated windows. She didn't know if it was the vast snow-covered ice or the clear, starry sky, the lit-up bridge in the distance, or the hills of Södermalm with their steep cliffs covered with buildings, but all she should think was that it really was exceptionally beautiful.

Then she was back in the concrete hell that blocked her view for the rest of the way to the hotel.

*

'WHAT DID YOU SAY his name was again?' asked the young man with a thin moustache behind the front desk, even though Dunja had already repeated it twice.

'Carsten Røhmer,' she said as slowly as she could. 'Carsten with a "c", and Røhmer with Danish ø and h after the ø. Should I write it down?'

'No, that won't be necessary,' said the man, giving her a smile to show that he didn't mind being disturbed from his book as his fingers worked on the keyboard.

Dunja could not understand what was so complicated about finding a room number. The front desk clerk was acting like he was hacking into a top-secret server. A few minutes later he took his eyes off the screen and pressed his fingers against his moustache.

'From what I can see he's the only one who's booked here.'

'Yes, but I'm his fiancée and surprising him. He has no idea I'm here.'

'Unfortunately, I can't give out room keys to just anyone.'

'I understand that, but I'm not just anyone. As I just explained, I'm his girlfriend.'

'I'm sorry, I don't understand.'

'I'm his fiancée and this is a surprise. That's why the booking only says one person.'

The man nodded, even if the smile had long disappeared. 'I'm sorry, but I can't—'

'Look. If it's about money, I have no problem paying for an extra person. As long as you give me a fucking key.' She extended her credit card and looked at him with an expression so insistent that he eventually had no choice but to go along with it.

The room was on the sixth floor and in the elevator on the way up she took the opportunity to fix her hair and refresh her lipstick. Once she'd found the room, she defied the pain in her feet and forced them into the high heels.

She opened the door slowly and went through the dark hall

into the room. It was bigger than she'd expected, and she couldn't see Carsten or the bed. But she could hear his mumbling voice and a phone receiver hit the cradle. And so he wouldn't have time to get suspicious, she hurried into the room, threw out her arms, and yelled, 'Tada!'

She didn't know what kind of reaction she'd expected, but she certainly hoped it would be more than what she got. Carsten was reclining in the bed with a bare torso, looking at her like he'd just been fired. She didn't know how she should interpret his response. Was he very surprised or downright terrified?

'Hello. It's me, Dunja. Aren't you happy?' She waved to him, and only then did he break into a forced smile.

'Sorry, honey. I… I didn't expect that you would—'

'Come to Stockholm. Well, that makes two of us.' She wriggled out of the heels. 'But it doesn't hurt to be a little surprised now and then?' She crept up to him on all fours and leaned forward for a kiss.

'Wait.' He stopped her. 'What's going on? Weren't you going to the Christmas party today?'

'Yes, but you know how it always is. And after all that's happened, it was the last thing I felt like, so I took a flight here to see you instead.'

'Okay, but…' Carsten scratched the back of his head, moving his gaze around before he looked her in the eyes again. 'How are you feeling, really? We haven't even had time to talk. It must have been horrible.'

Dunja nodded. She couldn't bear to answer all the questions, and silenced him with her mouth instead.

In the early stages of their relationship, a kiss could have gone on for ever. When they were first in love, it felt as if it would never end. Their lips met in an endless number of combinations, every one of which felt like small sensations. Their tongues couldn't get enough of each other, and she'd loved the taste of him, not to mention his warm, damp breath. They'd lost themselves and almost drowned in each other's gazes. She'd thought this was how it would be for ever.

But after a little more than six months, Carsten started to close his eyes. She'd considered asking him why, but chose to ignore it and hoped he would soon open them again. Instead, their kisses got shorter and his tongue seemed to have tired of playing with hers. After a while, she'd summoned up the courage to ask what was wrong or whether she smelled bad. Even today she could recall that he just shook his head and forced his way into her. Ever since then, she too had started closing her eyes, and a few weeks later they'd stopped kissing altogether.

But now they were kissing again, and he was even looking at her. Yet something didn't seem right. Something that she couldn't quite put her finger on. Was it his shifting gaze that kept looking past her? Or the tongue that was a little too eager in its movements?

She broke off the kiss.

'What is it?' he said. 'Do I have bad breath?'

'No, it's just that I have to... You know, after the trip and all.' She crawled backwards off the bed. 'I'll be right back.'

'What do you say about having a drink at the bar?'

'Absolutely. I'll just freshen up a little.'

'Yes, although—'

'I'll be quick. I promise.' She opened the door to the bathroom, went in and locked it, which she always did, even though they'd been together for almost five years. She never sat on the toilet when Carsten was standing alongside, struggling with his dental floss.

But that wasn't why she locked the door today.

She'd initially brushed it aside, but it had been obvious from the moment she had entered the hotel room. Maybe it was the front desk clerk's unwillingness to help her or the sound of the phone hitting the cradle that tipped her off. She couldn't say for sure. She had tried to tell herself that it was just that her nerves were on edge. But once they'd kissed, she could no longer blame it on stress. And everything was confirmed once she turned on the light in the bathroom.

One towel was missing from the hanger and the shower cap package had been opened. The glass with Carsten's toothbrush was turned over on the sink, along with the shaving cream and a green box of toothpicks wrapped in plastic. But she couldn't see the expensive aftershave she'd bought him for his sensitive skin. And the bathtub's shower curtain had been closed.

So fucking pathetic, she thought, as she took two soundless steps over to the bathtub and tore the shower curtain to the side. Neither of them said anything. Dunja could only note that evidently this was his type. She had long blonde curls going in every direction and breasts that behaved as if the law of gravity didn't exist. She was lying flat in the tub, trying to cover herself with the missing towel and had all of her make-up and Carsten's aftershave, which she had gathered up in a panic, spread around her.

Dunja didn't know how to react. The situation was so absurd that she was almost completely nonplussed. She was just as surprised as the woman when she leaned over, grabbed the bottle of aftershave, turned the shower on to its coldest temperature and left the bathroom.

'Are you ready?' asked Carsten, who was now out of bed and in the process of getting dressed.

'Yes. Quite ready.' She grabbed the high heels that were on the floor and turned to the door.

'Dunja. What is it now? Why—' She could hear him following after her. 'Say something. You can't just—'

She didn't hear anything else once she'd taken her winter coat and the bag of boots and closed the soundproof door behind her. To her own surprise she didn't feel the least bit sorry when she threw the bottle of aftershave into a wastebasket on her way through the hallway to the elevator.

86

FABIAN LEFT THE KITCHEN with fresh-brewed coffee and had to remind himself that he was actually in his own living room, not in an investigation centre far underground. With Tomas and Jarmo's help, he'd managed to tidy up after the burglary in less than two hours. They'd arranged the furniture so that the dining-room table, with all its leaves added, was in the middle of the room, and the couch and armchairs were along the walls. The whole investigation was unpacked and the walls were covered with the photographs, notes and leads that had disappeared from the original investigation room.

Even better, Jarmo had photographed everything before they packed it up at the police station, so most of it was laid out and categorized just like before. Niva had arrived an hour later with her equipment, and now all of their screens, computers and printers, and a number of black boxes with blinking lights were set up and connected.

They had never worked together this efficiently. The usual banter was on pause and everyone had a common goal: to identify and arrest the real perpetrator. The person who'd messed them around and fooled them with such detailed false leads that the investigation was officially closed.

'Hmmm,' said Jarmo, pouring the steaming coffee into cups. 'Should we get going?'

'I can start,' said Fabian, and told everyone about the events of the past twenty-four hours: the recorded cell phone call between Edelman and Grimås; how he'd found a passageway that linked Ossian Kremph's apartment to the condemned apartment; and explained that it was how the perpetrator was able to go into Kremph's place to replace his medications and plant various incriminating pieces of evidence. He told them about the concealed camera and that the perpetrator had almost certainly drowned Semira Ackerman and removed her right cornea just before he'd arrived. And he described how the tracks seemed to lead to a pathologist named Gidon Hass by way of the Israeli Embassy in Stockholm. When he was finished, silence reigned and no one said anything for several minutes. They all needed to digest and think before they could move ahead.

'That pathologist. Do we know anything more about him?' Tomas asked at last, shaking his protein drink.

'He's an expert on organ transplants and up until three years ago he was the head of the pathology institute in Abu Kabir. Since then, he seems to have gone to ground,' said Fabian.

'Abu Kabir. Isn't that a city in Egypt?' asked Jarmo.

'Yes, but it's also a district in Tel Aviv.' Fabian turned to Niva. 'Have you managed to find a picture of him yet?'

'I was wondering when you would ask.' Niva sent an image to print and handed it over to him.

Fabian immediately recognized the man in the photograph. He turned to the wall where all the other pictures were tacked up, and took down one of former Israeli ambassador Rafael Fischer sitting at a table flanked by his son Adam. 'That's him.' He pointed to the man sitting on the other side of the former ambassador, who was leaning towards him as if he was about to say something in confidence.

'Yes, of course,' said Jarmo, nodding. 'That explains the victims' connections to the Israeli Embassy.'

'In what way?' said Tomas.

'Instead of turning to the Swedish healthcare system in search of a new organ—'

'But they did look here,' Niva interrupted. 'I've looked at the victims' medical records, and all three were on waiting lists for several years until the middle of 1998.'

'And then what happened?' asked Tomas.

'They were taken off the waiting list before any transplants were carried out.'

'As far as his son Adam Fischer was concerned, I have no doubt that he connected him to Hass,' said Fabian. 'And when it comes to Carl-Eric Grimås, presumably he had to go through Edelman, who at that time had close contacts at the embassy.'

'So now he's doing all he can to sweep it under the carpet,' said Tomas.

Fabian nodded. 'But we still don't know what Semira Ackerman's connection is right now. Does anyone know when this picture was taken?'

'In August 1998, at Adam Fischer's sister's wedding in Tel Aviv,' said Tomas, emptying the protein drink.

'Tel Aviv again,' said Niva.

'Maybe that's when Adam Fischer got his new heart?' said Tomas. 'That would explain why he's the one with a cane, not his father.'

Fabian moved his head in agreement.

'Fabian, on a different topic…' Jarmo poured some milk into his cup. 'Exactly when did you find that passage between the apartments?'

'Last night, sometime after nine.'

Jarmo turned to Tomas with a significant expression, then looked at Fabian. 'So that was you I heard in the bedroom.'

Fabian nodded. 'It makes you wonder who broke into my apartment. Until the two of you arrived, I was convinced it was the same person who'd confiscated the investigation from the station.'

'Surely that's exactly what they were looking for, but we got there first,' said Tomas, smiling proudly.

'The question is, what do we do if they come back?' said Jarmo.

They fell silent and let the question hang in the air, as if it had only now occurred to them how little they really knew. The only sound was Niva's eager fingers on the keyboard.

'Listen, I've got an idea,' she said at last, taking her eyes off the screen. 'Actually, I take it back. It's too soon to start talking about it now, and besides I'm not even sure if it's going to work.'

'Come on, you've already started telling us about it,' said Tomas.

'Okay, fine. We can assume with relative certainty that the perpetrator has been at certain places at specific times. And we actually have several confirmed locations. For example, we know he left the parliament building from the rear door at exactly 3:24 on 16 December. We can also assume that he was in the condemned apartment on Östgötagatan right before Fabian was there last night. What other places do we have?'

'We have the surveillance video of him leaving the Slussen car park in Fischer's car,' said Tomas. 'We'll have to check the exact time, but I think it was some time in the afternoon of the eighteenth.'

'And he was at the Shurgard storage facility where we found Adam Fischer's body,' said Jarmo. 'He should have been there a number of times, although we don't know when.'

'How were you thinking about using all of this information?' said Fabian.

'If we analyse the cell phone traffic in the towers around each place at the relevant point in time, we should find at least one cell phone number that's recurring. After that, it's just a matter of locating and arresting the person in question.'

Fabian didn't know what to say, and it didn't seem like Tomas and Jarmo did either. But he was sure they were asking themselves the same question he was.

Why hadn't anyone thought of this before?

Fabian's phone started ringing. The call was from a blocked number.

'Yes, hello.' said Fabian.

'Is this Fabian Risk?' asked a stressed female voice.

'That's right. Who am I speaking with?'

'Carnela Ackerman.'

'Ackerman?'

'I'm Semira's sister. I think you saw me on Stureplan last Friday. Is it possible for us to meet? I know who was in your home.'

'Name the time and place.'

'Gondolen. I'm waiting at the back of the bar.'

There was a click before Fabian could respond.

87

IT WAS THE FIRST time Fabian had been to Gondolen since their department Christmas lunch four years before, and he'd almost forgotten how magnificent the view was from the restaurant. Despite the darkness and the heavy clouds preparing to release yet another snowstorm, it was stunning. Stockholm was literally under his feet. On his way through the restaurant towards the bar, he could see everything from the blinking Kaknäs Tower out on Gärdet to the illuminated Hötorget skyscrapers and the rotating NK clock in red and green neon.

He wasn't sure whether he would recognize Carnela from Stureplan because his focus had been on her sister Semira. But he was able to immediately identify her as the woman with a stressed expression who kept looking over her shoulder while nervously clutching her glass. He sat down beside her at the bar. She was very attractive and looked like a model with her long, golden-brown hair and leather boots, jeans, deep red polo shirt, and a necklace strung with thick stones.

'I don't know what information you've got from the police about your sister. But—'

'Semira would never go out on the ice like that,' Ackerman interrupted without taking her eyes off the glass. 'Never. I might do that, however. I've always thrown myself into the unknown and trusted that someone would be there to catch me.' She took a sip of wine and shook her head. 'My mother always said it was because of me she had so many grey hairs, although I never landed in her arms. It was Semira who was always there for me. She didn't let me down a single time over all these years, and when there was finally an opportunity to return the favour, it ends up like this!' She struggled not to cry, but was unable to hold back the tears.

Fabian handed her a napkin. 'How did you help her?'

'She suffered from bullous keratopathy, which affected one of her corneas. She was eventually more or less blind in one eye and was in so much pain that she couldn't do anything any more, not even read. And she loved sitting down with a good book.' Ackerman wiped her eyes.

'So you're the connection to the Israeli Embassy?'

Only now did she meet his gaze. 'How did you know that? I work there.'

'You said you knew who broke into my place.'

She nodded, unlocked her cell phone and showed him a picture of two men in suits getting into the same black Volvo that Fabian had seen outside his building entrance. 'These are the men that were in your house. They work for the Israeli Embassy and they're trying to arrest the perpetrator before the police do.'

Of course the embassy was conducting its own investigation. 'Do you have any idea how the crimes were committed and any theories about who it might be?' said Fabian.

Ackerman shrugged. 'I don't know, but there are rumours that someone managed to get hold of a list or some kind of document of all transplants that have been brokered through the embassy, which actually is not that strange. The whole office is one big mess right now because we're in the process of packing up and getting ready for the move to Nobelparken. I want you to know that you've arrested the wrong person, and that there are probably several people left on the list.'

Fabian nodded. 'You couldn't give me any names?'

She shook her head.

'Carnela, do you know someone by the name of Gidon Hass?'

Ackerman immediately got a strained look in her eye. 'What have you heard about him?'

'So you do know who that is.'

She nodded imperceptibly. 'He's a cousin of the ambassador, and he's here now—'

'Here, as in Stockholm?'

She nodded again.

'And do you know why he's here?'

Without answering, she looked over her shoulder and finished the wine.

'Carnela, if you have information that can help us arrest the person who—'

'I'm sorry,' she said, 'but this won't work. I've already said way too much.' She took her handbag and got down from the barstool.

'Carnela, wait. Has someone threatened you?' Fabian reached out his arm to stop her, but she pushed it away and hurried off to the exit.

88

BELIEVE ME, I SEE how you walk around and want nothing more than to be taken, he'd said with a laugh as if it was the most natural thing in the world – that slimy fucking asshole. Every which way so that you feel like you're alive, he'd continued, as she was almost suffocated by his sticky breath. Every cell in her body had hated him and would probably continue to do so for all time.

Yet she had to admit to herself that Kim Sleizner was right.

The revelation had come to her late the night before after a long walk along a snowed-over Götgatan in search of another hotel. She had wanted to get as far away from Carsten as possible, so it didn't matter that it took her until Medborgarplatsen to find one. She went to bed after taking a short bath to get warm. The next morning, she had hoped to get up early, have a quick breakfast and take the first available flight home. Then she would see about having the locks changed and hire a moving company to pack up all of Carsten's things and have them delivered to his parents' place in Silkeborg. After all, it was her apartment.

It was the perfect plan – if only she could have fallen asleep. Voices from partying Stockholmers kept making their way up to her room, so she lay there tossing and turning, feeling the crisp sheets against her newly bathed skin. It was then that it had occurred to her how right the slimeball had actually been.

She tried with her fingers, but that only made things worse. Just as he'd insisted, she wanted to be taken, *every which way so that you feel like you're alive*. And she decided it should start now.

She'd put on the dress and high heels again and followed the voices from the street to Kvarnen, a beer hall right around the corner from Götgatan. The line was long, but she managed to skip to the front, and once she was inside it didn't take long before she had locked eyes on her victim.

He was standing by the bar with a beer in hand, talking with some friends. With his curly red hair and freckled face he was the opposite of a classic beauty and not her type at all. But the low-cut shirt showed what good shape he was in, and his charisma had been impossible to resist.

She didn't need to do more than stand a few metres away and cast a few looks in his direction for him to leave his friends and come over to her. She tried to say something in Swedish, and he'd responded in English. She forgot his name the moment it left his mouth. Instead she would remember him as *the red-haired Swede*.

He'd shown her down to the basement level where ghost-like plaster casts pressed their way out of the stone walls and sweaty people collided on the boiling dance floor. They'd danced as if there was no tomorrow. She remembered how he'd stood behind her, so close that she could feel how much bigger he was than Carsten.

She had no concrete memory of leaving the dance floor. Everything felt like it happened in a split second and suddenly they were in her hotel room, emptying the mini-bar, and investigating each other like eager teenagers who finally had a house to themselves. At some point she must have finally fallen asleep and was only just waking up.

It was already ten thirty and, thank goodness, the red-haired man was gone. Considering the pounding ache between her legs, she couldn't possibly have managed another round. She laughed and realized that she'd probably made love twice as much during the past few hours than she had during all the years she'd been with Carsten. She vowed to make it a tradition.

Every Tuesday from now on she would go out into the night to top up her self-esteem. Men did it and it seemed to work. She hadn't been this happy and exhilarated in a long time. She didn't even have a headache. Her only rule was that each week should be with a different person. As long as she was turned on there were no rules on whom she could pursue.

Her ringing phone interrupted her thoughts. The call was from a Swedish number.

'This is Dunja Hougaard.'

'Hello, I just wanted to check in on you. You disappeared. At first, I thought maybe you'd gone home for the weekend, but then I heard what happened.' She heard a heavy sigh from the other end. 'To be honest, I don't understand how you could throw yourself right into that all alone. It must have been horrible.'

'I didn't think he would be there. And then it was too late,' said Dunja as she finally managed to place the voice. 'But, Klippan, I'm doing okay now.'

'Are you sure?'

'Quite sure.'

'That's good to hear. Then I'll take this opportunity to wish you a Merry Christmas.'

'Thanks, and same to you. Have a nice Christmas vacation.'

'Oh, I will. For once I've taken two weeks, even though we don't really get many days off a year. Berit insisted. In a few hours we're heading for the airport and then it's on to Thailand.'

'That sounds nice.'

'It cost a small fortune, but hopefully it will be worth it.'

'For sure. Have a good trip then,' she said, trying to end the call, which was draining her phone's battery.

'There was just one more thing, and I hope you aren't offended that I ask. Is it really true that he was in your apartment when you came home?'

'Yes.'

Her response was met by silence, and Dunja could almost hear Klippan trying to find words.

'It's so odd,' he said at last. 'Why would he let you live and lock you in a car with all the mutilated body parts, if he just wanted to kill you in the end? Which would have been much easier when he had you drugged in the industrial building out in Kävlinge.'

Klippan had had the exact same reaction she had.

'Because it's not the same perpetrator,' she said, even though she'd actually decided to drop it.

'Dunja, that's just what I suspected.'

'I think Willumsen was a decoy to get us on the wrong path. It was so well executed that he would have been convicted in any event. We even found his semen in Katja Skov.'

'He had nothing to lose and could just as easily find you, before you found him.'

'Precisely.'

'So what do we do now? Is there anything I can do before I leave?'

'Yes, actually. Maybe you can help me find the name of the owner of a car with Swedish licence plates? It's currently sitting at the bottom of Helsingør Harbour and I want to know why.'

'Absolutely. No problem. Just give me the number and I'll arrange it.'

'HXN 674,' she said without needing to look in her cell phone notes.

'Okay, I'll text you the response. Good luck. I hope everything works out.'

'I hope so too,' said Dunja, before hanging up.

She got out of bed, showered and washed her hair, and used all the free creams lined up on the sink. Then she pulled on the red dress, which was starting to feel a trifle unclean. When she was finished the text from Klippan was already waiting on her phone.

Don't know where you found the car, but the owner's name is Carl-Eric Grimås. He was the Swedish Minister for Justice before he fell victim to the 'Cannibal Man' just under a week ago. But that can't have anything to do with your case, can it? Klippan

She entered a brief reply: *No, it must be something completely different. Thanks and have a nice vacation! Dunja.* Then she went over to the window, pulled back the curtains and looked out over the snow-covered little park outside. Thirty or so pre-school children were playing at one end of the park, and two men were selling Christmas trees at the other.

She'd heard about the Cannibal Man who had suddenly started murdering again, several years after serving his sentence. There had been quite a bit about it in the Danish papers too. For a brief moment she'd actually toyed with the idea that there was a connection to her investigation. Two well-known perpetrators: one Danish and one Swedish, both of whom reoffend and leave obvious traces behind. But for lack of anything more concrete, she dropped the idea and continued with the Willumsen lead.

Now they were both dead and the investigations were closed.

Maybe the Swedish sports car at the bottom of Helsingør Harbour was exactly what she needed to bring her investigation and the Swedish one back to life.

89

Managed to get in. Think it's best you come here. As in pronto. N

FABIAN LOOKED UP FROM the screen, and saw a little red laser dot moving from one suburb to the next on the projected map of Greater Stockholm. He was in the meeting room along with Tomas and Jarmo, listening to Markus Höglund and Inger Carlén's briefing on the raid against Diego Arcas.

'We are targeting six apartments that we've located in a circle around the city,' said Carlén, looking down at a map.

None of them had an ongoing investigation of their own – at least not officially.

'Plus the Black Cat on Kungsholmen,' continued Höglund who was standing beside her at the short end of the table with a Danish cookie in one hand.

'And when were you thinking about striking?' said Fabian in an attempt to hurry up the meeting. Officially or not, the perpetrator was not only at large, according to Carnela Ackerman, but he probably had several more victims on his list. Not to mention, Niva had just succeeded in hacking into the cell phone operators' system after working day and night.

'Tomorrow night,' said Carlén.

'And I hope you really mean *we*,' said Höglund, looking each of them in the eyes. 'This is such a large operation that we're going to need help from everyone in the department.'

Fabian exchanged a look with Tomas and Jarmo, and could see that they hadn't received Niva's message yet.

'We understand that this comes at an inconvenient time, right before Christmas and all,' Carlén continued. 'But unfortunately, Diego Arcas doesn't break for holidays.'

Höglund pressed on the remote control and the map was replaced by an aerial photo of the block around the nightclub. 'As you know, the Black Cat is here in a big basement space facing Hantverkargatan.' He motioned with the laser pointer. 'But because it has three different exits we'll need to spread out...'

Fabian stopped listening. Tomas and Jarmo's cell phones had just started vibrating on the table in front of them, and he saw them click open the message from Niva.

'One response team is going to make their way in here, through the light opening in the courtyard,' said Höglund, pointing again. 'The other will be waiting in a bus around the corner on Polhemsgatan and will go in through the main entrance on Hantverkargatan at our signal. Questions?'

'No, I think it seems clear.' Tomas looked up from his phone. 'What do the rest of you say?'

'Completely clear,' said Jarmo, putting his phone in his pocket.

'The important thing is that no one gives the start signal until the show is in full swing,' said Carlén. 'It's then, and only then, when they're most distracted and vulnerable, that we go in. Okay?'

'Was there anything else? Otherwise I have a lot to do,' said Fabian.

'No, I think that was all,' said Carlén with a sigh.

'It might be good to take this opportunity to do some Christmas shopping now, when it's still so quiet,' said Jarmo with a smile.

'Good idea,' said Tomas, standing up.

'Wait a minute,' said Höglund, holding up his hands. 'Inger

and I have been working on this for over six months. It can't fall to pieces. Before you leave, I want to know that you're all sure that you understand all the details.'

'Quite sure,' said Tomas. leaving the meeting room together with Fabian and Jarmo.

'YES, I'M IN,' SAID Niva. 'But because I'm not at NDRI the fun will be over as soon as the spiders find me.'

'The spiders?' said Fabian, seeing Edelman come out of the kitchen with a cup of coffee in hand while he hurried through the corridor along with Tomas and Jarmo.

'Yes – the bots. The point is that I need more data, and soon.'

'Right, but this isn't a good time for me,' said Fabian as he tried to read Edelman's face, but he looked completely neutral. He had to try his best not to reveal anything, and gave him a curt nod without slowing down. Edelman echoed it and continued walking towards his office for what felt like an eternity.

'All you need to do is listen,' Niva continued. 'As I said yesterday, I need more places and times, the more specific the better. I only have two now: the door at the parliament building and the condemned apartment, which won't be enough. So Huey and Dewey need to go through that surveillance video and pull out an exact time the perpetrator was at the Slussen car park. You can work on Shurgard.'

'We're working as fast as we can.' Fabian rounded a corner and ran into a woman, who dropped her bag.

'Pardon me,' she said in Danish.

'I'm the one who should apologize.' Fabian crouched down and gathered the toothbrush and travel-size containers of shampoo and body lotion that had fallen on the floor, and put them back in the H&M bag that contained a red dress and a pair of high heels.

'You're from Denmark?' said Tomas with his chest muscles tensed.

'Yes, I'm looking for Malin Rehnberg. Do you know where she sits?' said Dunja.

'She's not currently sitting – she's lying down,' said Tomas, grinning.

'Unfortunately she's on sick leave and won't be back for at least six months,' said Fabian, giving the bag back to Dunja, who was dressed in jeans and a white blouse under an unbuttoned coat.

'But maybe I can help you?' said Tomas.

'Yes, this concerns a car that apparently belonged to—'

'Hello? Did I say it was urgent?' Niva's voice screamed through the phone.

'I'm sorry, but unfortunately we have to go. Tomas,' said Fabian, hurrying on.

DUNJA WATCHED THE THREE men head down the corridor and wondered how she should continue. Her only contact at the National Bureau of Investigation in Stockholm was on sick leave and would apparently not be back for quite some time. The consequences of her lack of sleep slowly washed over her. She just wanted to go home and pull the covers over her head.

'Excuse me, but you look a little lost. Are you looking for someone?'

Dunja turned to see a man wearing round glasses walking towards her. 'Yes. I actually came to speak with Malin Rehnberg, but apparently she's sick.'

'Yes, that's right. But I'm her boss. Maybe I can help you.' He held out his hand. 'Herman Edelman.'

'Sorry. I'm Dunja Hougaard from the Copenhagen Police.'

They shook hands and Edelman showed her to his office. 'Would you like something to drink? Coffee? Tea? I even have a little Gammel Dansk.'

'No, thanks, I'm fine. Actually a glass of mineral water might be nice.'

Edelman opened two bottles of Ramlösa and poured each into a glass.

'Also, would you happen to have a charger for my cell phone?' She held up her iPhone. 'It's completely dead.'

Edelman went over to the desk and came back with a charger. 'Be my guest. But how did you get in, by the way? From what I understand you don't have a scheduled meeting.'

'No, but as I just said, I wanted to surprise Malin,' said Dunja, pushing the charger into the outlet.

'And they just let you in?'

Dunja nodded, while Edelman shook his head.

'I hope you have better security at the Copenhagen police station. What can I do for you?'

'I'm working on a homicide investigation and we've discovered a car that belonged to your Minister for Justice.'

'Are you referring to Carl-Eric Grimås?'

'Yes. The licence plate is HXN 674.'

'And where did you find it?'

'At the bottom of the harbour in Helsingør. And from what I've understood, he was one of the victims of a major homicide case here in Stockholm.'

'Yes, that's right. But just so I'm completely clear: What homicide are you investigating?'

'I'm looking into a series of victims who have been raped and mutilated.'

'Of course. The TV celebrity and his wife.'

Dunja nodded.

'I thought that was closed.'

'It is, technically. I was just tying up some loose ends to make sure that we hadn't overlooked anything, when I discovered this connection.'

'Calling it a connection might be a bit of an overstatement, but obviously we'll get to the bottom of it. I'm sure there's a completely reasonable explanation.'

'And what might that be?'

'Well… Grimås was known for collecting cars – fancy cars – and it's not inconceivable that one of them was stolen and made its way into the underworld. Your perpetrator probably needed a car that couldn't be connected to him. But, as I said, I'll be sure to check this out and promise to get back to you as soon as possible.'

Dunja pulled the charger out of the phone and stood up. 'I would prefer if you get back to me directly.' She gave him her business card.

'Absolutely. No problem. And you'll be reachable at this number between Christmas and New Year, too?'

'I'm always at that number.' She shook his hand.

'When it's not dead, that is.' Edelman laughed and showed her out.

90

WHEN FABIAN CAME HOME with Tomas and Jarmo, they found Niva glued in front of the largest computer screen displaying a long list of various names and cell phone numbers.

'Don't tell me that all of those are suspicious,' said Tomas, looking over Niva's shoulder. She didn't bother to answer.

Only now did Fabian understand why he'd never heard about the possibility of triangulating an unknown cell phone number with a number of different places and times. The list of numbers and associated names seemed infinite. Even though Niva scrolled so quickly that the numbers and letters flowed together into a mishmash it never seemed to end. Although she wasn't done, he had to make an effort to control his scepticism.

'There must be something wrong. There just can't be that many,' said Tomas, who had started to exercise his biceps with an elastic resistance band.

'Hundreds of thousands of people must pass through Slussen every day, which is why I need more data,' said Niva with restrained irritation.

Tomas turned to Jarmo, who was sitting by the TV fast-forwarding through the surveillance video from the Slussen car park. 'How are things going at your end? You haven't started watching Fabian's private videos, have you?'

'I just found what I was looking for.' Jarmo froze the image of the perpetrator driving out in Adam Fischer's car with a gas mask on his face. 'He left the garage at 3:33 p.m.'

'Okay, we'll set a limit of 3:32,' said Niva, entering the command. 'And when do you think he got there?'

'He definitely wasn't in the car when Fischer drove in,' said Tomas, changing positions so that he could exercise his triceps. 'Fischer would have noticed, and it's obvious that he doesn't have the faintest idea of what's in store for him.'

'Please, stop that right now,' said Niva. 'It's noisy and smells like rubber.'

'So what's the problem?' Tomas gave Fabian a mischievous look.

'Did Fischer have a reserved space at the garage? Was his place nearby?' Fabian asked to change the subject. He'd regained faith in the idea.

'He had the coolest apartment at Mosebacke with a view that you couldn't help but be jealous of,' said Tomas. He finished up a final set before rolling up the band.

'So either the perpetrator followed Fischer in his own car, or else he was waiting in the car park.'

'I would guess the latter,' said Jarmo. 'I've gone through the video second by second, and I can promise you that he's not in any of the cars behind Fischer.'

Tomas sighed.

'How can you be so sure? It's not like he drove in with the gas mask on. He could basically be in any one of the cars that entered afterwards.'

'Well, in that case he's changed genders because there were only women behind the wheel in the seven cars that followed. But surely the expert must have a good explanation for that.'

'Okay, we're all tired here,' said Fabian.

'Not me,' said Tomas.

'Me neither,' said Jarmo.

'Well, then, it's just me. And actually it doesn't really matter. Let's just assume that he was there for at least as long as Fischer.'

'That was eleven minutes,' said Tomas, pushing a packet of *snus* under his upper lip.

'Okay, let's say ten to be on the safe side. How many are we down to now?' Fabian asked Niva.

'A few thousand,' said Niva with her eyes fixed on the screens. 'Hopefully there will be fewer once I've cross-referenced them with the numbers from the parliament building and the apartment on Östgötagatan.'

'Is anyone hungry besides me?' said Tomas.

'Take what you want from the fridge,' said Fabian, who was hungry himself, but couldn't tear himself from the screen where the list of cell phone numbers was getting ever shorter as the computer did its calculations.

When Tomas came back with a plate full of toasted marmalade and cheese sandwiches seven minutes later, the list was so short that it fitted on to a single screen.

'How many are we down to now?' asked Tomas as he wolfed down a sandwich.

'Forty-three.' Niva stretched in the chair.

'Is it done calculating?'

Niva answered with a curt nod, and Fabian felt disappointment pulling him back down into the fog of fatigue. Forty-three was, of course, considerably better than hundreds of thousands, but it was still too many.

'I don't understand. Can forty-three people really have been at three of these places at the exact same time?'

'Keep in mind that this doesn't take into account precise GPS co-ordinates,' said Niva, taking the last piece of toast.

'What the hell—'

'I've used a number of cell phone towers to triangulate an area as far as possible, but as I said, it's far from an exact science. Any number of these cars might have only just passed by Slussen.'

'I understand that too,' said Fabian. 'But the far exit of the building in the late afternoon when the snow is pouring down? Come on. There must be something wrong.'

'You're forgetting that it's not that far from the Central Bridge.'

'And what do we have on Östgötagatan?'

'For one thing, it's near Götgatan. But it was nine o'clock at night by then, so the majority of people who were there were probably residents.'

'Why isn't there a name attached to that number?' Tomas pointed towards the screen.

'It's a prepaid card.'

'Right, but surely he's not dumb enough to run around with a cell phone account in his own name.'

Niva looked up from the screen. 'Why didn't I think of that before?'

'So how many are we down to now?'

'One.'

'Just one?' Fabian repeated. 'Is it turned on?'

'Let me check.' Niva's hands were back on the keyboard.

'I need some *snus*,' said Jarmo, squeezing past Niva.

'Didn't you quit?' Tomas handed over a pouch.

'The cell is turned off right now,' said Niva, continuing to enter commands.

'Can you see if it's been anywhere else?' said Fabian, and Niva nodded.

'Axelsberg. Selmedalsvägen 38, 40 or 42.'

91

THE PAST WEEK FOR Carnela Ackerman could only be described as a never-ending nightmare. Every morning when she woke up she kept her eyes closed, clasped her hands and prayed that it would be a dream.

Two days ago Semira died. Besides her beloved sister, she had nothing else to live for, other than her job. It appeared that she had been brutally murdered for an innocent wish to be rid of her pain and to have her sight back – a wish she hadn't even dared to express out loud. Instead she had accepted her place on an endless waiting list.

She had no idea who had punished her sister, but two things were clear: Semira wasn't the only victim and the police had arrested the wrong person. Even that Fabian Risk knew it. He'd mentioned Gidon Hass, which was when she had changed her mind and realized the forces she was about to awaken.

She'd intended to tell him about the permits that were still not entirely in place and that constituted one final chance to stop the move. Soon that train would have also left, and if she didn't tell it would never come out. She needed to collect her thoughts and decide whether to contact him again. Actually, she should have called in sick and stayed at home. Instead she was sitting behind her desk trying to convince everyone that she was someone who could be relied on.

At the very least, she wanted to be left alone and not to have to talk to anyone, especially that woman from the district council who refused to take no for an answer. And now the woman from reception was calling her again.

'Yes, this is Carnela Ackerman,' she said in an attempt to sound as neutral as possible.

'Hi, this is reception.'

'Hello. What's this about?'

'I'm sorry, but it's that woman from the district council. She keeps calling, and now she's threatening an unannounced visit and fines if we don't answer her questions. I know that you would prefer not to take any calls today – I've really tried to put her off – but...'

'Okay, transfer her to me.'

'Oh, thanks a lot.'

Carnela awaited the transferred call and answered. 'This is Carnela Ackerman.'

'Finally. You're not the easiest person to get hold of, you know.'

'No, I have a very full schedule in these last few days of the year. Who am I speaking with?'

'Sorry. My name is Eva-Britt Mossberg, and I'm calling on behalf of the Östermalm District Administration. We are doing a study of your employees' work environment.'

'This can't wait until January?'

'Unfortunately not. The information has to be compiled before the end of the year, and you're the last on my list. I just have a few simple questions that won't take more than three minutes to answer at most. The alternative is that we come for an inspection, and you'll have to pay for that.'

'Sure, sure, let's get this over with.'

'Okay. Thank you. Do you use your own cleaning personnel, or are they brought in?'

'It's external.' Carnela did not intend to say a single unnecessary word.

'I see, and how often do they come?'

'Three times a week: Monday, Wednesday, Friday.'

'Do they come during office hours, or—'

'No, they come after office hours.'

'I see. And what company do you use?'

'Always Clean.'

'And are you satisfied with them?'

'Yes.'

'Very good, I'll take this opportunity to say thank you and to wish you happy holidays.'

'Are we finished already?'

'As I said, there were only a few questions. Bye now.'

There was a click, and Carnela Ackerman sat there, looking at the receiver in her hand.

MALIN REHNBERG EXHALED AND set the cell phone down on the table beside the bed. The call had exceeded expectations. She knew she was good at lying, but not this good. If she ever decided to embark on a new career, she could always try acting; or, even better, be a professional poker player.

She brought the bed up to a seated position, then opened her computer, entered the cleaning company's name in the search field of the browser and clicked to their website. It promised dazzlingly clean homes and offices and that they were both punctual and reliable. Unfortunately, there were no pictures of the staff or any information about whether they had male cleaners.

She had no choice but to assume another role, so she picked up the phone and entered the number. As the ring tones sounded, she used the opportunity to think about what she should do if they were already off for the holidays and didn't answer. Maybe she could ask her sister who worked at the Social Insurance Agency to get her information about all the employees. The risk was that she would tell Anders, who would totally flip out. Niva Ekenhielm was a much better alternative, however much it grated her to admit it. She could get the information as quickly as she could destroy a marriage.

'Welcome to Always Clean. How may I help you?'

'Hello, my name is Malin Rehnberg.' She was completely unprepared for anyone to answer and hadn't thought up a pseudonym. 'I'm looking for a cleaner to make my home as dazzlingly clean as you promise on your website.'

'Absolutely. Do you live in a house or apartment? And how many rooms—'

'It's big and this will probably be really expensive,' Malin interrupted. 'I would prefer to have male cleaners. Do you have any?'

There was silence on the other end.

'Let me underscore that this is only about cleaning. I've just had much better experience with men.'

'I understand. We should have several. But—'

'Marvellous! Perhaps you could email me a list?'

'I don't know. There—'

'And one more thing: can you please include their names and pictures, so that I can see what they look like?'

92

THE SHELF IN THE dark hall was filled with gloves, hats and scarves, and some winter coats were hanging on the hooks. Boots and shoes were on the shoe rack below. There was the outline of an old-fashioned telephone on a hall table beside a wicker chair further inside, but it was too dark to see whether it was an authentic one with a dial.

The angle was adjusted and the search for clues moved down to the floor. Suddenly the light came on and a pair of bare feet were visible in the small round, reversed image. They belonged to an elderly man who was scratching his grey hair.

Fabian withdrew the dental mirror, carefully closed the mail slot and hurried down the stairs.

The geographic position that Niva had given them by triangulating the cell phone towers was anything but exact. Selmedalsvägen 38–42 included three different entrances with access to nine floors each with between three to five apartments on each level. Then again, she'd only counted on a radius of fifteen metres, which was the best-case scenario. Fabian didn't dare think about how big it could be in the worst possible outcome as he glanced up at the light-brown concrete buildings that stood in a row; evidence of an architect's bad day.

It had taken them twelve minutes to get there, even though Tomas had run red lights and used every bus lane. To ensure they didn't lose any more valuable time, they split up with each of them taking a different entrance. Fabian had just finished the top two floors, and was on his way down to the seventh.

A mother disappeared into the elevator with her stroller. He waited until the elevator doors closed, before exhaling a big sigh of relief that he was finally alone. Fabian started studying the five apartment doors. There was another stroller and a tied-up garbage bag outside one of them. On the door beside it was a handwritten 'We live here' sign with all the family members' names, including 'Copper' and 'Old Boy'. The third door was not quite as easy to rule out. It said 'M. Carlsson' on the mail slot under the sticker that said 'No flyers, please'.

Fabian rang the bell with one hand and felt the shoulder holster inside his coat with the other. The service gun he usually didn't carry and that had never been used outside the firing range was in place. He couldn't say why, but carrying it always made him feel uncomfortable, like the feeling of wearing a tie when everyone else was in T-shirts. But Tomas and the others insisted that they should be armed, and he agreed it was probably a good idea. At any moment they could be under fire – the perpetrator might be ready and waiting behind any one of the apartment doors.

As he rang the bell again, Fabian wondered whether he would pull out his gun and pull the trigger without hesitating. Somewhere deep down, he knew the answer and could only hope he was wrong.

He had taken out the dental mirror, pulled out the shaft and was carefully guiding it down through the mail slot, when his cell phone started vibrating. He picked it up with his free hand and put it to his ear while he adjusted the angle of the mirror.

'Hi, Daddy,' he heard Matilda's voice at the other end.

'Hi, Matilda. How's it going out at Aunt Lisen's?' He scanned the hall and saw a dirty, illuminated terrarium containing something hairy with several legs, and a few guitars leaning against the wall.

'It's bad. Theo says I'm a piece of shit and that he's going to hit me.'

'Why would he say something like that?'

'Because I told Mummy he sneaked out through the window last night.'

'What did you say?' asked Fabian, as he watched someone go past a guitar and walk up right towards him. He pulled the mirror up again, but it was stuck.

'He left, and wasn't back until—'

'Matilda, I have to go now. We'll talk later.'

The door opened and a man in his mid-thirties came rushing out in tracksuit bottoms and a bare torso. 'I saw what you were up to!' The man reeked of beer and pushed Fabian up against the wall. 'Fucking peeping Tom.'

'I'm a police officer,' said Fabian, finally managing to dig out his identification and hold it up in front of the man. 'We're looking for a suspect in one of the apartments here and when you didn't answer I assumed you weren't at home.'

'So you started spying through the mail slot. Is that even legal?' The man let go of Fabian and grabbed his identification.

'We're in a race against time and this is the only chance we have.' Fabian coaxed the mirror out and took back his ID card.

'I see, and what happens now? Do I have to go in for questioning?'

'No, if anything comes up we'll be in touch again. One last thing: what do you know about your neighbours?'

'Basically nothing.' The man seemed almost disappointed that nothing more would happen. 'Although the kids in there shriek like pigs every fucking day starting at five thirty in the morning. It's so bad, I've thought about reporting them. Can I do that with you?'

'No, but as I said we'll be in touch if we need you.'

In order to make it clear that they were finished, Fabian turned around and rang the doorbell of the apartment next door. He waited for the sound of footsteps and the door being closed behind him, but when he didn't hear anything he turned around again to face the tenant.

'Like I said, we'll be in touch.'

'It's not illegal to watch, is it?'

'No, but I'd prefer it if you... Oh, forget it.' Fabian gave up with a sigh, and returned to the neighbour's door and rang the bell again. When no one answered he took out the mirror and guided it down into the mail slot.

'Is that thing allowed?'

Fabian tried to block out the man and focus on what he saw in the mirror.

'Well, there you go. You learn something new every day.'

The hall looked similar to the elderly man's apartment above, except the doors were open and let in enough light so that he could study the furnishings.

'Do you see anything cool?'

'No. It's just boring things,' said Fabian, slowly turning the mirror.

There were colours everywhere. The walls were painted red and a thin yellow cloth with tiny mirrors and sequins sewn in was hanging over a larger mirror with a gold frame. There were small shelves with tea light holders in various colours on the opposite wall and the rug that stretched through the entire hall was green and blue. Other than a grey sweater and a heavy black jacket, most of the clothes hanging on the hat shelf were bright.

He angled the mirror down to study the shoes on the shelf, but was met by one eye of a gas mask. The shock startled him and made him lose his hold of the mirror, which disappeared through the mail slot.

'Hey! What the hell was that?'

'I have to ask you to go back into your apartment now.'

'Did you see something important?'

'I said get into your apartment.'

'Nice and easy now.' The man backed up a few steps and stood on his own threshold without closing the door.

Fabian took out a picklock and a small bottle of lock oil and started working.

'So that's how it's done.'

After a minute or two he was able to turn the picklock around like a key and carefully open the door.

'Jesus, that can't have been the first time.'

Fabian looked around the hall of the apartment. There was a gas mask hanging on a hook in the far corner. It could be a coincidence, but who had a gas mask hanging in their hall? He continued further inside. The first door led into a bedroom, which was painted a rich hue, just like the hall. The walls were warm yellow and the bed in the middle of the room had a pink duvet cover spread over it and couldn't be wider than a metre. Fabian tried to put together the image he had of the perpetrator. He really wasn't sure what he had expected, but one thing was certain: it wasn't this.

A shimmering red silk cloth with several dozen candles and some incense burners were placed on top of a dresser along one wall across from the headboard. Right in the middle of the dresser was a framed photograph of a stone embedded in the ground and just beside it was an old record player with *At Last: The Best of Etta James* on the turntable. He pressed play. The record started turning, the arm lowered, and Etta James's most famous and haunting song, *At Last,* sounded through the speaker.

Fabian picked up the framed photograph to inspect it more closely. He realized that there was something written on the stone in small, unintelligible letters, but he could only understand two dates.

ןידי םירפא

1977–1998

רחא והשימ בהוא ינא םעפ יא םעפ ףא
רחא והשימל הכה יבל םעפ יא היהי אל םעפ ףא
רחא דחא ףא אלו התא

חצנ ךות לא לעו ,יח ינא דוע לכ
יל םג זא .הלוכ בוש לכוא בורקב.
בוש ונשגפנ ןכמ רחאל
ךילא ילש החטבהה

It wasn't Arabic, that much he could decipher. And it didn't look like an Asian language either. He figured it could be Hebrew; at any rate, the text reminded him of the embroidered letters that Edelman had hanging on the wall of his office. In order to be completely certain and to rule out Georgian, Armenian and all the other languages he didn't know, he would have to have someone look at it.

On the other hand, he was convinced that he was looking at a gravestone. But whose? And who was the grieving person? Was he even in the right place? He took a picture of the photograph with his phone and sent it to Niva, and then went back out into the hall and went into the next room.

One step across the threshold was enough for all doubt to disappear. The room differed markedly from the rest of the apartment. There were no warm colours or decorative objects to make it feel pleasant. The walls were more reminiscent of how it looked right now in his own living room, yet no investigative work had gone on here.

Instead this was where all the planning had taken place.

The wall to the left was covered with old newspaper clippings and photographs. He spotted Ossian Kremph at various ages and the security guard with the mannequins. Carl-Eric Grimås was also there, both as a minister wearing his typical hat and fur-collared coat, and as a young man when he worked with Herman Edelman at the National Bureau. Semira Ackerman and Adam Fischer were on the wall, too.

But there were also other faces that Fabian didn't recognize: a well-groomed woman with brown hair who Fabian could have sworn looked just like the wife of a Danish celebrity; and a muscle-bound man with bright blue eyes and a strong jaw. Connected to each person was everything from extracts of court reports and newspaper clippings to medical records and detailed notes, such as their work hours and commutes, as well as entry codes, where they did their grocery shopping, whom they socialized with, their favourite TV shows and taste in clothing. It was everything a stalker might need to inhabit these people's world.

The whole thing was linked with red, tacked-down bands that branched out over the wall. There was a timeline that ran horizontally along the top of the wall, starting on 8 December with Adam Fischer's kidnapping and moving day by day until 24 December.

Today was the twenty-second.

Fabian followed the two red bands towards the last two days, but both were incomplete. The nails were still in the wall, so the perpetrator must have torn off all the pictures and notes before he left the apartment.

Two days left.

Another two to go.

It couldn't mean anything else.

Fabian turned to the rest of the room. Rolls of protective plastic were leaned against one long wall and there was a shelf lined with gas tubes and another with scalpels and all kinds of surgical tools. A clothes rack was filled with various get-ups, including Joakim Holmberg's security guard uniform, and a bunch of wigs, fake beards and a moustache were piled on top of a vanity.

He spotted a number of keys and pass cards hanging in a key cabinet. None of them was marked, so he focused his attention on a work table with a pile of document folders and a large screen that was connected to a desktop computer under the table. He tried to start it, but once he realized there was no keyboard or mouse, he thought it might be best to take it home to Niva. Instead he opened up one of the folders.

It contained printouts from the pathology institute in Abu Kabir. There was page upon page of long tables. The first column consisted of a five-digit number, and the second contained a blood type. The third column listed every transplantable organ associated with the five-digit number, and the fourth column ranked the quality of each organ using a ten-point scale.

Another folder contained documentation on the organ buyers. Thousands of people must have been in contact with the Institute. Each file contained their medical records, which organ had been transplanted, and from whom they had received it. That is, which five-digit number.

A number of folders later he found the final link: the pictures of the dead. His heart sank as he turned the pages, seeing horror after horror. All those people who had been opened up and emptied without their consent, and then renamed with a five-digit number that was stapled to their forehead.

'Wow. This is what you might call the jackpot.'

Fabian turned around to face the bare-chested neighbour, who was standing right behind him.

'Imagine having this kind of neighbour. It's unbelievable,' the man continued, throwing out his arms.

Fabian was about to order him back to his apartment, and even made a move to draw his gun to show how serious he was, but he didn't get that far.

'Okay, I know, I know. I shouldn't be here. You just get so curious. It's not every day you realize you have a psycho for a neighbour. Stay calm. I'm leaving now,' the man said, disappearing back out into the hall.

'Wait a second!'

'Yes?'

'What do you know about your neighbour?'

'Pretty much nothing.' The man shrugged. 'But she's damned good-looking, that's for sure.'

'She?' Fabian was convinced that he'd heard wrong, until he saw the man nodding.

93

GOD KNEW, IT HADN'T been easy. Malin Rehnberg had used the whole range of her acting abilities before she managed to convince the woman at Always Clean to email her both names and pictures of their male cleaners. She'd even been forced to solemnly swear to have them clean her house once a week for at least six months. I'll have to see what Ursula says about this, she thought, clicking on her email's envelope icon to see if anything had arrived yet.

She'd been rapidly pressing on the icon for the past ten minutes, like a gambling addict in front of a one-armed bandit. Each time her inbox showed up empty she was on the verge of calling back Always Clean to show them who they were dealing with. She didn't need to restrain herself this time, though, because it had finally arrived.

Hi Malin,

I hope you find someone suitable. Six months is a fairly long time. ;-)

Kind regards,
Åsa

Malin typed out a quick response promising to get back to her as soon as she'd looked over the list.

The attached file turned out to be several megabytes, which meant that she must have included all the personnel. It wasn't that much of an issue other than it would be time-consuming. Then again, they couldn't have that many male cleaners.

She preferred to be left alone when she was working. The hospital staff had already given her two warnings about needing rest and threatened to confiscate both her phone and computer. Fortunately, she didn't think that the cleaning woman who was doing her daily round would tattle on her; otherwise she would have done it long ago, considering the number of times she must have seen her reclining with her computer.

She started at the top of the list, but she didn't get much further than halfway down the first page when the door opened and she had to quickly close her computer and hide it under the covers.

'There you are.'

'Dunja? What are you doing here?'

'Didn't you tell me to pop in if I was in the neighbourhood?' Dunja came in with a bouquet of flowers.

'How lovely. Are those for me?'

'Of course.' Dunja put the flowers in the vase on the night-stand.

'Should I get some water for them?' the cleaning woman asked.

'Yes, thank you, that would be very nice,' said Malin, making room on the bed for Dunja. 'What a lovely surprise! Although you could have called to warn me. I would have put a little make-up on.'

'Yes, you really need to.'

'You should have seen me a few days ago. Actually you did. Why didn't you say anything?'

'When?'

'In Denmark, when we met. I must have looked like a right sunfish.'

'Oh, come off it, you looked fine. What happened to you?'

'This,' said Malin pointing to her pregnant belly.

'Is everything okay?'

'Yes, but come sit down and tell me what you're doing here.'

'It's a long story.' Dunja sat on the edge of the bed. 'But the short version is that you were right.'

'Of course I was. May I ask about what?'

Dunja's smile disappeared. She was just about to start talking but stopped herself when the cleaning woman came back in with a pitcher of water and started filling the vase.

'It's okay. You can tell me.'

'It's Carsten… It's not going to work out for the two of us.'

'Obviously it's not. I could see that from a mile away. You weren't even in love.'

'No. But I thought I was. We almost never argued, and—'

'Listen, that doesn't mean a thing, I can promise you. My husband Anders and I fight all the time. Maybe fight isn't the right word… We bicker. As soon as we see each other we start up. But, God, how I love him. More than anything.' Malin stopped herself when she saw that Dunja had started crying, and hugged her. 'Listen, I know it's tough, but—'

'I'm just so tired, and to be honest I don't even know why I'm crying. I think I'm fine. In a way it feels like I've known all along and was just waiting to be humiliated enough to force me to leave him.'

'You can be happy it happened now, and not when you look like me.'

Dunja laughed and dried her tears. 'Unfortunately, I have to head out now or I'll miss my flight. It was really nice to see you.'

'I'll be in touch when I've got my head above water again – likely in twenty years!'

Dunja laughed again, got up, and walked out the door. Malin leaned back in bed and wondered when she had last told Anders how much she really loved him. She decided to call him, but not quite yet. First she had to go through that personnel list from Always Clean.

She opened the computer again, put in her password and started sifting through the information. As she expected, there weren't many male cleaners. After a quick review she deduced there were only three. Three potential suspects, all of whom had access to both keys and codes to get into the Israeli Embassy and clean after office hours. Any one of them could have been the leak that Grimås and Edelman were so worried about. She wrote down their names and personal identity numbers in an email to Fabian. She was about to press send when her eyes locked in on the face directly beneath the picture of one of the men.

She couldn't really pinpoint what drew her to it, except that there was something familiar about the woman. Only once she enlarged the image did she realize that she actually recognized her. Was she a distant colleague? Or perhaps one of the thousands of witnesses she'd met? She just couldn't identify her.

Suddenly she realized how she knew the woman and every muscle in her body tensed. She'd seen her every day since she'd been in the hospital, sometimes several times in the same day. It had been so often that she no longer thought about it. She'd been here ever since Matilda turned on the doll she'd had with her.

In fact, she was in the room right now, holding the mop in her hands and staring right at her.

THE STAFF IN THE ward were having a heated discussion about the open treasure chest that was bubbling out air to oxygenate the water. The question concerned how much money they should actually spend on brightening up the waiting room when the staff room was in an appalling condition.

Dunja didn't even notice the aquarium as she passed the waiting room on her way towards the elevators. She was completely absorbed in planning Carsten's move out of the apartment. He would be coming home late that evening, which would give her several hours to change the locks and pack up his things.

She pressed the elevator button and noted that it was twenty past twelve. It would soon be two hours since she'd seen Herman Edelman and he still hadn't been in touch. She couldn't say she was surprised. The chance that he would call before Christmas was negligible. In that respect, Sweden was exactly like Denmark: everything closed down for the holiday.

Everyone except the perpetrator.

She recalled the real reason she'd wanted to see Malin Rehnberg. She had wanted to tell her that their Minister for Justice's car had shown up in her investigation in a strange coincidence. But the conversation had been all about Carsten instead, and perhaps that was just as well. Malin looked really worn out and was surely overworked. She needed to recover and gather her strength before the delivery.

Or not?

Suddenly she felt hesitant. Maybe she could go back quickly and tell her , if only to get a reaction. It wouldn't take long, although it would mean she'd have to take a taxi to the airport so that she didn't miss check-in.

When the elevator doors opened a few seconds later, she was already on her way back to the ward. Right by the bubbling aquarium, she got the call she'd been waiting for.

'Hi, it's Herman Edelman. I don't know if you remember me.'

'Yes, of course I do.'

'You'll have to excuse my tardiness, but getting your information turned out to be more complicated than you might have anticipated. This is how it fits together: just a few weeks before Grimås was murdered he sold his Porsche 911.'

'Who did he sell it to?'

'I'm getting to that. I don't know how it works in Denmark, but here in Sweden the seller is responsible for sending in the change of ownership to the Transport Agency. Normally it only takes a few business days before the notification is registered, but in this case it didn't come in until yesterday.'

'Do we know why?'

'Apparently two numbers in the postal code were reversed. There's your connection.'

'So, who was the buyer?'

'Björn Troedsson at Arkitektgatan 2 in Malmö. Apparently he's no more than a stone's throw from Konsultgatan where Benny Willumsen lived.'

'The car was stolen?'

'Exactly. The police report should have come in to the Malmö Police on Monday, 14 December, but since the owner information didn't match, it was set aside. It arrived only while I was rooting around. I'll email you all the papers so you can see them with your own eyes, and if anything is unclear all you have to do is contact me again.'

Dunja thanked him for the help, hung up and decided not to bother Malin Rehnberg.

TIME HAD SLOWED DOWN and seemed about to stop entirely. Malin was sure that if she'd dared move her gaze to the clock on the wall, she wouldn't even have been able to discern the plodding movement of the second hand.

Normally she wasn't someone who got scared. It almost never happened. Even in the most stressful circumstances, facing a gun held in shaking, drug-addled hands, she would react contrary to most of her colleagues and become more calm and collected, which was often what was needed.

But this time she was scared.

And, for the first time ever, for her life.

Her children's lives.

Her hospital gown was soaked with sweat, and she couldn't move. Terror had drilled its claws so deep into her that all she could do was lie in bed, staring back at the woman. She didn't even try to reach the alarm button that was hanging down on its cord only a foot or so away.

Neither of them said anything. There was no need for words. The eyes said enough.

They both understood.

That there was no return.

Aisha Shahin, Malin repeated in her head. She was struck by how lovely it was – almost as lovely as the woman who was standing before her with golden-brown skin and clear blue eyes.

Fear started to release its hold on her. Maybe it was because the whole situation seemed so surreal. It should be against all the laws of nature that something so beautiful could cause something so horrific. It reminded her of the images from a little over eight years ago. They were so unbelievable that they almost looked like an action movie. Both she and Anders had to sit in front of the TV and watch the planes crashing into the Twin Towers over and over again, far into the night, to understand that it had really happened.

She mustered up the courage to reach one arm out towards the alarm button without taking her eyes off the woman. But she missed it and had no choice but to turn around and try to grab the swinging button again. With her hand trembling convulsively, she finally got hold of the plastic and was about to press in with her thumb.

But it was too late.

The cleaning woman was already on top of her and tore the call button out of its socket. Malin's arms started waving and tried to claw wherever they could reach. They'd never been in a fight for life and death, and were soon overpowered and locked against her chest. How strong was this woman?

A respiratory mask was pressed against her face. She hadn't noticed it before she heard the gas start hissing. She'd never been good at holding her breath and was always the first one up to the surface. But now there was no place to go. She was forced to stay down, despite the growing pain in her chest. She wouldn't manage much longer, and could already picture how soon she would be forced to give up.

Her lungs were about to burst. In a final desperate lunge she tried to get loose, but her arms were still pinned down. All she could move was her head, so she tried first in one direction, then in the other. She repeated the action with more force, which created a gap between the mask and her face.

She took a few desperate breaths, while she threw her head in every direction until the mask fell off. Without thinking she sank her teeth in the hand restraining her arms and bit down until she tasted blood.

The woman shrieked and eased her grip on Malin's arms. Malin rolled on to her side away from the woman, over the edge of the bed, and down on to the floor. She felt a pain in her hip, but what did that matter now? All she could focus on was getting out of there, away from the beautiful monster, and into the corridor where she could scream for help.

She tried to stand up, but something in her hip wasn't working properly. She slid forward on all fours, using her arms and one leg with the other dragging behind. She did everything she could to block out the pain in her hip even though it got more intense, and concentrated on pulling herself towards the door.

Once she got there, she started screaming for help as loud as she could, while she reached for the door handle to open it, but she couldn't get all the way up.

The hands that grasped her ankles were so strong and pulled her back across the floor like a newly slaughtered animal. She resisted, kicked the hands loose and managed to make her way back to the door to open it.

But only in her mind. Her body had given up.

With her broken hip, all the woman needed to secure her was a hard knee to the back.

'You should have taken the mask. It's not certain that they're going to survive,' said the woman behind her.

Malin didn't understand what she was talking about until she felt a stab between her vertebrae and a numbing sensation spread across her body, down into her legs and up over her belly.

94

3 April 2000

IT HAD BEEN THREE years since Aisha Shahin crossed the border out of Palestine. She'd managed to get all the way to Sweden using her mother's savings. It turned out that she had a talent for Swedish and was one of the best students in her language class for immigrants. She wasn't able to transfer her medical training, so she started working at a cleaning company instead. Slowly but surely, she built up a secure life for herself. But she'd never stopped dreaming about the day when she and Efraim would be reunited, leave everything behind and never let go of each other again.

It was the reason why she was back again.

She'd taken many risks on her way over the border to get to her old village of Imatin. But the letter had given her no other choice. The hand of God must have helped the letter find its way to her. She knew all the words by heart.

> Aisha, it feels like you're here and reading every word over my shoulder. I don't want to stop writing but strength has run out of my body. I must save my last bits so I can fold this up, put it in the envelope and drop it in the night.

It told her so much, but nevertheless ended in a question greater than anything else.

Was he alive?

Had he succeeded in the impossible? Or had it ended the way she had feared? The weight of the uncertainty rested on her chest and she felt as if it would suffocate her if she didn't get an answer soon.

God was with her in any event. She could feel it in her whole body, like the heavily loaded backpack that chafed across her shoulders, yet she hardly seemed to notice. The half moon in the clear night sky gave off just enough light so that she could keep her flashlight off, which was a major advantage. Although she could see from a distance that all the houses in the village were dark, it was far from certain that everyone was asleep.

As a little girl she had gone there a lot. She and her friends had loved to run around and play hide-and-seek among the trees and stones. Her mother warned her that she would be punished for playing there one day because there were strong forces that were hard to resist. But she'd continued without giving a second thought to what lay below her bare feet.

She'd only understood what her mother was talking about the morning after the electricity had been turned off and darkened the whole village. They had woken to find three dead bodies lying in a heap outside the wall, right at the spot where she would sit in the shade and count out loud with her hands over her eyes while the others ran and hid. She recognized all three of them, but the youngest she had known personally. They had played together after school almost every day, and she had never met anyone else who was as good at throwing stones as him.

It looked exactly as she remembered it: the trees that had provided shade and were so much fun to climb in, the benches on the inside of the stone wall, and the graves that were scattered all over the place. There were a few old ones with worn, overturned stones, but others were quite new.

It took no more than a few minutes to find what she was looking for. They were in a row at the far end of one corner. Even though it had been almost two years ago, the moulding in the ground was still clearly visible.

Rasin. Mihayr. Zakwan. Tamir. Muzaffar. Altair. Safi. Wasim.

Every name was familiar. Five of them were her brothers. The other three were neighbours.

But they weren't the reason she'd come back.

She was here for the last one.

The one that didn't even get a stone with an inscription.

The ninth grave.

She wriggled out of the backpack, unfolded the spade, and started digging. The ground was hard and dry. An hour later she got on her knees and brushed aside the dry earth from the thick industrial-strength plastic that had been wrapped several times around the body and fastened with heavy tape. With the help of a safety knife, she cut through layer after layer of plastic. When the body was finally exposed below her she saw exactly what she'd feared.

She had expected that the cut-open and emptied body would make her start crying. The sight of the gaping, empty eye sockets and heavy stitches from the throat all the way down past the navel would make her tears drip down over his mutilated body. But she did not shed so much as a tear, not even when she noticed the label with the five-digit number in black ink that was attached to his forehead with a staple.

All she could feel was hate.

She hated her father and brothers who had forced him out on the mission, and her mother who had stood by and watched. She despised the Israeli soldiers who had fired the shots and the doctor who had opened him up and deprived him of everything that made him whole. But most of all, she felt hatred towards everyone who walked around with blood on their hands and Efraim inside them; those people who had refused to accept the judgment of God. She carefully pulled loose the label from his forehead and folded it up.

Whoever they were.
Wherever they were.
They would all get their punishment.

95

FABIAN GOT IN THE car to drive the desktop computer over to Niva. On his way into the city his thoughts were whirling around as quickly as the snowflakes outside. After turning right on to Hornsgatan on a red, and coming within a centimetre of a collision, he put Kraftwerk's Computer World into the CD player in an attempt to regain focus.

It's not that he wasn't prepared for surprises. He'd realized long ago that this was an unusual investigation that required thinking outside the box. After all, they were dealing with a perpetrator who had devoted years to meticulous preparations and hadn't left anything to chance.

Yet the fact that a woman was behind it all had come as a total surprise. And to be honest, he still had a hard time imagining it, even though it was the reality. According to her neighbour, Aisha Shahin was both unusually pleasant and extremely beautiful.

So far they hadn't succeeded in locating a picture of her. But he was convinced that it was only a matter of time before Tomas and Jarmo, who were searching the apartment, would find one and send it over, even if it wasn't the highest priority. They were focused on producing leads to the next two victims as quickly as possible, even if the perpetrator's careful planning indicated that it might already be too late.

He parked in the disabled spot right outside his building entrance. The darkness had long since settled in. He took the computer from the passenger seat, locked the car and hurried through the snow that was now pouring down.

Once he was inside, he pulled off his snow-covered boots and went into the living room. He set the computer down on the table beside Niva's various computer screens, which were all displaying the same message: 'Work in Progress'.

Niva was nowhere to be found. He called her name without getting a response, and took out his phone to call her.

'Hi.'

'Where are you?'

'At your place. Here, I'll give you a little clue.' He heard the sound of splashing water.

Fabian walked over to the bathroom to find Niva in the bath, cell phone in hand.

'That was quick.' She set down the phone and started clapping her hands.

They were in the middle of one of the toughest investigations they'd ever been involved in and here she was relaxing in his bathtub. The only things missing were candles and champagne.

'Niva, what the hell are you doing?'

'There is a limit to how long you can sit in front of a computer without washing. Let's just say that this is long overdue, something that also applies to your highness, not to mention Huey and Dewey. Besides, I can't do anything until the machines out there are finished with their current task.'

'Has the text on the gravestone been translated yet?'

'It's on the table.'

Fabian turned back to the living room where he found some handwritten sentences in an open notebook.

Never again will I love another
Never again will my heart beat for any other
You and no other
As long as I love, and on into eternity

Soon you'll be whole again, and I will be too
Then we'll meet again
My promise to you

He read through the text twice, as if he couldn't get enough of the words and everything they meant.

'It really is beautiful.'

Fabian nodded and looked up. Niva was walking towards him in a white bathrobe.

'I couldn't find anything else, so I hope it's okay that I borrowed this.'

It was far from okay. She was wearing Sonja's bathrobe, which was anything but shared property. But he didn't have the energy to put up a fight and reinstate the boundaries. Besides, he still needed her help.

'Do you think all this is for his sake?' Niva continued, standing beside him.

'Yes.'

'Imagine being so in love with someone that you're prepared to go that far.'

Fabian nodded without saying anything.

'How far would you go for Sonja?'

Fabian understood exactly where she was heading. But this time he didn't intend to go along with her. 'As far as the law allows.'

'That doesn't sound especially romantic. Just think how much more I could do.'

'You?' Fabian met her eyes.

'Yes. How many laws have I broken?'

Fabian thought about how to respond, but his phone broke the silence. 'This is Fabian—'

'She's gone! They've taken her!' a voice screamed on the other end.

'Sorry, but who am I—'

'They've taken her and no one seems to know where she is!'

'Who's gone and who am I speaking with?'

'Anders Rehnberg! Who the hell do you think? They've taken Malin!'

96

WAS IT DOD WHO'D turned His back on her, even though He'd stood beside her the whole way? Was this His punishment? For the first time in a long while she felt uncertain about whether He was really with her. Or was it just a series of unfortunate events influenced by chance that had tripped her up? It couldn't be anything else. Not now, when she was so close to her goal.

She'd arrived almost an hour and a half too late. Not five minutes or a quarter of an hour, but eighty-eight whole minutes. When she was young she was late more often than not. But this was the first time it had happened since she'd set foot in Sweden. For twelve-and-a-half years she had been on time and today was not a good day to be late.

If it hadn't been for the hidden camera they'd unknowingly brought along with them in the rest of the investigation material, Fabian Risk would have almost certainly found enough in her apartment to arrest her before she was finished. She didn't quite understand how the woman who was no longer actually a police officer had managed to pull it off. It had something to do with her cell phone, that much she understood. But how it could have led them to her apartment was still a mystery. Several years ago, she'd travelled to Umeå to buy the anonymous prepaid number and had even had the cell phone turned off for the past few days.

To avoid catastrophe, she'd returned to the apartment in haste, and only taken the most important things with her in the stroller. She'd made it out of the apartment at the last minute before he arrived. He would find quite a bit, especially in the computer, but that didn't matter now. They wouldn't get there in time anyway.

The important thing was that under no circumstances could the finale be upended. Then everything she'd built up would collapse, and she wouldn't have a chance to carry out the most important part of her plan, the whole point of what she'd worked for over the past decade.

As if that wasn't enough, the pregnant policewoman managed to get hold of the cleaning company's personnel list and then clearly recognized her, which was not surprising given how long she'd been keeping her under observation. She also couldn't understand how the list had ended up in her hands in the first place, but she hadn't had time to figure it out. She'd been forced to improvise and take care of the situation in front of her, certain that somehow there must still be a point to it all, even if she couldn't see it right now. Despite everything, God must still be with her.

She'd promised herself that no innocent persons would be affected and that only those who deserved it would face her wrath. But she'd already been forced to make an exception in Denmark. The situation had slipped out of her hands and she'd had no alternative. The man had decided not to stay overnight at the apartment in Copenhagen and had come home several hours earlier than expected. Although in many ways, he'd been an accomplice, so she didn't have a guilty conscience.

On the other hand, that wasn't the policewoman's fault. She was just doing her job – really well at that. Her fate and the fate of her two unborn children was something she had to leave to God.

At last she found a parking spot on Pontonjärgatan. She changed clothes in the back seat, locked up and put the key on the left front tyre, before hurrying around the corner and making her way up Polhemsgatan through the fresh snow. She rang the bell beside the grey steel door and was met by the burly guy with rings in his ears, who told her off for being late. She'd made up a lie about how someone had jumped in front of a subway train, but he wasn't the least bit interested in listening, so she kept quiet and nodded, promising that it would never happen again.

At least she was being honest.

She hurried to the broom closet and took out her equipment. Many square metres needed to be vacuumed and scrubbed in the few hours she had left. Dried-up crud had to be cleaned up, condoms must be thrown out and bathroom stalls required new rolls of toilet paper.

All before the night's great event.

She would be forced to work quickly to make it fit her timeline. But stress was also working in her favour. The burly man, for instance, had seemed preoccupied. If the others were only half as stressed as she was, none of them would have time to notice her transformation.

97

FABIAN HAD FELT A nagging worry since he discovered Matilda fiddling with that camera in the doll at the hospital. He'd immediately made sure Malin had got a new room, but it had been too late. The perpetrator had found her anyway. But how and, above all, why? He had no idea, and could only hope that his worst fears would not be realized.

The ward where she'd been resting was deserted except for the reception desk, where some of the nurses were crowded behind a computer screen, exchanging confused looks.

'What happened?' he said, even though it was clear that they were as perplexed as he was.

'We have no idea,' the tallest one said. 'We switched to night shift an hour ago, and we're still trying to figure it out.'

'It says here that she was supposedly moved down to delivery, but we've checked and they never received her,' said the one sitting behind the screen.

Fabian hurried to Malin's room. Anders Rehnberg was sitting in a chair in the middle of it, his face buried in his hands. The room felt unnaturally empty now that the bed was no longer there. He wasn't crying, but when he looked up at Fabian his red eyes were evidence that it was all that he'd been doing for the past hour.

'You bastard! I hope you understand that this is your fault – yours and no one else's.' His eyes radiated such hatred that Fabian had to struggle against the impulse to turn around and leave.

'Anders, I understand how you feel, but we still don't know what happened.' He pulled out a chair and sat down across from him.

'Don't come here and say you understand, because you don't. You're even worse than Malin.'

Fabian couldn't figure out what he was talking about.

'I've talked with your wife, and do you know what she said? Huh?'

Fabian shook his head.

'That you're unfaithful every day you go to work, because that's all you think about. She said that living with you is like living with an empty shell or a shed skin. And clearly it's not just her and the kids who are in second place – it's everything. I thought you and Malin were friends.' He spat out the words as if they were venom.

'Anders, try to calm down now so we can—'

'Don't say that I didn't warn you. I explicitly asked you to stay away from her. But you couldn't.'

Fabian leaned over and put a consoling hand on Anders' shoulder.

'Don't touch me.' Anders brushed it away. 'She was sick. They said she was overworked, as in she worked too much. All she needed was to rest and recover before the delivery. But you couldn't leave her in peace.'

'Anders, let's not get ahead of ourselves now. We still don't know any information—'

'We don't?' Anders looked him in the eyes. 'So what do you think happened? That she just rolled out of here with the bed to buy a candy bar? And then what? That whet her appetite and she just kept rolling on out into the snowstorm?'

Fabian wanted to protest and bring up counter-arguments and evidence that Malin was in no danger at all. Even if they couldn't see it right now, there was probably a rational explanation for everything. But he couldn't muster up the strength. Anders was right. Probably more right than even he had imagined.

'So this is completely your responsibility...' He broke down. Fabian made an effort to move closer to hug him, but changed his mind.

'Anders, I promise to do everything I can to find out what happened. This will work out.'

Anders once again locked his eyes on Fabian and shook his head. 'Everything you can? That's not enough. It's far from enough. I want you to promise that it will work out and be fine again. Can you promise that?'

Fabian hesitated, but nodded at last. 'Okay, Anders, I promise.'

'Otherwise I'm coming after you. I don't care about the consequences. If you can't fix this, I'm going to see that you have to pay for it if it's the last thing I do.'

98

ONE LIFE STORY AFTER another was pushed in through the shadowy opening of the Black Cat on Kungsholmen. All of them were scantily clad, despite the icy cold. Each had a different story of what brought them here, but the look of terror was always the same, no matter where they came from or what language they were thinking in. It was a fear of what awaited them inside, of which they actually knew nothing, but had heard far too much.

The hands of the guards were everywhere, but mostly they were just pressing and shoving them, like cows being brought in for milking. It couldn't go quickly enough. The guards' eyes shone with stress as they kept watch over the otherwise peaceful back street that was desolate because of the storm.

A steep staircase led them right down into a massive pit of darkness. They could hear the steel door being closed and bolted behind them, along with the keys rattling and locks being turned. A row of bare bulbs in the concrete ceiling illuminated a long winding corridor with padlocked compartments on either side filled with worn-out furniture and packed-up memories that no one would ever share. They passed through another steel door followed by several layers of red, heavy curtains.

They were finally inside. It was still dark, but it didn't feel as impenetrable. Once their eyes adjusted to the dim light, they could see how big the room really was with its painted black walls and ceiling. Small spotlights shone down on red couches spread out in a big circle around an elevated round part of the floor – the stage they'd all heard about.

They were shoved through the space, past a hidden door in the black wall, through a blindingly light corridor with fluorescent fixtures in the ceiling and doors on both sides. They reached a large, tiled bathroom, with toilet stalls, mirrors and bidets. The guards ordered them to take care of their needs one last time and wash all their holes thoroughly.

IT HAD BEEN A nearly impossible race against time, but she'd almost finished cleaning everything. In some of the private rooms it hadn't taken more than a quick vacuum, and in one group room she'd only turned over the pillows and removed the most visible condoms. She had just hung up the overalls in the broom closet and pulled her bag with make-up and other clothes out of her backpack, when she heard the shouts of the guards getting louder.

She'd been forced to leave the broom closet with the clothes in her arms, and hurry ahead of the others through the corridor into the bathroom, where she'd locked herself in the last stall. Her heartbeat had been racing so fast it was impossible to make out the individual beats.

But once she'd put on the dress and shoes, and the bag of make-up was hidden safely in the water tank of the toilet, she'd felt calmer than ever. This was not simply one in the line of sinners who would get their punishment; it was something she'd looked forward to since the day she'd realized who he was. Diego Arcas was one of *them*, and this could be nothing other than God's way of showing her that He was with her all the way.

She could hear the washroom outside filling with the new shipment. None of them said anything, but she could clearly make out the smell of fear. She waited a little longer before she left the stall and started imitating the behaviour of the other girls: the worry in their eyes and their hesitant steps and hunched backs.

99

FABIAN RISK OPENED THE door that didn't lock, stepped into his hallway and took off his coat. The car ride home had been fine even though he was still intoxicated. It was the first time ever he'd driven while under the influence, but right now he was much too tired to really care. He felt like a wrung-out rag and was unsure whether he would make it all the way into the bedroom.

After Fabian had finally convinced Anders that he had his best officers out looking for Malin, Anders had agreed to leave the hospital and let Fabian drive him to the villa in Enskede. Once they arrived, he invited Fabian in for a whisky. Fabian tried to politely decline due to the late hour and the fact that he was driving, but Anders insisted, saying it was the least he could do.

It turned out that Anders was a member of the Swedish Whisky Society, and had an entire room in the basement dedicated to his collection. According to him, it was one of the biggest in the country. As predicted, they hadn't stopped at one glass and the mood between them became more relaxed as the alcohol thinned their blood.

He let Anders talk about everything between heaven and earth: the house, which was an endless renovation project, even though it was much too expensive; his job as an elementary school teacher in Skärholmen; and how all his colleagues nagged him to become a principal, even though power had never really interested him because he preferred being closer to the action.

After almost two hours, Fabian set down the half-filled whiskey glass, stood up and said thank you. *Sit down*, Anders said with a serious tone and look that gave Fabian no other choice but to obey. And with tears running down his face, Anders told him about Malin: he explained how much he loved her and how she was the best thing in his world; he told him that they'd met on a bus – the 54 as it was called at the time – and that Malin hadn't wanted to get off because it was pouring with rain, and that they'd finally taken the plunge together at Odenplan and shared his umbrella, giggling, before calling in sick from a phone booth.

After that he filled Fabian's glass, even though it wasn't empty, and asked whether he still loved Sonja. Strangely enough, he'd been completely unprepared for the question and was about to rattle off the standard response about how much he loved her and how well they complemented each other even though they were so different, but the words got stuck.

Instead, he'd tried to give an honest picture of things: he wanted nothing more than to still be in love, but their relationship had morphed into an increasingly difficult struggle and doubt was starting to make bigger gains. Anders had listened and nodded at his fumbling attempts to corral his emotions. It was almost like they were on their way to becoming friends.

Damn, you really messed things up, Anders said at last, getting another bottle. *Either you love someone or you don't. It doesn't have to be more complicated than that. Sure, the flame can be low, but then it's time to roll up your sleeves and start working on it. If, on the other hand, it's gone out, it's over. Then you might as well call the lawyer and look into getting the papers signed.*

Even though Fabian knew that the words were nothing other than banal platitudes coming out of a whisky glass, they'd stuck with him. The thought that he and Sonja were something to get over with as quickly as possible made him short of breath and caused him to get up and drive home, despite Anders' protests.

He stopped by the bathroom to grab a couple of Alka-Seltzers, before going into the bedroom. He didn't turn on any lights, but could tell from the glow of the streetlight that seeped in through the drawn curtains that Niva was sleeping in his bed. She was lying on top of the covers and was still wearing the bathrobe that had slipped up and showed just enough...

Why hadn't she gone home? Had she really been working that late? He wondered whether he should let her sleep or if he should put her in a taxi, but he was unable to make up his mind. And right then he understood what Anders had been talking about earlier: the hesitation he'd been feeling finally started to dissipate. In that moment, he just knew the flame was still alive, and could even see the little blue flame with his bare eyes. It shone faintly and was just about to go out, but it was still burning.

Strengthened by this revelation, he lay down fully clothed as carefully as he could on his side of the bed so that he didn't waken Niva. It didn't take long before her slow breathing made him relax, and with every breath he sank down deeper into sleep. And just before he was completely swallowed up by the world of dreams, he had an idea of what they could do to rescue the flame from going out completely; how he and Sonja could find their way back and be in the same room without wanting out.

As soon as this was all over, he would tell her. The idea was drastic and would involve a lot of work and a major adjustment for the whole family, not least for Matilda and Theodor, who would almost certainly protest. They would not only have to change schools, but make new friends. But what did that matter? *If that was what they needed to stay together, the decision wasn't hard*, Fabian thought, falling asleep with the conviction that there was positive change in their future after all.

100

SHE PULLED OFF HER panties, straddled an open bidet and started washing herself carefully everywhere, exactly like each new delivery was always ordered to do. Neither the burly guy nor the other two who were standing along one wall seemed to recognize her or notice that there was a new addition.

As usual, there was someone who had to be problematic. This time it was the bleached-blonde Pole right behind her who broke down and refused to wash herself. She couldn't have been over twenty, and evidently hadn't understood that this was serious.

'I want you to leave before I do anything,' she said audaciously through tears to the guards.

'You just want one thing,' one of them said in her face. 'Do you know what that is?' The woman responded with a defiant look. 'To do as you're fucking told!' He gave her a hard slap with the back of his hand. 'Understood?' When he didn't get a response he repeated the blow, but with clenched fist and full force.

The punch hit so hard that it looked as if her head was about to twist off her slender neck. She collapsed unconscious in a heap on the floor.

The guard clapped his hands until he had everyone's attention. Then he unzipped his fly and emptied his bladder on the woman. 'I want everyone to look really carefully. This is what happens when you don't do as you're told.'

They all stared at the unconscious woman whose hair was getting wetter and wetter.

'Okay, let's get a move on!' He zipped up his trousers and washed his hands.

Everyone except the lifeless Polish woman left the washroom and went through the corridor back out to the room filled with all the couches. Pulsing music sounded out of concealed speakers and they were ordered to line up in a row facing the stage. As if on cue, a struggle arose over who could stand as far back in line as possible.

She, however, wanted to be up in the very front.

'You there. Up on the stage. Yes, I'm talking to you, bitch,' said one of the guards, nodding at her to move along.

She did as she was told and stood in the middle of the stage, her eyes blinded by the strong spotlights in the ceiling.

'Turn around,' a voice said from somewhere in the blinding light. She obeyed the command.

'Stop.'

She stopped with her back turned towards the voice.

'Bend over – slowly.'

She lowered her upper body and made sure to stick her bottom out and keep both legs and back as straight as possible. His footsteps came towards the stage, then walked up the stairs, before they stopped right behind her.

None of the other girls had said a word the whole time. The silence was so dense that she was unsure whether they were even breathing. Then she felt his hand on the back of one thigh, and it continued up along the inside of her leg towards her vagina.

'Mmm, you shaved. I like that.' He let his finger slide into her. She moaned and pretended to be excited.

'So you like it?'

'Mmm, yes,' she said, rotating her bottom slowly.

'Want some more?'

'Oh, yes, please.'

'Take off your clothes.'

She stood up, let the dress fall to the floor, and stepped out of it, while Diego Arcas walked around her, studying her thoroughly while sniffing his fingers. Suddenly he stopped, held out one hand and felt her breasts.

'Are they real?'

She nodded.

'How old are you?'

'Never ask a woman her age.'

The reaction came lightning fast in the form of a hard slap that burned for several minutes afterwards. 'You're not a woman. You're property – my property! Never forget that.'

She nodded and let the pain in her cheek serve as a reminder not to get too comfortable and presume her victory in advance. After all, she wasn't done yet.

'On your knees and open my pants.'

She got down on her knees, unbuttoned his trousers and lifted out his half-erect penis.

'Do you like it?'

She nodded and forced a smile.

'I said, do you like it?'

She took it in her mouth and felt the veins starting to fill with blood.

'That's better.'

She continued to work back and forth, taking it in as deeply as she could, while caressing his balls.

'Every single one of you bitches watch and learn. This is how you give a good blow job.' He took hold of her hair and pulled harder and deeper, almost making her gag.

The pulls got faster and faster, and she could feel his testicles pulling upward. To help him on the way she carefully stuck one index finger into his anus and started caressing his G-spot. Thirty seconds later it was time. The first load she took in her mouth, but she stood up for the second. Arcas' eyes were closed and he was completely absorbed in his pleasure. It took him a few seconds before he opened his eyes and looked at her.

'Who the fuck told you to stand up?'

'No one,' she said, performing the movement she had practised so many times in front of the mirror.

She hit the mark on the first try and felt her index and middle finger penetrate deep into the eye socket and bend around the back of the eye itself. As soon as she felt the optic nerve between her fingers she pulled with full force, put on her dress, and left the stage.

101

FABIAN HAD NO MEMORY of having taken off his clothes. Yet now he was lying naked on his back, staring at the tiny peacock that had just landed on his chest and woken him up. The feet stuck like little nails through his skin, and he wondered if he could shoo it away. But the fear of how it would react made him stay as still as possible as he watched it wander across his stomach and further down over his exposed member.

Niva was riding him so intently that her breasts bobbed in time, Sonja's bathrobe tossed behind her. She must have been at it a while because she was close to climax. The peacock had jumped down on the floor and had walked out the door. He was hoping that if he could just get out of there, like the bird, everything would be undone.

This wasn't what he wanted. He'd made a plan. Yet he couldn't help but enjoy her movements. And she was clearly enjoying having him inside of her. He saw the look of victory in her eyes. She'd finally got what she'd lusted after for so long.

The sweat was running down from her forehead, along her neck and across her breasts where it slid off and hit him. She pulled her hands through her hair and stretched backward as she increased the tempo.

She was close now, really close. He could tell.

He responded to her thrusts with greater force until she threw herself back and forth and whimpered with pleasure. He was on his way too. It was irrelevant that he didn't really want this, just like the fact that he would regret it for the rest of his life. Nothing mattered any more and nothing could make him stop.

It was Niva who stopped and got off him without warning, and the frustration pounded so hard that it was painful. He expected her to get on all fours or lie on her back. Instead she straddled his face and started rubbing her pussy against him. He licked and sucked as much as he could, tasting her juices and playing with the tip of his tongue against anything he could reach.

He could hear her whimper again and did everything he could to help her. At the same time she pressed harder and harder against him, so hard that finally he couldn't breathe. He tried to get loose – he needed air – but her legs were much too strong.

He held his head still while the rest of her body prepared itself to be swept away by yet another wave.

102

THEY WERE ALL SCREAMING at the same time, not just the girls, but the guards as well. She wasn't concerned and had actually anticipated the chaos and panic. She knew some of the guards would be more quick-witted than others and come after her, but the only thing she hadn't expected was Diego Arcas' ear-splitting scream that cut through all the other sounds in the room. For some reason, she'd thought he would take it like a man.

She had managed to get several metres from the stage, and could hear two guards behind her. She fought the instinct to look over her shoulder. There was no time for hesitation. Instead she put all her energy into picking up speed. She'd practised a lot on the track and knew that velocity meant everything if she was going to get over the couches in the most efficient manner, and reduce the number of seconds to the surveillance room by more than half.

At first she'd thought it would be hard to get enough speed in high heels, but as long as the centre of gravity was in her toes she didn't have a problem. She jumped over the first couch as if it was hardly even there, and did the same with the second. She could hear that the two guards were already close behind her. Four steps later and she was over the third couch and only had a ten-metre-long stretch before she was at the door.

Certain that the charge of adrenaline improved her personal best by at least three seconds, she tore open the door, hurried in and locked it behind her. Even though the guards would be there any second, she took a few deep breaths and looked at the bloody eye in her hands. It was the last piece of the puzzle to make her beloved whole again.

They started tugging on the door handle, which quickly transitioned to powerful kicks against the door. She could see on one of the surveillance cameras above the control board that there were now four of them. Before too long, they would get out the right key and try to put it in the lock, and when they realized it didn't work they would take out their guns instead.

She took out the plastic tube from its hiding place behind the binders on the bookcase, unscrewed the lid and dropped the eye into the fluid. Then she closed it again and inserted it into her vagina. She cleaned her hands of blood with some wet wipes, pulled on the dress and took hold of the barely visible fishing line that was attached to a knotted rope.

She started heaving herself up the rope just as the first shots hit the lock. She was both light and agile and her arms had never been stronger, so she had no problem making her way up. But the most critical step was at the top. In order to close the inspection hatch behind her she would have to turn upside down and make her way into the ventilation conduit feet first.

She'd managed to do it without any major problems every time she'd practised, but she didn't have sweaty hands then and wasn't feeling the stress that the guards might force the door at any moment. At last she succeeded and could haul in the rope, put back the grate and start crawling backwards through the narrow conduit.

Less than a minute later she heard them break into the surveillance room, arguing about where she could have gone. Not long after they started shooting towards her.

The sound from the shots spread through the conduit, which acted like an amplifier. Even though she was a safe distance out of the corridor she was forced to cover her ears. In only a metre or two the conduit would branch off and then part again. It would become considerably more difficult for them to figure out exactly where she was. They would most likely have to split up and start randomly shooting into the conduits.

But she wasn't worried. It wouldn't be long before they had other concerns. At any moment they would be taken completely by surprise – again. But that was out of her control. If it had been up to her, she would have had exclusive rights to this particular night, which was the only time she could get close enough to Arcas.

The shots stopped, just as expected, and after a few seconds of silence she heard scattered shouts and screams. Uncontrolled panic broke out below her. She imagined this was what it sounded like when a tsunami struck. The corridor beneath her was filled with people, but now she was no longer the one they were after. Now the guards and women were the prey. She crawled out towards the main room and looked through the grate.

The police.

They were everywhere with their guns drawn, wearing bulletproof vests. A few were even on their way down from the hidden skylight in the ceiling. She could count at least ten who were trying to take control of the situation, ordering in English for everyone to get down on their stomachs with their arms and legs extended.

Some of the girls did as they were told. Others tried to flee, but were quickly apprehended and forced down on the floor one by one. Four of the guards were already on their stomachs with their hands cuffed behind their backs, and two of the police officers were on their way over to the stage where Diego Arcas was still lying in a pool of blood with both hands in front of his face.

She kept crawling through the narrow conduit as quietly as possible, making her way further away from the increasingly agitated voices of the police who were starting to realize what had happened.

As she worked her way through, she could feel the metal walls getting considerably colder. When the conduit suddenly turned upwards a metre or so before continuing straight she knew she didn't have far to go. It was now several degrees below freezing and she increased her speed so that her damp hands wouldn't get stuck to the freezing metal. The disadvantage was that she made more sound, but that couldn't be helped. Hopefully the police officers were fully occupied with other things.

A few metres later her high-heeled shoes hit the grate. One well-aimed kick later she was out in the courtyard. There was not far to go now. Her plan had gone as she'd hoped.

She had counted on the motion-sensitive light going on as soon as she had put back the grate, which would illuminate the way to the garbage cans. But it didn't.

It was already on.

She didn't understand the gravity of the situation until it was too late.

'Well, well, look what we have here,' said a voice right behind her.

With her hands in the air she turned around and saw the smiling SWAT team member emerge from the darkness with a gun in one hand and handcuffs in the other.

103

FABIAN WASN'T SURE WHETHER he was asleep or awake. Were his memories only a sick distorted dream or had they really happened? The details were so clear that they couldn't be anything other than true, except for a tiny peacock who'd been there and walked across his body. He didn't know why, but it had recently started showing up more often in his dreams.

It simply couldn't be true. He'd been quite sure he'd seen the flame and had a plan for how he and Sonja could get things back on track. So far he hadn't dared open his eyes. He felt relief in sleep, even though he was now fully awake. He knew the cold, hard truth would be staring right back at him and tried to put it off for as long as possible. Eventually the ringing phone gave him no choice.

'Where the hell have you been?' It was Tomas Persson.

'What do you mean? Has something happened?' Fabian sat up in bed.

'Happened? What planet have you been living on? Remember Diego Arcas?'

Of course, thought Fabian, noting that Niva was no longer there. Had she even been there in the first place? Yes, she definitely had. He was quite sure of it, just as sure as he was that he'd been naked, even though he'd gone to bed with his clothes on. But now he had them on again...

'Höglund and Carlén are absolutely furious with you and have evidently filed a complaint,' Tomas continued.

'A complaint for what?' Fabian felt a headache coming on and struggled to get out of bed.

'For oversleeping? I don't know. The thing is that evidently the worst of the chaos happened before the response team stormed in, because once they finally did it turns out that Arcas is lying there bleeding like crazy on the stage.'

Fabian tried to put together a steady stream of words into something with meaning on his way through the hall to the bathroom, while he looked around for Niva.

'You're supposed to ask why he was bleeding like crazy.'

'Tomas, I don't have time for this.' Fabian walked into the bathroom and splashed water on his face.

'You're boring. Jarmo and I weren't in the club to see what went down, so we contacted the hospital where Arcas has been admitted.'

'And? Did you get an answer?'

'He's missing an eye.'

'What do you mean, "missing an eye"?' Fabian dried himself with a towel.

'Hell if I know. Someone must have taken it. And my guess is that it was one of—'

'The girls.'

'Exactly! Nice to hear that you're finally awake.'

'Do you know if everyone was arrested?'

'No idea. But there are literally broads everywhere here.'

'At the department?'

'Yes, they're being questioned by borrowed uniforms and interpreters. Several of them can't even speak—'

'Tomas, listen to me right now. This is important,' said Fabian, putting on deodorant under his shirt. 'You and Jarmo have to make sure that every single one of them is handcuffed. No one is allowed to leave. Do you understand? No one.' He hurried out of the bathroom and saw Sonja walking into the hall.

'And how the hell would that happen? Höglund is almost boiling over already. He's never going to—'

'I'll take care of him. Tomas, I have to go now.'

'But—'

'Just do as I say!' Fabian hung up, tried to collect himself and went up to Sonja, uncertain whether he should hug her. 'Hi, darling.'

'Don't I get a hug?'

'Of course. I just didn't know if…' He fell silent and embraced her. 'Listen, I'm in the middle of a case and am actually on my way out.'

'Sure, no problem,' she nodded. 'I'm just going to grab some clothes from home and buy the last outstanding Christmas presents. You're coming out tonight, right?'

Fabian looked at her without saying anything. He wanted nothing more than to promise that he would come out and celebrate Christmas as planned. Maybe everything would work out for once and Aisha Shahin was already in custody. Then the only thing he'd have left to do would be to confront Edelman with the evidence and get him to realize that he had no choice but to tear up the old investigation. He'd already made far too many promises that went unfulfilled.

'Okay, I get it.'

'Sonja—'

'Fabian, it's okay. I understand that you're in the middle of something that you can't talk about, but it would be really nice if you came out and celebrated Christmas with the family.'

'All I want is to come, but—'

'I've thought a lot about what I said last Sunday, and…' She looked away.

Now it's coming, thought Fabian. She'd gathered up enough energy to be able to say she wanted to break up. And maybe that was exactly what they should do. Maybe his dream last night – or was it a reality? – was proof that the flame really had gone out and that their relationship was dead and should be buried before the decomposition had gone too far.

'If you want to, I want to.' She met his gaze again.

Fabian felt his strength returning, and made an effort to say something.

'Wait, I'm not done here. When this is all over, and when you're finished with whatever it is you're doing, I want us to start over – really start over.'

Fabian leaned forward and kissed her. He could feel her response for the first time in a long while and could tell that she was prepared to give them one last chance. But then her lips tensed and her tongue disappeared.

'A person could almost get a little jealous.'

Fabian whipped around and saw Niva coming in from the living room, fully dressed.

'You must be Sonja. Niva Ekenhielm.' She extended her hand.

'I know who you are,' said Sonja without so much as looking at her hand. 'On the other hand, I don't know what you're doing here.'

'She's helping me with the investigation. We've been working day and night,' said Fabian, wondering how he should continue.

'You'll have to excuse me, I didn't want to disturb you, but I have to tell Fabian something.' Niva turned to him. 'Tomas told me about your theory and I think it adds up. Apparently Diego Arcas had serious scar tissue in the middle of his left cornea. He'd been on a waiting list to get a new one for several years before he gave up.'

Fabian nodded very curtly to show her it had to wait.

'Which would support our information that Semira Ackerman had problems with her right eye,' Niva continued, handing over a printout.

'I guess I'll go,' said Sonja, making an effort to turn around.

'No, wait, tell me more about your day. You were going to pick up some clothes,' said Fabian. 'And shouldn't you put on some coffee?'

Sonja looked at them, clenched her teeth and shook her head, before leaving the apartment.

'Oh, boy, I hope she wasn't upset,' said Niva.

Fabian turned around and looked her in the eyes and tried to understand what was going on in her head and whether something really had happened between them. Was she just toying with him? Maybe that smile was sheer *schadenfreude* at seeing him fumble so desperately for answers. The last thing he intended to do was to humiliate himself even more and ask.

He would rather continue to hover in uncertainty.

104

UNTIL NOW THINGS HAD mostly gone her way. Other than a number of minor setbacks, which had all been remedied, only the issue of the Minister for Justice's car was still a concern. The Danish police had found it at the bottom of Helsingør Harbour, but the connection between the two countries hadn't been made for some reason. It was only a matter of time before the police on either side of the border put two and two together and started talking to each other. Then they would finally discover what was hidden beneath the surface and Gidon Hass would become a distant memory.

In an ideal world, she would have already been sitting in the rental car on her way out to the airport for the last time with all of Efraim's stolen parts packed in the ice that filled her watertight suitcase.

She'd even hoped that once she'd gone through check-in and security she would have time to celebrate with a glass of champagne. She'd never tasted it before and wasn't even sure she would like it, but she deserved it if she'd made it all the way to the finish line, even if it would be her last glass.

Instead she was now sitting handcuffed to a chair in the police station.

It couldn't be interpreted as anything other than a serious setback.

Yet she didn't feel the least bit worried. She simply hadn't taken into account the risk that the police might arrest her too.

Fortunately, she'd prepared a plan for how she would handle such a situation – a plan that she would have preferred to avoid, but now had no choice other than to implement.

The arresting officer from the courtyard had swallowed her story whole. She told him that she had managed to get away from the rest of the group and stayed hidden in the ventilation conduit. He'd tried to calm her, explaining that she no longer needed to be afraid. Then he'd shown her to the minibus where she blended in with the other girls.

Now she just looked like all of the other victims. The carelessly shaven policeman sitting across from her smelled of mould and was apparently clueless. She'd given him the expected answers and he had dutifully jotted them down in sprawling handwriting.

Fabian Risk was different. He had surprised her more than once already. Out of nowhere, one of his colleagues had come storming in and chained her to the chair, although he didn't recognize her. Nobody seemed to recognize her, even though she'd been there scrubbing the corridors, cleaning their desks and emptying their wastebaskets countless times during the past year. But soon Fabian would surely arrive, and he wouldn't be as easy to handle.

Despite that, she was happy that she'd let him live and left the condemned apartment before he got there. In the end, either he or maybe that Danish policewoman would connect all the leads. If it wasn't now, it would happen as soon as he looked at her computer. She wondered whether she should be more worried than she actually was. The plan was hanging by an extremely thin thread and not just one but a number of things could still go wrong.

But she felt as if that almost didn't matter now, as if she'd taken a sneak peek at the future and knew that it would work out. She felt completely calm even though it was contrary to all reason and in many ways unlike her, who always preferred to be safe than sorry. She was quite convinced that God, who had stood by her side the whole way, wouldn't fail her at the finish, so she leaned back in the chair and closed her eyes.

She was close now.

As close as she could ever have dreamed.

105

EVERY YEAR ON THE last workday before Christmas Eve, Herman Edelman and the rest of the management group gathered in Stadhuskällaren for a long Christmas lunch. It was a tradition that had grown so entrenched in recent years that not even a major operation, such as the one against Diego Arcas, could get them to break it.

Fabian actually didn't have time. If it turned out that Aisha Shahin was one of the girls in custody from the Black Cat, under no circumstances could they risk her slipping out of their hands. But he needed a green light from Edelman before he could officially arrest her, which would mean he would have to put all his cards on the table, however much he wanted to avoid it. Without approval they had no choice other than to release her again.

After crossing Stadshusbron, he made a sharp left turn across the opposite lane, forced the ploughed wall of snow on to the bike path, and parked in the middle of the broad sidewalk outside Stadshuset. Even though it was midday, the welcoming outdoor candles were already burning outside the restaurant entrance on the east side of the building.

He found them in the back of a private room under a stone archway. And judging by the noise they'd already managed to consume a fair amount. The police commissioner Bertil Crimson and prosecutor Jan Bringåker were there, as was Anders Furhage from SePo with Eva Gyllendal, chief of the Stockholm Police, sitting beside him. The group had expanded to include Ingrid Brantén, the head of department of the Ministry of Justice. Not unexpectedly, she was sitting next to Herman Edelman, and Fabian could only assume that the two had recently had a good deal of contact with each other.

'Fabian,' Edelman exclaimed when he caught sight of him. 'I thought you'd be home making gingerbread cookies!'

'I will be as soon as we've had a chance to talk.'

'As you can see, I'm a bit occupied here. Can it wait?'

'Unfortunately, no. But if you can't get up, we can discuss it here instead.' Fabian waited for one of the others to ask what it concerned, but no one said anything.

Finally, Edelman himself broke the silence with a disgruntled sigh.

'It appears you'll have to manage without me for a little while, but I'll be back in a minute.' He raised his schnapps glass, emptied it and stood up.

They went over to a vacant table some distance away. Before they'd even sat down the murmur of the others was back at the earlier level.

'What's this about?' said Edelman in a tone that made it clear he didn't intend to waste time on small talk.

'There's a chance that we've arrested the correct perpetrator, and I need your approval to—'

'I thought we were through with all this.'

'Yes, you might have been, but evidently we weren't.'

'Let me decide on that.'

'Herman, I know that Carl-Eric Grimås was guilty of buying an organ on the black market, and I know that you were the one who helped him contact the embassy and, by extension, the pathologist Gidon Hass.'

'Grimås wasn't guilty of anything.'

'No? What do you call buying yourself a new liver on the black market?'

'For one thing, it wasn't illegal in Israel at the time, but I also can't understand why a person should feel guilty about wanting to live. Who doesn't want to take one more breath and cling to the dream of immortality?' Edelman waved over the waiter, who was carrying a tray of schnapps glasses, and took two of them. 'It's easy for you to get on your high horse: you're no more than halfway through life. Even if you're aware that one fine day this will all come to an end, you live your life as if it's going to be eternal. I can promise you that once you're my age all of that changes, and some of us get more desperate than others. I wouldn't describe any of them as guilty, at least not until I was faced with the choice myself.'

'If you don't think it's a big deal, why would you make such an effort to conceal the truth?'

Edelman seemed completely nonplussed for a few seconds, before he lit up in a smile and started laughing. 'Young Padawan, I have taught you well.' He pushed one schnapps glass over to Fabian and raised the other. 'Cheers.'

Fabian took the glass and raised it – this time he didn't intend to make the mistake of refusing – and emptied it in one gulp. He would need all the help he could get.

'You know, it's funny. I feel like I'm seeing myself in the mirror when I look at you. Besides the beard and the belly, which I already had by your age, there's no great difference between us. Just like you, I was convinced that all investigations needed to be solved. I didn't care how many resources were required or what the consequences were: the truth was paramount and always worth the price. It was only in later years that I've come to see how wrong I was. The so-called truth is actually nothing but a chimera, and my constant search for it has cost me everything that really meant something to me. It's long since too late for me, but not for you. Take that as some good advice.'

'You were aware that Kremph was innocent the whole time and that someone else, someone who was far from finished, was behind this, yet you drove the investigation in the wrong direction to protect yourself and your own involvement. If it hadn't been for you, we might have been able to save Adam Fischer and Semira Ackerman. You want me to take advice from you? Bullshit.'

'Fabian, you can go at it as hard as you want. It doesn't matter to me. The perpetrator is arrested and dead. The case is closed and we're about to go on holiday. However much you want to believe it, there's nothing you can do about it now. Not one thing, so Merry Christmas to you.' Edelman stood up and turned to leave.

'Let me shut the door.'

Edelman stopped and turned back again towards Fabian, who was still sitting at the table with his cell phone in his hand.

'Don't tell me this is about that damned leak again.'

'Unfortunately it is.'

'In other words, they still haven't been able to close it.'

'No, but—'

'I knew it. This is exactly what I was worried about. I could feel it. I never would have agreed to go along—'

Fabian paused the recording from the wiretapped call between Edelman and Grimås, and set down the phone. 'We're done when I say we're done.'

Edelman stared at the phone on the table. 'So Niva is on board again. Interesting. She always had a soft spot for you. I assume you're aware that this is never going to hold up in court, not to mention that what you've done is a criminal offence.'

'You can report me if you want, but first I want you to sit down again,' said Fabian, putting the phone back in his pocket.

Edelman took a seat and looked Fabian in the eyes. 'What do you want me to do?'

'Open up the investigation again and give me free rein to lead it. Tell Höglund and Carlén that I'm going to need an interview room, and make sure that arrest order and the rest of the paperwork are ready within thirty minutes. Considering that Jan Bringåker is sitting at your table, I can't imagine it will take more than fifteen.'

Edelman looked sombre while he thought. When he finally nodded his okay, Fabian had already stood up and headed for the exit.

106

EVEN THOUGH FABIAN CLEARLY recognized the dirty-white walls, the brown fixtures that always contained at least two blinking fluorescent lights, and the patchy grey linoleum floor that was so worn it was impossible to get clean, he stopped after a few metres and wondered whether he was in the wrong place.

The usually calm and rather slow-paced department was now full of people and new faces. This wouldn't be quite as easy as he'd imagined. Even his own workspace was occupied by a uniformed police officer, who was on the phone while cleaning his nails with a ruler.

From what he could see, Tomas and Jarmo had cuffed the girls in the chairs they were sitting in. He overheard a number of questions: *Where did they come from? How had they come in contact with Arcas? What had they been subjected to?* But no one seemed to be asking the most important question: Who tore out his eye? Instead they were all being treated as victims of Arcas' human trafficking, which may be the case. Aisha Shahin could have escaped before they'd even arrived at the police station.

But he was far from sure. The operation at the club had been very extensive, so there was still a chance that she was at the department right now, making up credible answers and waiting for the right moment to slip away. She could basically be any one of the captured women, imitating their nervously shifting gazes and making fragments of their stories her own.

He hurried around to get a sense of how many women there were and what they looked like. He thought about how he could gather them all in the same room and study their eyes, which should indicate if any of them stood out from the rest. But there were no guarantees that someone had seen what had happened or that this wasn't the first time they'd met. He also thought someone should cross-examine their stories while Niva double-checked their information to find out which of them was lying. But that would take time considering all the language barriers.

Time they didn't have.

There was still one person whom he couldn't stop thinking about. The officers he had put on to Malin's disappearance were working around the clock, and Fabian was desperately hoping that, since Malin Rehnberg had never been involved in the illegal organ market, the killer would have no reason to make her the next victim. But, even if she was alive, Malin was likely tied up and terrified somewhere, and it was his responsibility to find her before it was too late. He'd made Anders a promise and if he failed he would never be able to forgive himself.

He hurried past the meeting room, which was also being used as an interview room, stopped and stuck his head in. Suddenly all his doubt disappeared. She was cuffed to the chair that Jarmo sat in each time there was a meeting. He had no idea what she looked like, yet he was certain: the long, golden-brown hair, the clear blue eyes, the golden-brown skin. It couldn't be anyone else. Her neighbour was right. She was exceptionally beautiful.

She turned towards him as he came in, and he could see in her eyes that she knew who he was.

'Aisha Shahin?' he asked.

The woman nodded. 'You took your time. I've been waiting for over five hours.'

'What? You can speak Swedish?' inquired the uniformed policeman, looking down at his note-filled papers. 'Aren't you from Iraq or something?'

'You can throw those papers away,' she said, as the policeman turned to Fabian, with a bewildered expression on his face.

'I'll take over from here.' Fabian sat down, surprised by her calm demeanour. 'Does this mean you intend to confess?' She looked as if she had been waiting for just this opportunity.

To his surprise, she nodded again.

'You admit to committing the murders of Carl-Eric Grimås, Adam Fischer, Semira Ackerman and most recently Diego Arcas?'

'I doubt Arcas is dead, even though he's the one who deserves it most. Besides that, the answer is yes.'

'Would you answer the same way during an official interrogation?'

'If you let me go to the washroom first. I've needed to go for an hour and a half.'

Fabian was about to say no. The last thing he wanted was to agree to any of her demands, but he couldn't deny her a visit to the toilet. He unlocked her handcuffs, took them off the chair, and attached the free end around his own wrist, before showing her to the washrooms.

He decided to let her use the disabled toilet. For one thing there were no windows, in contrast to the larger bathrooms that had several stalls in a row, and he could lock her to one of the handrails. The only problem was that she couldn't reach the door to lock herself in, but he solemnly assured her that he would stand right outside and wait until she was finished.

In the meantime, he took the opportunity to text Tomas and Jarmo, who were probably out having lunch, and informed them that he'd found her and intended to do a preliminary interview. He said that he preferred to do it alone, but would like them to come back as soon as possible after lunch.

No problem, Tomas texted back after only a second or two. Fabian admitted to himself that he had completely changed his opinion of him. Until now he'd mostly seen him as a cocky, steroid-popping young stallion without any analytical ability whatsoever. Initially, it had been impossible for him to understand how Jarmo put up with it or how Edelman could have hired him, for that matter.

But after the last few days, a different image of him had emerged. Sure, he was still just as irritating, but he was also more quick-thinking and focused than most of the others. Fabian was convinced that it was Tomas and not Jarmo who made sure to pack up the investigation so that nothing disappeared. Besides, he seemed to have an unusually strong sense of loyalty, both to the others in the group and with respect to discovering the truth.

Fabian kept looking at the clock. She'd been in there for almost ten minutes. He started to get the feeling that at any moment he'd be standing there with his trousers down realizing that he'd been fooled. There was something about her calm. It seemed to convey that she had nothing to worry about. Had he missed something? A crawl space? A way out that was so obvious that in retrospect he would never be able to figure out how he'd missed it?

He glanced at the clock again. Eleven-and-a-half minutes had now passed. Even though he could spend considerably longer in the bathroom, he knocked hard on the door and ordered her to hurry up. There was no response. Just as he knocked again, he realized what he'd missed and tore open the door.

Aisha Shahin was hanging from the wall hook with her legs barely on the floor and her cuffed arm angled straight out from the handrail. Her mouth was wide open and her eyes were closed; a twisted white hand towel was tightened around her neck.

Fabian hurried in, took her down from the hook and set her on the floor next to the toilet. He could feel her pulse, even if it was faint, but her breathing had stopped. He pressed his mouth against hers and filled her lungs with air over and over again, until she coughed and woke up.

'Do you remember me?' he asked, finally seeing worry in her eyes. 'You're not getting off that easy.' He attached one part of the handcuffs around his own wrist again and pulled her up. 'For your own sake I hope you've taken care of all your business because this is going to be a long interrogation.'

107

NORMALLY FABIAN WOULD OFFER his interview subjects a coffee or tea, and sometimes even something sweet. Experience had taught him that he tended to get more interesting answers when the person in question felt more relaxed. But this time he didn't offer anything. He was still annoyed about her trick to try to kill herself, even if he did understand it. She had apparently finished her mission and had nothing left in this world.

But he was anything but done. He wanted to know why. What horrible thing had happened in her life to explain her actions? He wanted to know how she had planned and thought, and not only managed to overcome all the obstacles, but always be one step ahead. There were so many questions, far more than could be covered in one sitting.

But he didn't intend to ask any of them now.

He started recording. 'This is Fabian Risk. The time is sixteen minutes past three o'clock in the afternoon on 23 December 2009. I'm here with Aisha Shahin, who has declined the presence of a lawyer.' He looked her in the eyes. 'Did you take the lives of Carl-Eric Grimås, Adam Fischer and Semira Ackerman?'

'Yes, that's correct.'

'Did you attack Diego Arcas and tear out his left eye?'

'Yes, that's correct.'

Fabian kept his eyes fixed on her. She did not show the slightest hint of being about to turn hers away. He wasn't even certain that he'd seen her blink. 'Have you kidnapped or abducted any others that I have not named who you are now holding prisoner?'

'Yes, that's correct.'

'Can you give me their names?'

'Sofie Leander and your colleague Malin Rehnberg.'

'So they're still alive?'

'So far anyway.'

'What have you done with them?'

'Which one?'

'Malin Rehnberg.'

'Let's start with Sofie. Malin is probably still sleeping, and as long as she continues to do so, she's in no danger.'

Fabian thought about what that might mean, but decided to drop it for the time being. 'Okay. So Sofie Leander. Which organ did you take from her?'

'The left kidney.'

'And why did you do that?'

'It wasn't hers.'

'Whose was it then?'

'Efraim's.'

'And who's Efraim?'

Only then did her gaze shift, and he could see her swallow. She was weighing her words with care.

'He was a man, a man I loved more than anything.'

'Was he your husband?'

She shook her head and wiped her eyes with her cuffed hands.

'The microphone only picks up sounds, so I'll repeat the question. Was he your husband?'

'No.'

'Boyfriend? Family member?'

'No.'

'But you love him more than anything?'

'Yes. Is that so hard to understand?'

'It depends on how you define hard. It's just a bit... How should I put it? A little...'

'Apparently you've never loved anyone that strongly.' She looked him right in the eyes.

Fabian lost his train of thought, and realized too late that he was the one who was now looking away. He'd thought the interview would be a struggle. Instead, he was sitting with a perpetrator who confessed to everything with a shoulder shrug.

'All the other organs you've taken,' he continued in an attempt to pick up his line of questioning again. 'Did they belong to Efraim too?'

'Yes, that's correct.'

'And this Sofie Leander. She's still alive?'

'You already asked that.'

'Where are you keeping her?'

'In a safe place.'

'I'll repeat the question: Where are you keeping her?'

'I can show you the way.'

'I would prefer if you could tell instead.'

'I'll repeat the answer: I can show you the way. The alternative is that you find it yourself, but she almost certainly will not be alive.'

'So you refuse to tell me where it is?'

'You've understood correctly.'

108

THEY'D DECIDED ONLY TO involve the absolute minimum number of people and as few outside persons as possible so that they didn't lose any valuable time. Besides, the majority of officers who were still on duty were occupied with the aftermath of the Black Cat raid.

The motorcade was only three vehicles long and they drove through a Stockholm so empty of traffic it was as if it had been cordoned off. It was the night before Christmas Eve, and most people had evidently taken the warnings of a powerful snowstorm that was said to be on its way during the night very seriously and had set off to their relatives in the country sooner than normal. The rest seemed to be staying indoors.

Fabian was behind the wheel with Aisha Shahin sitting alongside him in the passenger seat. Both her hands and feet were shackled, and the seatbelt was pulled between the chain holding her hands, just in case she got the idea to throw herself out of the car. He was in direct contact with both Jarmo and Tomas, who were in the car ahead of him, and with the paramedics in the ambulance behind, but not many words were exchanged. Not even the otherwise talkative Tomas said more than was absolutely necessary. Instead the mood was very focused, as if they were all fully occupied with trying to picture what they were about to see.

'Turn left at the light,' said Aisha Shahin, her eyes directed straight ahead.

'Left up at the light,' Fabian repeated in the headset to Jarmo, who got into the left lane and turned on to Drottningholmsvägen heading west.

The directions continued and brought them across Västerbron and Hornstull and further along E4 south. Even though it was pointless and wouldn't change the end result, Fabian couldn't help but try to figure out where they were going.

Not even when they left the highway, crossed a bridge and continued on to Älvsjövägen did it ring any bells. Only after a few more kilometres, when the road turned into Magelungsvägen after a roundabout, did Fabian realize that he'd been here less than a week ago.

But it was Tomas who said it out loud: 'She must have got a quantity discount.'

He could now see the illuminated lighthouse-like tower on the right side. A minute later they turned into the deserted parking lot outside Shurgard Self Storage in Högdalen.

Fabian tried to fit it together: she'd taken them back to where they'd found Adam Fischer strapped down and mutilated on a plastic-covered table. Hillevi Stubbs had vacuumed every square millimetre of the storage compartment for clues, yet she'd obviously missed something. Or was she intentionally taking them in the wrong direction?

'Okay, looks like we're here,' said Fabian to the others. 'Take a quick look and secure everything. We'll wait in the car.'

'All right,' said Tomas. Fabian could see him get out of the car ahead, checking his gun.

'I'll take the left, you take the right,' said Jarmo, hurrying off towards the building like a dark shadow.

About twenty minutes later, Fabian got the all-clear and released Aisha Shahin from the seatbelt and helped her out of the car. Just as predicted, the snow had started to pick up. Shahin shook with cold in her thin dress and high heels. There hadn't been enough time to get her any other clothes, but Fabian found a blanket in the trunk and put it over her shoulders.

They walked up to Jarmo, who was busy checking the contents of Hillevi Stubbs' two tool bags. When he was finished he closed them, took one in each hand, and nodded to the others that he was ready.

'Okay, let's continue,' said Tomas, constantly looking around with his drawn gun while Aisha Shahin showed them towards the entrance.

They did not move quickly. The high heels couldn't be more out of place in the frozen snow and the chain between her feet didn't allow any big steps either. But once they got to the door, she entered the code, which moved the door to the side and turned on the fluorescent lights inside. Tomas went in to check the inside of the building, while the others waited until he was back a few minutes later with the go-ahead.

Once inside, they were surrounded by warm air. Fabian could hear the electric motor start behind them, which closed the gate and shut out the winter. He looked around, but couldn't identify anything that stood out from the last time he was there.

With the foot chain dragging along the concrete floor, Shahin led them across the large hallway, straight towards the compartment where they'd found Fischer. Was that really where they were headed? The questions were piling up in his mind, but he knew there was no point in asking them. She wouldn't give him the answers he needed anyway. When the chain finally fell silent they were only a few metres in front of the compartment that was still cordoned off with tape. There was a round hole sawed in the door that had been covered by a temporary sheet of plywood.

'Remove the barricade and the sheet of plywood,' Jarmo said to Tomas. 'It would be easier if he retrieves the key that's up there,' said Shahin, nodding towards the cable cover that extended above the louvre gate all the way to the compartments.

Tomas gave Fabian a perplexed look. Fabian thought about

it quickly, but couldn't see any problem, and nodded the okay. Tomas made his way up with one foot on a fire extinguisher and the other on the compartment's code lock. He jumped down right away with a small violet plastic chip in his hand. He held it towards the code lock but nothing happened, except a red light came on.

'It doesn't work.' Tomas turned to the others.

'Let me try.' Shahin extended her cuffed hands.

Tomas was uncertain, but handed it over after both Jarmo and Fabian nodded. Shahin moved forward with her short, chained steps, but not towards the code box of the compartment. Instead she continued towards the compartment alongside. Fabian had no idea what was going on. It wasn't until she held the key against the code lock and entered the four-digit pin number that it occurred to him that she rented that compartment too. There had been another victim lying there the whole time, only a few metres away, on the other side of a thin steel wall.

After that everything happened very quickly.

An electric motor started up, and the gate started rolling up in front of them. At the same time, Shahin threw herself down on the floor. Before anyone had time to react she had rolled under the gate, which was suddenly on its way down again.

'What the hell!' Tomas shouted, attempting to stop the gate from coming down completely.

But it was too late and soon the gate was closed again.

'Nice work, guys.' Tomas looked at the others. 'What the hell do we do now?'

'Make our way in, of course,' said Jarmo, opening one of the tool bags. He threw a pair of protective goggles and a battery-operated angle grinder to Tomas, who got started on the gate. Immediately sparks started bouncing against the floor.

'Fabian, what the hell are you waiting for? Go and see if there's any way out of there from the back end. I'll take the other compartment.' Jarmo tore away the sheet of plywood and disappeared through the hole in the gate.

But Fabian stayed still. He already had a premonition of what she was up to on the other side of the gate, but he didn't want to mention it to the others. Instead, it was one of the paramedics who hurried away along the row of compartments.

'She's not in this one,' said Jarmo when he came back out of the compartment.

'She's not anywhere back here either,' said the paramedic who rejoined them. 'There are only more corridors and more compartments. This place seems endless.'

'We know she hasn't gone anywhere,' said Jarmo, looking towards Tomas, who had now made it halfway with the angle grinder.

'What do you think she's up to in there?' asked the other paramedic. 'Destroying evidence?'

'Who knows?' Jarmo shrugged. 'We already have more than enough evidence to convict her.'

'Besides, she's already admitted everything,' said Fabian.

After another six minutes Tomas turned off the angle grinder. They walked up to the gate with their guns drawn. While they were waiting, none of them said so much as a word. It was as if they couldn't move past the shock of what had happened.

'Anyone want to go first?' asked Tomas.

Fabian bent over and stepped in as carefully as he could to avoid cutting himself on the sharp edges.

She could have been pressed against the inside of the gate, prepared to attack him with a knife or some other weapon, or ready to take him hostage as her ticket to freedom. But Fabian wasn't met by an ambush or a knife against his throat. Instead he saw exactly what he'd expected.

'There's no danger. You can come in,' he called out to the others and walked over to one corner of the compartment.

She sat, shrunken and defeated, with her feet as far from each other as the chain would allow. Her dress had hiked up, revealing that she had no panties on, and her long, golden-brown hair hung down and covered parts of her face. The syringe was still in the crook of one arm, evidence of how right he'd been.

Jarmo had maintained that there wasn't anywhere for her to flee, but that's exactly what she had done. Fabian had managed to prevent the first attempt, but this time she'd made it all the way, and now she was so far gone that no one would ever be able to arrest her and bring her to justice.

The others came in one by one and looked over his shoulder, asking the expected questions. He nodded, but neither Tomas nor Jarmo seemed to trust him. Instead they squeezed past him and determined that the body was still warm, so they started searching for her pulse and checked her breathing. Convinced of what they would discover, he turned his back to them and went over to the plastic-covered table under the powerful lamp where Sofie Leander was strapped down in her bloody hospital gown.

A feeding tube was taped to her mouth. One arm was connected to a drip and the other to a droning dialysis machine. Her dirty hair was plastered to her sweaty forehead. Other than the dark circles under the closed eyes, her face was as pale as a porcelain doll. If it hadn't been for the barely perceptible movement of her chest and the weak taps against his fingertips, he would have assumed they'd arrived too late.

'What do we know about her?' Jarmo stood beside him at the table.

'So far nothing other than that her name is Sofie Leander and that she's had her kidney, which she purchased illegally, removed.' Fabian carefully lifted the hospital gown. Based on the blood on the bandage that was wrapped around her waist several times, the wound likely extended from the inside of the hip all the way up along the one side. 'But Niva is working on it and—'

He was interrupted by the ping of his cell phone. He looked at the screen, but could not help wondering whether she was eavesdropping on him somehow. 'Speak of the devil,' he continued, quickly reading the text message: *'She was born in 1969 and was on the waiting list for a transplant from 1993 to 1998. Somewhere during that time, she must have gone off the waiting list and left Sweden to settle in Israel. She only returned last summer with her husband, Ezra Leander. Her contact with the Swedish healthcare system ever since has solely been for her amenorrhoea, her ovaries, or general gynaecological visits.'*

'What's amenorrhoea?' said Tomas.

'Absence of menstruation,' said one of the paramedics, who was on his way in with his partner.

'Maybe she wanted to get pregnant,' said Jarmo, taking a step to the side to make room for them to come and examine her.

But Fabian didn't answer. Instead he repeated the name 'Ezra' to himself while he stared at the screen and read the message again.

'Fabian, what's going on?' asked Jarmo at last, and Fabian looked up.

'She's married to... her husband... is Gidon Hass.'

'Gidon Hass? How can you know that?'

'Ezra is his middle name. It can't be a coincidence.'

'What are you trying to say?' said Tomas. 'That she's married to that transplant expert?'

Fabian nodded. The revelation, and what it all meant, made him feel sick.

'Okay, so he arranges a new kidney for his wife,' said Jarmo, who still appeared to be struggling to understand how this fitted together.

'Unless that's how they met,' said Tomas.

'But there's one thing I don't understand,' said Jarmo. 'She must have been here a long time, maybe for several weeks. If she's married to Hass, surely he must have missed her, and been fully aware of what she'd been subjected to.'

'You're wondering why he didn't report her missing,' said Fabian.

Jarmo nodded.

'He probably didn't want to risk the truth coming out.' Fabian lowered his eyes towards the unconscious woman strapped down between them.

'So he sacrifices his own wife instead,' said Tomas. 'What a fucking swine.'

'Is it okay if we take her out now?'

Fabian nodded and helped cut away the straps and disconnect the feeding tube, the drip, and the dialysis machine. Then the paramedics moved her over to the stretcher and disappeared through the opening.

'I don't know what the rest of you think,' said Tomas. 'But if she's not in immediate danger, shouldn't we leave and bring in that asshole right away?'

'Wait a minute,' said Fabian, scanning the compartment, without knowing exactly what he was looking for. He wasn't ready to leave – not yet.

The reason was Malin Rehnberg.

Aisha Shahin had promised to tell him where she was. *Let's wait with her. Malin is probably still sleeping, and as long as she continues to do so, she's in no danger*, she had said, and he'd trusted her.

Now he was stuck, without so much as a clue as to how he would find her, assuming Shahin hadn't left any clues behind. Maybe there was a key to a third compartment? He started searching more thoroughly under the plastic-covered tables, among the hoses that led down into various buckets and containers, through the surgical tools and the rolls of gauze bandages, and in the piles of documents that described every step of the operation in detail.

'Fabian, excuse me, but what the hell are you doing? Are we going to leave?'

'Soon, I'm just going to—' Fabian crouched down in front of Shahin and opened her hands.

'I'm just going to what? How big a head start should we give him?'

'Tomas is right,' said Jarmo. 'There's no reason to—'

'Dammit! Can't you shut up so I can concentrate?' Fabian shouted, taking a few deep breaths while sensing that Tomas and Jarmo were exchanging glances behind him. He rolled the body over and felt below her with his hand, but he couldn't find anything there either.

He had searched everywhere and couldn't think of a single place that he hadn't looked in. Yet he couldn't make himself leave the compartment. There was something that didn't add up; something that irritated all his senses and was making his body itch; something that made him feel completely duped.

The missing piece was a brown stain on the back of the foot shackle by her right ankle. Suddenly, everything fell into place: the suicide attempt in the washroom and her controlled calm. How could they have missed it? Had they been that stressed? He turned to Tomas and Jarmo, who were sighing impatiently.

'It's not her.'

'What do you mean, "not her"?' Tomas said sceptically.

'What in the hell are you saying?' said Jarmo, hurrying up behind them.

'She's changed places with her victim, that's why she brought us here,' Fabian continued. 'See for yourselves.' He drew his fingernail over the brown shin so that the white skin below emerged. 'It's just brown cream. And this…' He took hold of the long, golden-brown hair and tore it loose from Sofie Leander's close-cropped head.

109

THE WINDSHIELD WIPERS WERE working at top speed, but could not sweep away the snowflakes, which were as big as crushed coconut balls, fast enough. The paramedics hadn't been in Shurgard for longer than forty-five minutes, and the roads were already completely snow-covered. *If the snow kept up like this,* thought Måns, *it was doubtful that they would make it to Stockholm South General Hospital at all.*

Although it was his turn to sit behind the wheel, they were both aware that Stefan was a much better driver, so he didn't protest when Stefan got into the driver's seat. Driving in the dark was one of his least favourite things, especially when the weather was so bad that it was impossible to turn on the headlights without being blinded by all the snow

They hadn't said a word since they got into the ambulance, which was probably a first in the almost five years they'd worked together. They usually talked about everything under the sun or listened to the radio and made snide comments about the music.

Most of the time they agreed on what they liked, except when something by Coldplay was on. Personally, he thought they were the greatest, but for some reason Stefan couldn't stand them and always insisted on changing stations or pointedly turning the radio off.

He'd confronted him once and got a long explanation about the guitarist Jonny Buckland's shortcomings when it came to

Chris Martin's song writing. After that Stefan started to rattle off a long list of guitarists who did meet his expectations. Somewhere between John Frusciante and Jonny Greenwood he'd decided never to ask again.

But now they weren't even listening to the radio.

To a certain extent, it was probably due to the weather. But that wasn't the whole truth. It wasn't the first time they'd visited a homicide scene and seen a dead person. They'd seen much worse than what was inside the storage compartment.

No, it was something else. He had a strong but nagging worry that was creeping under his skin, and he was sure Stefan felt the exact same way. He'd seen it in the policemen's eyes, especially in those of one of them.

There was something about this case that didn't add up.

Suddenly they heard a bang, as if something in the back had fallen to the floor, something hard, metallic. He turned to Stefan, who met his gaze.

'Did you hear what I heard?' he said, and Stefan nodded.

'Should we stop and check it out?' said Stefan.

'Maybe we should just try to get there as soon as possible.' He wanted nothing more than to drop off the unconscious woman in the back and finish his shift.

Then they heard it again. The same metallic bang that echoed throughout the vehicle. This time Stefan slowed down, put on the hazard lights and stopped by the side of the road on Huddingevägen.

He sighed in protest before he pulled on his hat, opened the door and jumped down into the snow. He left the door open so that Stefan would feel the biting cold too, and walked along the side of the ambulance while he considered the source of the noise. Maybe one of the doors hadn't been properly closed or it was a punctured tyre.

But there was nothing to suggest that either of those things had occurred. Everything looked exactly as it should. Then he heard another sound. This time it wasn't a bang, but more of a scraping, almost like someone was moving inside. He must have heard wrong. The victim was unconscious and strapped down. But clearly something in there was making a sound.

He put his hand on the ice-cold door handle, and immediately regretted his decision not to put on gloves. Then he opened the doors and climbed into the ambulance. He turned on the overheard light, and could see that the woman was lying on the stretcher and appeared to be sleeping just as deeply as when they found her in the storage unit.

The only things that didn't look right were the straps. The one over her legs looked loose and the two that were supposed to be over her body were hanging down with their buckles on the floor. This might explain the two bangs, but it certainly wouldn't explain the scraping sound. He gazed over the tools and instruments that filled the walls, but could see nothing that deviated from the norm. One of the emergency bags was hanging a little crooked and wasn't completely closed, but that was the only thing that was remotely off.

He looked at the woman again and tried to understand what had happened – if anything at all. At last he gave up with a sigh, leaned over to pick up the strap and tightened it across her hips. When he was done he straightened her hospital gown and accidentally grazed the inside of her thigh.

It might have been the soft, warm skin or simply the fact that no one would notice anything anyway. Maybe it was the heat of the moment. But something made him carefully lift the gown and look under it.

She had no panties on, which he hadn't expected. Actually he didn't really know what he'd anticipated. Although he did think it should be hairy and bushy. After all, she'd been strapped down in that compartment for some time. But it wasn't. She could have removed all her hair permanently with one of those laser treatments.

He dismissed his forbidden thoughts and pulled the gown

down again. Suddenly he noticed what was in her left hand – the syringe that explained everything. It accounted for the unclosed emergency bag and why the straps had come loose. It even explained her shaved vagina.

Unfortunately, much too late.

110

THE SNOW WHIRLED AROUND the snowploughs with yellow flashing lights that inched along three abreast, making it impossible to pass them. In truth, it didn't really bother Fabian that much. He was driving aimlessly towards the city so that he could be alone.

The revelation that it was Sofie Leander and not Aisha Shahin lying dead on the floor of the storage unit had come as a shock not just to him, but to Tomas and Jarmo as well. Keeping your victim alive for weeks simply to ensure that her body would be still warm when it was discovered was so calculated that even Tomas had been on the verge of collapse and kept repeating that this was absolutely the worst thing he'd ever seen.

It took several minutes before they were able to talk more or less sensibly with each other. After a number of failed attempts to get in contact with the ambulance they agreed to split up. Tomas and Jarmo would make their way as quickly as possible to Stockholm South General Hospital and try to find out what happened to the ambulance, and Fabian would go home and continue working with Niva from there.

But what would he do at home? If he needed to talk to Niva he could just call her. *And as soon as Tomas and Jarmo arrived at the hospital his phone would almost certainly light up*, he thought, only realizing now that he and the three vehicles in front of him were on their way up Västerbron. At this speed it would take several minutes before they were completely across.

He decided to defy the no-stopping rule, turned on his hazard lights and lowered the seat.

After Shahin's suicide attempt in the washroom he'd been convinced that death was her escape route. He'd wrongly assumed that she had nothing left to live for now that she was finished with her revenge. But it had only been an act to trigger that exact response. He thought about the text on the gravestone, framed on the altar in Aisha's apartment, and realized that the answer had been right in front of him this whole time.

Never again will I love another
Never again will my heart beat for any other
You and no other
As long as I love, and on into eternity
Soon you'll be whole again, and I will be too
Then we'll meet again
My promise to you

He knew it by heart and repeated the third last line out loud to himself: *Soon you'll be whole again, and I will be too*.

She wasn't finished yet. The organs may have been collected, but it wasn't until they had become part of his body once again that he, and by extension she, too, could be whole. She was on her way to his grave.

But where was it? Was she planning on flying out of the country? And in that case under what name? Or was she already on board one of the ferries to the Baltic countries? Perhaps she would try fleeing north across the Finnish border. The possibilities were endless. She'd fooled him not just once, but several times over.

The same thing had happened with Malin Rehnberg. He'd counted on the fact that she would tell him before it was too late. Now he no longer knew what to believe. *Malin is probably still sleeping, and as long as she continues to do so, she's in no danger*, she had said. But what would happen when she woke up?

His cell phone started to ring and he quickly picked up.

'Jarmo here. The ambulance never made it to the hospital.'

'And what happened to the paramedics?'

'The only thing we know is that they're missing. But the vehicle is equipped with GPS, so Niva is already working on tracking it down. Where are you, by the way? Niva said—'

'I don't have time to explain.' Fabian hung up, put the seat back and called Niva.

'What are you doing up on Västerbron? Something exciting, or are you just stuck in the snow?'

'Don't you have an ambulance to locate?'

'What says that one thing cancels out the other?'

'Because time is something we don't have right now.'

'It's on Pontonjärgatan 10.'

'Pontonjärgatan. Isn't that close to Hantverkargatan?' It was only a few minutes from where he was, so he immediately turned off his hazard lights and shifted into gear.

'Yes, it looks like she's back at Black Cat. Wait a second—'

'What?'

'Let me just check something... Yes, it's true.'

'What?'

'Malin Rehnberg's cell phone just turned on again and it's in exactly the same spot.'

Fabian hung up and immediately called Malin's phone as he tried to keep one eye on the road.

'Hi, Fabian. That was quick.'

He hadn't held out any hope that Malin would answer, yet still he felt the disappointment spreading like poison through his body when he heard Aisha's voice. 'What have you done with her?'

'Is it that Niva again?'

'You promised, and I trusted you.'

'Who you choose to trust is completely your responsibility. Besides, I didn't say anything except that she could wait.'

'Wait? How long will that take? She's in her last trimester, dammit!'

'Until I'm sure that you will leave me alone.'

He turned right on the exit ramp at the end of the bridge and continued around Rålambshovsparken on to Rålambshovsleden east. It wasn't far now. In only a minute or two he would be there. 'And what makes you think I'm ever going to do that?'

'I'm not the only one who made a promise.'

She must have heard his conversation with Anders at the hospital. How many cameras had she actually planted? 'And what happens when she wakes up?' He turned left on to Polhemsgatan. 'You said there was no danger as long as she was asleep.' He didn't expect a response. The important thing was just to make the time pass.

'Then she'll be face-to-face with the real problem. Let's just say it's in her best interest to sleep a little while longer.'

'What kind of problem?'

'What you should be devoting your resources to instead of hunting for me.'

Fabian turned on to Pontonjärgatan and saw the ambulance. 'You've murdered at least four people, who admittedly had questionable morals, but from a legal standpoint they haven't committed crimes that are even close to what you've done.'

'What law? In Sweden it's a crime to buy a stolen bicycle but okay to transplant a stolen organ.'

Fabian opened the car door, let the engine idle and crossed the street towards the ambulance, while he unbuttoned his shoulder holster and pulled out his pistol. 'They haven't kidnapped, tortured or killed anyone.'

'Maybe not with their own hands, but their money made sure that Efraim's body was cut up from the top down. He was violated and emptied of all life. The only thing that was his, besides me, went to the highest bidder.'

Fabian came up to the driver's compartment of the ambulance and saw that it was empty. 'I agree it's disgusting, and I can understand if you're—'

'You don't understand anything. You never will.'

He went round to the back of the ambulance. 'And why shouldn't I understand?' He tore open the back door and aimed his pistol into the darkness.

'Because you have never loved anyone that much.'

The two ambulance drivers were lying lifeless on the floor with something glowing on the stretcher between them.

'You never seem to have loved anyone at all. Good luck with your promise.'

She ended the call and Fabian climbed into the ambulance. Both men had a pulse and were breathing, and the glowing object on the stretcher was a cell phone.

Malin's cell phone.

He picked it up and studied it while he called for another ambulance. Suddenly Malin's phone vibrated in his hand. He read the message.

Nobelparken.

He didn't need any other information. Fabian understood exactly what it meant.

111

MALIN REHNBERG SCREAMED OUT loud in the darkness as she woke up, and only managed to calm down once she realized she was alone. Confused and uncertain, she tried to review what had happened. The last thing she remembered was lying on the hospital floor, fighting for her life with the cleaning woman, who turned out to be the perpetrator. She recalled her fall from the bed and how she had struck her hip so hard that she was forced to crawl to the door. Now she was lying in a hospital bed once again, but this time in a different model; it appeared to be brand new with plastic around the side handles.

The room felt similar. Even though it was so dark that she couldn't see a thing, she realized that it was smaller than the room at Stockholm South General. It even sounded different when she screamed. Plus, she sensed there was a wall along one side of her and there was only a wall at the head of the bed in the old room. But most of all, it was the smell that made her certain that she had not only been moved to a different room, but that she was somewhere else entirely.

And then, of course, there were the straps that made it impossible for her to move. They were tightened from her feet all the way up over her chest. The more she thought about it, the closer she was to panicking and she had to force herself not to waste her energy on screaming. Instead it was crucial to think creatively and be observant of details. She noted, for example, that the pressure from the straps eased a bit when she exhaled. Ten minutes later, she'd been able to wriggle both her arms out.

But the joy over that partial victory ended abruptly once the kick hit her ribcage on her right side. She couldn't figure out what it was, but after the third kick she remembered that she was pregnant with twins. How could she have forgotten? What kind of drugs had they pumped into her? She put her hands on her stomach and felt movement on the right side. The left was quiet, a little too quiet.

She had to get out of there as quickly as possible to get help. She tried to loosen the straps, but couldn't find any knots or buckles. She extended her left arm to search the wall with her hand, but she didn't find any switches, breakers or anything else that could be pressed. Then again, she did notice that the bed moved a little each time she pressed her hand against the wall.

So the brake was not on.

She put her left hand against the wall and pushed off with full force. The bed moved at least several metres through the darkness before hitting the opposite wall. After feeling around with her hands, she finally found the panel she'd been searching for that was filled with controls, taps and buttons to push.

The light flickered on. Just as she'd suspected, everything in the room was brand new. The protective plastic was still on in several places and there were signs on the wall around the door indicating that it was freshly painted. The drip bag hanging on her bed was empty, so she pulled the cannula out of the crook of her arm and pressed in with her thumb to stop the blood.

There was an Internet port and phone outlet on the panel above her, but she couldn't see a computer or phone. She pulled herself over towards a wall cabinet where she found a supply of compression bandages, tape and various pairs of scissors. She took the sturdiest one and started cutting strip after strip.

When she was finished she tried to get out of bed, but had to give up. The pain in her hip was still so intense that the joint felt like it was moving around freely as soon as she tried to move. Instead she had to keep using the bed as if it was a canoe, pulling herself over towards the door.

The built-in spotlights in the ceiling turned on, revealing that she was in a broad corridor with doors along both sides. Presumably they led to rooms similar to the one she'd just been in. There were even signs saying that these doorframes had been freshly painted, too.

She'd already understood that she was in a hospital. But which one? A private clinic? And if that was the case, why was no one else here? Actually, it didn't matter. Nothing mattered other than getting out of there as fast as possible.

Without no idea which direction the exit was in, she chose to go right and started pulling herself along the wall towards some double doors at one end of the corridor. She pulled on the cord, which opened the doors, before continuing in. The spotlights woke up in time with her movement and shone down on dazzlingly smooth surgical tables under large ceiling lamps. She saw a number of different instruments attached to cables and hoses and shiny round metal tables filled with various surgical tools. The operating room looked so new, she wondered whether it had ever been used.

Desperate to find something to communicate with, she made her way over to a counter with cabinets and drawers. Suddenly she heard agitated voices coming from the corridor she'd just left. She looked around for somewhere to hide, and noticed an open door opposite her.

'Didn't you see the car outside? And why do you think the lights are on? Ghosts?' one of the voices said as they got closer.

Malin pushed away from the surgical table with all the force she could muster and rolled off in the direction of the half-open door. But before she got there the doors behind her opened and three men came storming in and stopped when they caught sight of her.

'What did I say?' the man in the middle declared, pointing at Malin.

The expressions of the other two men did not change.

'Excuse me, but who are you and what are you doing here?' said the man with a strong accent, pulling his fingers through his grey hair.

'My name is Malin Rehnberg and I work at the National Bureau of Criminal Investigation here in Stockholm,' said Malin, thinking that she recognized the man. 'I have no idea why I'm here. I don't know even know where "here" is. But maybe you can help me with that and get me home.'

'Bureau of Criminal Investigation, you say?' The man came nearer to her.

'Homicide investigator.'

'I understand.' The man nodded. 'Unfortunately, I can't help you.' He looked at the other two men. 'Take her to room three.'

'What do you mean? Okay, if this is a secret location, I won't tell anyone. Just let me go home.'

'I'm terribly sorry.'

As the two men rolled her away, she realized where she recognized the man from.

112

THE SNOWSTORM HAD PICKED up even more, and by the time Fabian passed Sergels torg a few minutes past midnight he couldn't even see the glass obelisk despite the millions that had been invested to make it light up. The message from Aisha Shahin said Nobelparken, and he had understood what it meant immediately.

It was the location of the new Israeli Embassy.

He'd read about the neighbourhood protests and how the final political decision had still not been made, but just as Carnela Ackerman had hinted, no one really anticipated that it would be rejected and it seemed that the move was already in full swing. He actually knew the charming building well. The Swedish Forestry Institute had formerly been housed there and he had walked past it countless times with Sonja back when they still held hands.

En route he'd contacted Tomas and Jarmo who would join him as soon as they could. It was possible they were already there. Although they had been at Stockholm South General and had a longer way to go than him, they had both the Söderleden freeway and Centralbron at their disposal and could avoid countless traffic lights and intersections.

He passed the Royal Motorboat Club at the far end of Strandvägen, followed the curve to the left and turned off the car lights before turning right up the hill and stopping the car. He had initially wanted to park further away in order to quietly explore the place on foot, but Malin could regain consciousness at any moment, if she hadn't already done so. And even though he had no idea what awaited her at that time, the mere thought frightened him more than he could bear.

He continued up towards the building, which resembled a fortress with a tower in one corner. There were piles of building material wrapped in tarps that were flapping in the wind all over the place. He couldn't see Jarmo and Tomas' car anywhere. Although he could hear a car picking up speed on the curve down on Strandvägen. When he turned around he saw its headlights turn up the hill and shine straight into the thousands of snowflakes that reflected the light in all directions.

He barely had time to formulate the question of why the hell they didn't turn off their lights and stop, before he realized the answer: it wasn't Jarmo and Tomas at all. Instinctively he threw himself down into the snow, and crawled on all fours behind a pile of boards. The headlights lowered and the car turned in and stopped in the courtyard only a few metres from him. He heard the sound of doors being opened and closed and thought it sounded like there were three of them, but it was impossible to hear exactly what was said.

'No, no, no, listen to me. The car down there...'

He didn't recognize the voice, but he made an educated guess that it was Gidon Hass – the man right below Aisha Shahin on the list of persons he wanted to arrest.

'... Alarm doesn't go off by itself...'

The voices trailed off and Fabian saw them disappear through a door into the building. He got up and hurried over but it was locked, so he went around the back of the building where most of the façade was covered by scaffolding. No lights were on in any of the first- or second-floor windows, so they had to be somewhere in the basement.

Fabian managed to make his way up along one of the scaffolding posts without gloves or real winter boots. Once he had reached the second floor, the gusts of wind were so strong that the snowflakes stuck to his face like nails. At last he was able to break a window and make his way into an unfurnished room that was full of paint cans and brushes. Using his phone as a flashlight, he hurried out.

After walking through a long hall, he took a wide staircase down to the first floor, where the renovation seemed to have stopped. The floor was torn up and loose cables were hanging from the ceiling. After some searching he found a narrow spiral staircase that led to the basement level. He continued through a thin corridor that had protective paper on the floor and smelled of fresh paint. Every five metres or so, he stopped and listened. The third time he heard them.

The footsteps were getting louder and louder.

He turned off his phone, and groped his way forward with his hands along one wall until he came to a door. He slipped in as quietly as possible, but it was too late: his movement had triggered the spotlights that bathed the room in light a few seconds later.

But that wasn't the worst part. The room, which looked so new and shining, had been used not that long ago. He walked towards the operating table. It had been wiped off, to be sure, but in haste. There were traces of blood on the underside of the tabletop and on one of the legs. When he lifted the perforated cover of the floor drain a metre or so from the operating table and put his hand down in the dark water of the trap, he fished up large coagulated clumps of blood, pieces of cartilage and strands of hair.

He stood up and caught sight of a heap of tied-up black garbage bags beside a door that stood ajar into an adjacent room. He suspected what was in them, but was unsure whether he could stand opening them and looking in.

He took a few steps towards the pile and pictured himself walking up to the house in Enskede and ringing the doorbell.

Anders would answer, and Fabian could immediately see in his eyes that he understood what had happened and would break down in front of him. He expected that Anders would start screaming and become aggressive, but instead he collapsed with one hand in front of his mouth. Fabian got down on his knees and could do nothing except hold him.

He untied one of the garbage bags and saw two severed arms and a foot. Parts of the legs were in one of the other bags. But it was only in the fifth that he found what he was looking for.

It was Carnela Ackerman's head.

His reaction made him feel guilty, but he couldn't help it. He was relieved that it wasn't too late. There was still a chance.

113

MALIN REHNBERG KICKED AS hard as she could to get their hands away from her while she waved her arms and screamed. It wasn't because of the pain in her hip, which was now so severe that she was about to faint. She was screaming for her life, even though she knew it was pointless and that she would never be able to get away. The two men's hands were much too strong. Before long they would hold her so tightly that all she could do was scream.

Only then did the grey-haired man, who she surmised was none other than Gidon Hass, come towards her. 'This is going to make you feel a little better,' he said in broken Swedish, holding up a syringe.

Malin made a final attempt to get out of their hold, but her strength was used up. Drops of sweat were now running from her forehead in a steady stream.

'Turn her around.'

The two men, who still hadn't said a word, rolled her over on her side with her back turned towards Hass. She couldn't feel the needle prick, but the effect hit her almost immediately. The muscles in her body relaxed and the pain finally subsided. For the first time since she woke up she wasn't in agony.

'Admit it. Isn't that better?'

She was about to nod, but forced herself not to. Agreement was the last thing she wanted to give him. 'I want to go home now. Do you understand me? I have to leave.'

Hass burst into laughter. 'She thinks she can leave.'

The others started laughing too, while they tied up her feet and hands with new straps.

'What the hell do you want from me?'

'Leave her with me and start searching the building.'

The two men nodded and left the room.

'What do *I* want?' He put his hand on his chest. 'You're the one who's intruding here.'

'I have no idea where the hell I am. Please.' She held back tears.

'We've already been through this. I want you to tell me whether there's anyone else here, or if that's your car parked out there.'

'I told you that I don't know. I was at Stockholm South General and the cleaning woman attacked me.'

'The cleaning woman?'

'Yes, I had just realized that she was the perpetrator in the investigation that I—' Malin interrupted herself. Suddenly she understood how it fitted together. 'Am I at the embassy?'

The man nodded curtly. 'Now perhaps you understand why you can't go home.' Hass turned his back to her and went to retrieve something.

'But wait. You can't just—'

'That's exactly what I can do.' He turned around with a smile and another syringe in hand. 'You should be grateful. You're going to fall asleep and won't even have time to realize that it's over.'

'But the babies?' She could no longer fight the tears. 'I am actually pregnant with twins.'

Hass came up and placed one hand on her stomach. 'You *were* pregnant with twins. One has already given up. Haven't you noticed it? Here we have life.' He placed his hand on the right side of her stomach and then on the left. 'And here, not so much. But what does that matter now? Soon you're all going to be reunited anyway.'

All she could think as he set down the syringe and tightened a strap around her upper arm was that this wasn't the way it was supposed to end. She was completely defenceless and pregnant. What had she done to deserve this?

'I've found a suitable vein,' he said, picking up the syringe again.

'Wait. Please, wait. You have to tell Anders, my husband, that I love him more than ever. I haven't said that in a very long time, but promise me that. Please, you have to promise.'

'Your husband will never hear from us and he'll never find out what happened. You suddenly disappeared one night and never came back. Of course, he's going to have theories about this or that, but he'll never get close to the truth. Over the years he's going to think less and less about it and get on with his life, maybe with another woman. Who knows, maybe even with twins to top it off.'

Malin spat in his face. 'I hope you burn in hell.'

He responded with a guarded smile. 'I may be wrong, of course, but I don't see you as someone who believes in heaven and hell. Although maybe that's the sort of thing that changes when you find yourself in your—'

Hass was interrupted by a shot and shouts from the corridor. After that there were another two shots in rapid succession. The silence that followed was broken only when the radio in his chest pocket started crackling.

'*It's safe to come out now.*'

114

TOMAS PERSSON DIDN'T USUALLY get scared, but if there was one way to describe how he was feeling right now it was exactly that. He was so afraid that he'd emptied his bladder and had felt the warm urine working its way down the inside of his legs. It was the first time he'd been hit by a bullet, and he'd expected that it would hurt a lot more. Now he felt almost nothing other than a dull, throbbing pain. Maybe it was just the surge of adrenaline, and once that subsided he would really experience how it felt to be shot.

The bullet must have passed through his right thigh because the blood had already stained his jeans dark and started dripping down on the white-tiled floor. There was so much blood that one of the two men who had forced him down on his knees and was now tying his hands behind his back with his own handcuffs had to move one foot to avoid getting blood on his shoe.

He'd never believed in any god, and he certainly didn't now, but still he repeated the same refrain over and over again in his head: *I promise to become a better person, if you just let Fabian get here before it's too late. Please, I beg you. I promise to become a…*

'What have we got here? More police?'

The two men nodded. Gidon Hass looked at Tomas and Jarmo, who were on their knees beside each other with their hands tied behind their backs. 'Are you from the Bureau of Criminal Investigation, too?'

Tomas and Jarmo bowed their heads.

'And are there any others?'

Both Tomas and Jarmo continued looking down at the tiles without changing their expression.

'I said, are there any others!?'

'No. It's just us,' said Jarmo.

'That's what you say, but where's your colleague, Fabian Risk?'

Jarmo shrugged. 'At home celebrating Christmas with his family, like almost everyone else in this country. It's a fairly big holiday here.'

Hass nodded at the men. One of them took a step forward and kicked Jarmo so hard right in the face that he lost his balance and fell to the side.

'I know what Christmas is, just like I happen to know that Risk isn't at home with his family. Now get up.'

Jarmo made an effort to stand, but was unable to.

'I said, get up.'

One of the men grabbed Jarmo's hair and dragged him up.

'Well? How do you think we should resolve this?'

'Come with us to the station and confess,' said Jarmo.

Hass started laughing. 'At least he's got a sense of humour. But I don't have anything to confess. You see, I'm going to be seen as a hero by all of those people who want to get their lives back and are prepared to pay a little for it. People who are currently prepared to go abroad and let some alcoholic doctor who lost his licence perform the operation in a dirty hotel room. The best thing about all this is that it won't even be on Swedish soil.' Hass threw out his hands.

'So this is sanctioned by Israel?' asked Jarmo.

'Israel,' Hass snorted. 'They have no idea what they've created. They think the need for fresh organs diminishes just because they passed a toothless law that prohibits it.'

'You were aware of what your wife was subjected to,' said Tomas. 'Yet you chose not to contact us. That's called withholding information and is punishable under Chapter 17 of the Criminal Code.'

'Oh, boy. I didn't think you would dare say anything, especially since you peed your pants and all.' Hass crouched down in front of Tomas. 'Yes, that's correct. I had my suspicions, but why risk all of this, which has taken years of planning, for a wife who does nothing but complain and has only offered the missionary position once a month since I got grey hair?'

'Because you love her.'

Hass laughed again. 'Another joker. You should have been comedians instead of cops.' He got up and turned to the two men. 'Kill them both.'

The two men walked over and stood a few metres from Tomas and Jarmo. Both drew their pistols, chambered a round and aimed at their heads.

'No, please don't. I'll do whatever you want,' Tomas screamed. 'Please! I'm begging you!'

Jarmo said nothing. Instead he simply closed his eyes.

FABIAN COULD HEAR TOMAS screaming for his life. Through the crack in the door he saw the two men in suits aim their pistols at his colleagues, who were on their knees with bowed heads. He recognized the men from the picture that Carnela Ackerman had shown him at Gondolen before she left him. Now she was cut up in a number of garbage bags.

He couldn't make any sudden moves or the light would go on again. But at last he managed to slowly bring one hand down inside his jacket and pull out his pistol and chamber a round without triggering the light. While Tomas screamed louder for his life, he slowly raised the pistol and aimed through the crack in the door. His colleagues' fate now rested in his hands.

But he couldn't do it. Or to be more precise, his hands couldn't stop shaking. They were completely useless and couldn't even manage a simple task, such as pulling the trigger, however much he tried.

Instead he just stayed hidden in the darkness, listening to them getting a final chance to tell them where he was. Jarmo denied having any knowledge of his whereabouts, even though both he and Tomas must have counted on him being there. He suddenly realized how this would end.

When the bullets penetrated their skulls and they collapsed to the floor, Fabian had long since given up and lowered his pistol.

After the shots echoed it became silent.

Completely silent.

But only for a moment.

Because soon he could hear them again, even though he'd seen them curled up with so much blood pouring out of the back of their heads that it reached all the way to the floor drain a few metres away.

The screams were back.

And they were louder than ever.

115

'TAKE THEM TO THE embassy and make it look like they were trespassing and were killed in self-defence. Meanwhile, I'll clean this mess up after I'm finished with the fat one,' Gidon Hass said.

Fabian's whole body was shaking. He could see the men in suits grab the legs of each of his colleagues and drag their bodies across the floor and out of some double doors.

At the same time the accusatory screams refused to fall silent. They kept getting louder, until eventually he stood up. Seconds later, the room was once again illuminated. Without any thought of the consequences, he pushed the door open a few centimetres further with his foot. He could see Hass standing with his back to him, putting on a transparent plastic apron and visor.

Then he walked over to a cabinet, took out a battery-operated surgical saw and selected the sturdiest blade. He started it up, ensuring that the battery was charged, and left through the same set of doors as the two other men.

Fabian dried his tears and tried to collect his thoughts, but it was impossible. The screams from his two executed colleagues drowned out everything else. He accepted total failure. Feeling that he didn't have anything to lose anyway, he walked into the operating room and followed the two trails of blood towards the double doors. He opened them, and saw that the trail continued along the corridor. Hass was nowhere to be seen, and the doors on both sides of the corridor were closed.

One by one he kicked them open, holding his pistol in a

two-handed grip in front of him. All the rooms were freshly painted and unoccupied, though some were furnished with beds and nightstands. Cables were still hanging down from the ceiling in some of them. Other than the protective plastic covering some of the furniture, the renovation looked finished in the room where Hass stood leaning over Malin with a syringe.

'Step away from the bed,' he heard himself shout.

Hass turned around with the surgical saw in one hand. 'Risk, so you were here after all.'

'Shoot already!' screamed Malin, who was lying strapped down to the bed with the syringe hanging loosely in one arm. 'What the hell are you waiting for? Shoot him!'

The sound of all the screams was almost drowning her out. 'Away from the bed,' he repeated instead, continuing into the room.

'I suspected that you were around here somewhere,' Hass said, backing away.

'Drop the saw and put your hands over your head.'

Hass did as he was told, while Fabian hurried up to the bed, pulled out the syringe, and started loosening the straps around Malin's wrists.

'You saw what happened, didn't you?' asked Hass.

Fabian didn't answer, and continued loosening the straps, keeping his pistol aimed at Hass.

'I can't help wondering why you didn't do anything. I mean, you're holding a gun in your hands. Maybe it isn't loaded, but I don't think so.'

Fabian was now again holding the pistol with both hands.

'Do you know what I think? Actually it's not what I think, it's what I know. You can't do it. Isn't that right?'

'Shut up!'

'Not even when your colleagues have guns pressed against their heads.' Hass lowered his hands.

'What the hell are you waiting for?' Malin screamed while she struggled to get her other hand loose.

'He's not waiting. He's powerless.' Hass leaned over and took hold of the saw that was on the floor.

'Drop it,' said Fabian. His hands were shaking from the exertion.

'What are you going to do otherwise? Shoot me?' Hass stood up with the saw in one hand. 'Didn't think so.' He turned on the toothed saw-blade and waved it in front of him. 'Why don't you just shoot me!'

Fabian was so focused on getting his shaking hands to pull the trigger that he didn't manage to duck and avoid the saw that came flying through the air. It hit him right above the hairline before falling to the floor.

The pistol slipped out of his grasp as he touched his head. A piece of his scalp was missing and the skull was exposed. The bleeding was so heavy that blood had already run down into his eyes and started dripping on the floor.

Nausea struck with such merciless force that he had to support himself against the bed so that he didn't lose his balance. He held on to the open wound with the other hand as hard as he could, but the blood still streamed between his fingers and worked its way down his face. Somewhere between the sound of his own heartbeat, and the screams from Tomas and Jarmo, he could hear Malin screaming too. But not what.

Hass was now down on all fours, crawling towards him. He looked as if he was searching for something. Of course, he'd just dropped the pistol. Maybe she wanted him to kick it away, but he couldn't see it. He could hardly see anything because of all the blood in his eyes.

Then the shots went off.

First one, then another, and then a third in rapid succession.

Fabian expected to feel pain in his stomach and see even more blood before he collapsed on the floor just like Jarmo and Tomas. But he didn't collapse, and he couldn't feel where he'd been hit. Had he started with Malin?

That bastard shot Malin. He turned towards the bed, but it was empty.

Fabian couldn't figure out what was going on. He tried to wipe the blood away from his eyes to see better, but more kept coming and a large pool had already formed under him. Then he saw her on the floor, lying with the pistol in her hands.

'Get moving!'

He heard the words, but still couldn't fully comprehend them. He turned around to see a shadow disappear through the door.

'He's wounded, but we have to get out of here before he comes back,' said Malin. 'You have to help me up.'

Fabian felt the energy running out of him as quickly as the blood, but at last he finally managed to get her up on to the bed and pushed it out of the room. He had no idea where the exit was, so he followed the two trails of blood through the long corridor. Hass was nowhere to be found.

An elevator with automatic doors brought them up one floor and opened right out into the snowstorm. But he couldn't feel the cold winds. Once again he heard Malin's voice, without comprehending a single word. He understood anyway and ran his hands under her armpits, pulled her from the bed that had got stuck in the snow, and started dragging her down the hill. He fell, but struggled back up, before falling again. Finally, he reached the car and got her into the back seat.

The car started on the first try. Despite all the blood that was pumping out of him making it almost impossible to see, he managed to back the whole way down the hill without getting stuck in the snow.

But he wouldn't remember any of that, or how he drove along Strandvägen, missing the left turn on to Hamngatan outside the Royal Dramatic Theatre, continuing along Birger Jarlsgatan at too high a speed before skidding right into the 'The Hawk and the Dove' statue on an equally deserted and snow-covered Stureplan.

116

GOD HAD ONCE AGAIN proved that he was fully by her side. He stepped in and acted as soon as she needed Him, whether she was aware of it or not. The pregnant policewoman, for example. She never wanted to hurt her. In fact, she didn't want to hurt anyone except those who had stolen from Efraim. But if it hadn't been for her, she never could have made it out to the airport and then on to Tel Aviv via Istanbul. Fabian Risk knew where she was going, but his need to find his pregnant colleague had given him no option other than to let her slip out of his hands.

Aisha Shahin picked up the checked baggage and got it through customs without being stopped, and from what she could see none of the melted ice had leaked out. The reserved Jeep had been waiting for her, and the drive to Imatin took less than four hours, just as planned. Even the checkpoints let her through without so much as a question about where she was going or what business she was conducting.

She almost felt as if God was rewarding her and rolling out a red carpet in her path for the work she'd done over all these years; all the training and planning she'd undertaken, and all the doubt she'd been forced to overcome. She actually hadn't dared to believe that she would succeed, but with God's help she'd outdone herself and was now almost at the point she'd dreamed about for so long.

She parked the car outside the village and waited for darkness. Then she opened the watertight container in the suitcase, took out the plastic bag with the organs that would make Efraim whole again, and walked the last stretch with the full backpack on her shoulders.

The gravestone was still in the same place where she'd put it almost ten years ago, but the text had been bleached out by the sun. She started by taking out the ink and filling in her words. Then she unfolded the spade and started digging. When she got deep enough she brushed the dirt from the plastic that covered his remains.

The last time she was here, the heavily stitched scar filled her with a bottomless dark hatred, but now she couldn't see it. The last drop of all that blackness had run out of her, and all she could feel was love; a love so deep and warm that she wasn't the least bit cold despite the low temperature of the night.

She took the folded-up plastic from his chest, which consisted solely of his ribs, and opened the watertight bag.

She carefully unscrewed the two lids of the contact lens case, and took out the corneas, first the left and then the right, and placed them in the eye sockets of the skull. Now he could see her again. Then she took his lung and carefully set it down in its place under his right rib, so that she could feel his warm breath against her cheek. The liver and the two kidneys would keep their love pure. At last she gave him his heart, which would beat for them from now on.

Once everything was in place, she settled down on her back beside him as close as she could. She held her cell phone in her hand, pressed play and set it on her chest. It was a sound that had streamed from his radio that one time, and which she had listened to every night she'd gone to bed alone ever since. She took out the little tin holding the pill, put it in her mouth and swallowed.

There wasn't far to go. They would meet again soon, and from now on nothing would ever separate them again. She looked up at the stars, which shone brightly that night, and realized that she had never been as happy as she was right now.

EPILOGUE

22 December 2009–14 April 2010

WITH MIXED EMOTIONS, DUNJA Hougaard got on a flight back to Copenhagen. She was surprised to discover that there had been an explanation for why the murdered Swedish Minister for Justice's sports car had ended up at the bottom of Helsingør Harbour. It might have been a little strange and roundabout, but it was still completely credible, which meant that she still lacked a concrete argument for opening the investigation again. And if that wasn't enough, she'd caught Carsten being unfaithful.

But despite everything, she felt stronger than she had in years. She was almost exhilarated as the wheels skidded against the runway. She didn't know exactly how it would work out, but from now on she would follow her own compass. No one would ever be able to bully her again, not a Hesk or a Carsten, either.

Not to mention that slimeball Sleizner, who almost certainty expected her to crawl back into her shell and submit a request to be transferred to a different department. But that was the last thing she intended to do. Instead she would stay put, awaiting the right time, and be the sharp stick that would never stop poking him in the eye. And once that opportunity presented itself she intended to strike with such force that he wouldn't know what hit him.

WHEN CARSTEN CAME HOME with a bouquet so big it barely fitted through the entry, his key no longer fitted in the lock. It reinforced the anxiety he'd been feeling all day. He'd tried calling

Dunja, but got an automated message saying that the number he was trying to reach was not in service. He sat down in the stairwell to wait. An hour later his mother called from Silkeborg to ask why a moving van with all his things had parked in the driveway.

IT TOOK MALIN REHNBERG a full twenty-three minutes before she managed to get out of the back seat in the car, where smoke and hissing sounds were coming out of the dented hood. It took another six minutes for her to dig out Fabian's phone and contact the emergency response centre. The woman on the other end was doubtful that it really was an emergency, but finally agreed to send an ambulance.

Even though Fabian's wound was not particularly large, he had lost over two litres of blood and needed a blood transfusion. But Fabian had an O Negative blood type, which was only compatible with O Negative blood. Normally the hospital kept a large supply of the blood because it was a universal replacement for almost all other blood groups, but on this particular night, there was an unusually large number of traffic victims, despite all the warnings about slippery streets, and the entire stock of O Negative at Stockholm South General had been used. Fabian had to be sedated while they located and transported the right blood.

In the meantime, Malin had an emergency C-section. A pale little boy weighing 4 pounds 11 ounces was delivered and placed on his mother's breast. Anders, who had made it there just in time, had the honour of cutting the umbilical cord, and soon the boy had a healthier colour.

After endless name discussions, they had agreed that if it was a boy he would be called Nils. But when Malin felt the warm little body against her chest, she asked Anders if he could imagine changing it to Love. He could.

The girl, who was delivered a few minutes later, was 2 pounds 1 ounce and never regained her colour. But she got to lie on her mother's chest alongside her brother for a long time, while her parents gave her the name they had agreed on: Thindra Siv Elisabeth Rehnberg.

On Monday 28 December, Fabian was well enough to leave the hospital. It was already past two in the afternoon, and Herman Edelman had asked him to come to the police station.

All he wanted was to be reunited with his family, but part of him looked forward to the debriefing where he would be able to give a complete account of what had happened the night of 23 December. Then the team could make headway in the investigation of the two murdered policemen and the arrest of Gidon Hass.

But there wasn't a debriefing or a plan of how they would move forward. He was told they wouldn't be continuing the investigation. According to Edelman, the case was closed and there was no reason to open it again. In addition, the Israeli Embassy had filed an official complaint about unlawful entry and use of weapons, despite the fact that Jarmo Päivinen and Tomas Persson had died and the embassy's own personnel had only been wounded.

The embassy had sent bullets in for analysis, which proved they were from Fabian's own service weapon.

Edelman presented him with the option of signing a letter of resignation and receiving six months' pay or becoming the subject of a police inquiry on illegal entry, persecution of an ethnic group and attempted murder.

Fabian was convinced that with the help of Malin Rehnberg and Niva Ekenhielm's testimony he would be exonerated of all charges, even though Aisha Shahin's apartment in Axelsberg had been emptied and all its contents destroyed.

He was equally convinced that if they worked together, they would be able to produce sufficient evidence to convict both Hass and his cousin the ambassador. It would not only drag Edelman and major parts of the Ministry of Justice into the case, but probably bring down the whole government. The truth would come to light, and whatever plans had been made for the operating room in the embassy would never be put into effect.

But he decided to sign his letter of resignation. It didn't matter what low opinion he had of his former mentor any more. However much he'd wanted to show Edelman that he was wrong and that the truth would always come out, he couldn't let the hunt for justice cost him the only things that mattered.

Something told him that this was his last chance to show Sonja and the children where he stood. He had to be prepared to bet everything on them. He had no idea whether Sonja was still willing to give them one last chance or if she would listen to his idea that they should start over in his old hometown of Helsingborg.

The only thing he knew for certain was that he could never forgive himself if he didn't try.

AFTER THE UPROAR AROUND the strange actions of the two policemen Tomas Persson and Jarmo Päivinen had settled down at the end of March, the Israeli ambassador was called home, only to be replaced a few days later by a new one.

The change did not receive much attention in the Swedish press, and no one questioned the official line that there were personal reasons behind the move.

It was not reported anywhere, either, that the ambassador's cousin, Gidon Hass, had been sent home in connection with the change. No official trial has taken place yet, but according to unconfirmed sources, the two cousins have been taken to Camp 1391 – Israel's own Guantánamo. At the time of writing it is unclear whether they are still alive.

X

4 January 2010

He'd heard them, but didn't believe in them. The rumours that no one talked about out loud, but which had spread like wild-fire behind closed doors and drawn curtains throughout the country. He had considered them made-up stories, much too incredible to be taken seriously – at least during the first few years. But all that changed on Sunday 15 September 2002. That was over seven years ago, and now he was painfully aware that the rumours actually under-estimated what was really going on.

An acquaintance – he'd never had any real friends – had asked him if he wanted to be part of a group that met in secret to practise Falun Gong, the prohibited Qigong-inspired form of meditation and martial arts. It promised spiritual enlightenment and bodily perfection.

He had asked the dice for advice. He'd done this ever since he'd read Luke Rhinehart's *The Dice Man*. He'd thrown a four, which was a yes, even if it was a hesitant one. He had no choice other than to follow it.

As a direct consequence of his decision, he now found himself in the Masanjia Labour Camp in the Yuhong district right outside Shenyang in north-east China. For seven years, three months and twenty-two days he had to survive on fare that couldn't be described as food, in a cell so small he could barely stand up.

Since his capture, he'd spent fifteen hours a day in one of the many factory halls under strict observation, performing forced labour: he cut loose threads from knock-off clothing or assembled toys and string lights for export to the US. Every mistake was punished with branding.

If it hadn't been for the dice and his conviction that one day it would take him away from there, he would almost certainly have broken down like the others around him. Once you'd realized what was really going on, all you could do was hope that death was on the horizon.

They weren't there primarily to be tortured or to perform slave labour in horrific conditions. While they did bring in a certain amount of money to the state, it was nothing compared to what they took out of them the day they were cut up and sold.

Organ by organ.

It was the real reason for all the tests and medical examinations and it also explained why the torture never extended to parts of the body that had a high dollar value, or why prisoners disappeared at regular intervals, never to return. He, on the other hand, was not the least bit worried. Over the years, he felt increasingly convinced that, in reality, this was his ticket out of there.

The revelation had come to him almost three years ago when, for the first time, they'd stormed into his cell without assaulting him or turning everything upside down. It was in the middle of the night, and he'd been placed on a stretcher out in the corridor that was then carried, under strict supervision, through all the gates and doors and outside the barricades.

It was the first time he'd been outdoors since he'd been taken prisoner. He could still remember how he'd filled his lungs with the night air and looked right up at the starry sky savouring the few seconds that passed before he was put in the ambulance and driven to one of Shenyang's many medical clinics.

He'd been anaesthetized once they'd arrived and woke up only when he was back in his cell, a bloody bandage around his trunk. Underneath was a carelessly sewn wound, several inches in length along the left side of his body where one of his kidneys had been. They hadn't even asked for permission. The Chinese government acted like they owned his body and could bring him in again at any time to harvest another one of his organs.

After a week or so, he'd been ordered back out to the factory halls to resume the slave labour, but since then nothing else had happened.

Until now.

Four days ago he'd been led away to an examination room he'd never seen before where a doctor had asked him to remove his dark-blue uniform jacket. He listened carefully with a stethoscope on the left side of his back for a long time and then on his chest. Maybe it was his heart they were after this time.

Obviously there was a risk that they'd already taken someone else's heart or that his beat irregularly or had some other defect that made it unsuitable, but he still kept himself constantly prepared. If they came to get him, he knew this would be his absolute last chance.

Out of the tens of thousands of prisoners in the camp, no one had managed to use the situation to their advantage. They had been broken down and brainwashed to the point that some didn't even remember their own names or that they were basically good people. This was where he had his great advantage: he'd never been good.

No one believed it when they met him. Most people thought he was pleasant, charming and considerate, but they couldn't be more wrong. For as long as he could remember, he'd enjoyed seeing others suffer. As a little boy, he'd taken advantage of animals, but later in life it was people, too. And maybe that was why his thinking was still sharp compared with the others'.

It had taken his parents several years before they finally realized things weren't happening accidentally and that it wasn't the other children's fault – their cute little adopted son was mean.

His father had immediately washed his hands of him. His mother, on the other hand, tried everything she could to help him, from bringing in psychologists to letting him start boxing. But when nothing had worked, the hope had gone out of her eyes too. Some years later, after his mandatory schooling, and inspired by Rhinehart, he'd let the dice decide his route. He told his parents that he intended to leave them and they had a hard time concealing their joy.

Something creaked. He sat up and could clearly hear the security gate at the far end of the corridor being unlocked and opened. It was the middle of the night and just like the time before he could hear the stretcher rolling on screeching wheels.

He took out the dice, shook it in his cupped hands and opened them with tense expectation, as he heard the creaking stretcher coming closer. It was exactly what he'd hoped for: two rows of three dots. The colour had long since worn away so only the small depressions were left. But it was a six nonetheless. A six he so longed to implement.

They were almost at his door. In a few seconds, a key would be stuck into the lock and turned, and he would be led out of his cell strapped to the stretcher. He quickly put the dice in his mouth, swallowed, and then put his hand under the pillow and down into the hole in the mattress where he'd kept the scissors from one of the factory halls hidden for over two years.

The door opened and he looked as surprised as possible when the guards came storming in. They shoved him out of the cell and rolled him on the stretcher through the same worn corridors, security gates and elevators as they'd done three years prior. But tonight there were no stars. Instead the rain was pouring down with drops so big he could quench his thirst simply by opening his mouth in the few seconds before he was put into the ambulance.

His prison clothing was completely soaked and was now plastered to his body, which he hadn't counted on. If any of the guards happened to glance in the direction of his right forearm they would immediately see the outline of the scissors under his shirt sleeve. But none of the tensely wandering gazes noticed anything during the trip to the clinic, and once they arrived, the hospital personnel took over and rolled him further through the illuminated corridors.

They were hurrying, so he guessed it was urgent. Just like the last time, everything was prepared when he came into the operating room. A team wearing green surgical gowns, mouth masks and latex gloves, was waiting, ready to saw open his chest, take his heart and almost certainly the rest of his organs. Then they would dump his body into a container where it would await cremation.

The anaesthetist raised his left hand in the air, massaged the back of it with his thumbs to improve the blood supply, and then expertly guided the needle into the biggest vein. At the same time, one of the nurses cut open his wet shirt and started washing the area around the heart with an alcohol-scented damp sponge, which she held in long forceps.

The syringe in his hand was connected to a thin transparent tube, which went up into a venous catheter. It was most likely filled with fluid that would make him drift off for ever as soon as it had worked its way down through the tube.

He had hoped there'd be an opportunity when their attention would be focused on something other than him. But everyone in the operating room, except for the man who stood with his back to him and held his arms out while a plastic apron was tied around his waist, had their eyes locked on him. Besides, the fluid from the venous catheter had already covered a third of the tube.

It was time to get started. He let his right arm fall out over the edge of the operating table and caught the scissors right before they fell to the floor, just as he'd practised every night for an hour over the past few years. The anaesthetist must have noticed because he immediately started shouting to the others.

He tried to tear his left arm loose from the tube and sit up, but the anaesthetist held his arm in place and pressed down on his chest. His right arm was still free and this was his last chance to act before it was too late.

The stab hit right exactly where he intended. Even though he couldn't see, he could sense that the tips of the extended scissors had forced their way into the man's throat on either side of the larynx. He started screaming as if he didn't quite understand what had happened.

Only when he closed the two blades of the scissors did the screams stop and morph into a hoarse gurgle. At the same moment the hands released their hold on him and went to his wounded throat in an instinctive attempt to stop the intermittently pumping blood.

He tore the tube from his left arm, and threw himself up against the others who were coming to overpower him. He aimed his slashes in all directions, so they would do the most damage. He'd never seen so much blood. It was everywhere. There was so much that he almost slipped several times on his way across the floor towards the man in the plastic apron who had taken refuge near the door. As soon as he'd been rolled into the operating room he'd realized that this was the surgeon and probably the only person in the room who was important enough not to be sacrificed.

He threw himself forward and slid across the floor feet first, kicking out the surgeon's legs so that the man landed on his belly and hit his face on the floor. He could hear several of the others on their way behind him, but he was already over the surgeon and had forced him up on his feet by locking his right arm behind his back and pressing the bloody scissors against his carotid artery. The others stopped dead in their tracks and allowed him to leave the operating room with his hostage firmly held in front of him.

In the corridor, the clinic staff stopped and obeyed his order to lie down and let him pass. The ambulance was still waiting outside, but the two guards who had come with him were nowhere to be seen. They could have been lingering over a cup of coffee in a staff room or maybe they were already on their way back to the camp in another vehicle with someone who'd just become one kidney poorer.

Once they reached the ambulance, the surgeon started to resist and begged and pleaded for his life. He just shook his head and explained that it wasn't up to him: the dice had shown a six, and there was nothing either he or anyone else could do about it.

He forced the surgeon down on his back, took hold of the scissors with both hands and stabbed him over and over again in the chest. He created a large enough hole, so that he could force his fingers between the ribs, break open the ribcage and expose the heart, which was still beating faintly.

Even when he'd torn it out of the body and held it in his hand, it had continued beating as if maybe there was still a slight chance it would make it.

But a six was a six, and not something that he could question, he thought, letting the organ fall to the ground, before crushing it under his boot. He got behind the wheel of the ambulance and drove off. His own heart rate was pumping so loud that it was impossible for him to hear anything else.

Finally, he was on his way to the place the dice had made him leave without so much as looking over his shoulder. For over fifteen years he'd been gone, and he'd never once thought about going back. But now he'd decided. Or, to be more exact, the dice had decided. It had given him the same answer every time he'd asked it the past few months. In other words, there was no doubt that he should return.

Back to Helsingborg.

ACKNOWLEDGEMENTS

Mi

Because you endured, even when it was very hard. You've been such a wonderful and completely necessary support. Your thoughts and feedback have been so much more than just one more contribution among the rest. Without you... No, the thought is impossible.

Kasper, Filippa, Sander and Noomi

Because you understand why Dad is sometimes somewhere else altogether, even though he's sitting and eating at the same table.

Jonas

For your time and energy, thoughts and ideas. A better sounding board doesn't exist.

Adam, Andreas and Sara, and all the others at Bokförlaget Forum

Because not only are you the best publisher, but you're also the most fun.

Magnus

Because you shared all your medical knowledge with me, and were more than happy to spend time discussing how big an eye is compared to a pearl onion.

Lars

Because you are so eager to explain how to chamber a round and all that other stuff that goes on behind the curtain.

Mikael and Jenny

Because you are two of my very best friends, and because you bought thirty(!) copies of *Victim without a Face*.

Ellen at the Akademibokhandeln bookstore in Helsingborg, and Sven-Åke and the whole gang at Väla

Because you read, liked, talked up, and got so many others to read my first book.

And finally a big thanks to all of you who went out and bought *Victim without a Face* in the summer of 2014 when no one else had even heard about it. Thanks to all of you, and to all of your friends you recommended it to, who in turn recommended it to their friends. Because of you, I can sit here and write the third book about Fabian Risk.